MW01128305

# Asherex
## *of* Adreia

E. CLAIRE

WESTBOW
PRESS®
A DIVISION OF THOMAS NELSON
& ZONDERVAN

WestBow Press books may be ordered through booksellers or by contacting:

WestBow Press
A Division of Thomas Nelson & Zondervan
1663 Liberty Drive
Bloomington, IN 47403
www.westbowpress.com
844-714-3454

ISBN: 978-1-6642-8233-9 (sc)
ISBN: 978-1-6642-8234-6 (hc)
ISBN: 978-1-6642-8232-2 (e)

Library of Congress Control Number: 2022919812

Print information available on the last page.

WestBow Press rev. date: 11/08/2022

I want to thank Tonya for being my sounding board while I was writing. Without you, I would still be working on this book, which took me six years to finish. Thanks for sticking it out with me over the years.

# Chapter One

Asherex

I stood in the small bathroom connected to the tiny room assigned to me during the summit meeting. For six days now, I had endured the madness of seemingly random meeting schedules and an endless list of useless formalities that only seemed to apply to Adreia's war council. There were twelve members of the council. Each had served at least twenty years as a high commander. Once a person was accepted into the councillor position, the position lasted until the day he died.

The purpose of the war council was to interact with the high commanders set over ten thousand soldiers and their commanding officers. The high commanders oversaw the commanders of a thousand, who were over the heads of hundreds. The heads of hundreds were over the unit leaders, who had ten soldiers under them. The war council was presided over by one man, the commander in chief. There were only three ways to obtain that high honor. A new commander in chief could be appointed to the office by the previous commander in chief or rise to power through a challenge, or the war council could temporarily promote a high commander to fill the position. A temporary commander in chief would serve a term of two years and then either be voted back into office at his request until he retired or lost his position or return to his high commander position and allow another to be appointed to serve in his place.

At times, the politics of the military were confusing. I had wanted to be a soldier since I was five years old, and now at twenty-six, I was the youngest man to reach the position of high commander. My father was trying to persuade me to reach for commander in chief, the second-most-powerful position in all of Adreia. The commander in chief ruled over all of Adreia with a people-elected senate to keep him from focusing entirely on the military and neglecting the needs of the people. There were thirty senators in all, and I knew them all personally and was glad I didn't have to deal with them on a daily basis.

Adreia was a strange place, even for those born and raised within its borders. During the two hundred years following the Global War, the elite had built the floating continent referred to as the World Above. The war had left the planet's surface scarred. One-third of it was uninhabitable because of the biological and nuclear attacks. In the aftermath of the Global War, the wealthiest and most intelligent people left on Earth had come together to build the World Above.

After its completion, they had selected the best of the best to live in the World Above, which the builders somehow had fixed just outside Earth's atmosphere. Anyone with a genetic defect or below-average intelligence had not been allowed entrance. It had been paradise above the surface of Earth for a time, but it soon had come crashing down around the people. The government had made it their mission to blot out everything they perceived as a threat to the security of the World Above. Thousands of years of history had been discarded as irrelevant, and strict rules had been implemented to give the people a sense of security. Just a few generations after its establishment, the World Above had forgotten what it was like to live on the Surface.

That detachment from the rest of humanity had brought about the ruin of the World Above. Four hundred years after the Global War, a new war had begun. Two men had opposed each other on the policies enacted upon the people on the Surface. Senator Asherex Adreia had politically challenged Commander in Chief Brashex. Brashex had imposed a harsh tax on the people of the Surface, causing many to fall into poverty and enslaving those who couldn't meet harvest-time quotas. Because of Brashex's cruelty, the people of the World Above had suffered due to the decrease in crops.

Senator Adreia had rallied the people behind him as he threw his political career into overdrive. Adreia, well loved by the people, quickly had stolen away the support of the majority of the military. The war had started the day Brashex struck Adreia during a press conference. The crowd had erupted into full-blown violence, and in less than thirty-six hours, the World Above had divided into two factions: the East and the West. Some had followed Brashex and believed that the Surface was theirs to command. The others had devoted themselves to Adreia and set about trying to make a way for the people above and below to live together without being unfair and cruel.

Now, nearly seven hundred years later, the two countries of Adreia and Brashex were still at war with each other. Unlike those on the Surface, who fought against one another, the World Above adhered to strict rules governing warfare. Nearly all fighting occurred either on the Surface or in the skies below the floating continent.

Every trip to the Surface posed its own threats. The natives had become immune to the deadliest disease released during the Global War, which had mutated and had no cure. Once a person was infected, he or she had less than two months before death came. The disease, known as Zeron's disease, was highly contagious until it reached the final stage, when blood-to-blood contact was the only means of transference. Because of this, people who suspected they might have been infected entered quarantine on the Surface for seven days. If no symptoms were present, they were free to go home. If they showed signs, primarily a cough that wouldn't go away, they went into quarantine on the Surface. After two months, if they didn't show symptoms, they received a full medical workup and went home if the results were negative for the disease.

An announcement came over the intercom system, snapping me back to reality, reminding the ten high commanders that our meeting with our commander in chief was in sixty minutes. I had been high commander for nearly four years and had participated in three summit meetings. This was the first time Commander in Chief Vaxis was meeting with us. It was exciting—or it would have been if I hadn't been feeling so poorly.

I'd started feeling sick two days ago. The doctor had given me antibiotics and a steroid shot to knock out whatever I had. Unfortunately, I felt worse today, and I had an appointment to have blood drawn and tests done after the meeting. It was the first time in my life I'd ever been sick. I'd never even had a cough, except when I'd tried to be a fish and breathe water, but that was a different story.

I swallowed that day's round of antibiotics, chased it with a good sixteen ounces of water, and then stared at my reflection in the mirror. My ash-brown hair was longer than I liked, but I was sure my wife would love it. She loved to run her fingers through my hair, but if I let it grow any longer than the half inch it was now, it would start to get those silly curls in it. A fever now darkened my once-bright eyes, which were sky blue with just a hint of green around the pupils. I felt much worse than I looked.

My plex rang, so I walked into the other room, picked up the inch-and-a-half-long handle, and scanned my fingerprint to pick up the call. Instantly, a holographic screen projected, and my wife, the most beautiful woman in the universe, came into focus. Her infectious smile immediately lightened my mood. Laughter danced in her amber eyes, and I longed to hold her close to me and enjoy her presence.

"Oh, Lillie, my sweet and beautiful wife, I love you more than all the stars in the sky."

She bit her lip, looked down, and blushed. My heart warmed at the sight. We had been married for six years, and still, I was able to make her blush, which only made her more beautiful.

"You keep talking to me like that while I'm at work, Asherex, and I'm going to have to cook all your favorite foods when you come home and make a date of it." She winked at me while attempting to flirt—something she wasn't good at. It endeared her to me even more.

"Don't you know that I don't need all those fancy things?" I lowered my voice. "I only need you in my arms on the beach under the stars. To feel your heartbeat next to mine and not do anything more than just enjoy you being mine."

A woman in the background of Lillie's workplace made some kind of gushy, romantic sound, and Lillie blushed again. "You know"—Lillie stared deeply into my eyes—"just when I was beginning to think I couldn't love you any more than I do, you go and surprise me. I love you more with every minute that passes us by." She sighed after a few moments of looking into my eyes. "Are you still not feeling well?"

"I go to the doctor later to find out why there's no improvement with the antibiotics they are giving me, which have nanobots in them. But enough about me. Can your mom go with you to your doctor's appointment this afternoon?"

My wife and I had been trying to have a baby for the last three years with no success. The last time I had been home on leave, I'd gotten tested, and everything had checked out. Now it was Lillie's turn to hear the results of her tests. Lillie was the third oldest of ten children, and she hadn't wanted any kids, but I had convinced her to have at least one. If, for some reason, we were unable to have one of our own, we planned on adopting. She liked the idea of adopting more than being pregnant. I guessed the outcome of that day's appointment would determine which road we walked down.

"No, she wasn't able to find a babysitter. Dad had to go see Nathan off to basic training, so he left her with all the kids and no way to get around. Honestly, though, if you can't be with me today, I don't want anyone there. It's not the same without you."

I smiled at my amazing wife as my heart fluttered in my chest. How had I been so lucky to find her?

"Oh, hey, my dad's calling. Call me to tell me what the doctor says after your meeting with the commander in chief. It will be nice for you to finally meet your friend in person. I'm so excited for you! Well, I'd better go. Love you bunches!"

"I love you, my Lillie."

She blushed once again as she hung up.

I set my plex aside and curled up on the bed. My body was cramping up. For the first time in my life, I was at a loss as to what to do. My father had kept me up to date on the latest in medical advances to prevent me from ever being sick, so I didn't know what was normal or if I was supposed to feel as if I were dying. *Maybe a quick nap before the meeting would help me feel better.*

# Chapter Two

## Asherex

I felt as if I were dying. My body ached as every muscle cramped from head to foot in a daunting rhythm that had me wishing I were anywhere but there. I tried not to break formation with the nine other high commanders as another spasm attempted to rip me apart. My heartbeat quickened as it became harder to breathe, and I knew someone had poisoned me.

The commander in chief of Adreia passed me by, and I quickly wiped the sweat from my brow, hoping no one would notice. I had to be extra careful of what I did or said, because I was the youngest high commander to rise through the ranks. Even though I had spoken to my commander in chief many times during various war campaigns, this was the first time I had been in his presence. I couldn't afford to die in front of him and risk damaging my father's reputation. My father had fought fiercely for his senator position, and as his only child, it was my duty to be a representative of his house. If I displayed weakness in front of the ruler of Adreia, I couldn't imagine what my father would say.

I fought through the urge to allow my legs to buckle beneath me as I pulled my hand away from my face and nearly lost my balance as I noticed that my sweat was bloody. I couldn't do it. I wouldn't live much longer if I didn't say something and get medical attention. My father's reputation would have to take a blow on this one. I just hoped he would forgive me.

I opened my mouth to speak to the high commander on my right, but no sound passed my lips. It took every ounce of strength I possessed to reach out and take hold of his arm as little gray spots began filling my vision. He turned to me with a scowl on his face that quickly turned to a look of alarm as he broke formation with a shout and lunged to catch me before I fell to the ground. I felt myself being lowered to the floor. The last thing I saw was the commander in chief's face full of concern before the darkness overtook me.

It seemed as if only moments passed before I opened my eyes again, only to find myself in a hospital room. The soft beeping and whirring of machines comforted me, until I tried to move and found myself tied to the bed. Panic set in as I fought against the bonds holding me back, but I didn't have the strength to do more than gently tug at the padded cuffs. Images flashed through my mind of when I had been a captive during my various war campaigns, causing my heart rate to increase.

The computerized beeping matched the rhythm of my heart, fueling my panic. The door to my room burst open, and three nurses rushed through, attempting to calm me, but my irrational, panicked brain refused to listen. Their soothing yet alarmed voices only made it worse. The one on my left grabbed a syringe and moved around the machine filtering my blood, and my fight-or-flight instinct killed the panic and turned it into pure rage. My strength returned in a crashing tide, and a battle cry ripped from my lips as I snapped the cuff holding my left hand and grabbed the nurse with the needle. As I made contact, my mind was no longer in the hospital room but transported to a grimy enemy prison where I'd spent three months.

◆ ◇ ◆

The dark-haired man with lifeless green eyes stood over me as I struggled to breathe. He picked up another instrument and ran it over the open flame, the only source of light in the room.

"I'm going to ask you one more time." His hollowed-out voice, devoid of all emotion, raked over me, causing adrenaline to surge through me once again. "Where is your high commander stationed? Tell me, and I might let you live as a slave in the copper mines."

I couldn't believe what I was hearing. The copper mines were worse than torture. *I would much rather die here than be shipped off to Earth's surface to mine for copper in the land controlled by the Brashex.*

My voice, barely more than a whisper, was without an ounce of fear. "I would die to protect Adreia and all her soldiers. Better for me to die than give up my brothers."

The angry fist of the commander overseeing the interrogation slammed into my face, causing me to pass out.

Freezing water brought me back from the darkness, and the interrogator started in with the questions once more. I could do this. I only had to outlast them or die before I gave in. I only wished I had spent more than four months with my wife after the wedding before returning to the battlefield.

The room seemed to melt away as I remembered the day I'd stood in Central City Militia Hall, watching, as the most beautiful woman in the world walked down the aisle with her grandfather by her side. At that moment, seeing her in that white dress, I had been utterly lost. She was my everything, and I would have given anything for her.

A tear slipped from my eye, drawing me back to the interrogation room. The commander stepped from the room, and the interrogator grabbed a gun and pointed it at my head before squeezing the trigger.

◆ ◇ ◆

I jerked awake in a panic as the chaotic sounds of hospital equipment crashed down around me. I couldn't move, and breathing had become more difficult than before. Short, clipped commands filled the room, and it took a few minutes before I recognized the voice of the man giving the orders and calmed down.

Six heavily armed soldiers were holding me down to prevent me from disturbing the various tubes and wires attached to me. The dead silence at that point nearly had me panicking again. Something terrible had gone down, and no one wanted to tell me. My eyes darted around the room, noticing the absence of my wife, until my gaze landed on my commander in chief.

Instantly, pain pierced through my heart. When I noticed the look in his gray eyes, the pain increased, as if someone had twisted a blade through my chest. "What—" I couldn't finish the question. I was too afraid.

He looked around and dismissed the soldiers before crossing the room and sitting on the edge of my bed. "The other nine high commanders are receiving treatment for radiation poisoning and the nasty cocktail of other poisons they ingested, but they only had one day's exposure. You've been exposed for at least six days. The good news is that they will be fine, and with a month or two of treatments, so will you."

His jet-black hair glistened in the harsh hospital lights as he looked away from me as if trying to put the right words in order. He blew out a sigh filled with resignation. "Someone tried to kill you, Asherex." He met my gaze once again. "Your in-laws are on their way here. Your father too."

Another round of knife-twisting pain lanced through my chest. "Lillie?" My voice, barely more than a whisper, was full of unrestrained terror. Where was my wife? What had happened to her that she hadn't been the first one there?

"Asherex, I don't know what to say. She's here at the hospital, in surgery."

My breath exploded out of my chest in one anguished exhalation.

"Someone hit her on her way home from her doctor's appointment."

Tears flooded my eyes, and I could no longer see the face of my commander in chief.

"The other driver fled the scene, but we have the voice recordings of her phone conversation with her father and the dash camera footage from her car as well as the—"

I no longer heard his voice as my world shattered around me. The love of my life had been in an accident and was in surgery. I knew deep down inside that she wasn't going to survive. We had married as soon as I turned twenty-one and had been together for six short years. She was my anchor, my world, my everything. How could I live without her by my side?

Strong hands gripped my face, and I blinked back the tears enough to see the commander in chief's face. He said nothing as silent tears rolled down his cheeks. He knew how much I loved my wife, because of the four nights and three days we had been in radio contact during a siege gone wrong four years back. We'd kept each other sane while cut off from the other soldiers and pinned down. Our conversations had started professionally, but soon we had poured out our souls to each other as if we had been the best of friends for years.

"Asherex, I'm sorry."

"Commander—"

"I told you"—his voice was a soft, tear-choked command—"to call me Drayen."

"I'm sorry, Comm—Drayen."

Another wave of tears threatened to overtake me, and Drayen pulled me against his chest. I broke down and let the tears fall until I couldn't cry anymore.

# Chapter Three

## Emet

"Emet? Emet?" The soft-spoken voice of one of the mobile mediunit nurses roused me from sleep. "Sir, they need you back in surgery. More troops just arrived."

A moan of protest passed my lips as I curled into more of a ball on my harder-than-a-rock bed. "I'm up. Be right there."

The door slid shut as she said something else, and my eyes closed once again. It seemed I was asleep for only a few moments before the door slammed back open, and the nurse returned. She shook me almost violently, and my sleep-deprived body protested.

"They've been waiting for you for an hour. You have to get up now."

With a sigh, I uncurled from the ball I had been sleeping in and swung my legs over the side of the bed. The nurse's gasp drew my attention, and I tried to focus on her, but all I wanted to do was lie down and sleep after thirty-six hours of nonstop surgeries.

"Did you not shower after your last operation?" Her question was full of concern.

I looked down at my soiled scrubs plastered to my body. I wanted to be disgusted but couldn't seem to muster up the necessary emotional response. "No, I don't imagine I made it that far." I looked across the room to where the showers were and decided that if I had a choice between showering or going back to sleep in my nasty clothes, I was going back to bed.

"Go shower, but make it quick. They really need you. How much sleep have you had?"

I turned my face to look at the little clock on the wall, squinted, and focused on it as if it contained all the secrets of the universe. The civilian twelve-hour clock glowed red in the darkness. It took a few minutes before my foggy brain deciphered the numbers enough to tell me that I'd had either sixteen hours of sleep or only a little more than four. Judging by my inability to perform simple tasks, I was going to go with four.

"My last surgery ended at zero five hundred hours."

"Oh my! Four hours isn't enough sleep, but your commander has requested you. I can buy you twenty minutes to shower, but don't make me come back in here." With that, she flew out of the room.

With a sigh of resignation, I began the short walk to the shower, peeling my bloodstained clothing off as I went. I leaned against the stall wall as the warm spray covered me. Weariness crept over me like a heavy weight upon my shoulders, and I slid down the wall onto the floor.

"Oh, Yehovah, be my strength." I drew my knees to my chest, wrapped my arms around them, and laid my head with eyes closed on my knees. "How much longer must Your servant be a slave among this people? Will You return me to my people or bring me into a place with other believers? Must I waste away in a place made by man, never again to take in the fullness of Your creation?

"From my youth, I have kept Your Torah before my eyes, and have I not observed all Your commands that I have been taught and suffered at the hands of my master for so doing? I know You have good purpose for me, as You did for Yoseph while he was a slave and prisoner in Egypt. I believe You will deliver me, even though I cannot see Your deliverance coming from the bottom of this pit. Redeem me, O Yehovah, from the hand of my oppressors!"

Bitter tears cut my prayer short. I wished to have the ability to freely worship Messiah Yeshua and to praise Him with song and dance as I had in the time before I was ripped from my family and sold into slavery to a man who forced me to become a doctor and then loaned me out to the Adreian military. I didn't have anything against my brothers-in-arms, but I longed with an unquenchable desire to be among others who were part of the spiritual nation of Yisra'el.

The door to the shower room crashed shut, causing me to bang my head on the wall behind me. I realized I had fallen asleep, and the water now poured down on me in a freezing cascade. How long had I slept? How had I slept in the shower?

"Emet?" The voice of my unit leader, Roark, pierced through the silence before he ripped the shower door open and stared at me in disbelief. "Get up. Get dressed. You are needed for emergency surgery in Adreia."

Adrenaline surged through me, and I was on my feet and cranking the water off before he fully turned away. I burst into the room, realizing then that I was completely naked and hadn't brought clothes with me or grabbed a towel. Roark threw a towel at me and disappeared into the barracks. It took me precisely thirty-two seconds to dry off, and when I turned around, there was a set of fresh scrubs waiting for me on the counter.

I pulled on clothing as I walked toward my bunk, but before I could sit down to put on my boots, Roark stopped me, saying, "Take 'em with you. We don't have time for that right now." He was already nearly out of the room, and I struggled to snatch up my boots and catch up with him.

"What's the emergency?" I asked. As we headed outside the mobile mediunit and toward the temporary hangar bay, the other soldiers stopped and stared at us—or maybe it was just me.

"Thirty minutes ago, our high commander's wife was involved in a hit-and-run." Roark turned to bark orders at someone near his cruzer before returning his attention to me as we entered the small airship. "She's in surgery as we speak but not expected to make it. You're being brought in because miracles happen around you, and Senator Reach requested that we do all we can to save her."

He strapped into his seat and took off before I was sitting and before the hatch door fully closed. Terror filled me as I lost my balance and rolled toward the closing hatch. Nearly falling out of an airship piloted by a maniac was unnerving.

"Strap in, Emet! We don't have time for you to get knocked out or injured."

"Did High Commander Reach give the order?" I scrambled into the seat and buckled in as he hit the thrusters and raced toward Adreia. I had heard stories of how much my high commander loved his wife. Every man I spoke to longed to have the same kind of loving devotion evident in Asherex and Lillie's relationship.

"No. High Commander Reach is in an emergency operation because someone attempted to kill him during the summit meeting between the commander in chief and the high commanders. This order came straight from the commander in chief himself. Seems that Asherex and Drayen are friends, so the kid gets special treatment."

It didn't surprise me that Asherex had befriended Adreia's military leader. From what I had heard, he was one of those people who loved life and put all he had into whatever he did. Not everyone was happy to be serving under a twenty-six-year-old, but few spoke ill of him, which said a lot about his character, seeing as how he was head over ten thousand soldiers and their commanders.

We landed on the hospital roof, and I quickly jumped out of my seat, only to have Roark grab me by the arm before I could look for the boots I'd lost during takeoff. I barely heard my friend's grumbled command to leave the boots over the roar of the engines he had left running in his haste to get me into the hospital. The hospital staff whisked me away, shoving me through doors and dressing me before I could protest. Before I knew what was going on, I was dressed, scrubbed in, and ushered into the operating room with the various displays of Lillie's broken body.

After five seconds of looking at the scans, I knew there was no saving this woman. Everyone in the room knew it. We could maybe buy her a few hours in the hope that her husband would be able to come say his goodbyes, but that was it. With a heavy heart, I turned to the poor woman and began working. I prayed for her under my breath, not really knowing if I should be praying for a quick death or for the hope that she would still be alive enough for Asherex to see her one more time.

The fourteen-hour surgery seemed to pass so quickly that I was surprised when we closed her up, and I walked out of the room. I knew she wouldn't survive much longer, because of the extensive damage, but everyone seemed to think she would live through it just because I had been there. Due to my relationship with the Creator of the universe, Yehovah, I'd earned a reputation as a miracle worker. This, of course, had caused many problems with people believing I could heal any sickness or fix any medical issue. Although it was true that my God and King had endowed me with great skill as a doctor and surgeon, He was the only one capable of healing someone. He could choose to work through me, but ultimately, it was up to Him.

Weariness crept over me as I stepped out of the shower in the private room I had been given to rest in. I wanted nothing more than to curl up on the bed and sleep for days, but as I walked into the room in a fresh pair of scrubs and noticed Roark sitting at the end of the bed, I feared I wouldn't get the chance.

"Emet"—Roark looked up from his small military-grade plex with a weary smile—"I have orders to have you stay here and rest until we know what's going on with Lillie and High Commander Reach. After she—" His green eyes darted to the floor, and his blond hair fell forward, obscuring his face. He looked like a little kid trying not to deliver bad news. After a moment of silence, he lifted his eyes to mine and cleared his throat. "After it happens, your master will be by to collect you before you are allowed to regroup with us back on Earth's surface."

All the energy I had left drained out of me upon my hearing that I would be going back to my master's house. Nothing good ever came out of my being near him. He hated me with a passion I didn't understand. As if sensing my thoughts, Roark patted the bed next to him. I plopped down, thinking about how blessed I was that my boss was my best friend.

He sighed and lay back. "Remember that time we were entrenched for two weeks in nonstop rain and had to sleep in shifts to keep each other from drowning?"

I smiled at Roark's twisted sense of nostalgia. It seemed the closer to death he came, the more precious the memory was. "Yeah." I lay back next to Roark, wondering if this was what it would have been like if we had grown up together. We had a bad habit of keeping the others in the unit awake when we started talking before we went to sleep, and the conversations didn't end until one of us passed out. "How could I forget that? Saith and Seth got into a fight in two feet of mud over who would take Doug's last RPG and go all suicide bomber on the enemy."

Roark's laughter stopped me, and a smile crept upon my face. "Oh!" He slapped me on the stomach in a playful manner. "And when Zach hacked their drone and used it to bomb their camp and, by some miracle, hit their hidden cache of weapons and nearly killed us all!" He busted up laughing as if it were the funniest thing in the world. "And Doug, that mad assassin, had just captured one of their tanks. Remember how mortified we were when that flaming tank came hissing across the battlefield toward us? Those were the good days. How did we not die?"

"Roark, only you would call those two weeks good days. The rest of us would have less-than-good things to say about it."

"Yeah." Roark yawned, drawing my attention. His eyes closed, and a smile crept across his face as if he were the only one in on a joke. "But you told us that story about that Yoseph guy and how he saved his whole family and an entire nation from a famine by interpreting—" Just like that, he was asleep.

I smiled, grabbed the pillow from the head of the bed, placed it between us, and turned to face the wall before allowing myself to finally drift off.

# Chapter Four

Emet

I awoke hanging halfway off the side of the bed where Roark had fallen asleep; my face was smashed into a cold drool spot. I had slept like the dead. I moved over onto the pillow enough to get out of the wet spot and prepared to go back to sleep, when the door slowly opened.

"Emet?" Roark's quiet voice pierced the room. "Are you awake?"

"I am now."

"Good." He stepped into the room, waving the lights on as he entered, and immediately, the room was flooded with brighter-than-natural light. "You've been asleep for seventeen hours."

I sat up abruptly. I couldn't believe I had been allowed to sleep that long. Roark was spoiling me.

"It's time for you to go do the doctor thing. They found another bleed, this time in Lillie's brain. Asherex says it's up to you if you want to try another surgery or if it is too little too late. If you decide not to operate, you will be legally bound to take her off life support. She's been on it five hours longer than the law permits, but no one wanted to wake you just yet."

"Has her family been in to see her?" I sent up a silent prayer for the family. I couldn't imagine watching a loved one fade away, knowing I couldn't do anything.

"Her mom and siblings have all gone to say their goodbyes. No one can reach her dad, even though he was on the phone with her when the crash happened. Asherex can't get out of bed to see her due to an incident earlier wherein he attacked a nurse and dislodged a lot of important tubes. They had to restart his treatment."

"Why did he attack a nurse?"

"He woke up cuffed to the bed."

Waking up in a strange place tied up was every soldier's nightmare. I couldn't believe the hospital staff would have been careless enough to leave a man diagnosed with PTSD tied down. I shook my head, slipped out of bed, and followed Roark to Lillie's room.

Roark took a call on his plex, leaving me to enter Lillie's room alone. A single nurse sat by the monitors, and she gave me a sad smile as she stood. "She's breathing on her own, but it's shallow and irregular. She's woken up a few times, but she will die almost immediately once the machine is shut off."

I nodded, and the nurse quickly left the room, as if the impending death were contagious. I prayed aloud: "O Yehovah, if Your servant has found favor in Your eyes and it pleases You, I ask for a chance to speak the words of life to this dying woman." I knelt at Lillie's bedside and took her hand. "Her people, her ancestors, have never known You, Yehovah. These people were left without You by man's design many centuries ago. They worship not idols of wood or stone, as my ancestors in Yisra'el did when they turned from You, but have instead worshipped power, intellect, and technology. Instead of looking into eternity, where You dwell, where the corruptible becomes incorruptible, they give themselves over quickly to things that lose their value the moment they come into their hands.

"I know, O merciful Father, that You have no pleasure in the death of the wicked but that You want them to turn and live. So give ear to Your servant, O Yehovah, and grant me my petition in Yeshua's name! Amen!"

A gentle squeeze on my hand made me jerk my head up in surprise. Lillie's bright amber-colored eyes were looking at me with a gentleness that spoke to my soul. *Blessed be Yehovah, who shows mercy to the dying and answers His servant's cry!*

"That was the most beautiful thing I've ever heard." Her voice faded in and out, causing me to read her lips. "What does it mean?"

I opened my mouth to speak and was amazed at the love and peace that came forth as I told Lillie about the Good News of Yehovah. The next twenty minutes were filled with the story of creation; the lives of Avraham, Yitshaq, and Ya'aqob; and how Ya'aqob's name had come to be Yisra'el. I spoke of Yisra'el's slavery, which had ended with the marriage between the nation and Yehovah through the Torah. They had committed to obeying without question, and I told of the blessings and curses that came for either obedience or disobedience.

Lillie's eyes filled with tears as I spoke about the disobedience of the house of Yisra'el, which had caused Yehovah to divorce her and scatter her into the nations, as promised in the Torah. Upon hearing the plan for salvation through Yeshua, the Messiah—salvation that would allow the divorced Yisra'el to be remarried to Yehovah without breaking Torah, because a man wasn't allowed to remarry his former wife after she was defiled by another—Lillie's tears stopped. A soft smile tugged at her lips.

However, I didn't stop there. I spoke to her about the resurrection into eternal life for those who feared Yehovah, believed in Messiah Yeshua, and walked out Torah. Understanding flooded Lille's eyes as everything I told her started coming together, and I couldn't restrain my enthusiasm as I told her about the New Yerushalayim and how we would no longer need the light of the sun or moon, because Elohim would be our light. We would dwell with Him forever and ever.

"I can't imagine the kind of love that would give everything for people who would forsake Him." Lillie's hoarse, broken voice betrayed the emptiness inside that I now saw in her eyes.

"You too, Lillie, can be joined to Yisra'el and attend the marriage supper of the Lamb. Just call out to Him, and He will answer."

She closed her eyes, but the streams of tears continued to flow down her cheeks. I looked away as her lips moved in silent prayer. This was her intimate moment with the Creator of the universe. I didn't want to distract her, so I prayed silently, thanking my Elohim for His loving-kindness.

Time seemed to stop as we prayed, but all too soon, it resumed as her hand touched my face. With one look at her, I knew without a doubt that everything I had endured up to that point had been worth it just to see my God and King shining back at me in those bright amber eyes, which were full of peace. Full of shalom.

She smiled at me and then closed her eyes, completely at peace for the shortest moment before the machine flat-lined. Tears of joy spilled down my face as the nurses came in, and I called the time of death, rejoicing inside that it was just the start of a time of rest before eternity began for her.

Tears still ran down my cheeks as I left the room and came face-to-face with Senator Reach. I felt terrible that I couldn't comfort him with what had just transpired in that room, because I knew he wouldn't understand the concept of God or even what the word *god* meant. I stood frozen in place for a heartbeat before he crossed the distance between us and wept upon my neck.

I comforted the senator for quite some time before I looked down the hall and saw my master leaning against the wall with a twisted smile on his face. Senator Reach finally pulled away from me, cleared his throat, and, in a soft whisper, asked, "Are you going to tell my son? I don't think I have the heart to do it."

Without thinking twice, I answered, "I would be honored, sir, to tell High Commander Reach."

He thanked me and led the way to Asherex's room. As we neared the door, I suddenly realized I still didn't have my boots, and in my haste to get to Lillie, I had forgotten to put on those silly paper-thin cloth shoes. I was padding around the hospital barefoot. I hadn't brushed my hair either, so I could only imagine what I must have looked like.

I knocked briefly on the door before letting myself in. The darkened room was large enough for a private waiting room, with two couches and two recliners filled with sleeping children and an exhausted-looking woman. A noise drew my attention, and I quickly bowed with a clenched fist over my heart as I realized the commander in chief was sitting next to the hospital bed where Asherex lay. He ordered me to relax, and I looked at Asherex for the longest time before finding my voice.

What could I say to this man? I knew that no words would make the news any less devastating, and I feared what he would do. I knew my master was waiting on the other side of the door, and if I incurred the wrath of my high commander, who happened to be a senator's son, my master would have me stripped and beaten. I had to tread carefully, so I took a risk and called High Commander Reach by his first name.

"Asherex, Lillie passed away twenty minutes ago while still connected to life support."

His eyes filled with tears, and his face paled. The woman on the couch sat up to hear what I had to say.

"She was conscious, and I spoke with her until she slipped away peacefully. I did everything I could to ensure she was as comfortable as possible."

Asherex nodded and held a hand out to me. I crossed the room and firmly grasped it. He gently pulled me down and whispered, "Thank you for being with my Lillie. It is a great comfort to know that you were with her in her last moments. I wish I could repay you for your kindness."

Tears pricked my eyes. This man had just lost his beloved wife and been unable to go see her one last time, but he thanked me instead of being furious for being unable to save her. He gave my hand a gentle squeeze and thanked me again before I stepped away.

The commander in chief was speaking softly with the woman, presumably Lillie's mother. *Yehovah, comfort these people in their grief.*

I bowed with my closed fist over my heart to my high commander and the commander in chief before exiting the room. My master was waiting for me in the hallway, and I braced myself for the coming onslaught of insults that usually followed a failed operation. I, however, was shocked when he simply nodded, turned, and began to walk away, expecting me to fall in line behind him. The unusual behavior had my heart pounding as we walked down sixteen flights of stairs and climbed into the waiting armored car.

My master, because of my surgical skills, had amassed a small fortune that I hadn't seen a dime of. If I needed something, I had to beg him for it and hope he was in a giving mood. It had taken him three years after he purchased me to buy me a bed, and he had done so only because he learned it was my twelfth birthday and only after I scored the highest on a specialized test that put him in a position to further his political career. That had been twenty-two years ago, and I still slept on that same bed, with its worn-out mattress. Roark had bought me every piece of clothing I had.

"You seem deep in thought, Emet. Care to share?"

I looked into his dark brown eyes, trying to ignore his shoulder-length salt-and-pepper hair hanging loose around his face. His high cheekbones, pointed nose, and sharp chin gave him a predatory look that made many men cower back from him. He was a predator from the inside out, a true politician.

"I've had a long week and am weary. Please do not take my silence for disrespect."

He smiled at me with his incredibly white, perfectly straight teeth and said, "It's a tragedy that Senator Reach's daughter-in-law died, but seeing as how you were there to comfort both Senator Reach and his son, perhaps I can make an ally out of him as I reach for a senatorial position."

My heart wrenched in my chest. How could this heartless man try to use a woman's death as a way to further his own career? Did he not know how much the family was grieving? Obviously, he didn't care.

"I have a present for you when we get home. I know it's something you will love."

I was quiet for the rest of the ride home while my master talked on his plex. I was too terrified to learn the reason behind my present. Once we arrived at the posh mansion, I waited for my master's permission to be dismissed to my room, but he spoke with someone for half an hour before shutting down the holographic screen and sliding the slim plex handle into his front shirt pocket.

He snapped his fingers, and a servant, who had been waiting patiently, entered the room with a rectangular object wrapped in brown paper. She handed it to me, and I was surprised by its weight. It must have weighed almost ten pounds.

"I picked that up"—he pointed at the object in my hands—"at a museum the last time I was on the Surface. It cost me a lot of money, but I figured it would keep you busy while you were home and keep you out of my way."

I opened my mouth to thank him, but he interrupted me.

"Tomorrow morning, Saz is having surgery, and you're going to be the lead surgeon. It's not supposed to be high risk, but seeing as how any operation could end in death, no one would be surprised if he didn't pull through."

"I thought you and Saz were allies and good friends."

"We are. He just knows too much now, and besides, when he doesn't survive the surgery, I will be able to fully take over our business, which means more political pull for me in the next election."

I couldn't believe what I was hearing. He wanted me to kill his best friend so he could further his own career. *How selfish.*

"Oh, before I forget: that book is contraband, and if someone discovers it in your possession, I will deny any knowledge of it, and you will be punished accordingly. Are we clear?"

I nodded at his question, which was more of a command. With

a wave of his hand, he dismissed me, and I climbed the stairs to my room two at a time to get away from him more quickly. Shutting myself in, I tossed the gift onto my bed and threw myself facedown on the floor. I pleaded with Yehovah to provide a way of escape for me not to have to murder someone. I knew I wouldn't do it, just as I hadn't been able to the seventeen times before that. If someone died on me, it was because there was nothing more I could do.

Yehovah had blessed me and proven Himself time and time again when my master had ordered me to kill someone in the past. I knew without a shadow of a doubt that my Elohim would keep me from sinning, and I was fully prepared to be beaten by my master for disobeying his wicked order. In the past, something had gone wrong to prevent me from making it to the operating room, or scheduling issues had arisen, and one time, the patient had miraculously recovered.

After my heavenly Father calmed my fear of breaking Torah, I began to simply worship Him with all I had. I recounted the miracles He had performed on my behalf and spoke of His deliverance in my life. I talked to Him as if I were a love-stricken teenager talking to the one I loved. I spoke in Hebrew, my native tongue, and recounted the Shema, one of the few scriptures I'd memorized as a child.

I praised Yehovah for the blessing of witnessing His mighty deliverance and mercy at the hospital. The praise faded into prayer for Asherex and Lillie's family and ended with a heartfelt prayer for my master to come to know Yeshua and be saved.

It seemed as if I had been praying for only a few moments, until I tried to stand, and my stiff body protested the movement. I checked the time on my plex and realized I had been on my face for six hours, but I was more awake and alert than I'd been in days. All I needed was time to spend with the Savior.

Feeling refreshed, I plopped down onto my bed, realizing I had forgotten the present from my master as it poked me in the thigh. Apprehension swirled through me as I sat up and unwrapped the book. Certain bound books were forbidden in Adreia and could land someone in exile on the Surface. The back of the book looked like a picture taken of the rippling surface of a swimming pool. Curiosity got the better of me as I pulled the rest of the paper away and flipped the book over.

The sight of the gold lettering on the cover caused my breath to rush out of me. My hands trembled as I ran my fingers over it. It was an Interlinear Bible, and the front cover stated that it was in Hebrew, Greek, and English. Emotion overwhelmed me as I ripped the book open and touched the name of Yehovah, written in Hebrew, with reverent awe, as if it would vanish from my sight. When it didn't disappear on me, I crushed the book to my chest and wept.

# Chapter Five

Asherex

Earlier that day

I had been in and out of consciousness for what seemed like an eternity. My father, my mother-in-law, and all nine of her children had come to see me as we all waited to see what would become of my Lillie. Drayen had left a few hours ago with a promise to return quickly. He had to check on his twenty-two-year-old daughter from his first marriage since she was home from college. I hoped he didn't come back, because he rarely got to see his daughter, but I knew he wouldn't leave me alone. I wasn't sure if it was because he genuinely considered me a friend or because he thought he owed me a life debt because I once had saved his life.

◆◇◆

I had just returned from my honeymoon, when my high commander called me to come in because our commander in chief had disappeared during a siege of a Brashex stronghold. I accepted the mission, and as commander of a thousand, I handpicked the best units under my authority and set out on the mission that would change my life forever. I had thirty soldiers and three unit leaders in the cruzer with

27

me as we flew through hostile territory on a search-and-recovery mission to find the sixty men with our commander in chief and extract our leader.

An EMP blast killed our cruzer and all our communications, causing us to blindly crash behind enemy lines. We fought our way to the last known coordinates of our troops. It took two days to make the trek through the rugged, mountainous terrain before we found the remnant of the sixty men. One of their communications officers handed me a makeshift plex without the holographic screen. It was the only thing they had managed to salvage. The other plex, given to the commander in chief, only had a range of six miles.

I took the plex, half expecting it to short out and electrocute me, and took half my troops on a mission to the mountain's peak in the hope that I could establish radio contact with Drayen. Our mission, met with heavy enemy fire, separated me from my men during the night. After taking a bullet to the shoulder, I fell over the edge of a cliff. I woke with the sun's rising to find myself tangled up in a tree and a bunch of scraggly vines.

It took several attempts to free myself before I finally rolled the other twenty feet down the steep incline. The pain of my wounds was almost unbearable, but I forced myself to keep putting one foot in front of the other until I came to the ruins of an old shack. As soon as I was out of sight in the shack, I collapsed. My mind began chasing around the same old thoughts I had whenever death seemed imminent. Was there a greater purpose to this life? Was death the end of life, or was there more? If there was more, what was it? Why didn't I have any answers to the questions I had spent countless hours researching? I couldn't believe this was the purpose of life. There had to be something more; I just couldn't find the answers.

"If there is more to this life than just dying, please give me a sign!" I screamed out my frustrations at the empty walls. I didn't know why I bothered. No one was around to hear me. Tears welled up in my eyes, and panic set in as I felt the weariness associated with blood loss. I was going to die out there in the middle of nowhere.

Thoughts of Lillie, my beloved wife, filled my head, and I tried to take strength from them, but I was just too weary. Fear consumed me, and I wept without knowing why there was a desperation deep inside that I couldn't explain. I took hold of that desperation and called out again to the nothingness around me for a sign of something more.

"Anyone copy?" The staticky radio transmission pierced the silence, and I dragged myself to the plex in the room's far corner. How had it gotten so far from me?

"This is Commander Reach. Over."

"Commander Reach, this is Commander in Chief Vaxis, but considering the circumstances, you can call me Drayen. What's your status? Over."

His voice calmed me, and I took stock of my situation. I had a wound from a bullet in my shoulder and most likely a few broken ribs. "I hate to be the bearer of bad news, Commander, but I've been hit and separated from my men. I have the only other working plex, and the sun is going down. I have one day's worth of water and no food. My ammo supply is nearly exhausted, with only sixteen rounds left. Over."

His sigh of resignation reverberated through me. "You must be about six miles from me. I have food and water but only two rounds left in my rifle. I'm pretty sure my right arm is broken, but I think I will survive. I've taken refuge in an old copper refinery, but the area is crawling with Brashex soldiers. I don't see a way out of this one. Over."

"Don't worry, sir; my people can track my location as soon as they get a transmitter up and running. I invented a shielded tracker that I've installed in the rifles of those under my command. Over."

Silence filled the decaying shack, and my eyes slowly drifted closed. I groggily opened my eyes as the panicked voice of my commander in chief filled the air. I assured him that I was still alive, and he walked me through patching up my wounds, a task made difficult by the ever cooling night and my lethargic body. Once finished, I rifled through my pockets to find the small tool pouch I carried for emergencies and worked on the plex in the hope that I could fix it so that we could talk with each other at our convenience instead of using the plexes like walkie-talkies.

Drayen forced me to talk him through the repairs I was doing, so he could ensure I hadn't passed out on him. I got shocked quite a few times, which caused Drayen to laugh at me. At least one of us was having a good time. By the time the first rays of dawn broke through the darkness, I had the plex fixed. We could see each other as distorted gray blurs on the fractured holographic screens.

We spent the next two days forcing each other to tough it out for just one more minute. He grew more concerned as my meager water rations ran out, and I lacked the strength to search for water. I feared he would have to watch me die.

As the sun set on the third day, my men awakened me from a fitful sleep. They quickly gave me nanos to repair the damage and drugs to make the pain manageable and set me up with fluids. We spent all that night in contact with Drayen, hoping we could come up with a plan to save him, but it was hopeless at that point. I knew there was only one way we could get him home safely, and he wouldn't sign off on it.

I picked up the plex, stared at the grayish blur that was my commander in chief, and said, "Commander, I have a plan to rescue you, but I need you to fully trust me. Do you trust me enough to not ask questions?"

Every eye in the shack was upon me, and confusion was plastered on my men's faces as the sun broke over the horizon. Drayen said, "Asherex, I trust you—"

I quickly powered off the plex without hearing what more he would say, fearing he would talk me out of what I was about to do.

"Commander Reach, did you just hang up on the commander in chief?" The question was more of a demand for an explanation from my second-in-command.

"Wes, I need you all to be ready. Gear up for extraction, and be prepared to get into the copper mill and save our commander in chief. We roll out in twenty minutes."

I walked out of the shack with thoughts of Lillie running through my mind. I would never see her again. I just hoped she would forgive me for what I was about to do.

A hand on my shoulder drew my attention to Unit Leader Wes. He stood there looking as if someone had just run over a puppy. "What's the plan, Commander Reach?"

"I'm going to surrender to the Brashex soldiers," I said. He stopped me with a sound of protest, and I grabbed his forearms to force him to look me in the eye. "It is better that one of us dies to save the ruler of Adreia. As the highest-ranking officer, it is my duty to be that one. The Brashex will never believe we would put forth this much manpower to rescue anyone with a lower rank than mine. They will take me and pull out of the area when I surrender, giving you a very small window to extract Commander in Chief Vaxis. I need you to be in charge and get him home safely. Can I count on you?"

He nodded as tears filled his eyes. I had once been in a unit under his command, and he had recommended me for promotion. He was a good soldier and a wonderful father to his five boys and one girl. Even if he could have taken my place, I wouldn't have allowed it. He had to be there for his family, watch his children grow up, and walk his daughter down the aisle one day.

I ripped my name patch off my uniform, removed my tags, and placed them in Wes's hand. "Give these to my wife, Lillie." Tears pooled in my eyes as he nodded.

That one decision led to three months of torture by the Brashex's best interrogator. When the Adreian military, led by Drayen, began closing in on my location, the interrogator put a gun to my head, but before he could squeeze the trigger, his high commander burst into the room and killed him. It surprised me that he had turned on his own people, until a few days of wandering around in the wilderness with him passed.

He had been conflicted by the decisions made during my interrogation. My unwillingness to give up my brothers-in-arms had affected him in a way I still didn't understand. Seth-Lucius cared for my injuries for a week before confessing that he had saved me because he was dying, and he couldn't allow someone who had fought so hard for the lives of others to die. Even though we had fought for opposite sides, I found my heart allying with him.

After eight days of our wandering around together, he decided to return me to my people but fell ill. I cared for him for two weeks, and during that time, I learned that Seth-Lucius was a twin but had been born with major problems with his internal organs. Within the first two hours of his birth, his parents had sold him to a research company, where the staff had experimented on him. The experiments had worked enough to determine he would live but not have a normal life, and he had returned to his parents after thirteen months.

He'd spent his whole life in and out of hospitals, until one day, he'd decided he wasn't going to sit around waiting to die. He'd joined the military and fought his way through the ranks to force his family to see that he was fully capable of taking care of himself. I admired his will not only to survive but also to thrive.

◆ ◇ ◆

"You are either deep in thought or really drugged out." Drayen's voice pulled me from my trip down memory lane.

"I'm not drugged. I refused the pain meds."

"Why?" His voice was full of concern.

I looked up into his gray eyes and noticed that anger boiled just beyond the surface. "I don't like not being in complete control of myself, and I want to be clear-headed when the doctor tells me that Lillie died."

Drayen recoiled at my bluntness, and Larissa, Lillie's mom, let out an anguished sound. I looked at her, wishing I could go comfort her, but I still had three more hours left of this round of treatment for the many poisons in my system.

"I don't like the man I am when drugged," I added. "I get violent and angry. I don't want to blow up on the doctor when he comes in. It's bad enough that his patient passed away; he won't need me making him feel worse for it."

"Wow." Drayen's voice was full of awe as he pushed his jet-black hair out of his face. "You really do care about other people too much, Asherex."

"That's what makes him special." Larissa's voice was full of pride and tears, causing me to smile for the first time since the new round of treatment had started. She had been best friends with my mother, and after my mom had passed away, she had taken over caring for me. Larissa had taught me to clean house and do laundry and had even attempted to teach me how to cook. Sadly, I had failed miserably at that. I couldn't even boil water correctly—something Lillie never had let me live down while we were growing up. Lillie always teased me that I was the dumbest smart person she knew, because I had been able to do college-level schoolwork at age six but couldn't figure out how to boil water without burning the house down.

"So what were you thinking about that caused you to completely miss your dad leaving about an hour ago and me coming in twenty minutes ago?" Drayen asked.

"The time I handed myself over to the Brashex to save you."

He gave me a puzzled look. "You were thinking about being tortured?" He kept his voice a mere whisper so as not to upset Larissa.

"Only a little." I teased, but he looked unamused and as if he wanted to strangle me. "I was mostly thinking about the three weeks afterward that I spent with their high commander."

Drayen stood straighter and eyed me as if I were about to give him the most precious treasure in all of Adreia. "In your report, you just said you were wandering around in the mountains; you failed to mention that one of their high commanders was with you. In fact, you refused to speak of it to the appointed therapist, and everyone just assumed you had been tortured and cracked. What could have been so important that you allowed your reputation to be compromised?"

"We became friends. And I didn't know how to explain to anyone that I could have returned after the first week but chose to stay with him."

He sat on the edge of the bed and stared at me for what seemed like an eternity. Leaving Seth-Lucius while he was still sick had left me feeling conflicted, but he finally had talked me into returning to my wife. I had felt like a terrible husband for abandoning her without an explanation, but I couldn't tell her the truth, because she would have reported it to my high commander, whose troops would have gone after my friend and killed him.

"He must have been really something for you to befriend him. What was his name?"

"High Commander Seth-Lucius Thane."

Drayen let out a disgusted sigh at the mention of my friend.

"You know him?" I asked.

"Yeah, we've fought each other quite a few times. The world would be better off if he died."

I was appalled. How could he say something like that to me about one of my friends? He knew I defended those I considered close and hated it when someone spoke ill of them. I had even defended Drayen quite a few times from those who wished him dead.

He must have seen something in my eyes that gave away my thoughts, because his face paled a bit as he stood. Drayen apologized and then retreated to the other side of the room with Larissa and the kids. He eyed me with a smile on his face from his position, which brought me a small measure of comfort to know he was still watching over me.

# Chapter Six

Asherex

I drifted off again after Drayen's retreat, only to have the nurses awaken me when they removed the empty IV bags and unhooked me from the blood-filtering machine. After that, my father slipped out of the room, telling Larissa the nurses were going to wake the doctor up. I assumed he was talking about the surgeon who had operated on Lillie.

After the nurses left, Drayen was back at my side, and Larissa went to read to her restless children. Within ten minutes, the kids were asleep, and Drayen was filling me in on my beloved wife's condition. They had found another bleed in her brain, but she had been on life support for much longer than the law allowed. It was up to me if I wanted to have another operation done. With a heavy heart, I signed the decision over to the doctor on my plex and hoped he let her die quickly.

Nearly an hour passed before a knock at the door signaled an incoming nurse or doctor. The door opened to reveal a six-foot-tall wall of well-toned muscle. His olive-colored skin betrayed him as a native from the Surface, probably from the Middle East. His curly black hair was loose around his face and looked as if he hadn't had time to brush it. His brown eyes seemed to glow with inner peace, and I knew I needed whatever he had that had put it there.

He glanced around the room like a well-trained soldier, and Drayen cleared his throat, drawing the doctor's attention. The doctor quickly bowed with a clenched fist over his heart, a sure sign that he was a soldier. Drayen dismissed the salute, and the doctor stood. I searched for a name tag that would allow me to virtually stalk this man to discover the secret to the peace deep inside him. My search turned up a simple gold ball earring in his right ear. No one in Adreia wore jewelry unless he or she held a high position, was married, or was a slave; and considering those in the first two categories only wore signet rings or simple wedding bands, I knew the earring meant he was a slave.

I wondered who owned him, if his master took care of him, and if I could buy him through the foundation and set him free. Thoughts quickly began swirling in my head about the proper channels I would have to go through and the months of paperwork I would deal with before even considering purchasing the doctor in front of me.

"Asherex." His soft voice full of warmth drew my attention. "Lillie passed away twenty minutes ago while still connected to life support."

My heart shattered into a billion pieces at his statement, but the life I heard in his voice comforted me.

"She was conscious, and I spoke with her until she slipped away peacefully. I did everything possible to ensure she was as comfortable as possible."

I nodded and held out a hand to him. He quickly crossed the room and took hold. "Thank you," I whispered to him with every ounce of gratitude I could, because I knew that somehow, my Lillie had found comfort in the presence of this man and whatever was inside him that beamed out through his eyes as soft, warm light. "For being with my Lillie. It is a great comfort to know that you were with her in her last moments. I wish I could repay you for your kindness."

I noticed the tears in his eyes, and I gave his hand one last gentle squeeze and thanked him once again before he stepped away.

He bowed to me in the traditional military way and once again to Drayen before leaving the room. Who was this man?

I could feel Drayen's eyes on me as I stared at the door through which the doctor had just left, as if my only chance at true life had disappeared. "Drayen, who was that?"

"Hold on. I'll go check." He disappeared for a few minutes and returned holding his plex. The holographic screen whizzed through pages of information. "His name is Emet. He's the highest-ranked surgeon in Adreia. It looks like he has had an apprenticeship under every high-profile doctor in Adreia and has more specialty degrees than anyone else in the business. He has a contract with our military and only gets pulled from duty when a high-profile client requires him."

I was impressed. Not many doctors attempted to get specialty degrees once they were established, but if that had been what his master wanted, he would have had little say in the matter. "What division does he serve under? I've never seen him before."

Drayen eyed me suspiciously for a moment as I reached for my plex. "It looks like Emet is under you in the Crimson Division. Asherex, there's no way you can know all the men under your charge. You are over ten thousand men and their commanding officers. That's a lot of people to handle, even for your photographic memory."

I began searching Emet in the military and civilian files simultaneously. "I've met all but five hundred of the men under my charge, and I remember all of them. I even know a third of the other soldiers under the other nine high commanders. I have yet to forget a face or name; I even remember every kid I went to preschool with. The nasty little boogers."

Drayen laughed as I shuddered. My early school years had been a nightmare. Unable to communicate effectively with children my age, I had found it challenging to fit in. They had been interested only in eating boogers and making messes, while I had been figuring out advanced patterns in the college books of my teacher, who'd been trying to get a new degree. The teacher had had the audacity to recommend that I be kept for another year in preschool, so I'd had to repeat it. Thankfully, Lillie's younger brothers had been with me that second year, and the triplets had taught me how to pretend to be a kid and make friends. I never would have survived without them.

Laughter from Dane, one of the triplets, drew my attention. "He did a good job of hiding the fact that he was a genius, until he was seven and got caught doing Lillie's homework one night when she was babysitting."

I glared at Dane before returning my attention to my plex. Drayen returned to the lounge area in the room and started probing my family for embarrassing details of my life. I read everything I could about Emet and was unhappy with what I found. Victor Rayas, known for his unrelenting cruelty, was his master. The only thing Victor was concerned about was obtaining a seat in the senate. Rumor had it that he resorted to blackmail and outright physical violence toward his opponents. Of course, no one could prove that he was behind the sudden deaths or injuries of those who ran against him in whatever political race.

When I started reading his medical records, I had to stop because I saw red. The head of a hundred over him had ignored more than sixty cases of abuse documented by Emet's unit leader that had led to hospitalization. It wasn't against Adreian law for a slave owner to beat his slave as long as the beating didn't go too far, but because Emet had a contract with the military, the law protected him as if he were a free man in the army.

After the third warning, a military court should have convened, tried Victor for the abuse of a soldier, and then hanged him. I was livid and knew I would end up doing something impulsive that would get me in trouble if I wasn't stopped, so I paged a nurse to come finally give me the much-needed pain meds. My father came in, looking as if he had slept in his clothes, and the nurses entered and immediately noticed that I was furious.

My father didn't ask me anything; he just took my plex and began reading through the files I had left open. His expression quickly turned from weariness to outrage. My father had teamed up with Lillie in a campaign to end slavery in Adreia, and he hated slave abuse almost as much as I did. It was the reason I poured billions of dollars per year into buying and freeing slaves through the foundation my wife and I had started.

My plex gave out a chime that echoed throughout the room. "Well"—Dane sighed—"it's official now. I guess we are all banned from working for the next forty days so we can mourn Lillie's death."

Tears threatened to overtake me as the reality that my beautiful wife would no longer be by my side hit me. The worst part was that for the next forty days, I wouldn't be able to work to get my mind off her passing. How would I survive the next forty days? Sometimes I hated the Adreian Law of Loss, which prevented anyone from being able to do anything work-related for forty days after losing a close loved one. Some considered it a time of healing to spend with family. My mind, however, defiantly kept working, refusing to let emotional loss drag it down.

My father returned my plex to the bedside table. He eyed me for a moment before squaring his shoulders and walking out of the room. I knew he was hurting, but he and I hadn't been close since my mother died when I was nine and he completely ignored me for years as he sought a senatorial position. By the time he'd tried to come back into my life, I had been fifteen and already a unit leader in the army, and I had been indifferent toward him.

The rift between us had been the source of many arguments between my wife and me. She had tried to get me to at least tell my father how I had felt about growing up without him present, but my foolish pride had kept me—and still kept me—from speaking to him about it. I knew he thought I hated him, but I couldn't find the strength to kill my pride and tell him the truth.

I let out a sigh as the pain medicine rushed through my veins like ice water, and within minutes, my eyelids closed, and I drifted off to sleep.

# Chapter Seven

## Emet

I awoke and stretched just as the sun was coming over the horizon. Every joint cracked in protest, and a sharp pain lanced through my side. I quickly rolled out of the twin bed only to realize that I had fallen asleep with my Bible, which was the cause of the pain. I smiled as I picked up the book and held it to my chest as I did my morning prayers.

As soon as I finished praising Yehovah, I started scanning pages of my Bible into my plex. I knew my time was limited, so instead of eating breakfast, I stayed in my room to ensure I could get the most out of my time. I managed to get all of B'reisheet and Shemot and nearly half of Vayikra scanned in before one of my master's servants came to collect me for the awaiting surgery.

I quickly hid the Bible under the floorboards beneath my bed, dressed, and rushed downstairs to keep Victor from having to wait on me. He was busy messaging people on his plex as I entered the foyer, and he barely glanced at me before walking out the door. Gavin Blane, one of the best lawyers in Adreia, stood with the door to the armored car open for us. He was just an inch shorter than I was at five foot eleven, he had white-blond hair, and his eyes reminded me of moonstones and made me cringe when they seemed to change to blue in certain lighting.

A chill ran down my spine as Gavin stepped into the car and shut us in. His appearance unnerved many people, and if he hadn't been so tan and I hadn't seen his medical files myself, I would have believed the rumors that he was an albino. Gavin sat across from our master and me and began talking about legal issues, leaving me to ponder the task ahead of me.

A series of detours due to construction had us stuck in traffic for several hours, and I drifted off. I awoke to a heated discussion between Gavin and Victor about murdering people. Although Gavin was a lawyer, he was Victor's secret slave and had trained from a young age to be an assassin. Victor somehow forced Gavin to kill people, and Gavin often had no memory of the event afterward, even when I would patch him back together after something went wrong. I couldn't figure out how Victor pulled it off and knew from our talks that once Gavin discovered that secret, he would expose Victor. It was going to be a nasty legal battle ending with our executions because of Victor's wickedness.

"I will not murder anyone else for you!" Gavin's vicious shout caused me to flinch backward.

I watched as Gavin reached into his suit and began withdrawing a blade to kill Victor. My breath caught in my throat. *Yehovah, stop Gavin from getting himself killed!* Out of the corner of my eye, I saw a series of bright flashes of light, and suddenly, Gavin froze in the middle of drawing his blade.

"Why don't you just relax, Gavin?" Victor's words were soft and velvety smooth, unlike anything I had ever heard come out of his mouth.

Immediately, Gavin sheathed his hidden blade and just sat there with a blank look on his face. Every muscle in his body was relaxed, and at that moment, I was more terrified of Victor than I'd ever been in the past twenty-seven years. If he could command one of the greatest assassins in Adreia with just a few flashes of light and a soft voice, I could only imagine what he was capable of.

Victor turned to me and said, "Saz's surgery begins in an hour and a half, but we might end up being a little late due to traffic. They will have him prepped and ready for you and, depending on our timing, will start the initial cuts, so all you will have to do is scrub in and start away." An evil smile crept upon his face, and his pupils dilated. "I don't care how you want to ensure that he doesn't survive; all you have to do is make sure he doesn't get back up again. You have one job, and I expect it done right."

"I won't do it." As soon as the words passed my lips, I knew I was in trouble. Why had I spoken up? I swallowed my terror as a blood-hungry look blossomed in my master's eyes. He pulled out a small black box about a half inch long by three-quarters of an inch wide and about as thick as my pinkie finger. My body involuntarily flinched backward as two prongs slid out of the end of the Taser at the swipe of Victor's thumb.

"Why is it that today all of my slaves have decided to be rebellious? I can't touch Gavin because he's a public face, but not one single person cares what happens to you, and it seems we have nothing but time for me to change your mind." Victor punctuated the last few words with a crack of electricity arcing between the prongs.

I pushed myself into the door to put more distance between us and caught a glimpse of a bright flash in the sky above. I turned my head in time to watch as a construction cruzer carrying fuel to the megacranes broke apart in a fiery explosion of twisted metal. Everything seemed to go in slow motion as adrenaline flooded my system. I pushed Victor across the bench seat, lunged across the carpeted space, and buckled Gavin in before throwing myself into my seat. I clicked the buckle into place just seconds before the wreckage slammed into the streets around us. It hit the front of the car, causing us to flip, and my skull violently bounced off the bulletproof glass before everything darkened.

I awoke to the sounds of screaming sirens and raging flames. Pain engulfed me. I attempted to open my eyes a few times unsuccessfully before I was able to focus on my surroundings. The car was on its side. I was pinned to the bench seat by the seat belt but hanging in the air. Gavin was still in a trance, unfazed by the fact that he was bleeding and had a severely broken arm that hung limply from his side into the open space between him and the door that was pinned to the ground.

The air was hot, and it felt as if we were in an oven. I knew if the flames outside continued to go unextinguished, we would bake alive in the armored car. At least I didn't have to go kill someone in the hospital.

A series of vile curses drew my attention to the mess of broken glasses and alcohol bottles as Victor struggled to his knees in the debris. He looked up at me, and his fury ignited. "You!" His voice was more of a snarl. "This is all your fault. Yours and that God you serve!" He launched to his feet and, in his enraged state, ripped the seat belt off me.

I slammed into the broken glass below and didn't even have a chance to catch my breath before Victor was on me, taking out his fury with his hands and feet. I curled into a ball in the glass and did my best to protect myself as I fought passing out. I knew I had a concussion and couldn't afford to lose consciousness.

Eight minutes into the beating, Victor suddenly stopped, and I heard a loud metallic popping sound as I closed my eyes. When next I opened them, I was on the sidewalk, in a fabric triage tent coming off the side of a building. There were people on either side of me as far as I could see. Most of them were sitting up, with only minor injuries.

The doctor within me wanted to get up and help, but my body refused to obey even the smallest order of lifting my hand. I hurt so badly that I was surprised I was awake. *Yeshua!* I weakly cried out as a tear slid from the corner of my eye.

The paramedics and military medics passed me by as soon as

they saw the chalk writing at my feet. I was sure that my master had refused me medical treatment and that these people just thought I was wasting a perfectly good place on the sidewalk. My eyes closed for a moment, but a gentle shake of my shoulder woke me up.

"Emet? Emet, can you hear me? I need you to wake up."

I recognized the voice and complied. The man kneeling beside me was a unit medic I had previously worked with. He walked me through his actions as he gently sat me up against a propped-up back brace and helped me to sip some water. He examined me, although others yelled at him for disobeying orders. Because he couldn't give me a more thorough exam, he gave me a few mild pain pills, all he had left, and reluctantly left me to tend to other people.

I could feel the plex in my pocket vibrating, but no matter how hard I tried, I couldn't get my hand to cooperate, so the plex just sat there, trying to vibrate a hole into my leg. My eyes closed despite my best attempt to stay awake, only to flutter open sometime later. I thought I had heard my name over the din of people and sirens, but as quickly as it sounded, it was gone. Was I imagining things? My eyes fell closed once more.

Rough hands grabbed my face, forcing my eyes open. It took a few moments for my foggy brain to recognize Roark and took even longer before I realized he was talking to me. "Roark?" My voice was nothing more than a hoarse, cracked whisper, and the look of concern on his face frightened me.

# Chapter Eight

## Roark

I stood there holding Emet's face in my hands and could tell he wasn't aware of anything around him. He had a glazed-over look in his eyes, and I was terrified that if he went back to sleep, he wouldn't wake up. I didn't understand why his master refused him medical treatment. Didn't Victor know that Emet was close to death?

"Roark?" Emet's voice was barely a whisper, fading in and out. His eyes drifted closed again, and I began shaking him, but I couldn't rouse him this time. Fear gripped me. My best friend was dying right in front of me, and no one cared.

"What do you think you're doing?" Victor's booming voice pierced through the din of noise filling the streets. Pure rage filled me as I stood and turned to him. There would be no mercy for him this time.

He strutted up the sidewalk toward me, with his wounds already halfway healed. Victor was a man accustomed to getting exactly what he wanted, and up to that moment, I had respected Emet's request not to harm his master, but as he neared me, I knew without a shadow of a doubt that if I attacked him, he was going to die unless someone stopped me. My unit's assassin had come with me to find

Emet after we learned of the accident, but he was nowhere near me at the moment.

As soon as Victor was within arm's length, he began to snarl orders at me to back away from his property. I noticed several military personnel stop what they were doing to watch the drama unfolding on my little square of sidewalk. I tried to hold back my rage, until Victor began to degrade Emet's God.

My fist struck before I was aware that I was going to throw it, and for a brief moment, I was stunned. I didn't believe in Emet's God and had even had many conversations about why I wouldn't, but there I was, defending an invisible deity I didn't even know for sure existed. What was wrong with me? Was I just looking for a fight?

Victor wiped the blood from his face and met my gaze with a murderous look in his eyes. I felt something predatory rise up in challenge within me. My lips peeled back from my teeth in a snarl before I lunged at him like a predatory cat. I felt his bones breaking beneath my fists before three soldiers dragged me off him. Two others pulled Victor away in case I broke free of those restraining me.

Victor coughed and looked around in confusion before his gaze settled back on me. He was dazed, but an evil light in his eyes spoke of violence and defiance. "Mark my words, Roark No-Last-Name: you will regret the day you crossed me."

"Are you threatening a ranking military officer?" The question from the Opal Division's high commander was more of a demand for a satisfactory answer. There were strict laws governing attacking and threatening military personnel. Breaking the law usually ended in a public execution to discourage anyone else from attempting the same.

Victor quickly looked away with a calculating look in his eyes. "I would never, High Commander."

The high commander eyed Victor wearily before turning his attention to me. He and his men had been on the scene from the beginning. It was obvious he wasn't looking to put anyone else in a body bag. His eyes roamed over me as if he were checking for wounds. "Where's your unit medic?"

I pointed to Emet's prone body behind me on the sidewalk. "I came to collect him as soon as I heard about the accident. He's the number-one surgeon in all of Adreia and would be doing a lot more good if he weren't about to die."

Confusion filled the high commander's hazel eyes as he looked at Emet. "Because your medic is a slave, you must get proper permission from his master to perform major operations on him, but under the law, he should be given high priority and up to ten nano treatments. Anything more will have to be approved by your commanding officer in your division." He sounded weary as the last statement passed his lips. "I'm sorry, Unit Leader Roark, but that's all I can do for you."

"Thank you for your assistance, High Commander Bane." I bowed with a clenched fist over my heart to respect the man in front of me. It wasn't every day that someone other than those in my unit tried to help Emet.

He gave a slight customary bow in return before calling his troops back to work. He ran a hand through his graying brown hair as he gave us one last look and then walked back into the fray. There was still so much to do. I didn't envy him his job.

"Well, that was a pleasant surprise."

I nearly jumped out of my skin at the unexpected statement from my unit assassin. Doug was an intimidating man who stood head and shoulders above most at six foot seven. As if that weren't scary enough, he always wore wraparound sunglasses that hid his pale green eyes, which seemed to glow with an almost neon effect. The dark sunglasses contrasted against his tan face and red hair, which he wore in a ponytail that trailed to the middle of his shoulder blades.

He smiled at me, knowing he had caught me off guard and enjoying every moment of it. "The rest of the team will be here in ninety seconds to collect Emet. I got him a place in a mobile mediunit heading to the Surface, but we can't do much without the higher-up's permission. We both know that Rayas isn't going to approve of anything since you not only gave him a taste of his own medicine but also humiliated him in public."

No sooner had Doug finished speaking than my unit arrived and loaded Emet onto a stretcher, and we headed toward our cruzer. I couldn't help the anxiety that tried to overwhelm me as I sent a request to my head of a hundred, knowing he hated me and would deny the much-needed medical treatment for Emet. I had sent more than sixty medical reports for abuse to him, and all had gone unnoticed by the man. I didn't care if he had a problem with working with a ward of the Adreian government who had grown up in an orphanage and still didn't have a last name because no one wanted him, but he needed to leave Emet alone.

It seemed only moments had passed before I was pacing a hole in the floor of the mobile mediunit, trying to convince someone with a higher rank than mine to approve of getting Emet better medical treatment than nanos. He would need nanos later, after he had surgery and was stabilized. Right now, he required scans and at least one surgery, but I couldn't find anyone willing to bend the rules to help. Victor's reputation permeated even the military ranks, and many were too afraid to cross him.

I returned to the officers' barracks, where Emet was lying on my cot. His face was paler than I had ever seen it, and his bruises were darkening quickly despite the nanos in his system, a clear sign that there was a lot of internal damage. I carefully sat on the frame above his head and attempted to rouse him again but only managed to get a soft moan out of him. I didn't understand why no one would help him. He was the first to get pulled in to help our higher-ranking officers, but when it came time for them to return the favor, they forgot about him.

"Unit Leader Roark?"

I looked at my old friend Unit Leader Zazis of the Jade Division. He looked worn out, and his eyes were darkened by disappointment as he shook his head to let me know he had been unsuccessful in persuading his commanding officers to help. I nodded at him, and he gave me a soft smile before apologizing and slipping from the room.

My heart was shattered. My best friend, my only family, was slowly dying in front of me, and I was helpless to stop it. Tears threatened to overtake me, and I quickly jumped to my feet and began pacing. I didn't know how much time passed before I threw myself back down onto the edge of my cot, ripped my plex from my pocket, and angrily fired up my messenger. I hesitated for a brief moment as the anger drained out of me, and I stared at my high commander's name on the holographic screen.

I blew out a sigh before clicking on it and composing the message. I briefly explained who I was, the situation with Emet, and what I needed from him. As soon as I sent the message, panic set in, and I quickly went into the meeting and break room for the officers. I couldn't believe I had just messaged High Commander Reach while he was mourning. His wife had just died, and I was being selfish. I was the worst scum of the universe.

My plex chimed, drawing the attention of the officers I had been pestering for the last several hours. I opened the message without thinking and stopped dead in my tracks when I read Reach's reply: "Thank you, Unit Leader Roark, for bringing this matter to my attention. I am now aware of Emet's situation and former reports filed by you. I will take care of everything."

It was the shortest message I had received that day, and it terrified me like nothing else. This grieving man, banned from doing anything work-related, had broken the Law of Loss by replying to me. I wanted to believe he would do something, but right now, under penalty of the law, he couldn't do anything to help me.

I pocketed my plex as Commander Fain's plex rang. Everyone in the room went dead quiet as Fain's high commander appeared on the holographic screen. "Fain? What's going on? I need to talk to Unit Leader Roark of the Crimson Division."

Every eye was on me as Fain stuttered through a short briefing and brought me his plex.

"High Commander Kays." I gave a quick bow with a fist over my heart before he dismissed it.

"Enough with the formalities; call me Ivian. I received a call from Asherex informing me that you are having trouble getting medical attention for your unit's medic. I'm signing off on any medical treatment you need for him and putting in a transfer to have him taken back to Adreia and treated at Central City's hospital. I don't care why no one stepped up and helped, but that will change now.

"My boys will personally see to it that everything is taken care of, and if Emet's master says one word to you, I will charge him with attempted murder of military personnel and have him executed before he can beg for mercy. If anyone else attempts to delay you or if you have any other problems for the next forty days, just call me, and I will take care of it on Asherex's behalf."

"Thank you, Ivian." What else could I say? How could I thank my high commander and Ivian for their quick reactions to my cry for help?

"No problem, kid. Now let me talk to that cowardly commander of mine again."

I handed Fain his plex and walked back to the barracks. It didn't take long before a medical team prepared Emet for the emergency flight back to Adreia, where he would receive the best care possible. Before I knew it, we landed at the hospital, where doctors rushed Emet into the radiology department for scans. A nurse escorted me to a private patient room set aside for Emet at High Commander Kays's request, where I waited for the surgery to end. Alone, I paced the floor, unsure what would come next, as I contemplated the illegal action I had taken to help my best friend.

# Chapter Nine

## Roark

I had been in the deepest sleep I'd ever had and couldn't figure out why I had suddenly awakened. My back cracked as I pulled away from the corner I had propped myself in to be able to see the entire hospital room. The small, poorly padded chair beneath me protested my movement as I wiped drool off the side of my face while scanning the room.

My eyes lingered on Emet's prone body lying on the hospital bed. The seventeen-hour surgery to save his life had been almost more than I could bear. My heart broke to see him on life support to give his internal organs a rest before the next surgery later that day. Seeing him like that made me glad I didn't have any family to worry about. Worrying about Emet was a full-time job, and I'd only known him for ten years.

A soft knock on the door drew my attention, and I invited whoever was on the other side in. My breath caught in my throat as my estranged childhood best friend stepped through the doorway. Contessa was as beautiful as I remembered—maybe even more so. She was two inches shorter than I at five foot six, and her beautiful dark blonde hair seemed to glow in the hall light spilling into the room behind her. I wondered if her blue eyes still held the stormy passion that once had reigned there.

She cleared her throat as she closed the door behind her. "It's been a while, Roark." Her voice was softer than I remembered, and my heart did that silly flip-flop thing when she spoke.

"Yeah, I guess dropping out of high school to join the military kinda puts a damper on a personal life." As soon as the words left my mouth, I regretted them. The last full conversation we'd had before I walked out of her life haunted me to that day. I had been rude to her, and even though what I had done and said had been completely honest, I knew I could have handled it much better.

"How's he doing?" Tess's soft voice drew me from the past disaster into the current tragedy.

Without hesitation, I began filling her in on Emet's condition and the proposed treatment. I didn't realize I was in unit-leader mode until I finished briefing her, but her father was high commander of the Imperial Division, so I was sure she was used to being talked to like that. It still didn't make me feel better. I wasn't good at social interaction outside of work. Emet was her friend and Hebrew teacher, and she needed something more than a military-style briefing.

"I'm sorry, Roark. I can't imagine how hard this is for you." Tess's voice trailed off, and the room filled with an awkward silence, causing me to panic.

What was I supposed to do now? I once had loved this woman but had destroyed our friendship because I'd gotten tired of her only treating me like a friend when no one else was around. I still loved her but was too terrified to speak up. I was pathetic.

My stomach growled, much to my embarrassment, breaking the silence. I was glad Emet, in a medically induced coma now, couldn't witness this. Thankfully, it was dark in the room.

"Roark, would you like to go grab some lunch with me? It would be nice to catch up, and there's nothing we can do for Emet right now. Besides, he wouldn't want us sitting around here in the dark."

She was right. If Emet found out I had forsaken the outside

world while he was in a coma, he would lecture me about how I was wasting my life instead of living it to the fullest and enjoying every moment. I could almost hear his voice telling me to find the light of life even in the darkest of storms and keep pushing through.

"It would be nice to get away for a bit and stretch my legs. Besides, we have a lot to catch up on, Tess." I stood and crossed the room, and we walked out of the hospital without saying much.

The restaurant was six blocks from the hospital and a bit fancier than the places I usually frequented. I felt out of place as the hostess seated us. Tess came from old money, and I had just spent all but $400 out of my life savings to make a trip to Yerushalayim to learn how to make tzitzit for Emet. Because I was an Adreian citizen, I'd had to pay a fee and a tax just to enter the gates of the capital city, not to mention that everyone there spoke Hebrew, while I only knew about ten words, so I'd had to pay a translator. Then I'd had to find someone willing to teach me and house me for the Sabbath because the city would not allow anyone to enter or leave through the closed gates, to keep threats of terrorism down.

Even though their children had protested, a lovely elderly couple had taken me in. Apparently, years ago, they'd lost one of their boys to an Adreian-Brashex battle. They'd welcomed me into their home, and the man had spoken a bit of the common language, so there hadn't been a complete language barrier when my translator left me. We'd shared a meal together, and I'd listened to the older boys read through the Torah in Hebrew to begin the Sabbath. It had been pleasant and completely worth my $60,000.

The waiter interrupted my thoughts, but before I could order, Contessa took charge and did it for me, just as she used to. She smiled at me, and we began to talk. I learned that she worked at a publishing company and loved her job. She was single again, which surprised me. The last time we had run into each other, she'd had a fiancé. As I studied her, I noticed she had the same spark in her eyes that Emet carried. I guessed she had given herself over to Emet's religious propaganda. So much for Hebrew lessons to learn a foreign language.

"So," I asked Tess, "did you break it off with your fiancé because of the whole God thing, or was there another reason?"

She looked at me in surprise and said, "Not that it is any of your business, Roark, but yes. According to the Torah, I am part of Yisra'el now and not allowed to marry outsiders. And even if he had converted, it wouldn't have been fair to him for me to marry him when I love someone else."

I stared at her as if she had just grown another head. "Why would you even get engaged to someone if you loved someone else?"

"Because I thought if I moved on with my life, I wouldn't have to think about it anymore, but I was wrong. It doesn't matter anyway because the man I'm in love with hates me. After all, I was foolish, and he isn't a believer."

My heart sank. "I don't hate you, Tess."

She looked up at me in surprise. Her mouth opened as if she would speak, but no sound came out. It was adorable.

"The last time we talked—" I blew out a sigh. "The last few times we talked, I was indignant because I was upset, and I know that's not a good excuse, but I don't hate you. I've never hated you. I'm going to be completely honest with you, Tess: I've been in love with you since the day we met, when I saved you from those men trying to kidnap you on the way home from school when we were seven. The last time I saw you, I was going to tell you, but then you told me you were getting married, and I lost my temper.

"It wasn't right of me, but I knew if I had spoken up, you would have left that guy and then ended up resenting the decision. I have absolutely nothing to offer you, and your dad hates me. I couldn't be the one who causes you not to have a relationship with him. I get this silly religious thing you're doing, so I would appreciate it if you don't tell me that you love me, because you've already said nothing will come of it. I would rather not know than be haunted by what could have been."

There were tears in her eyes as she nodded in agreement. Why couldn't I just keep my mouth shut? Once again, I felt like the biggest wretch in the universe.

Tess opened her mouth to say something but stopped as her father entered the room. He walked straight up to her, and his stony face melted into a smile as he approached Tess. Keller wasn't the most intimidating man. In fact, he looked more like a movie star than a high commander. Tess had gotten her stormy blue eyes from him, but other than that, they looked nothing alike. His black hair, combed out of his face, looked as if a professional had styled it. He wore a fancy suit custom-tailored for him that doubled as light body armor. Keller's usual fedora was absent today, which was all right by me because the man already stood at six foot two and didn't need the extra height.

"Sorry I'm late, cupcake." Keller's smooth voice flowed into the room and commanded attention as he hugged Contessa and took his seat. "I just left an active investigation in the lower ninth ward and barely caught a cab here."

"I thought the Opal Division handled crimes and investigations in the city. Why would you be there, when you are supposed to be at the hospital, getting treatment for nearly being poisoned to death a few days ago?"

"The Opal Division does handle investigations, especially ones involving murder, but seeing as how one of mine is involved, it is beyond their jurisdiction." Keller spoke in a hushed tone to prevent the other patrons from eavesdropping.

"One of your division was murdered, and you're taking care of it?" I spoke before I could stop myself. I had been doing a good job of being invisible, but I couldn't help but be curious about a fellow soldier's fate.

"No one in my division was murdered today that I know of, Unit Leader Roark. They found High Commander Bane's wife dead in their bedroom, and his blood was everywhere, but he was gone without a trace. There were obvious signs of a struggle."

My heart stilled a bit. I had just seen High Commander Ezekiel Bane less than twenty-four hours ago. "Zeke's been taken? I know he didn't kill his wife and leave."

"We don't know anything for sure right now, and I don't want to jump to conclusions." Keller's plex rang, interrupting his briefing. He spoke on his private earpiece as the waiter brought food to our table. Contessa and I began eating as the conversation unfolded between Keller and a doctor of some sort about his treatment.

With a sigh, Keller ended the call. He apologized to Tess as he gave her an affectionate hug while mouthing a death threat to me over her shoulder if I so much as thought about touching her, and then he left us alone. Tess and I made small talk as we finished our meal, and I was amazed that it wasn't awkward to be around her after telling her I loved her. Maybe it had been a mistake, but then again, perhaps this was the first step in the right direction for me.

"Roark?" Tess's nervous tone caught my attention and stopped me from pushing back in my chair as I prepared to leave the restaurant. "I think someone has been following me for the last couple of days. I don't feel safe. Will you please walk me home?"

I nodded at her in full alert mode. I hadn't paid much attention to the nervous looks over her shoulder before, and now I was kicking myself for it. Tess's father had begun backing a well-known political figure who recently secured a position in the senate, and because of it, Keller had received many threats and a few attempts at blackmail. Of course, no one who had taken the time to figure out why Keller Thaz was a high commander instead of a politician or clothing model would have attempted anything in the first place. Keller was a man who took vengeance to a new level and had the support of ten thousand well-trained soldiers to back it up.

We left the restaurant through the more secluded patio and slipped into the crowded streets. I held Tess's hand tightly as we navigated the maze of streets and headed toward her home. The situation was a tactical nightmare, and I longed to have the support of my unit behind me. Unfortunately, they were all home on leave while Emet was in the hospital. Besides, I already pulled them off leave too often to keep Emet from being alone with his master. I simply couldn't ask them to leave their families to help me.

We made it six blocks, when I spotted a black Ravager that had passed us at least three times. The large vehicle was popular with active families who had kids on various sports teams, rich individuals who wanted to drive in luxury, and those about to kidnap someone—at least that was the vehicle I would have used. They were common, and the seats conveniently folded into the floor, making enough room behind the sliding side door to stash a body or two. Another Ravager pulled to the curb ahead of us, and drawing my sidearm, I dragged Tess through the alley behind us.

They cornered us in the alley, and I knew I couldn't fight my way out of this one without getting Contessa hurt. Without thinking twice about my safety, I pushed Tess against the wall behind me and made a show of pulling my gun into a firing position. I slipped my thumb through the old rubber grip and carefully removed the paper-thin clear tracking chip. High Commander Reach had made them standard issue for his soldiers. They had been created to be removable and inserted into the eye like a contact. The chip was perfect for situations like this. I just wished it didn't feel so uncomfortable.

The chip went into my left eye without a problem just as six men dressed in black body armor filled the alley. I popped off a few rounds just to make a show of it before one of them hit me in the shoulder, and another bullet hit me in the hip. Pain shot through me as they attempted to disarm me and reached past me to grab Tess. I knew she was as good as dead if they took her, so I clamped my hand on her arm so tightly that I feared I would break my hand.

Contessa looked at me. Her eyes were wide with panic and pain, but we both knew I couldn't let her go. The men attempted to pry her free of my grip while someone else shouted at them. I could hear sirens heading our way in response to my unsilenced gunfire, and they decided to take us both. I did my best to keep myself between the woman I loved and those trying to abduct her and stay conscious through the pain of my wounds as the men forced us into the Ravager.

As soon as we headed down the road, Tess attempted to stop the bleeding. Why couldn't she stick to the kidnap victim's guidelines that every military father taught his children? She needed to stay still so I could hang on to prevent our captors from dumping me off somewhere without her. We needed to sit tight and wait for an opportunity to escape, and if that wasn't possible, then I would have to convince them to torture me instead of her, which would be easy considering I was an expert in making people want to kill me.

# Chapter Ten

## Emet

I awoke slowly, as if emerging from a thick fog, and waited for the pain to return before opening my eyes. After a few moments of nothing, I finally opened my eyes and breathed out a thankful prayer that I was in a clean hospital room. Roark must have been able to get me the medical attention I needed, and I hoped he hadn't had to do anything illegal.

I sat up, careful of the IV line in my left arm, and looked around the room, expecting to find my friend lurking about. A twinge of disappointment pierced my heart when my search turned up with nothing. It wasn't like Roark to leave me alone after I was hurt, but maybe he had finally listened to me and not sat around tormenting himself with his inability to help me, as he usually did.

After a few moments of assessing myself, I snagged my chart and began flipping through the electronic doctor's notes while taking my blood pressure. I knew my wounds were bad but hadn't realized just how close to death I had come. I wondered how Roark had managed to get me into surgery and then placed in a recovery tank before I got my own private room. It was somewhat strange to be alone, and I took full advantage of it as I pressed the call button for the nurse and bowed my head to pray to Yehovah for my recovery and for Roark.

Twenty minutes passed by the time I said amen and lifted my head, yet there was still no nurse. The IV bag was empty, and according to my chart, I was due for a quick wellness exam and a discharge, but no one seemed interested in following the doctor's orders for my care. If the nurses had worked under me, they wouldn't have neglected one of their patients, especially when it was past the prescribed discharge time set by the doctor, because the hospital lost money at that point. I pressed the button again and waited another twenty minutes before becoming impatient and removing the IV myself.

Thirty minutes later, I showered, dressed in the clothes Roark had left for me, and walked to the nurses' station. Irritation and a bit of anger briefly surged through me when I noticed six nurses sitting around gossiping about a doctor having an affair while the muted call lights flashed. I cleared my throat, and all the women looked at me as if I had just called them every name in the book.

"You're the patient from room 710B. What are you doing out?" one of them said.

"That's Dr. Emet to you." I looked at the young blonde nurse who'd spoken to me with such disdain and tried to keep my tone polite. "And I am an hour past my discharge time. I took the liberty to give myself the wellness exam and am discharging myself from your care."

The women looked at one another, stunned. They recognized my name and knew exactly who I was, and they all knew I would have to file a report against them for neglecting their patients. I reached across the desk and unmuted their call-board. They all looked ashamed.

"Emet!"

I quickly turned at the authoritative tone of the man calling out my name, half expecting him to be there to punish me for something. It took me a moment to realize the man rushing out of the elevator was High Commander Thaz, my friend Contessa's father. He was in front of me in a matter of moments and grabbed my shoulders in a viselike grip.

"Someone was supposed to tell me the moment you woke up. I need your help. Come with me now." With that, he rushed back toward the elevator, and I had to shove past my confusion as I raced after him. So much for filling out the discharge paperwork.

As soon as the elevator doors closed, Mr. Thaz gripped my shoulders again with a murderous gleam in his eyes. "Someone took Contessa and Roark. I need you to find them," he said, and my heart stilled. "They've been missing for two days, and I don't know what to do!"

"Calm down, Mr. Thaz." I kept my voice level as my military training kicked in. "Have you tried tracking Roark yet?"

He looked stunned as he released me and walked out the open elevator doors, heading toward a waiting car. I quickly followed him, and we headed toward the capital city's military headquarters.

"What do you mean by tracking Roark?"

"High Commander Reach designed special tracking chips and paid for all his men to have one installed in every weapon they carry. The weapons shield them from EMP blasts, and a smaller tracking chip can be inserted over the iris if the need arises."

"And how exactly do we track the chips?"

"I haven't got a clue. Roark takes care of that, but I can message his commanding officer and request his location."

Mr. Thaz nodded as I pulled out my plex and sent the formal request to my unit's head of a hundred.

Twenty minutes passed, bringing us into the military HQ and a part of the building I never had known existed. The place, reserved for ranking officers, made me feel out of place. The massive collection of holoplex stations scattered everywhere tracked every camera in Adreia and showed live feeds from the Adreian satellites of the Surface. Everywhere I looked, real-time footage of wars or places of interest played across the holographic screens. It was terrifying.

Mr. Thaz bounced around among the holoplex stations, giving

orders to ground troops while trying to get some information about where his daughter was. No one seemed to be able to get through to a higher-ranking Crimson Division officer to pull Roark's tracking data. Everyone either was engaged in active battle, as the Crimson Division always was, or had been placed on the no-contact list. There were ten commanders of a thousand and one hundred heads of a hundred in the Crimson Division, and for some reason, we couldn't get a single one of them on the plex. It was irritating, and I now understood why Roark kept me away from the politics of the ranking military. I couldn't handle the protocols that one had to go through just to call a higher-ranking officer, especially if the officer was in a different division.

My plex chimed, and I quickly opened the message from my unit's head of a hundred, only to have disappointment flood me. It read, "Emet of unit C1086, I regret to inform you that you have broken the chain of command by sending me this request. Any and all correspondence to me should be through your unit leader. Roark No-Last-Name is not my concern or priority. It is his responsibility to defend the captured civilian with his life."

He hadn't even bothered to sign it or to pretend to care that the civilian was High Commander Thaz's daughter. Roark had told me many times before that people hated him for no other reason than he was a ward of Adreia. He had grown up in an orphanage, and no one had adopted or wanted him, which was why he had no last name. It didn't matter that he had joined the military and become a ranking officer all on his own. He even held several records at the training academy that few came close to. The people of Adreia were horribly judgmental.

I sat down and prayed for guidance. I felt hopeless and unable to help anyone. My racing thoughts came to a crashing halt as I remembered Senator Reach and his past military career, during which he had hacked into Brashex satellites. My heart raced in excitement and fear as I told Mr. Thaz I would be back and left HQ.

The cab ride to Senator Reach's house had me on edge because what I was about to do and ask for was illegal by Adreian law. Before I knew it, I was in front of the massive black door that led to the senator's large three-story home. My heart pounded as I rang the doorbell and waited. Five minutes passed before I rang again, praying that the senator hadn't left. It was only six thirty in the morning, and seeing as he wasn't allowed to work because he had lost his daughter-in-law, I couldn't imagine he would have gone far.

I was about to give up, when the door opened, revealing a shirtless Senator Reach. His tousled black hair looked as if fingers had been run through it repeatedly, and his light bluish-green eyes held a hidden passion. I couldn't help but notice that he was extremely muscled, as if he had never stopped training from his days of being a commander of a thousand. He looked as if he were ready for battle and even had a handgun strapped to his thigh; plus, he was taller than I was by three inches. With all that added up, I found myself intimidated by him.

It shouldn't have surprised me that this man was one of Adreia's Crimson Soldiers, a high honor that only seven people in Adreia's history had achieved. A Crimson Soldier could pull military rank over the commander in chief and do just about anything he wanted without backlash. What could anyone say to someone who could decide to take over the country at any moment?

"Senator Reach, I need a favor."

He looked me over before throwing the door open and inviting me inside with a sweep of his arm. Silence filled the room as he closed the door behind us and walked through the foyer and into the lavish living room. As we walked, I noticed the lone tattoo just under his right shoulder blade. It was a shaded gray horse made up of interlocking geometric patterns that seemed to endlessly swirl into one another. The horse stood knee-deep in a river with a slightly red haze to it, and I was curious about the unusual, tribal-looking tattoo, but I had come here for Roark and had to keep my focus on that. He snagged a light jacket, pulling me from my thoughts, and shrugged it on as I noticed several small children asleep on his couches. I was sure they were the same children from Asherex's hospital room.

"I'm babysitting," he whispered as he looked back at me, but I didn't believe it for a moment.

"It's not my place to question the day-to-day affairs of those in the political world." As soon as I said it, I knew I should have kept my mouth shut.

Senator Reach looked at me with a conniving smile similar to the one my master displayed when he knew a worthy opponent had verbally assaulted him.

We walked into a back room that appeared to be his office, and he shut us in, but unlike when my master did the same thing, I wasn't afraid. I felt only peace and a rare boldness as Senator Reach took his seat.

"Well now, you obviously didn't come here to spy on me for Rayas, so what do you need?"

"I need you to hack into your son's program and track my unit leader for me. He was taken two days ago while trying to defend High Commander Thaz's daughter. There's nothing else I can do, and I know you are capable of doing this."

He sat back with a smug smile and then shook his head. "You know I'm not supposed to be working, and hacking is illegal. In fact, I've been trying to get my son to stop doing it for years. On the other hand, if I don't do this and Asherex learns I had a chance to save one of his soldiers and did nothing, he will hate me even more than he does now." He sighed and then leaned forward and, with a swipe of his hand, brought up his holoplex station built into his large desk. "Who am I to refuse such a request?"

"What is this going to cost me?"

Senator Reach looked up at me in disbelief. "Can a man not do what is right for no other reason than because he is asked to? I am a senator because I want to make a difference in this corrupt political system and change Adreia for the better, unlike Rayas, who is only interested in the power that comes with the position. My father was a captive from the Surface, forced into citizenship, and never happy here. I want to ensure that no one gets treated like that."

With that, he began diving into the world of computer code. I studied him while he intently watched the ever-changing code made up of several different languages. He didn't once type anything on the projected keyboard, but I could see his eyes noticing a pattern hidden within the code. Then the corner of his mouth quirked up, and he dove in. After five minutes, he sat back.

"Unit Leader Roark of the Crimson Division, unit number C1086. Resides at 1436 North Qualiet Avenue in the sixth ward. Quite an impressive résumé. I'm surprised he hasn't taken a promotion to commander of a thousand yet." Senator Reach mumbled in another language for a few minutes before he stood up, causing his chair to fall over. "Aha! Got him! He is being held at 1990087 ZX-C9 40." He looked at me apologetically and said, "Sorry. I forgot you don't know military code for addresses. It's the old shipyard factory in the city's forty-second ward of the Upper East Side. Building number seventy-six in the northeast corner. First floor."

"Thank you, Senator Reach."

"Azriel."

I looked up at him in surprise at hearing a Hebrew name in Adreia. "Excuse me?"

"My name is Azriel. I'm not allowed to be a senator right now, and I've always hated being called Mr. Reach, so call me Azriel."

"Thank you, Azriel."

He gave me a strange look as his name rolled off my tongue in my native language, but I couldn't help but smile as the meaning of the name struck me. Elohim was indeed using him to answer my prayers to help Roark.

"Well, you'd better be going now and help your friend." Azriel's gentle tone and quick smile comforted me as he sent a short message on his holoplex before powering it down. With a flick of his wrist, the door to his office opened before he reached it, and he motioned for me to follow him back through the living room.

The woman from Asherex's hospital room was checking on the children as we passed through, and she froze when she saw me. She wore a disheveled, expensive men's button-up shirt, and she bit her lip in fear as I passed by.

Azriel didn't even glance her way but led me into the foyer and opened the front door. He stepped outside with me as a cab pulled up to the curb.

"Emet." His authoritative tone stopped me from going down the steps.

"Yes, sir?"

"I heard what you said to Lillie at the hospital."

My heart stopped for a moment. If he turned me in for speaking about my religion, I could be in serious trouble with my master. *Yehovah, please watch over me.*

"If I were a lesser man, I would turn you in, but you comforted my daughter-in-law with it, so I will keep my mouth shut for my son's sake. My father once tried to speak to me of such nonsense." He shook his head as if trying to dispel a bad memory. "Be careful in the future not to get caught talking about whimsical things."

With a boldness that surprised me, I turned to him and said, "It is easy not to believe because you cannot see. It takes great strength to have complete faith in a Creator who loves and watches over His creation. I will pray for your eyes to be opened." With that, I turned and walked to the cab and told the driver where to take me. I wanted to spend a few minutes praying, but knowing that time was of the essence, I pulled my plex out and called Mr. Thaz.

He answered before the first ring was finished, and relief washed over me as his face came into view on the holographic screen. I told him where to go, and he bribed my cab driver to get me there as fast as possible. After he hung up, I bowed my head in prayer for Roark, Contessa, and Azriel.

It took twenty-seven minutes to reach the old shipyard, and

the military was already swarming the place. Mr. Thaz was quickly at the cab, paying the driver, before I could even open the door; and before I could figure out what was going on, I found myself inside the building, giving Contessa a quick medical exam. I wasn't surprised that she only had a few bruises and scrapes. She kept trying to get me to leave her alone and look after Roark, but I knew her father would be unhappy if I didn't look her over first.

Once finished, I followed a soldier to the interrogation room where Roark was. When I walked in, I hesitated at the doorway because he was slumped forward in the metal chair with his back to me. He was a bloody mess and wasn't moving. "Is he—" I couldn't bring myself to finish the question.

# Chapter Eleven

## Emet

A moment passed before I heard a soft groan and watched Roark lift his head and look around as if he were searching for me. I stepped in front of him, and he flashed me that smile of his as a playful light filled his pain-darkened green eyes. Without hesitation, I knelt before him and tried to examine him, but he kept moving away from me like a drunk child.

"Emet." His voice was a loud whisper, as if he were trying to tell me a secret. "I was tortured."

"I know. Now hold still so I can take care of you."

He finally let me begin my exam. "They recorded it. Do you think I'll be able to watch it later?" His playful tone irritated me but caused some in the room to laugh.

"How much pain medication has he been given?" I asked the medic assisting me.

"Nothing yet. We couldn't get him to sit still long enough, and he passed out right before you walked into the room."

"Emet, I'm good. Just untie me so I can go home and take a nap."

The soldiers trying to preserve the crime scene echoed the muffled laughter throughout the room, and my frustration skyrocketed because it distracted Roark and made him move again. He leaned close to my face and, in an attempt at a loudly hushed whisper, said, "Why are there so many people? I'm on edge right now 'cause I don't know who they are!"

"Roark, they are High Commander Thaz's men. There's no reason for you to panic. Please calm down, and let me finish my exam. Okay?"

He smiled at me as if he were enjoying a joke and then sat back in the chair. "Okay! I'm calm. You just do what you need to do, boss, and I'll just sit here. Yep, I'll just sit right here and do whatever it is I'm supposed to do. What am I doing? Oh yeah! I'm going to take a nap."

Before I could do anything, Roark passed out on me. That made it easier for me to do my exam, but I couldn't help but fear for his life as we packed him into an ambulance and raced off to the hospital. Once at the hospital, I oversaw his six-hour surgery and attempted to rest during the six hours he spent in the recovery tank before he was transferred a room.

Mr. Thaz pulled me into the hallway and asked for a briefing, and I filled him in on the surgery and recovery plan. Of course, Roark would have to see a psychologist before returning to work, because this was the first time he'd been tortured. I felt sorry for whoever got stuck with that job, because Roark had an odd outlook on life.

My master made his way into our conversation and enjoyed every moment he had with Mr. Thaz because of his place in the political world. It didn't surprise me that my master would do such a thing. He didn't even pretend he was interested in Roark's health and well-being, which was fine with me. I didn't think I could have stood back and said nothing if he'd started faking interest right then.

"Victor, I was wondering if I could ask a favor of you," Mr. Thaz said.

My master's eyes gleamed with a predatory look at Mr. Thaz's question. "And what might that be?"

"Could I borrow Emet? I know he is a certified psychologist, and given what has transpired in my household, I find myself in need of the best Adreia has to offer."

"For you, High Commander Thaz, I will gladly loan you Emet's services free of charge."

"Wonderful!" Mr. Thaz quickly brought up documents on his plex for my master to sign, which would transfer me into Mr. Thaz's employment for as long as it took for me to sign off on my patient's mental well-being. As soon as Victor signed the documents, Mr. Thaz said, "Now I can rest easy, knowing that Roark is going to be receiving the best care possible."

I had to bite back my laughter as my master's face paled, and his eyes widened. "Roark?" His voice barely restrained his horror.

"Why, yes." Mr. Thaz's voice was triumphant, his smile was predatory, and his stormy blue eyes sparkled with victory. He knew about Roark's attack on my master while I was unconscious, and he knew how much it would bother Victor that he wasn't even going to get paid for my service. "I can't have my future son-in-law having a psychotic breakdown before I've had a chance to apologize and give him permission to marry my daughter. And if anyone messes with him, I will bring the wrath of Adreia down on their head." Mr. Thaz's last words, punctuated with his knuckles cracking, made my master step back in fear.

My master stood there awkwardly for a few more minutes, feigning interest in a political matter that Mr. Thaz was dragging him into, but I could tell he just wanted to run away and lick his wounds. When a doctor came to take Mr. Thaz for his treatment for the assassination attempt during the summit meeting, my master finally got the chance to leave, and I slipped back into Roark's room. Exhausted, I curled up on the small sofa near the windows and passed out.

The sound of Mr. Thaz's voice woke me, and I became a spectator as he talked with Roark. It was strange to hear him relay his point of view of his daughter's friendship with Roark, which had ended badly in high school. Contessa had told him the truth about what happened while Roark was in surgery. Mr. Thaz apologized for being so hateful toward my friend and gave him permission to marry Contessa. I knew that Roark and Contessa loved each other, but they had many issues to work out before a relationship could happen. It was like something out of a movie, and I sent up a small prayer for Roark and Contessa's reconciliation.

Roark's prescribed discharge time came, and we found ourselves outside the hospital, waiting for our taxi to arrive to deliver us to Roark's home, which was a two-hour flight from the capital city. We didn't speak much as the cab ferried us home, and Roark arranged for the taxi company to deliver his cruzer from the hospital. All too soon, we were inside the small one-story, two-bedroom house. Roark didn't believe in furniture, so the house contained only a small two-foot-tall table and several lounge pillows in the sitting room off the kitchen. There was no holoscreen to watch anything on or a radio, only a few pieces of exercise equipment. The items, neatly tucked away like decorations, bore extensive wear, giving away their regular use.

The larger of the two bedrooms had a full-size bed and one dresser, with a few decorations on the walls. That room was the one Roark gave me when I stayed with him when my master didn't require me to stay at his mansion. I preferred to be here, even if I slept on a few blankets on the floor, as Roark did. This was my home in Adreia, even though my heart belonged to Yisra'el.

A loud curse from Roark drew my attention, and I turned just in time to watch him punch a hole in the wall. "Roark!"

"Don't start on me, Emet. I've had a terrible week, and I don't want to hear some lecture from you, especially if you're going to throw your religious nonsense around."

"I'm sorry."

My apology only seemed to upset him more, and he turned around to face me. Something dark in his eyes spoke of violence, and I involuntarily took a step back. I had seen that look in my master's eyes many times right before he attacked me, and even though I believed Roark would never hurt me, I couldn't help my response.

"Roark, I am your assigned psychologist."

"I'm not talking about my feelings with you." His voice was harsh and barely restrained. "I was tortured for two days. I'm angry and tired, and I'm fine!"

"You are not fine. No one could go through that and not be affected." I tried to keep my voice level and calm, but the fire in his eyes only grew brighter.

"You want to talk about being tortured? Fine. Let's talk about all the times you've been tortured by that psychopath who owns you. He beats you to within inches of your life on a regular basis, and still, you defend him like he's something worth saving! In the meantime, you pray to your God as if He's going to make it all stop. Where is He? Where was He a few days ago while you were dying on the sidewalk? Nowhere—that's where He was. I was the one who ran around trying to save you! I was the one who broke the rules to save you, not your God! If your God loved you so much, why didn't He kill Victor and set you free long ago?"

"Yehovah doesn't need me to be who He is, and He takes care of me. I might not understand why I am here, but He will turn it to His purpose."

A round of curses filled the air, and I flinched back. I knew Roark was only lashing out at me because of the mental stress he had undergone while being tortured in front of the woman he loved, but it still didn't comfort me to see my friend acting like an enemy. *Yehovah, bring peace to my friend, and heal his mind. Open his eyes to see You, his ears to hear You, and his heart to receive You in Yeshua's name. Amen.*

"His purpose!" Roark walked toward me with a murderous look in his eyes. "It's all about 'His purpose' with you. Do you know what I think? I think Yehovah abandoned you and doesn't care about you at all, and that's why you are a slave to the most evil human being in the universe." Roark was in my face now, and I feared he would hit me.

"His ways are higher than my ways, and His thoughts are higher than my thoughts. Who am I to question Him?" It took everything I had to keep the fear out of my voice as I spoke.

He pushed me against the door. "If your God were real, He would set you free. You are so devoted to Him, yet He has left you utterly alone. How could anyone believe that your God is real if He can't even take care of you?" With that angry question, Roark turned and walked toward the bathroom.

"Yehovah hasn't abandoned me. He brought you into my life, didn't He?"

Roark stopped for a moment, stepped into the bathroom, and slammed the door behind him. My legs suddenly went weak, and my heart felt as if it were being shattered into a million pieces as I slid to the floor. I didn't know how long I sat there holding back tears before pulling myself to my feet and walking out the door. I wandered around feeling numb and ended up in the park a few miles from Roark's house.

It was dark, and the stars were incredibly bright, so I sat beside a tree and stared at them. I wanted to fall into prayer for Roark and pour out my heart to Yehovah, but words eluded me. I covered my eyes with my hands. "Yehovah—" Suddenly, the tears broke through, and I wept.

Hours passed by, leaving me drained and feeling homesick. I longed to be back home in Yerushalayim and behold the Western Wall again. I longed to see the twelve guard towers that loomed into the sky, covered in solar panels that supplied the city with power, and to lay my face against the capital city's outer defensive wall and let the sun-warmed stone radiate into me.

I missed the din of noise of the people going about their daily business and the remarkable beauty of the city during the Sabbath. *O Yerushalayim, how I long to be in your shadow, to only see you once more.* I would even have happily stayed in utter darkness in the tunnels beneath the Temple Mount and spent the rest of my days alone. That would have been enough for me.

I sat there for a while longer, trying to recreate my homeland in my mind from my memories. I might have been five when they took me from my family, but I still remembered them and their love and faith. With a sigh, I pushed myself to my feet and began the walk back to Roark's place.

Uncertainty and trepidation washed over me as I let myself in but quickly dissipated when I saw Roark asleep on the floor next to the table. After locking the door behind me, I went to him and attempted to get him to stand so I could put him to bed. He barely woke enough to help me. As we entered his room, which was empty except for a small three-drawer dresser, a blanket pallet on the floor, and a new cardboard box in the corner, Roark looked at me through half-lidded eyes and groggily said, "I'm sorry, Emet. I'm not fine. I'm just not fine."

"I know, Roark. Just let me take care of you, okay?"

He nodded as I lowered him onto his bed, and he passed out as soon as he hit the pillow. I turned to leave the room but paused as I noticed a small wooden box on top of his dresser. Curiosity got the best of me, and I found myself in front of it and, without thinking twice, flipped the lid open. My breath caught in my chest at seeing a bunch of prepaid credit chips with $500 apiece, which happened to be a little more than 10 percent of Roark's weekly paycheck. On the lid of the box was a list with the names of an orphanage, a home for the widowed, and a nonprofit financial-assistance charity for the poor written in Roark's handwriting. There was probably about six months' worth of chips in the box.

My heart warmed at the sight. My friend was giving to the poor, the widow, and the orphan with a tenth of his wages. He might not believe in Yehovah, but he had adopted an essential biblical concept. With a smile, I returned the box to the way it had been when I found it and stepped out of the room. After a quick shower, I slipped into bed, thinking about the long weeks ahead, and prayed until I fell asleep.

# Chapter Twelve

## Asherex

It was storming so badly that I couldn't see the lake five hundred feet from my backyard. Lightning flashed continuously, but the sound of thunder never made it through the soundproof walls. When building the small mansion for my wife, I'd included soundproofing as a precaution to prevent my PTSD attacks from triggering during a storm. A sigh passed my lips at the thought of Lillie. It had nearly been forty days since she died, and my life was already rising up from the ashes as if she had never been there. It was strange how it felt as if she were right beside me at times, and then I would remember that she was gone.

I couldn't even have a dream with her in it without my brain reminding me that she was dead, and upon waking, it would be as if I had lost her all over again. How did normal people cope with loss? Did it ever get better?

"What do you want from me?" I spoke aloud to the nothingness around me again, as if someone were there to hear it. How many times in my life had I done that? Was there something out there listening to me and watching over me? If so, where was it?

Another flash of lightning drew my attention and brought back memories of Lillie and me sitting in the plush window seat that protruded from the back of the house. It was about half the size of our bed, and we had spent many lazy afternoons here, curled up in each other's arms, counting heartbeats between lightning flashes. I smiled at the memory. A mechanical beep as the last round of meds coursed through my system interrupted my thoughts.

The hours couldn't pass quickly enough. It would be another six hours before I was free of the IV tubes and blood-filtering machine. I hated the drugs I had to take, because they left me feeling perpetually angry, and I could feel that my brain wasn't functioning at full capacity. I knew that my servants were avoiding me because of my mood swings, and several times, I'd had to apologize to them for my outbursts, but they always made me feel worse when they told me I had nothing to apologize for.

The door to the library opened, and Lazerick walked into the room as if he owned the place. Lazerick was one of the first slaves I'd bought and set free, but he refused to leave and had been by my side ever since. He was a former Brashex assassin taken as a prisoner of war, and even though I had procured the proper paperwork for him to return home, he wouldn't leave. Instead, he had stayed by my side and helped me rise through the military ranks. He was a blessing, except for the fact that he loved to mess with me every chance he got.

Lazerick smiled, flashing his perfectly white teeth, and said, "Master, you have a visitor. Shall I send him away?"

I glared at him for calling me *master*, and his smile broadened. He knew I couldn't stand that title. "Who is it?" My voice was a little harsher than I intended, and amusement danced in his champagne-colored eyes. He tilted his head to the left, and his curly, shoulder-length blond-and-silver hair framed his face, making him almost appear boyish instead of forty-eight. Or maybe it was the fact that he was only five and a half feet tall that made him appear to be a teenager.

"Your father-in-law." Even though his eyes held amusement, his voice betrayed the underlying threat of violence. The fact that he didn't use Veris's name let me know how much he hated the man.

Lazerick believed that not acknowledging someone's name was a way to curse him or her.

Before I could tell Lazerick to send him away, Veris walked into the room and dismissed Lazerick. Lazerick bared his teeth at my father-in-law in a show of aggression before stepping out of the room.

"I would have him put down for that if I were you, Asherex."

"Well, I'm not you. I actually value the lives of others, Veris." My tone was anything but friendly, and his laughter was unexpected.

"So I hear they caught the man who killed my Lillie and tortured him to death."

Veris's tone was full of delight, but my heart sank. I understood why they'd interrogated the man to ensure someone hadn't hired him to kill Lillie, because her death had happened at the same time someone attempted to murder me. The poor man hadn't deserved to be tortured, which was my fault. If someone hadn't tried to kill me, the guy would have been charged with unintentional manslaughter and fleeing the scene and had a swift death, and his family would have been able to bury him. Instead, they'd incinerated his body and tossed the ashes over the edge of Adreia.

"I feel sorry for his family."

"What!" Veris shouted. "He killed my daughter, your *wife*. He deserved everything he got!"

"Lillie drove in a state of emotional turmoil because you drugged her and illegally took her to the Surface to have her sterilized before she married me. You broke the law and stayed away until now because you knew you would have to face judgment and death. Everything you've ever done is under review, and your family will suffer because of it. You probably came here because you think I will save you somehow, but I can't. Even if I don't press charges, which I won't, my father will because you have deprived him of an heir to the Reach name, and he will charge you for the murder of the potential grandchildren he would have had."

Veris took a step back as the smug look fell from his face. He stood there in silence before saying, "I know who tried to kill you,

Asherex. I will give you the evidence if you arrange safe passage for me to the Surface."

My anger flared. I might have occasionally broken the law to hack into things to help my soldiers, but I would never have helped a criminal escape justice. "No. You will face judgment for what you've done. I know you will find a way to escape, and when they ask me to hunt you down, I will accept without hesitation. I won't kill you, and I won't let anyone else kill you either. I will ensure you have a proper trial before your execution. There is nothing you can give me that will change my mind."

Vile curses filled the air as Veris turned and fled from the room. I knew my servants had already alerted the authorities that he had been here, but he would be long gone by the time they picked up on his trail. Weariness crept over me as my anger dissipated, and I closed my eyes and drifted off.

A gentle hand shook me awake, and I automatically knew I had been asleep for only forty-six minutes and twenty-three seconds. With a groan, I opened my eyes and came face-to-face with my father. What was he doing here?

"How are you feeling?" His voice was uncertain, as if he feared I would send him away before talking to him. Guilt pierced my heart, and I opened my mouth to say something, but nothing came out. Before I could try again, my dad stood up and walked over to the shelves where I kept the book chips I had read over the years. He ran his fingers over their spines and said, "I wanted to check on you after Veris showed his face here. I was told that he stole a cruzer and crashed somewhere on the Surface and that he was selling Adreian secrets to rebel groups. His whole family will bear the weight of his mistakes."

"Will Larissa be banished?" My heart sank. I couldn't imagine never again seeing the woman who had been like a mother to me since I was nine.

Dad turned to face me and said, "No, she won't be banished, but she has no income and small children, not to mention that all their property will be seized, and if her parents don't take her back, then she will have nowhere to go and will lose the little ones."

"They won't be out on the streets. They can come live here if they need—"

"No." He cut me off midsentence. "You will not ruin your rank and reputation by bringing them into your home."

My anger flared. How dare he think I cared about that superfluous garbage instead of family? "Dad—"

"Asherex! This is not up for debate!" He cut me off again, and I was ready to rip out the tubes holding me back from hitting him. "Larissa is pregnant! If you take her in, you will be charged with committing adultery and face possible death charges without an investigation to see if you are responsible or not. For once in your life, Asherex, listen to me! I know what I'm doing and want to keep you safe."

"What have you done?" I couldn't hold back my anger and disappointment. He had slept with a married woman, and if her father pressed charges, he was a dead man. "What were you thinking? Never mind. I know you weren't thinking! How could you be so irresponsible?"

He flinched as if I had slapped him before his anger surfaced. "Don't you dare act like you've never broken the law before, Asherex Reach. You're not the only one who lost Lillie. I know you have problems functioning like a normal human being, but maybe if you stopped acting like an emotionless robot and let someone in, you would understand how the rest of us feel."

With that, he turned and walked out. I shook with rage as my heart shattered from the vicious verbal attack. I didn't even notice Lazerick sit down next to me, until he pulled me into a gentle hug around the various tubes and wires attached to me.

"It's okay, kid. Just let it out. You know he didn't mean it. He just doesn't know how to handle you on your meds."

I clutched his shirt tightly in my fists and let my anger explode in hot streams of tears that tried to tear me apart. I hated these drug-induced mood swings. Soon an icy feeling began coursing through my veins, and I knew Lazerick had given me drugs to make me relax and sleep. For once, I welcomed the oblivion.

I awoke to the sound of laughter, and it took me a moment before my foggy brain recognized that it belonged to my wife's twin sister, Nayomi. The machine next to me beeped, letting me know that the last round of meds emptied into my system. I must have been drugged pretty heavily not to have noticed when they unhooked me from the blood-filtering machine, which was now nowhere to be found. What had Lazerick given me?

My plex chimed, and I dug through the blankets to find it. Without hesitating, I opened the message from the foundation worker I had asked to assist me in purchasing Emet. Even though I wasn't supposed to be working right now, I couldn't let it go. His message didn't tell me anything I didn't already know, including that it would take up to two months for his freedom documentation to be completed, even though we had started the paperwork two weeks ago. It was strange how someone could go about setting free a man he didn't have possession of yet, but I wasn't complaining. There was no price I wouldn't have paid to set Emet free.

"Asherex Reach! Are you working? You still have forty-two minutes before that's legal."

Nayomi's voice pulled me from my mental walkthrough of the proper paperwork and other arrangements necessary before a slave could be set free.

"Of course I'm working. I don't know how not to work, Nay; you should know that by now."

"I can't believe you." Her playful tone made me smile as she appeared in the doorway. She turned to someone in the other room and said, "Can you believe it? He's working already!"

"What are you talking about? He never stopped working." Drayen's voice boomed through the room and instantly made me feel better. There was something healing about hearing my best friend's voice, even if it was teasing. "He's probably checking on how fast the snail's pace of the bureaucratic world of freeing slaves is going. I'm going to make a prediction that it is now further along than when first filed but not seen by anyone at the capitol building."

I shook my head as they burst out laughing before I removed the IV line from my arm and powered down the machines. I had been waiting all day for Drayen to show up and was anxious to see my friend. Nayomi hugged me as I entered the sitting room full of strange furniture that Lillie and Nayomi had bought to fill the large space intended for entertaining guests. It looked as if ancient steampunk furniture had had a baby with modern art and then thrown up all over my white-and-gold marble floor. The only excuse Lillie had given me for keeping the look was that there was no wrong way to sit in or on the furniture. It had seemed as strange to me back then as it did now, except now the room matched what I was feeling on the inside; everything was chaos trapped inside a perfectly painted room designed to look like everything else in the house.

I sat on what looked like a melting sofa and joined in the conversation going on about some kind of dress that looked like different colors to different people. It was probably the dumbest thing in the world to have a debate about, but as it went on, I found myself laughing more and more. The picture of the dress was flashed around many times on Nayomi's plex, and after the third time she practically shoved it into Drayen's face, I noticed they looked at each other the way I had looked at Lillie. When had that happened?

We were still deep into the dress debate, when Nayomi's and my plexes chimed with the message that our forty-day mourning was officially over. Silence hung heavy in the room for the longest time before Nayomi left Drayen and me alone. He looked at me as if he were debating whether or not to say what he was thinking.

"Asherex"—he sighed—"as the high commander of the Crimson Division, it is your duty to put together a team to catch a terrorist. I wouldn't ask you to do this, but Veris cannot escape punishment for his crimes against Adreia. You have twelve hours to put your team together before you launch to the Surface."

# Chapter Thirteen

Asherex

It was dark and drizzling, even though the full moon still shed its light in the forest. I didn't know where my men were or if they were alive. We had tracked Veris down, but he'd ambushed us and scattered us into the night. The last time I had been conscious, my second-in-command and a few other men had been with me, but that had been three explosions and one cliff ago.

The cold seeped through my body armor, and I shivered, causing pain to lance through me. I closed my eyes and welcomed the cold rain on my exposed face, thankful that my air-filtering machine was still intact and working correctly. If it busted, I would have to spend seven days in quarantine before returning to Adreia, in case I picked up the incurable disease known as Zeron's disease.

I did my best to curl into a ball while my body protested the slightest movement. Before falling over a cliff, a nearby tree had burst apart, and the wooden shrapnel had embedded itself in my armor. Some had broken through into my left side. I didn't know how bad the damage was, but I knew nothing vital had been hit, or I would have been dead by now. It had been about seven hours since then, and all I wanted to do was go to sleep, but I knew I wouldn't survive the night if I did.

Movement in the brush caused my heartbeat to quicken, and I reached for my sidearm and aimed at the sound's source. Relief washed over me as my second-in-command burst through the undergrowth awakening from a long winter. His face, half covered by his respirator, was a welcome sight, and relief washed over me to see that he looked fine except for a slight limp.

"High Commander Reach!" He limped to me and began a quick examination, which caused me to pass out from the pain.

When I came to, he was sitting next to me, and my pain-filled moan drew his attention. He looked at me briefly before saying, "There are too many of them, and they know these woods like the back of their hand. Our backup is on its way but still at least five hours out. The enemy will find us here soon, so we need to move."

He stood and leaned down to help me, but I stopped him and said, "Lance, you need to go. If you move me, you could kill me. It's a miracle I'm not dead now; we both know it. You have a wife and five children waiting for you at home; please don't kill yourself for me."

"I won't leave you, Asherex." With that, he reached for me again, and I grabbed his wrists with all the strength I could muster.

"Leave me. That's an order, soldier. I will hold them off as long as possible to buy you time to escape."

His eyes were full of protest, but after a few minutes, he relented, and with slumped shoulders, he left me. I pulled myself a few feet and propped myself up against a rock to get a better vantage point to defend myself and buy Lance some time to escape. The cold bit into me again as a cloud swallowed the moon, and the silence became deafening.

"Is this what you wanted? For me to die here?" My whispered questions seemed to fall right off my lips to the cold ground. My heart felt as if it were breaking as I realized that this would probably be the last night I was alive, and I still didn't have the answers I had been seeking my whole life. "If you are out there, please show me who you are. I can't live like this anymore, not knowing if I'm insane for believing you are there. I just need to know. Please." My voice trailed off as the tears fell. This couldn't be it, could it?

I must have passed out again, because Lance awakened me. He looked worried and slightly panicked until I groaned and grabbed his arm to make him stop. Without saying a word, he dragged me to my feet despite my pain-filled protests and forced me to limp with him. He started hooking us into a makeshift repelling harness and said, "There were too many of them, and I ran out of bullets before they ran out of men. I came back here thinking I could repel down the cliff, but there was no way I was going to leave you to die."

I looked past him down the cliffside and panicked at the sight of a raging river several hundred feet below us. "There's a river down there, Lance!"

"Yeah, I know, Reach. There is also a ledge, and according to the maps I have, there is a cave about thirty feet from the current water level. People once used it to smuggle goods down river."

"You can't be serious right now. If we fall into the river, we are as good as dead."

"Asherex, if we stay here, we are dead. At least this way, there is a slight chance we might survive the night, and a slight chance is better than no chance."

I tried to swallow back fear as Lance brought us over the edge of the cliff and began the hard work of keeping me still while slowly making his way down the cliffside. All I could think about was drowning in the freezing river below us; drowning happened to be my biggest fear. I was so lost in my tangled thoughts of dying in the water that I didn't notice the people firing upon us, until a bullet struck the rock near my head. Lance shouted something at me a moment before the rope busted from a bullet. I watched seemingly in slow motion as it unraveled, and we fell.

As soon as I hit the freezing water, my breath ripped from my lungs, and I began to sink. The last time that had happened to me, I had been five, and I felt as helpless now as I had back then. The freezing water stole my pain and soon my consciousness.

# Chapter Fourteen

**Roark**

I was running. I had been running for six hours now and getting nowhere. My thoughts raced through the events of the last couple of months over and over again. It took everything I had to maintain my pace of twelve miles an hour instead of running as fast as I could until I dropped and the treadmill threw me into the wall, something I had done about a week ago and wasn't looking to repeat.

Emet had left a few days ago, and because I hadn't talked to him the entire time about being tortured, he refused to clear me for active duty. His report was open across the room on my dining table, and I had memorized every word. He had said I was emotionally unavailable; was unwilling to accept reality; and, my personal favorite, had a savior complex and was compelled to recklessly sacrifice myself for others, causing me to be a danger to myself. Did I sacrifice myself for others or just those I considered family? Yeah, that was totally me—not. Or was it?

Why was I questioning myself? Anger surged through me at the thought. I was perfectly fine, except for being a little messed up in the head from being tortured. I didn't need Emet telling me how to live my life; I knew what I was doing.

*There is a way that seems right to a man, but its end is the way to death.*

As the thought slammed into me, I could hear Emet's voice, and my anger kicked up a notch. With a growl, I began running faster, trying to drown out my thoughts with the sounds of my feet slamming into the treadmill beneath me. *The wicked flee though no one pursues.* The thought hit me like a bat upside the head, causing me to miss a step and slam into the wall four feet from the back of the treadmill.

I lay there on my back, looking up at the ceiling, and listened to the treadmill running without me. That was the way life went, wasn't it? It kept going even after it knocked the breath right out of you and left you helpless on the floor. Why was I so angry about Emet, my best friend, being honest about how dysfunctional I was?

He had tried hard to get me to talk just to help me, and I hadn't even considered that he was upset about what had happened to me. If he had been in my place, I wouldn't have left his side until I knew he was fine. I had been selfish and forced him to put up with me without treating him like a friend and sharing even the smallest detail about what I had been through or how I felt about it.

Cold chills broke out across my body as my sweat-drenched clothes clung to me and sucked up the air-conditioning. I closed my eyes and tried to ignore the cold, only to have a heavy knock at my door disturb my peace. With a sigh, I stood on shaky legs, shut the treadmill off, and headed to the front door.

Three heavily armed soldiers dressed in black with gold trim along the armor greeted me with deadly stares. They were part of the war council's Secret Service division and probably would have been intimidating to most, but I just stared at them as if they were pests on my porch.

"What do you want this time?" I couldn't hide my irritation. It wasn't the first time the Secret Service had been at my door, and it probably wouldn't be the last. Because I held several records at the most prestigious training facility in Adreia, they often selected me for special operation missions. In fact, the only one who had broken any of my records was Asherex Reach. Even though I had refused every promotion that came my way, I still had to answer to the war council and do their bidding whenever they wanted to sic me on someone or have me go fetch something for them.

"You have five minutes to shower, dress, and be in the cruzer."

The one on the left spoke, and I gave him the dirtiest look I could muster before slamming the door in their faces and quickly walking to the bathroom. I cranked on the cold water and soaped up my clothes before peeling out of them and hanging them on the hooks at the back of the shower to dry. Weariness began to creep up on me, and with a groan, I shut off the water, patted myself dry, and went to my room to dress.

My worn battle suit desperately needed replacing, but I couldn't afford it. Because my head of a hundred had cut my unit's budget, I'd bought all their armor out of my pocket for the last five years, so I had been putting off buying anything for myself. The men didn't deserve to suffer because someone hated me for having no official social status. It wasn't my fault that I had grown up an orphan and that even now, no one wanted to officially adopt me and give me a last name, which would have granted me an official social status. Not that I cared. I was perfectly fine being Roark No-Last-Name, even if those who said it meant it as an insult.

With a sigh, I pushed my hair from my face, plugged my feet into my boots, and stepped outside. They were waiting for me. The neighbors stared at us in disbelief as I boarded the cruzer and headed off. Why couldn't the neighbors keep their noses out of my business?

Conversation was nonexistent as we flew three hours to the capital city and walked into the capitol building, where the war council and the senate were located. As we passed the senate chambers, we strategically maneuvered through the halls to avoid disrupting the senators scattered about in various conversations. They were preparing for the busiest time of the year, when every farming contract with the Surface was up for renewal. If they didn't renew every contract, they weren't paid, but millions of contracts were up for renewal, and they only had two months to get through them all. They had to approve price increases for grain and requests to increase the price of the harvested crop as well as new farm equipment or repairs.

It was stressful for everyone involved because the business owners who relied on the crops had to wait to set prices on their merchandise until they were sure they would have a product to sell. The senators usually didn't get every contract approved and lost their pay. Those on the Surface who didn't have their contracts renewed were stuck with a bunch of crops they legally couldn't sell to anyone in Adreia and faced the death penalty for selling to anyone else, because the food they grew belonged to Adreia. They could keep it for themselves, but without the money to bid on a new contract, many lost everything they owned. Man, was I glad I wasn't involved with any of that.

The armed guard shut me in the war council's chamber, and I found myself facing the twelve men and their assistants. They sat around the massive, heavily polished table, waiting for me to walk to the center of the room. I made them wait a few minutes before I crossed the room and bowed with a clenched fist over my heart to show my respect. As the bow was dismissed, I had to bite back my questions while waiting patiently for them to brief me on the mission they were about to send me on.

"Unit Leader Roark of Crimson Division unit C1086, you have been summoned here today for a retrieval operation. Six months ago, the *Racaquor* went down behind enemy lines, and the black box was lost. One of our undercover allies retrieved the box from Brashex control and confirmed that it hadn't been hacked yet. The operative disappeared four days ago, and we have tracked the black box to a compound in the Borderland. Your mission is to infiltrate and retrieve the black box before anyone discovers what it contains. You will be alone on this mission, and if you fail, no one will be coming for you; if you are captured and tortured, your mission in the Borderland will be denied."

"Not to be a buzzkill here, boys," I said, "but my shrink says I'm not fit for active duty."

"That is irrelevant." The councilor to the right of the head speaker stood. He looked across the room at a small panel of people behind me on the left. "What do you think of young Roark, Dr. Cavet?"

"I do believe that Mr. Roark is clinically insane and agree with the professional opinion of Dr. Emet. However, I wouldn't send a sane man to do this kind of work. Roark, we need your unorthodox tactics here due to the poor relationships with the clans of the Borderland. I would recommend one of our Crimson Soldiers, but they are both occupied at the moment, so you are the next best thing."

I couldn't believe what I was hearing. Had the most well-known psychologist in Adreia just called me clinically insane and told me I was perfect for a job? Had I just had my skills compared to those of the two Crimson Soldiers in Adreia?

"It is settled then. You are cleared for active duty after you complete your mission. Now, go bring the *Racaquor*'s black box back before Adreian secrets fall into the hands of terrorists," the head speaker said, dismissing Roark.

Before I could speak, the armed guard removed me from the room and escorted me outside, where I had to call a ride to fly me back home so I could get my cruzer and head out on my top-secret mission. Once in my cruzer, I had to go through all the red tape around taking a personal airship to the Surface, which took twenty minutes, before the best Adreian pilots escorted me through the hangar tunnels. When I entered Earth's atmosphere, the sight of Earth from just outside the World Above's border was breathtaking, and I wondered what it would have been like to grow up there.

With a sigh of resignation, I punched the thrusters and began my descent to the Borderland. It was a place controlled by many clans and under neither Adreian nor Brashex control. The natives, who were savage brutes, enslaved many who survived crashing in their territory. Occasionally, someone would return from enslavement in the Borderland and talk about cannibalism and other horrendous acts of violence against other human beings within the territories. I was sure that not every king was like that, but I didn't want to find out.

The trip took about seventeen hours, and finding a suitable landing place that would hide my cruzer took another hour. I lay down for a few hours to rest before suiting up and heading out. The compound, most likely heavily guarded, required surveillance before I attempted anything. I had no clue what I was in for. This was going to be fun.

# Chapter Fifteen

## Emet

I cut the water in the shower, took my time drying off, and wrapped the towel around my waist. The last thirteen hours in and out of surgery had been therapeutic and helped take my mind off Roark. I hadn't signed off on him to return to active duty, because after thirty days, he still refused to talk about being tortured. He wasn't happy about it, and now he had to convince another psychologist that he was mentally fit for active duty. *Poor Roark. He may not be able to return.*

With a sigh, I opened the door to the small doctor's sleeping room and stopped dead in my tracks at the sight of Senator Reach leaning against the room's door. He was dressed in full body armor, with his Crimson Soldier patch on his arm and a look of murder in his eyes. His piercing gaze made me uncomfortable, and I became even more aware that I was naked except for the towel. *I should start taking clothes into the bathroom with me, even if I have locked the door to the room.*

"My son has gone missing, and you will help find him."

I just nodded, and he left me alone in the room. It took me a moment before I noticed the brand-new set of body armor laid out on the bed and the change of clothes. I had been hoping to be able to sleep a little today, but that was out of the picture now. With a sigh, I began dressing and praying for Asherex.

When I stepped out of the room, Mr. Reach was waiting for me, and I fell in line behind him as he briefed me on the mission. Two men who had been with Asherex were dead, and Asherex and one other were missing. The destroyed or disabled tracking chips were not transmitting. I couldn't help but wonder if the Reach family would ever get a break from tragedy and drama.

Mr. Reach flew us in his top-of-the-line personal cruzer to the hangar bay where my unit was waiting minus Roark. No one spoke a word as we neared the fleet about to take off, and Mr. Reach began briefing the assembled teams on what to expect when we reached our destination. The briefing was nearing its end, when another cruzer landed, and my master walked toward us. He looked furious.

"What do you think you're doing, Reach? You cannot just take my property without my permission!"

My heart beat faster with every step my master took toward me. He was furious, and I knew he would beat me badly, if not kill me, because I had left with the senator. Mr. Reach stepped in front of me, and his body language told the story of how he had come to wear the Crimson Soldier patch on his arm. My master must not have noticed that a greater predator was in front of him, and I knew he was caught up in his own bloodlust and would fight if he wasn't stopped first.

My master stopped a few feet from Mr. Reach with a wolflike, predatory gleam in his eyes, and I wondered if he realized he was up against a silent killer I could only liken to a panther. There was no way my master would come out of this confrontation unscathed, if he came out alive. The air around us fell silent; not even the sound of a cruzer engine interrupted it. I wondered if all the soldiers gathered around to watch the inevitable fight could hear my pounding heart.

Everything seemed to unfold in slow motion as my master decided he would fight, and as soon as his muscles flexed, Mr. Reach was on him. A quick one-two punch to the throat and face nearly brought my master to his knees, but before he could recover,

Mr. Reach grabbed him with one hand, wrenched him off his feet, and slammed him into the nearby cruzer. My master was pinned about a foot off the ground, and I caught a glimpse of Mr. Reach's face and was terrified at what I saw. No emotion was evident in his blue-green eyes, not even the anticipation of a kill.

"If you ever come after my family or me again, Rayas, I will make you wish you had never been born," Mr. Reach said. My master struggled to suck in a breath as Mr. Reach got in his face and, in a deadly whisper, added, "My father warned me about you before he died, you snake."

As quickly as the fight had begun, it ended as Mr. Reach released my master, turned back to the men, and finished his briefing as if he had never been interrupted. I didn't dare look at my master, fearing I would set him off again. I knew if he actually got hurt, it would come back on me later. The only thing I could do was pray that my master's anger would melt away. I also hoped he would realize that when a Crimson Soldier told someone to do something, the person didn't have any choice. He or she had to obey or would face worse punishment for disobeying the highest-ranking person in Adreia.

"Emet?" Mr. Reach's soft tone drew my attention, and he looked at me like a parent concerned for his child. "Are you all right?"

I noticed then that everyone else had already gone off to his assigned place, while I was left alone with the senator. It was both disconcerting and somehow peaceful to be alone with him after such a public display concerning my master. "I just—I'm sorry about my master's behavior."

He looked at me in a strange way, raised an eyebrow, and said, "You cannot apologize for someone else's behavior. It's not your fault that Rayas is pure evil. Besides, when Roark returns, you won't have to worry about Rayas anymore."

Mr. Reach left me with more questions than answers. I was confused. What had he meant by "when Roark returns"? Where had Roark gone, and why would his return solve my problems with my abusive master?

"Don't you just hate it when people drop something like that on you?"

I jumped as my heart pounded at Doug's unexpected question. "Doug, you have to stop scaring me like that!"

He chuckled at me before slinging his arm around my shoulders, even though he was seven inches taller than I, and herded me toward our cruzer. The other units we were sharing the airship with gave us odd looks, probably because Doug wore those dark wraparound goggles that added to his deadly aura, and the fact that he was nearly seven feet tall didn't help matters any. As we took our seats, someone made a comment directed at me about not needing nonessential personnel on a search-and-rescue mission. The comment stung, especially considering I had performed life-saving surgery on the soldier in a triage tent a few months ago when no one else would touch him.

As soon as he heard the remark, Doug shot to his feet and got in the man's face. I couldn't hear what Doug said to him, but soon all color drained from the soldier's face, and he looked at me in fear. I quickly became fascinated with my new boots and tried to be invisible. Everything seemed to go much better when no one noticed me. *Father, be with me. As it is written in Tehillim 18, "I love You, O Yehovah, my strength. Yehovah is my rock and my fortress and my deliverer, my God, my rock, in whom I take refuge, my shield, and the horn of my salvation, my stronghold. I call upon Yehovah, who is worthy to be praised, and I am saved from my enemies." And so I call upon You, my King, to deliver me from the snares of the wicked and give me shelter beneath the shadow of Your wings. I thank You, Yehovah, that You have placed mighty men in my life to pull me from the hands of my oppressors. I realize that these men are given strength to accomplish Your will in my life, so I ask only that You draw them to Yeshua that Messiah might point them back to You. I long for them to see Your loving commitment and loving-kindness, repent from their sins, renounce the ways of the world, and take up the banner of Your Torah. May Your will be done, O Yehovah, in this place and in these people. In Yeshua's authority, I ask this of You, Almighty Father. Amen.*

When I looked up from my prayer, Doug was staring at me—at least I thought he was looking at me. It was hard to tell with his wraparounds. He smiled for a moment before catching me off guard and asking me about Yeshua feeding the five thousand. At first, I was uncomfortable answering in front of the other soldiers. As Doug pressed me further, I began to relax, and soon everything else seemed to fade away as the others from my unit started asking questions.

We landed four hours later and joined the others who were already searching for High Commander Reach. It was a lot of organized chaos, and I felt out of place as people began coordinating off search grids and establishing possible scenarios that could have befallen our high commander. Forty-five minutes later, my unit still didn't have an assignment. Frustration was setting in, and I did my best to stay out of everyone's way while tempers flared.

I was in the perfect position to watch as a unit returned dragging a well-muscled teenager. The boy couldn't have been more than fifteen, and he attempted to free himself from the soldiers, but to no avail. They chained him up to a tree and began questioning him. He looked at me, and I could see a fierce fire burning in his eyes, a look I had seen many times in Gavin's eyes when he was defying our master. This kid would get hurt, and my heart broke for him. Without thinking twice, I crossed the clearing, heading toward where Doug was sitting.

"I told you that I don't know anything!"

The kid's frustrated but level tone seemed to fill the air and brought all activity to a screeching halt. I was the first to resume movement, and as I passed him, he called out to me in perfect Hebrew, "Man of El! I can help you escape your slavery and free you."

His words pierced my heart with warmth, and I stopped to look him in the eye. I smiled at him before answering in Hebrew, "If you want to help me, find my high commander. The rest is up to Yehovah."

He nodded at me as if I had just given him the greatest mission in the world before his eyes went past me. I turned my head just in time to see Doug before he could open his mouth and startle me. I scowled at him, and he smiled back and asked, "Whatcha talking about over here? I understood 'Man of El,' and that was about it."

"May I ask you a question, Doug?"

"Fire away."

"When did we start kidnapping underage children and holding them against their will? What we are doing here isn't lawful."

"We don't." Doug turned his face to the kid and asked, "Do you know what transpired here last night?"

"I already told them I don't have a clue what anyone is talking about. I run a salvage yard and have all the paperwork to come here to scrap out the junk airships that are up here. I've been doing it for five years, and if you don't believe me, just look at my permits."

Doug turned to one of the soldiers who had chained up the kid and ordered him to release the boy. The soldier began to argue but quickly changed his mind when Doug reached for one of his throwing knives. A minute later, they released the kid, and he turned to me and said in Hebrew, "You are not alone. I will do as you have asked." Then he turned and ran away as fast as he could.

*Blessed be Yehovah! Thank You, Father, for blessing Your servant and reminding me that I am not alone in You!*

# Chapter Sixteen

Asherex

I was drowning. Water filled my mask meant to filter the air I breathed, trapping it against my face. I struggled to breathe and began blindly twisting about, attempting to find a foothold but slipping farther beneath the water's surface. The water was still cold this early in the year, and a strong current from recent rains attempted to pull me farther under into the murky darkness. *Please don't let me die like this!*

The respirator violently dislodged from my face as a dark figure came closer. Warmth seeped into me from the contact with the shadowy man while he pulled me with him against the current. I broke through the surface, gasping and sputtering in an attempt to breathe, but something beneath us sucked me under again. Once more, the shadowy man dove for me, and I felt him pull at something holding me back. It seemed like an eternity before it released me, and my lungs involuntarily expelled the last of the air in them.

When I finally regained consciousness, I was lying on my back, looking up at the ever-darkening sky. The wind whipped around violently, and I could barely hear other people's voices but didn't have the strength to look at them. I closed my eyes against the painful numbness in my body, only to have someone shake me awake moments later.

"Are you the high commander they are looking for?"

I could only nod at the teenager in front of me.

He smiled and said, "I thought you were dead. I couldn't find a pulse. Don't worry; I will take care of you, but we have to move you because of the storm." He paused as if waiting for me to respond.

I remembered the injuries I'd sustained before falling victim to the raging river. I managed to mouth a quick "Okay" before he continued.

"What's your name?"

Darkness began creeping up on me again as I weakly said, "Ash—" before passing out.

I awoke slowly and knew I had been unconscious for three days, four hours, and fifty-six minutes. Sometimes it was hard to live with a built-in clock in my head. A loud boom of thunder caused me to jackknife out of bed and fall onto the hardwood floor beneath as the sound shook the whole house. My heart was pounding, and to calm myself and prevent a PTSD attack, I started counting backward from a thousand while ignoring the pain lancing through my body.

I reached five hundred before my pounding heart slowed to a normal pace, and I slowly pulled myself to my feet, using the sturdy wooden poster bed. I took a couple of deep breaths before looking around the small bedroom, which had been done in earth tones, with a beautiful dark red-and-black comforter on the queen-sized bed. The furniture looked old and had been handcrafted, giving the room a welcoming feel. A quick glance at my bandages reassured me that I hadn't pulled any stitches that might have been there.

I slowly made my way to the bathroom, where I discovered a note telling me not to get any of my bandages wet, along with a pair of sweatpants, boxers, and a plain gray T-shirt. It took me a bit to clean up with a washcloth and pull on the clothes left for me. With a sigh, I finally looked at my reflection in the mirror and winced at the sight. The right side of my face was mostly black and blue and scratched up. I was surprised it didn't hurt other than being a little sore. My biceps had bruises in the shape of someone's hand. I was in bad shape, but at least I wasn't dead.

The sound of clanging pans drew my attention, and I slowly made my way to the hallway, using the wall for much-needed support. My room was the third from the stairs leading to the main floor of the house. The staircase was made of old wood, and I feared it would give beneath me as I slowly made my way down. Every step creaked, and the handrail seemed to struggle under my weight.

I stepped off the last step as a woman walked out of the kitchen. Her surprised looked quickly turned to one of concern. Her bright green eyes looked me over like those of a mother whose only child had fallen off his bike, and I had to bite back the smile that threatened to break across my bruised face. As she stepped toward me, some of her golden-brown hair slipped from the clip it was in, and the wavy curls immediately took their rightful place alongside her neck. She was beautiful in a way most women attempted to make themselves with costly makeup.

"Ash, are you all right? I should have checked up on you so that you didn't have to come downstairs by yourself. The doctor said you had to be monitored closely because of your injuries."

She gently pulled my arm over her shoulders and led me to a chair at the small bistro table in the kitchen while I tried to figure out why she had called me Ash. It took me a few minutes to remember that I had passed out before telling that kid my full name. I guessed he hadn't read my name patch on my uniform.

"What's your name?" My voice was hoarse, and I winced at hearing it.

She turned to me with an apologetic smile and answered, "Forgive me! I forgot my manners. I'm Kyandra, but everyone calls me Ky. I run this bed-and-breakfast with my brother, Michael, but he isn't here right now. He escorted some people home after Pesach and won't be back for at least a week."

She turned and began removing various pots of food from the fridge and busied herself with the food cooking in the oven.

Confused by the word *Pesach*, I didn't notice that we were no longer alone, until a hand landed softly on my shoulder. With a startled glance, I looked up and once again found myself staring into the dark brown eyes of the teenager who had pulled me from the river. His warm smile was infectious and instantly made me feel at home.

"It's nice to see that you are up." His voice was full of cheerfulness and expectation that I couldn't comprehend. It was almost as if nothing could ruin the day for him, and he wanted to ensure that everyone around him felt the same. "My name's Jonathan, just in case you don't remember. I told you before, after pulling you out of the floodwaters, but you were so out of it that you were babbling in many languages. Can I get you anything?"

"Jonathan, he needs some water, and see if he will eat anything," Ky said. "Maybe take him outside so he can get some fresh air and a little sun before Shabbat begins."

What in the world was Shabbat? What language were these people speaking? Was this how other people felt when trying to talk to me about what I did outside the military?

"Yes, of course! I will gladly take Ash outside and help him around for the night."

Jonathan helped me to my feet and walked me outside. The effort was almost too much for my battered body, and by the time he helped me into a lounge chair on the patio, I was shaking violently. He disappeared for a moment and returned with a light blanket and a large glass of water. I greedily drank the water but refused the pain meds Jonathan tried to give me. After the second refill, I was no longer shaking and began to relax.

"Ash?" Jonathan's concerned voice drew my attention. He sat there in the afternoon sun with a weary smile. He released a long breath, pushed his shaggy black hair out of his face, and said, "I hate to ask this of you, but people around here hate Adreians, especially Adreian soldiers. Everyone figured out that you are from Adreia, but I hid all your gear and armor so they would take you in and treat you." He looked away, and sadness crept across his face for a brief moment before he looked back at me. "I would hope that everyone here would've put aside their hatred and helped you, but I don't think they would have. Ash, you can't tell anyone that you are a soldier."

He looked torn and ashamed of the lies and deception, and I knew the kind of people he was talking about. Many people held a generational hatred for Adreia. They didn't understand the way the Adreian government functioned, so they feared. Others fell victim to their harvest contracts' not making it through the senate and, because of it, became financially ruined. Sometimes civilians were caught in the middle of an Adreian-Brashex skirmish and were drafted to help fight or killed in the crossfire, which bred hatred for soldiers. No matter what we did, people were going to hate us.

"Jonathan, I understand your concerns, and for their sakes, I will not tell them that I'm a soldier. It doesn't change this fact: if they refuse me medical treatment or throw me out of town, there are consequences. I am a ranking officer, which means that mistreating me can result in the death penalty. I need you to fully understand what you are asking of me."

"I know. Eight years ago, this community suffered from an Adreian draft, and my father was among the ones put on the front lines. It took a year before the battle ended. He'd become a unit leader over people from the community during that time. After it was over, everyone treated him differently—well, they always had treated him differently because he wasn't a believer, but this was different. It got really bad, so he moved us fourteen miles away, taking his business out of the community, and many people lost their jobs. I still live there and work for myself, even though my parents died in a car crash five years ago. Not everyone here likes me being around, because of what my father did, but I've learned to ignore them and focus on Elohim."

*Elohim?* What language was he speaking? What did it mean, and why was this kid focusing on this Elohim?

"Jonathan," I said as he looked at me intently, "I'm sorry about your parents. I lost my mother when I was nine, and my father left me with his friends and disappeared for an entire year while he was grieving for her. We still don't have a good relationship."

"Well," Jonathan said with a note of cheerfulness in his voice, "until one of you dies, you have time to fix that problem. That's a blessing that a lot of people would love to have."

"Jonathan, how can you be so cheerful?"

His genuine laughter danced around us like music, and it shone through his brown eyes, lightening them. "I can't take credit for any of it. It's all because of Yeshua."

*Yeshua*—another word I didn't understand. I closed my eyes and exhaled slowly before opening them and asking, "Can you please explain some things to me?"

"Of course! That's what I'm here for." He playfully winked at me.

I found myself smiling. His joy was infectious, and he reminded me of Aiden, my pilot and apprentice to the empire of cruzer repair and innovation. I had taken him in when he was young. I loved that kid like my own, and I felt that if I spent time around Jonathan, I would also end up loving him.

I said, "I need you to define these words: *Pesach, Shabbat, Elohim*, and *Yeshua*."

# Chapter Seventeen

## Asherex

I awoke to the beautiful sight of the sunset painting the clouds in fiery hues. Jonathan's words still chased themselves around in my mind. It was almost too much to take in. Pesach was a feast of Yehovah, who was also Elohim. He had created everything on Earth and beyond through and for Yeshua, who was the Word of Elohim made flesh and somehow the Son of Yehovah at the same time. Pesach signified redemption for Yisra'el through the blood of a lamb. It also pointed to Yeshua being the sacrifice for all of mankind. Yeshua had been slain from the foundation of the world so that everyone from the first man, Adam, to the last one born could be redeemed and brought back into right standing with Elohim.

Shabbat, also called the Sabbath, was a day of rest that pointed back to the story of creation, because Yehovah had labored for six days and rested on the seventh, thus establishing a day of rest that the entire world was to observe. Somehow, this Sabbath day pointed to Yeshua and His kingdom on Earth. None of it made any sense.

The sound of a truck in dire need of a tune-up and some repair drew me from my thoughts. Jonathan and another man stepped out of the extended cab and walked toward me. Jonathan came directly to my side, while the other man went into the house and began carrying out the food that Kyandra had been diligently tending to since I got out of bed. It looked as if they were preparing to feed an entire army.

"How are you feeling, Ash?"

"I slept for a bit but don't feel rested, and I'm starting to feel every bruise, but I am alive, so I can't complain too much."

Jonathan smiled at me with his infectious smile and helped me to my feet. We started toward the truck, and he looked at me and said, "Normally, we don't use the truck on Shabbat, but seeing as how the whole community has dinner together after praise service to usher in the Sabbath, we decided we would use it to get you there. No one wanted you to have to walk half a mile to the dining hall."

"I don't think I would have made that walk tonight."

He just smiled at me and continued to lead me to the truck. Getting into the tall metal-framed death trap without causing myself more pain was more challenging than going through basic training. Once I was settled, Jonathan quickly checked my bandages to ensure I hadn't started bleeding again. He was a sweet kid with a servant's heart, and I couldn't help but wonder why he continued to live outside the community. If he had been in Adreia, because his dad had served in the military, he would have been given a pension until he turned eighteen and discounted college tuition.

Jonathan slid into the seat next to me with a gracious smile still on his face and carefully buckled me in as if I were breakable. My heart warmed at his actions, which spoke volumes about his character. Had his parents raised him to be like this, or had he come into it on his own?

It didn't take long before the other man, who introduced himself as Westly but said everyone called him West, climbed into the driver's seat. After a few attempts, he started up the truck and slowly drove across the small town to the dining hall. Once we arrived, two men came to help Jonathan get me out of the truck and into the large, ornate building. On the outside, it looked like a small metal warehouse. The inside, decorated with brilliant banners and painted themes that flowed into one another, held a welcoming atmosphere. There was a large area set up with tables with fancy tablecloths made of fine linen, and each table had a fresh bouquet of bright-colored flowers and two small glass oil lamps.

The whole atmosphere was inviting, and I longed to just sit there listening to the chatter of the people. Jonathan placed me at a table near the entrance, where there would be less foot traffic, which meant fewer chances of someone accidentally bumping into me. Almost immediately, people began trickling by to introduce themselves and let me know they were praying for my recovery, whatever that meant. Everyone seemed welcoming and sweet, unlike those in places I had been in Adreia, where people pretended to be welcoming while plotting to stab you in the back at the first opportunity.

There was a lull in the flow of people, and I took the time to look the place over again. I noticed a small platform about a foot off the ground with various musical instruments. It had been a long time since I had seen that many instruments in one place. I knew how to play all of them except for the twelve-stringed guitar. I decided I would have to look into playing one of those after the hole in my side healed up, which wouldn't be much longer if they could get me to the hospital. Hopefully, the floodwater would recede quickly so I could contact my men and get proper medical treatment.

A gentle touch on my shoulder drew my attention to Jonathan. He'd been helping in the kitchen and was now back at my side with a glass of water. He asked me if I wanted anything to eat, but I declined. My stomach was upset because of the pain I was in, and I didn't want to throw up, so I just sipped on some water.

Soon the band went up to the stage, and someone opened the service in prayer. It was the weirdest thing I had ever heard. *But then again, I talk to something or someone I'm not even sure is there, so I can't judge them too much on the prayer thing.* As soon as he finished speaking, the band played, and people flocked to the large dance floor. Jonathan left me and joined them after the first song played.

It was obvious to everyone that the decision to leave me tore at his heart.

I lost track of time just watching the dancers move in almost perfect sync with every song that played. I had never seen something so beautiful. It spoke to something deep inside me that I had always tried to ignore. Every song was about Yehovah, Elohim, or Yeshua, and even though I didn't understand most of what they were saying, I knew they were worshipping with everything they had. The musicians poured themselves into every note, the singers held their hands up with eyes closed, and the dancers smiled while some sang along as they flowed across the dance floor.

"Is this what you wanted me to see?" I whispered the question, hoping I would get an answer this time. Whoever I had been talking to all these years hadn't spoken to me since I was five, and seeing as I had been told I was dead during that time, I was not sure I could rely on that memory. But maybe this was where I was meant to be, and this Yehovah was the one I had been looking for all these years. I guessed I would have some time to find out; all I had to do was learn what these people believed and observe their actions to see what was in their hearts.

One song flowed into another with an occasional worship message from one of the singers. The scene was so captivating that I almost didn't notice the man sitting next to me. He was probably in his late forties or early fifties, but he wore his age well, so I couldn't be sure. His once-black hair was more silvery than black, and his dark blue eyes contained much wisdom. His face, however, held a weariness that went beyond the physical.

"Are you all right?" I asked.

He turned to me with a slight blush creeping across his face and said, "I should be asking you that." He let out a weary sigh. "It's been a tough week. Well, I guess it's been a tough year so far. I lost my wife of thirty years last week and buried my parents on the first of the month. I'm hanging on by prayer and the skin of my teeth, but praise Yah that I'm still here to minister to my flock."

I didn't completely understand what he was talking about, but by how he looked around the room, I assumed his flock were the people gathered around in the building. My heart went out to him for losing his wife, and I wondered how he was here instead of being in mourning for her. I knew that the people on the Surface didn't observe the forty-day Law of Loss, but I couldn't imagine burying someone and then returning to work a week later.

"I lost my wife a few months back." I twisted my wedding band around my finger. I hadn't had the strength to remove it after Lillie passed away. "It's been pretty hard, and sometimes I wake up thinking she's right next to me, only to find an empty space where she should be."

"Does it ever get easier?" His voice was full of grief.

I placed a hand on his shoulder and replied, "It does a little at a time. Sometimes it is one step forward and then twenty steps back, but as time passes, it becomes easier to focus on all the good things without feeling like your heart is breaking into tiny shards all over again. I guess you have your Elohim to help you through this, so you are one step ahead of me already."

He looked at me with a sad yet happy smile on his face. He seemed like a genuine person, and I longed for him to find comfort. "You're right, son. Thank you." He gently squeezed my hand and then excused himself and joined the dancers.

I repositioned myself in the chair, only to have pain lance through me from my side. It shot through me like molten fire, robbing me of breath. Within moments, Jonathan was at my side. Concern was plastered across his face. He asked me a lot of questions before agreeing that I should go back to the bed-and-breakfast. West and a few men loaded me into the truck, and after the fourth attempt to get it started, the engine roared to life.

It took three of them to get me up the stairs and into the bed, where Jonathan cleaned and redressed my wounds. The others left, and the sounds of the truck sputtering before it was quiet let me know that the metal death trap was no longer operational.

Unfortunately, I believed that truck was the only way out of town and to the hospital.

"Ash?" Jonathan's worried voice drew my attention back to the room. He held a glass of water and a bottle of pain pills. "I know you don't want to take pain meds, but please take them. If for no other reason, then take them so you can sleep. Please?"

How could I argue with that face? "I will take them if you promise to go back, enjoy the rest of the night, and not worry about me."

He looked down at the bottle of pills and then back at me and replied, "I will promise to go back and enjoy the rest of the night, but I can't promise I won't be worrying about you."

"All right, I will compromise." I held a hand out for the pills and hoped they wouldn't turn me into an evil, hateful monster, as every other pain med did. Maybe I would be sound asleep by the time everyone came back, and no one would face the venomous beast I became.

I swallowed the pills and chased them with the glass of water. Jonathan sat at the end of the bed, and we didn't speak as I closed my eyes and waited for the medication to kick in. It was nice to have someone around, even if we didn't speak a word. I wondered if Jonathan realized just how special he was.

# Chapter Eighteen

Asherex

I awoke to the gentle rumble of thunder and the sound of steady rain on the metal roof. It was a strange way to wake up. I was used to my soundproof house, where storms were nothing more than beautiful pictures in my windows. I hoped the storms would cease soon and the waters would dry up so I could get the medical help I needed.

The sounds of people chatting drew me out of bed. I stepped onto the cool tile floor in the bathroom and took my time getting ready for the day. My sore muscles protested every move as I gave myself a sponge bath and changed my bandages. The shrapnel wound in my side looked infected. I needed to get to the hospital soon.

Dressed in fresh clothes, I headed down the stairs. I wasn't sure which protested more, the old creaky stairs or my battered body. Once at the bottom, I looked over to the living room and noticed at least twenty people crammed into the space. All of them were holding books and taking turns reading out of them, occasionally stopping to discuss something they had just read.

The young man sitting in a comfortable chair nearest me quickly got up and motioned for me to join them and take his seat. I was a little reluctant to do so, but the man moved to another spot across the room, and everyone was staring at me, so I slowly made my way to the chair. Within seconds of my sitting down, Jonathan came in the front door, wearing a good-quality rain slicker, and he smiled when he saw me.

I couldn't help but smile back as he hung up his coat, removed his muddy boots, and made his way across the room. He stopped next to me, opened a book to a certain page, and handed it to me before disappearing into the kitchen. The woman sitting next to me pointed to the fifth verse in the eleventh chapter of the book titled Vayikra. I found the place and read along with those taking turns around the circle. Jonathan returned from the kitchen with a glass of water and some cut-up fruit for me. Then he sat on the floor and immediately joined in the discussion about clean versus unclean animals for food.

It was strange to hear the list of animals their Elohim commanded them not to eat. None of those animals were considered food in Adreia, because they were unhealthy. I wondered if the early dictators of the World Above had used that passage as inspiration when deciding what was healthy or if they had relied purely on scientific research.

"Ash?" Jonathan's inquiring tone pulled me from my thoughts. "Do Adreians eat pork and shellfish?"

Every eye in the room was on me as I answered, "No. There is too much evidence of pigs, shrimp, crabs, and other bottom-feeders causing disease. They have a high toxicity level and low nutritional value. Health is very important in Adreia. Most people find it offensive when they come to the Surface and someone eats those things around them."

"So do you eat everything we have talked about so far that is considered clean?" one of the women sitting across from me asked, and I again found myself the center of attention.

"Adreians do, but I have never eaten red meat or dairy products.

My father kept me on a strict diet as a child, and I never changed it when I moved out."

They gave me strange looks, and a few exclaimed that they wouldn't have been able to give up certain foods containing dairy products. I finished off the bowl of strawberries, kiwi, and apple slices Jonathan had given me while they continued their discussion before returning to the reading. Being in the midst of these people seemed strange but somehow right. The love they had for one another was tangible.

The wound in my side began to throb, distracting me, and I shifted in the chair, hoping to relieve the pain. I settled back in, ignoring the pain, and tried to find my place again. It took a moment before I found that we were at the end of verse forty-five. As soon as the beginning of the verse was read aloud, my head snapped up. Instantly, my hair stood on end, and goose bumps broke out across my body.

Had they just said *Torah*? I knew that word. I didn't know what it meant, but I knew that word. I sat there in disbelief as they finished the chapter and began discussing the last of the reading. With a desperation I hadn't felt in a long time, I looked back at the verse, and sure enough, there was the word *Torah*, written four words into the forty-sixth verse. I couldn't believe what I was seeing.

Without saying a word, I set the book aside and went into the kitchen. The pain of my wounds was completely forgotten. I paced around the large kitchen island while trying to reconcile what I had just heard in the other room. To think that for all these years, I'd thought I was disturbed for believing what I had witnessed as a child when I supposedly died after drowning in a frozen lake. A man who had held me and kept me warm had told me I would bring Torah to Adreia.

Now here I was, hearing that word again after twenty-one years. Was I deranged? Was I dreaming? *This can't be real.* I hadn't spoken a word about that moment to anyone since it happened, for fear the doctors would do more tests on me, so no one could possibly have been playing a joke on me. I was going to have a panic attack.

Jonathan grabbed my arm, causing me to stop pacing. A look of concern was plastered on his face. He spoke softly as he made me sit, trying to calm me while taking my blood pressure. I wanted to ask him a million questions, but I held my tongue. How could I say anything without him thinking I'd lost my mind? What was I going to do? When I reunited with my men, they would interview the people to determine my state of mind, and I couldn't receive a negative report if I was going home.

"Your blood pressure is high, Ash." Jonathan's face was full of concern as he took the cuff off my arm and then checked my bandages. "You've pulled your stitches too."

"I need to go to the hospital."

"I know, Ash, but there is no way to get you into town right now. If I put you on my four-wheeler, we would have to drive thirty miles out of the way and through a lot of floodwater to get there. I'm not even sure we could make it. I barely made it here this morning."

I sighed and asked, "Is there any way I can call someone?"

"No one here has a plex. The community has a few landlines and mobile phones, and that is it."

It was hopeless. The Adreian plex system didn't allow unlisted numbers from mobile phones or landlines to reach a plex. I didn't even have a way to hack into the system and patch myself through to someone. I had to tough it out until the floodwater receded and the truck was fixed.

"Maybe you should go lie down and rest. I will try to patch you up and find someone to restitch this since the doctor isn't around."

I consented and soon found myself back in my room. Jonathan watched in both fascination and disgust as I sewed my wound closed again. As soon as I finished, he cleaned the rest of the wounds and replaced the bandages. He tried to get me to take the pain medication again, but I refused, even though he insisted for twenty minutes. It took even longer for me to convince him to return downstairs and join the others before I attempted to take a nap.

An hour and forty-five minutes passed after I fell asleep, and I protested the gentle hand shaking my shoulder. With a reluctant groan, I opened my eyes and glared at Jonathan. He gave me an apologetic smile and helped me sit up, piling pillows behind me to recline.

"Anna, one of the women you met last night, brought you some vegetable soup, which is completely vegan, for lunch. The main service is about to start; then we are all having lunch together. If you want me to, I will stay here with you since you're in no condition to leave."

I looked from Jonathan to the large bowl of soup on the nightstand, and my stomach growled. He laughed. I looked back at him and said, "You shouldn't let me keep you from going. I will be fine. Trust me, I've been through worse. Thank Anna for me for the soup."

He nodded and asked, "Is there anything else I can do for you? I feel like I'm not doing enough and keep running off."

"Jonathan, you have done more for me than my servants back home, and they consider me family. Now, go enjoy your Sabbath, and do whatever it is that you people do at this main service of yours."

He grinned at me with laughter dancing in his eyes before he checked my bandages and left. As soon as he was gone, I grabbed the bowl of soup and ate. It was delicious, and it took all my self-control to take my time and enjoy it rather than scarfing it down. After it was gone, I drank the glass of water Jonathan had left me and opened one of the six water bottles on the nightstand. Once I was satisfied, I eyed the bottle of pain medication and, with a sigh, took the prescribed amount before settling down again.

# Chapter Nineteen

## Roark

The last three days had been full of setbacks and lots of surveillance of the compound. I finally found a way into the place but still had no clue what was waiting for me inside. As I pried the cover off the air vent and lowered myself into the unknown, I wished I had my unit with me. Guilt pierced my heart at the thought that Emet was alone with Victor right now instead of being by my side, where no one but me could hurt him.

I was going to have to apologize to him, and I hoped he would forgive me for being a fool. Of course, I knew he would forgive me because that was just the way he was, but I had to wonder if things would be different between us afterward. Would he remember it and not let it go? Maybe he was better off without me; all I seemed to do was make things worse for him.

I shoved my thoughts aside as I lowered myself through a vent onto the floor in a dark room lit only by the glow of an old, nearly burned-out lightbulb. It was eerily quiet as I scanned the room. Disgust filled me at the sight of the room littered with torture devices. It smelled of urine and dried blood. The urge to vomit nearly overtook me as memories of my recent bout of being tortured swirled in my head.

A muffled groan drew my attention. I turned and immediately threw up at the sight of a man hanging by his wrists from the ceiling. When I looked up again, he stared at me as if he were ready for me to torture him. With a sigh, I crossed the room, removed his gag, and hoped he didn't alert the whole compound that I was there.

"I'm not going to hurt you." I whispered as quietly as possible but felt as if my voice carried and boomed throughout the room. I knew it was only my nerves getting the best of me, but I strained to hear anything beyond the room just in case.

"You're Adreian?"

His question seemed more like an accusation, and I replied, "What gave it away? The Crimson Division patch on my arm?" I tried my best not to sound sarcastic, but I couldn't help it. Sometimes people asked dumb questions with obvious answers, and for some reason, I had a hard time being respectful with my reply.

He smirked and called me a bad name before asking me to get him a drink of water from the sink in the corner. I looked at him in disbelief before doing as he asked. If I had been him, I would have asked to be set free, but that was just my insane reasoning.

I brought him back a handful of water because I couldn't find a clean container to put any in, and after he drank it, he said, "I'm a Brashex soldier."

"Well"—I couldn't stop myself—"technically, you are a prisoner, and you used to be a Brashex soldier."

He looked at me for what seemed like an eternity before a smile crept upon his face. "I like you, Adreian."

"Wow, that's a first. Normally, people hate me after the first couple of words leave my mouth."

"I can see why."

I couldn't tell if he was being serious or joking, but before I could say another word, the door opened, and I quickly replaced his gag before ducking behind the counter. Two armed men walked into the room, talking in a language I didn't know, and I pulled my sidearm as one of them approached the chained Brashex man. The man jerked the guy's head back by his hair, got in his face, and then said something in a serious tone before releasing him and slapping him across the face. The other guy near the door laughed as he turned around and walked out of the room, followed by the other guy.

I had half a mind to put a bullet in both of them, and it took all my willpower not to pull the trigger. I had to keep focused on the mission; nothing else mattered. *Not the people walking out of the room or the man hanging from the ceiling.* As soon as the thought crossed my mind, guilt pierced my heart. I couldn't leave the Brashex soldier here to be tortured to death. I was sure if our roles had been reversed, he would have left me there to rot, but I couldn't do it.

I didn't know how long I sat there holding my gun and listening for someone else to come walking down the hall and into the room. Finally, I convinced myself to get up and move to the pulley system keeping the soldier hanging by his wrists. It took a few minutes to figure out how to work it before I gently lowered the guy to the floor. When I made it to his side, he stared at me in disbelief as I removed his gag before picking the locks keeping him in chains.

"You are wasting your time, Adreian. I'm in no condition to escape." His whispered tone was full of authority, and I instantly knew he held a ranking position in the Brashex army. I wondered how he had ended up here alone.

"Yeah, well, I don't leave people behind, and I have a feeling I might need a hand escaping. As long as you can pull a trigger, you are useful. I just ask that you don't put a bullet in me in return for getting you out of here." He began to protest again but quickly shut up when I plunged the needle for the vial of nanos into his arm. It was my only vial, and I wished I had taken the time to restock my cruzer, but I would have had to pay out of my pocket, and I didn't have that kind of money right now.

I spent the next couple of hours tending to his wounds while he told me everything he knew about the compound. The two men who had been here earlier came only during the day and left every evening, so they wouldn't be back for a while. They were responsible for torturing the soldier and keeping him alive so they could torture him more.

Once satisfied that he wasn't going to fall apart on me, I left him and continued my search for the black box. I finally found it and ran a quick diagnostic scan to ensure the encrypted data was intact. It only took ten minutes, but those ten minutes seemed like an eternity, and as soon as my plex confirmed that the data was intact, I packed up and headed out the door. My heart pounded in my chest, and adrenaline shot through my veins as I stealthily made my way back to the Brashex soldier. Every swiveling camera I had to evade added to the hype, and I was starting to imagine sounds, or maybe I was hearing people talking.

I rounded another corner only to find no people there. I was starting to feel extremely paranoid. I made my way down the hall and paused before rounding the next corner. My heart was trying to beat its way out of my chest, and I took a deep breath before rounding the corner, only to run right into a Borderland soldier. He recovered before I did and drew his sword as I scrambled to my feet.

The blade sliced through the air next to my head before he kicked me to the floor. I rolled just as the heavy blade smashed into the floor where I had been. With a choice curse, I managed to give him a quick kick to the kneecap and heard something crunch. He went down with a cry of alarm, and I drew my silenced gun and shot him point-blank in the head.

Without a second thought, I jumped to my feet and fled. As I ran toward the room where my wounded backup was, I could hear the angry shouts of highly trained, brutal killers closing in on me. Several bullets whizzed past me as I rounded another corner and threw myself into the back entrance to the torture room. I quickly knocked over a rack of torture implements to block the door, but I knew it wouldn't hold them off for long.

The Brashex man quickly pulled himself to his feet. I handed him my rifle, slung his arm around my shoulders, and pulled him toward the other door. We shot our way through the maze of hallways, and his weight wore me down after a while. My side was killing me, and he could tell I was getting tired. He tried to get me to leave him and save myself, but I refused to leave him, even though I was out of ammo, and he soon would be as well. I had made it out of worse places than this, and we would get out of here alive, even if it killed me.

We barricaded ourselves in an office of some kind and busted out a window that was barely big enough for us to squeeze through. Once outside, we hightailed it to the forest and headed straight for my cruzer. The enemy was close on our heels; the bullets continued to fly, and the pounding of horses' hooves in the dark forest spurred us on. We knew death was waiting for us if we slowed down.

He fired off the last round as we rushed into the opening hatch on my cruzer. The enemy gunfire continued to assault us as the door closed. I had never realized how slowly the back hatch sealed. I took a moment to take a few deep breaths before throwing myself into the pilot chair, firing up the engines, and taking off as fast as the old beast would allow.

I could hear the Brashex soldier rummaging through my stuff, but I didn't dare take my eyes off the sky. My vision was beginning to blur, and I felt queasy. I rubbed my eyes and noticed again that my side was killing me. I shook my head, trying to dispel the weariness, and when that didn't work, I shifted in the pilot chair. I immediately felt a cold chill run up my spine at the feeling of warm liquid in my seat.

"Brashex, you need to come pilot right now."

I heard him making his way toward me as he said, "This ancient thing is a manual and belongs in a museum. I haven't got a clue how to steer the thing, let alone keep it in the air."

"I guess you are going to learn fast."

"Why?" His concern quickly turned to alarm when he reached my side and no doubt saw the blood all over my white pilot chair. He cursed a bit before saying, "Tell me how to drive!"

I opened my mouth to respond, but nothing came out as the silver spots crowded out my vision. He sounded as if he were miles away as he shouted something I couldn't make out just before I fell forward into the steering column and faded away.

# Chapter Twenty

Emet

We had looked for High Commander Reach for two days before the search was called off due to terrible storms and massive flooding that made it impossible to track him. I had spent most of that time praying for the Reach family, but Roark was never far from my mind. I couldn't help but feel responsible for his not being with us while we searched for High Commander Reach. He wouldn't have let us stand around waiting for someone to give us an assignment; he would have taken the initiative and picked a direction for us to go despite what everyone else said.

Of course, when I returned to Adreia, my master forced me to work through the Sabbath as punishment for leaving with Senator Reach. It was the longest day I had worked in a long time at the hospital. Even though I was busy from the time I got there, time seemed to flow slowly. If Roark had been around, he would have pulled me away for some made-up reason concerning the unit and let me have the Sabbath off. I missed him, and even though I had been doing my job, I still felt responsible for Roark's not being on duty. Deep down, I knew he would have lectured me if he had seen me moping around about that, but I couldn't help it.

I tried calling Roark's plex again as the cab neared my master's house, but once more, it rang until the automated message picked up. It gave me the option to leave a message, but I just hung up. I wasn't sure what to say to him, and part of me was afraid he was still mad at me. The other part of me was worried that he hadn't answered after the second call. What if something had happened to him? *Yehovah, my King, my strength, Your servant asks that You be with Roark and bring him home safely. Guide him by Your righteous right hand, and lead him beside the still waters so that he may know peace. Soften his heart to receive Your love and mercy, for You, O Yehovah, are a merciful Elohim. You are patient and compassionate, and it is Your desire that no one would perish in sin but that all would turn from their wicked ways and find everlasting life in Yeshua, Your Son. O Yehovah, Your servant asks that You reveal Yourself to Roark in a great and mighty way so that he cannot deny that You alone are Elohim. In Yeshua's name, amen.*

The cab stopped in front of the mansion. After paying the driver, I climbed out and made my way up the steps. Weariness crept into me by the time I made it to my room, but I forced myself to crawl into the shower, thankful it had a bench for me to sit on. The water cascaded over me until my skin was waterlogged and wrinkly. I stepped out, wrapped up in my robe, and lay on my uncomfortable twin bed.

Within moments, I dreamed of floating in a warm, sunbathed lake near my house in Yisra'el. With my eyes closed against the bright sun, I listened to my older brothers play on the beach. It was the most peaceful thing in the world. I knew my mom and dad were watching over us, and I had nothing to fear. This was paradise.

A loud knock at my bedroom door startled me from my peaceful dream, and a moment of fear speared through my chest at the possibility that my master was on the other side of the door. I quickly cleared my throat and invited the person inside. The sight of Gavin's nearly white blond hair instantly calmed me yet made me uneasy at the same time. He gave me a sad smile, and tears glistened in his moonstone-colored eyes.

"May I come in?" His voice, choked up with unshed tears, was calm.

I motioned him inside as I sat up, ensuring that my robe wasn't revealing anything, and I wished I had dressed before getting in bed. One day I would learn that it was a good idea to take clothes into the bathroom and get dressed there. Of course, if I did that, I figured I would end up walking out of the shower to find someone waiting right in front of me. I couldn't win.

Gavin sat on the edge of my bed, gazed down at the mattress with a strange look, and then glanced back at me before saying, "Your bed is awful. Why didn't you tell me you were sleeping on a rock? I would have made Victor at least buy you a new mattress."

"It's more comfortable than half the places I've slept before. Gavin, are you okay?"

He shook his head and answered, "I miss Kress. Emet, Kress has been missing for twenty-seven years to the date, and the worst part is that I still don't know if my brother—our brother—is dead or alive." He pulled me into a hug and began sobbing. It broke my heart to see him like that, and I did my best to comfort him.

Kress Rayas had been Victor's only child. Kress's mother had died while giving birth, due to medical complications caused by the doctors, leaving Kress with almost complete hearing loss in both ears. Victor had handed over control of their company to Saz to stay home with his handicapped child while he fought a legal battle against the doctors responsible for his wife's death. After three years of fighting, Victor had lost the lawsuit, and if it hadn't been for Kress, the outcome would have crushed him.

Because of the enormous financial drain, Yo'ash Reach, Victor's best friend, had given him the money to start a new company, and within two years, he had recovered the millions he'd lost during the lawsuit. The new company had caused him to spend less time with Kress, so Victor had attempted to adopt a child but failed. In light of the many complications, he'd turned to Saz. It hadn't taken long for Saz to procure Gavin from the black-market slave trade. Victor had feared that if he didn't take him, Gavin would end up as a child sex slave. Because of that, he'd participated in the illegal transaction. Nevertheless, Victor wasn't a fool, and he'd hired people to act as Gavin's parents, even though Gavin was Victor's slave.

When Kress had turned six, Victor had brought eight-year-old Gavin home for the first time. From all the stories Gavin had told me, they had been inseparable. They had done everything together, from sleeping in the same bed to studying for the careers Victor was preparing them for. Kress had planned to be a programmer and work with his dad to invent a better-quality hearing aid. Gavin, of course, had decided to be a lawyer so that no one else would suffer the kind of loss Victor had and come out empty-handed.

When Kress had turned ten, he'd wanted another brother, so Victor had found me at an auction house and decided to buy me, even though I had already been sold four times. Because I barely had spoken their language, the staff at the auction house had kept me for four months before he could take me home. I had been seven at the time and hadn't understood why they'd taken me from my family. I remembered Victor being kind and trying his best to reassure me that I would be safe.

Two months before I had gone home with Victor, Yo'ash's house had caught on fire, and his body had burned beyond recognition. Two weeks later, during a school field trip, a cruzer with Kress on board had exploded and crashed. They never had found his body but had recovered the bodies of the other thirteen children and six adults. Losing Kress had changed Victor; by the time I had come to be his official possession, he hadn't been the same man I had met. He had been despondent and quick to lose his temper. Within two months of living in his house, Victor had told me I would be a doctor and forced me to begin studying. For the first year, he'd allowed Gavin and me to be around each other; then he'd sent Gavin away and become more violent.

Victor had started getting more and more involved with the darker side of politics. With each passing week, I had grown more terrified of him, and I'd hidden myself to pray or cry. If Victor had found me crying or praying, he had beaten me and locked me in my room without food for a couple of days. Now here we were twenty-seven years later, and Victor still abused me for whatever reason he imagined, but I didn't hate him. How could I after knowing what he had gone through?

"Emet, can I stay here tonight?" Gavin asked me in a childlike tone that seemed out of place coming from the assassin.

"Of course. I'm not going to make you leave."

In one fluid motion, he stood up, told me we were not going to stay in my room, made me get dressed, and dragged me into one of the guest rooms. I had never been in any of the guest rooms before, so I was surprised when we walked in. It was beautiful! Gorgeous greens and gold made the room feel like a king's chamber. My room had plain white walls and an unpolished hardwood floor. I was in awe of the place.

Gavin flopped down onto the king-sized bed and tossed a throw pillow at me. I smiled as I threw it back at him and sprawled across the most comfortable mattress I had ever touched. Gavin didn't let me get comfortable before throwing more pillows at me, starting a war. I had never had a pillow fight before and found myself enjoying it. Our laughter filled the room for a long time before he called a truce, and we settled down.

"It's so peaceful when Rayas isn't here." I spoke my mind and immediately regretted it.

"Yeah, it is. Victor went out of town with Saz for a few days on a so-called business meeting." Gavin air-quoted the last two words and then made a disgusted sound. "There are better ways of saying you are going to go break the law and spend time with your boyfriend." He sneered the last word with contempt.

My heart stilled, and I sat up. "What do you mean by *boyfriend*?"

Gavin looked at me and replied, "Boyfriend. A boy who is more than a friend and someone you might share intimate moments with."

"That's illegal, and they both can be hung if they are caught! Are you sure that's what they are doing?"

"That is something you cannot unsee, Emet. Trust me, I've tried."

"And you didn't report them?"

Gavin sat up and looked at me seriously for what seemed like an eternity. "If I spoke up, Victor would have me hanging next to him. Do you know how many people he has forced me to kill over the years? I don't, but I'm sure he has kept a list. Otherwise, I wouldn't have secretly married my wife and had a son with her. I can't do anything that would jeopardize my family, including you. If there was a legal way to turn him in without both of us paying for it, I would have found it by now." He blew out a sigh and fell back into the pillows. He covered his face with his hands and said, "Emet, will this nightmare ever end? I try to have faith in Yah, but I hate Victor so much. I lost my little brother. It was my job to protect him, but I was sick that day, so I couldn't go with him. It's my fault." Tears choked out the rest of his words as I fought back my own.

I didn't know what to say, so I just began to pray aloud for Gavin. He pulled me into another hug, weeping upon my neck, while I continued to pray for him. Hours passed before he passed out, exhausted from the emotional drain, and I watched over him until I couldn't keep my eyes open any longer.

# Chapter Twenty-One

Asherex

Two days after the Sabbath ended, the truck still wasn't running. West and a couple of others tinkered with it, and when I offered to help, they refused. Apparently, I was in no condition to fix a vehicle. I had been in worse shape before and fixed my cruzer so I could get medical attention.

Frustrated by my inability to help, I wandered outside into a barn with an old, broken-down harvester. Inside the barn was an old-model mini-mega-lift, a device used in airship repair to carry multiple-ton objects. It operated remotely and did everything a mechanic could except weld. The lift was an innovator's best friend, and I finally got the old girl up and running with Jonathan's help.

Jonathan shouted in excitement as the lift headed toward the harvester for the first time in ten years. The excitement on his face made me smile, even though smiling hurt my bruised face. His enthusiasm reminded me of Aiden's first build with me. That had been one of the best days of my life; I'd seen the kid come alive after all the trauma he had suffered when he lost his mother and was placed in foster care.

"So, Ash, do you think we will get this old rust bucket fixed before they get the truck done?"

"I would bet ten grand on it. I read all the manuals for it last night, and you have all the parts we need for any repairs. There's no way we will fail."

Jonathan looked at me with an infectious smile plastered on his face and light dancing in his brown eyes and said, "That will teach them not to let us help fix the truck."

I tried not to laugh and hurt myself as I replied, "After we are done with this beast, we can fix the metal death trap as well."

Jonathan's laughter erupted throughout the barn, and it brought me hope that I would soon receive medical attention. I couldn't wait to heal up, but I was going to miss this place when I left. I just hoped I learned whatever I was fated to learn here.

# Chapter Twenty-Two

## Roark

I awoke slowly with an awful taste as my tongue cleaved to the roof of my mouth. It left me feeling as if I'd been dumped in the middle of a desert. The aches in my body let me know that I was alive but in worse shape than before I'd passed out. No doubt we had crashed, and I hadn't been strapped in at the time. I just hoped I could get us back in the air.

The sounds of tools clanging around, followed by some choice curses, brought a smile to my face, and I slowly pushed my battered body out of my bunk. On the way out of the back hatch, I snatched a couple of bottles of water and followed the cursing. The Brashex soldier had removed one of the damaged exterior panels and was attempting repairs. It was obvious he had no clue what he was doing with my rig.

"You're going to tear it up, Brashex."

He quickly slid out of the hole in my cruzer and looked at me in disbelief. "I'm surprised you're not dead right now. By the way, your ancient piece of junk belongs in the scrap yard."

"Sh! She can hear you!" I reached out and gently rubbed my cruzer and, in a soft tone, said, "It's okay; he didn't mean it, girl. He's from Brashex, so you have to forgive him. I know there's nothing wrong with you, and you're going to fly just fine."

He stared at me in disbelief, and I threw a water bottle at him before shooing him out of the way so I could work on my cruzer. Squeezing into the small space hurt my already damaged body, but I dealt with it and began working. Brashex handed me tools as needed. He also pulled me out of the hole to take breaks and have my wounds rebandaged. It took all day and most of the night to get all but one line repaired, and no matter what I tried, I couldn't get the thing to stay clamped with the patch.

Irritation and frustration flooded me once again as I tried to get the clamp tightened up over the patch. The tool slipped, and I busted my knuckles so hard I could feel it in my spine. A long string of curses left my mouth before I forced myself to take a few deep breaths and devise another solution. "Hey, Brashex, can you get the metal tape out of the supply cabinet in the back?"

"That's your solution—metal tape? That stuff is for repairing cracks in a ventilation system!"

"My unit's medic uses it as a waterproof bandage wrap on the battlefield, so I'm pretty sure it will hold up long enough for us to get somewhere else where I can repair it better."

I heard him walk away muttering something about using tape. My eyelids fluttered shut, and I did everything I could to shut out the pain of my wounds as I waited for him to return. My chest felt tight, as if a massive weight were pressing down on me while a vise squeezed my ribs together. I couldn't tell if they were bruised or broken at this point, but I knew it was only a matter of time before a Borderland patrol found us, and we needed to be ready to fly as soon as possible.

Brashex was taking too long, so I lay there with my eyes closed, concentrating on my breathing: a slow, controlled inhale followed by an equally slow and controlled exhale. Over and over, I did this, until the pain in my body seemed to disappear, and my mind quieted. This was peaceful.

A hard slap to my face jerked me awake, and I stared into the soldier's eyes. He looked panicked. It took me a minute before I realized he had pulled me out of the hole in the side of my cruzer, and I was now lying on the warm ground under the stars. *I must have passed out. Whoops.*

He sat back hard on the ground beside me as I slowly pushed myself into a sitting position and rested my arms on my knees. "How long was I out?"

He shoved his shaggy strawberry-blond hair out of his eyes and answered, "About twenty minutes. I thought you were going to go ghost on me there for a minute."

"Nah, I can't die on you yet. I haven't had the chance to annoy you." I lightly punched him on the arm.

He gave me the dirtiest look one human being could give another before smirking and shaking his head. "Adreian, are you all right in the head?"

"Nope. My shrink says I'm certifiable."

He looked at me in disbelief before saying, "Then why are you here? I don't know how they do it on your side of the wall, but in Brashex, a man has to be fit for duty before he can go on solo missions."

"The war council wanted someone with psychopathic tendencies to run this errand for them, but both of their Crimson Soldiers were busy, so I was the lucky dog who got to go play fetch for them," I said, and he laughed. It was one of those hard laughs that kept a person from breathing. "Brashex, that would scare most people."

He caught his breath and replied, "I'm not easily scared. I was an assassin and interrogator for fourteen years before becoming commander of a thousand in the Shadow Division. I grew up in the slums and have had to fight for everything I have since the day I was born. You don't scare me, but you are insane, and your ancient flying ghost-maker scares me. I don't even know how it still flies with all the fix-it-quick patches you have going on in there. I will be surprised if we make it somewhere else without being ghosted by the death trap."

I let out a laugh that sounded evil. "Chewing gum"—I reached out and snatched up the metal tape from beside him—"and tape are all that holds this beast together."

The look on his face was priceless as I crawled back into the hole in my cruzer and began taping the cool-air intake pipe. I knew we would be fine as long as there wasn't a crack that let air escape. If it busted on us in the air, the engine would overheat and explode. That was the only drawback to owning an old manual airship.

Fifteen minutes later, the panel was back in place, and Brashex was helping me into the pilot's chair. A quick preliminary flight check showed me that everything was in good enough shape to take off. The right wing of the cruzer wouldn't be able to fold up when we landed, but that wouldn't be a problem as long as the town we went to had an air control to guide us to a proper landing zone.

Brashex strapped in as I lifted us off the ground and began our ascent. The manual steering was more difficult to control than usual, putting strain on my arms and aching chest muscles. This flight was not going to be fun.

An hour passed before we cleared the massive forestland and headed out of Borderland territory. I was sweating profusely and shaking from the pain I was in and the added strain from flying without power steering. The crash must have caused a leak in the fluid that made flying a manual possible. It was getting harder to breathe, and my vision was blurring on me again. I wanted to keep flying because we were only about an hour from the nearest town, but my body wasn't going to hold up that much longer.

With a sigh, I descended into an open field. My new friend took the copilot's chair and attempted to help me land the beast. Once we were safely on the ground, he looked at me and said, "How in the world have you been piloting this thing with that horrible steering?"

"Sheer force of will and psychopathic tendencies."

He laughed at my reply as he came over to help me to my

sleeping quarters, which contained a single cot built into the wall, with three small drawers beneath for clothes. Lying down only seemed to worsen the pain, but I was so exhausted that I didn't even try to find a more comfortable way to sleep. Brashex removed my boots and checked my wounds before leaving me alone in the dark. It didn't take long for me to pass out.

# Chapter Twenty-Three

Asherex

I had been sleeping peacefully for the first time in months, but the feeling of fingers running through my hair stirred me awake. I didn't want to open my eyes, so I just lay there enjoying the warm sunlight on my back and the smell of salty air through the open windows. *Could this moment be any more perfect?*

"Asherex, how long are you going to pretend to be asleep?"

I couldn't help but smile at my wife's question. We were two months into our honeymoon, and I didn't know how I could ever love this woman more than I did now. I opened my eyes to find her beautiful amber eyes staring at me intently. My heart swelled with love as she slid down on the pillow until we were face-to-face.

"Asherex, are you going to retire from the military so I don't have to worry about you not coming home every time you leave?"

"And what, dear wife, would I do? I'm a commander of a thousand, so I can't just retire like a normal soldier. I have a ten-year contract to fulfill before I can consider retirement. Besides, I'm not a stay-at-home-dad kind of man."

She laughed, and my smile broadened. "You can do a million things, Asherex. You own several businesses, and you can come work with me at the foundation. You can do anything you set your mind to, which is why I love you."

"I don't know about working at the foundation. I have no problem giving you the funds to buy and free slaves, but I couldn't do it. I like seeing results, and it takes too long to even file a single application. I would go insane waiting for it to go through the two-month process of being approved and sent back. It only took me six months from start to finish to design, build, and program the cruzer line I developed when I was sixteen, and now it's the most widely used design in both Adreia and Brashex. I'm afraid I wouldn't be engaged enough to go through the process of buying and freeing slaves. That's why I have you. I make the money, and you take the money and use it to buy and free people."

She smacked me playfully on the shoulder and said, "Asherex Reach! If you met these people, you would want to help them. You bought Lazerick, didn't you?"

"And now he won't leave me alone! I couldn't get him to move away if I burned my house down. Don't get me wrong; I've come to love the guy, but he has a way of getting under my skin and enjoys every moment of it."

"You can't stay in the military forever. That was part of our agreement when I said I would marry you." Her tone was playful and serious, but I knew she expected me to keep my end of the bargain.

"I know. I'm locked in for another ten years at least, but then I will retire, and between now and then, we can figure out what we will do."

"And what happens if they promote you and you get locked into another contract?" Lillie's face showed her concern.

I touched her warm cheek to reassure her that all would be well and replied, "I would have to accept the promotion and the contract that comes with it. We would discuss it when it happened. The only way I could be promoted without my consent is if the commander in chief or the Crimson Solder ordered it, and then I would still be in my old contract. Don't worry. I want to be around to raise our children, and by the time I retire, we should have a few little ones running around."

She shook her head at my teasing tone. I was still trying to convince her to have children, but she didn't want any. Her family was huge, and she'd helped with the younger ones so much that she'd decided long ago not to have any of her own. She'd promised me she would consider having one child later, so I had to be patient with her, or else I would push her away.

My mind raced through the possibilities of what I could do when I retired. Lillie was right that I could do anything, but I wanted to do something I was passionate about. I loved my job and the men under my care. I knew them all by name and invented new armor and weapons to keep them safe in battle. Almost everything I did was for them, and I didn't want to stop doing my job. Why couldn't my wife see that this was my passion? She didn't want me to have anything to do with the military, including weapons manufacturing. These people were my family, and I wanted to protect them.

With a sigh, I rolled onto my back. The military had been my passion since my first memories formed after the accident when I was five. I didn't know what else to do with my life. I felt this was where destiny had led me, and if I stuck with it, I would one day have the answers I was searching for.

"Asherex?" My beautiful wife's voice drew me back to her. "What are your dreams? There has to be something you want out of this life."

*Dreams?* She kept talking, but that word was chasing itself around my mind. Something wasn't right about all of this. I looked at her, and she didn't seem to notice that I wasn't paying attention to what she was saying. This wasn't real, was it? This was a dream—no, a memory.

As soon as the thought crashed over me, I turned again to Lillie and reached for her. Before my fingers could make contact, the vision faded, and I found myself lying in a strange bed miles away from home. My hand rested upon the cold pillow next to me as pain lanced through my chest. My Lillie was dead. Gone. Never to be seen again. Tears welled up in my eyes, and I turned into my pillow, ignoring the pain of my wounds, and sobbed into it so that I didn't disturb anyone else in the house.

The tears stopped a few hours later, leaving me feeling numb. Thanks to my internal clock, I was painfully aware of every second that had passed since I woke from the dream. I just wanted to sleep and not wake up for a long time but was too terrified to close my eyes. Jonathan and I were supposed to finish putting the harvester back together today, but I couldn't bring myself to get out of bed.

I ignored a soft knock on the door but heard the floor creak as someone walked toward me. Jonathan soon came into view with a concerned look on his face. He sat on the edge of the bed, lightly touched my shoulder, and asked, "Ash, are you okay?"

"Does the pain of losing someone ever go away?"

He sighed and looked away before answering, "Not really. They leave a hole inside of you that nothing else can fill. It gets a little easier after a while, as if you forget that they are not there, but then you hear something or see something, or something happens, and it's suddenly like they are gone all over again. I learned not to try to fill the hole and just to be kind to others and help as much as possible because everyone has holes inside. Maybe what I do or say can help someone forget for a while."

"Tragedy makes wise the youth."

He looked at me as a sad smile spread across his face. "I hate to say it, Ash, but you need to get up and do something to help take your mind off it. Besides, we need to get you into town as soon as possible because your wounds are infected. I spoke with the doctor earlier, and he said he would be in town tomorrow and the day after before heading back out to the other small town nearby to take care of his patients there."

He was right; I needed to get up and finish the job we had started, so I could get closer to making it to town. It wasn't fair of me to lie here wallowing in self-pity while my father was left wondering if I was alive or dead. My family deserved to know I was alive, so I couldn't waste another moment being selfish.

Jonathan helped me up and changed my bandages before we headed back to the barn to finish putting the harvester together. It took about four hours to get everything bolted into place using the lift, and we decided to take a small break to eat. We ate outside and watched West and some of the other men attempting to fix the truck. It was painful to watch, and as soon as I finished eating, I walked over to where they were and offered my services again.

They, of course, declined with a long string of excuses as to why I couldn't work on the truck. My injuries were at the top of that list. After fifteen minutes of attempting to explain to them that I worked on airships and owned cruzer repair shops, my frustration was mounting. I wasn't sure if they were only hearing what they wanted to hear or if they were genuinely concerned about my wounds, but it was driving me mad.

Finally, I threw my hands up in surrender and told Jonathan to drive the harvester over. He quickly ran off to the massive ancient beast, and when it roared to life, everyone around stopped what he was doing and watched in disbelief as it rounded the corner and came to a stop in front of us.

"Now"—I looked at West—"can I please fix your truck so I can go to the doctor?"

# Chapter Twenty-Four

Asherex

We had worked throughout the night and the next day to fix the truck, and many times, I had sent Jonathan back to his machine shop to fabricate something or out to his junkyard for parts. It was nearly four in the morning, and I was fighting sleep to finish putting the engine block back together. Jonathan was asleep at the workbench and snoring away. *Maybe I should get some rest as well, because I won't be able to hoist the engine back into the truck by myself.*

With a sigh, I woke the kid and helped him into Kyandra's house. I put him in his guest room, and he was dead asleep as soon as he hit the bed. I watched him sleep for a few minutes, recalling when Aiden had been fifteen. There had been many nights when I carried him to bed from the workshop. I missed him.

I made my way to my room, did my best to wash up, and then replaced my bandages before lying in bed. My body ached, and I was exhausted, but sleep eluded me. My mind replayed every step we had gone through in taking the truck's engine apart and replacing parts. That was what happened to me when I was stressed out. Some people drank, and others stress-shopped, but I replayed repair scenarios on repeat in my head until I went insane.

A noise from downstairs drew my attention, and I quickly

got out of bed, changed out of my pajamas, and headed down to investigate. Kyandra hummed along to one of the songs from their Shabbat service the other night while preparing some kind of bread. I cleared my throat to get her attention so I wouldn't scare her when she turned around and saw me.

She turned around with a soft smile and said, "You are up early, Ash. I'm just starting the cinnamon bread for breakfast, but you are more than welcome to make something if you are hungry right now."

I laughed at the thought of cooking, and she looked at me funny. I said, "If you like your house, you don't want me even sitting in your kitchen. I can't boil water correctly."

Kyandra stared at me in disbelief as I sat at the small kitchen table by the large picture window. "I'm surprised to hear that. Cooking is just a bunch of math and chemistry, and you are probably the smartest man I've ever met."

"I completely understand how cooking works, but getting my brain and hands to put it together is like watching a train wreck in slow motion. In fact, I might just be the only person in Adreia kicked out of the easiest beginners' cooking class with a full refund. The teacher told me I had three options for food in my life: eat everything raw, order out, or hire someone to cook for me."

Kyandra's laughter filled the room, and for a moment, I thought she would fall to the floor. It took her several minutes to recover before she could finish kneading her dough. After covering it, she made us herbal tea, and we sat at the table, talking. She told me about her brother, who seemed like a respectable man I hoped to meet soon. Kyandra's love for him was evident with every word she spoke about him, and I wondered if people ever figured out that I didn't have that tone when I spoke of my father.

Shame filled me at hearing Kyandra talk about her brother. Lillie had tried for years to get me to give my father another chance to be intimately involved in my life. Perhaps it was time for me to kill my pride and reach out. I wasn't sure if he would accept it if I did. Or maybe he wanted the same thing. *How would I even do it? What could I say that wouldn't end in an argument? Should I even hope that things could change between us?*

With a shake of my head, I pulled myself away from those thoughts, focused on watching Kyandra pull the cinnamon bread out of the oven, and realized I was alone with her. It wasn't right for an unmarried man to be alone with a woman, especially since my father was a senator. If anyone found out about this, the media would grab hold of it and ruin both my father's reputation and mine. However, I'd just found a way to sit comfortably without feeling any pain and didn't want to move.

"So," I said, trying to hide my sudden awkwardness, "your brother seems like a good man. I hope I get the chance to meet him before I leave."

Kyandra looked over her shoulder as if she had forgotten I would leave soon. She shyly smiled, darkening her green eyes, before turning back to the bread. I wasn't sure if she was messing with the bread or if she was making herself look busy. Maybe she realized she was alone with me as well.

"Michael took after our dad for sure. He is always running off to help other congregations. He would have been back by now, but he stopped to help our brothers and sisters devastated by the storms. He used all the money we had saved up for repairing this place to rebuild people's homes." She turned around and leaned against the counter with a proud grin before continuing. "He says Yehovah knows what we need and will provide more than we could imagine, but we have to give everything first. My brother is the first to empty out the bank and trust for financial blessing in return. I hope I can have that kind of faith one day."

"Maybe I can help you with that." My words caught her off guard, and she quizzically looked at me. "Because you run this place and I have been staying here, you will be compensated for my room, plus one-third of my total income for the days I am here. And if you allow me to stay here for the mandatory quarantine time, you will be paid a minimum of a thousand dollars a day for my lodging, food, and medical care, plus one-third of my total income during the quarantine time."

"How much is one-third of your income?" She sounded bewildered at the thought.

I shrugged. "I can't honestly answer that question without taking a couple hours to think about it. I own several businesses but have the best people over them, so I hardly have to think about them. Plus, I have royalties from several patents and the income from my primary job."

"You're really rich, aren't you?"

"My assistant, Aiden, told me the other day that I'm on the top-five list of the richest people in Adreia." I looked away from her, embarrassed to admit it. I hated that the media kept a list of the wealthiest people in Adreia. It bothered me that other people could learn about it and try to take advantage of me. I didn't mind helping people who needed it, but I'd had my fill of fake people pretending to like me just to get their hands on my hard-earned money.

The sounds of heavy footfalls on the stairs drew our attention, ending our conversation. A moment later, Jonathan came rushing into the room. His shaggy black hair was a complete mess. He looked at me as he said, "I can't believe I fell asleep! We were so close to having that thing put back together."

I couldn't stop the chuckle that burst from my lips, which caused my injuries to send shards of pain through me. I ignored the pain as best as I could and addressed Jonathan. "Relax. We can put the engine into the metal death trap later. Why don't you have some breakfast and maybe brush your hair? Then we can get back to work."

Jonathan touched his hair, groaned, and ran back upstairs. Kyandra and I laughed at his reaction. We were still laughing when he returned and sat opposite me at the small kitchen table. Kyandra plated us both a serving of cinnamon bread with a dipping cup full of homemade icing. I looked at it for a moment while watching Jonathan devour it.

"I've never eaten anything like this before." I caught them both off guard with my statement. My strict diet had kept me away from most sugary things; if it wasn't a natural sweetener, such as honey, I hadn't consumed it.

"If you don't like it or it's too sweet for you, I can make you something else." Kyandra watched me closely as I tore a piece of the bread off and dipped it into the icing.

I hesitated for a moment before putting it in my mouth. The flavor overwhelmed my taste buds, and I didn't know what to think. It was very sweet, so I tried a piece without icing and found that I liked it much better. "This is really good."

The smile on Kyandra's face caused me to smile as well, and I noticed that her bright green eyes lightened even more. The sight warmed my heart, and I quickly busied myself with finishing the rest of the bread, hoping she hadn't caught me studying her. Why was I acting like this?

While Jonathan worked on a second piece, I ate an apple and a banana. We headed back out to finish the truck as soon as he was finished. West came over to help Jonathan wrangle the engine back into the truck, and after a couple of hours, the thing roared to life, filling me with relief. I was ready to go see the doctor.

About an hour later, the truck was loaded up, and I was on my way to town with West and someone who hadn't introduced himself to me yet. We were silent as the truck crept over the washed-out road. Every bump sent pain lancing through my body, leaving me longing for a nice, smooth cruzer ride. I was spoiled.

"I've never been in a gasoline-powered vehicle before, West. To be honest, the thing terrifies me because gas is highly flammable."

West chuckled, and the other guy looked amused. "Well, kid"—West's southern accent thickened as he called me *kid*—"people used gasoline for centuries before all those fancy alternative fuel sources were thought of. In fact, people are more likely to be shot down in an airship and blown up than burn up in a truck fueled by gas."

I looked at him and wasn't buying it one bit. "I would have to check the statistics before saying anything about it. I've only been in one cruzer that blew up, which was my fault. I ended up burning down my dad's house while trying to fix an old manual; they explode when the cooling pipes get damaged and the engine overheats."

The guy in the backseat burst out laughing, and West moved the rearview mirror to eye him before saying, "I wouldn't be laughing if I were you, Earl. If I'm not mistaken, you've destroyed more cars than anyone I've known, and a few of 'em burned down to the ground."

Earl's laughter quickly died, and the two started talking about all the gasoline-powered vehicles they had wrecked and totaled over the years. By the time we reached the small gravel-road trading post, I was starting to think I had picked the wrong people to ride with. I was now more terrified than ever of the metal death trap we were in and couldn't wait to get out of it.

Relief flooded me as I climbed out of the truck with Earl's help and headed toward the small stone building where I would be able to report in. It was one of the smallest, most neglected outposts I'd seen. There was one holoplex station in the back corner, along with a desk piled with books. One guy manned it and didn't even bother to look up at me when I entered the building. I would have to talk to someone about how lax things were here.

I walked over to the holoplex station, scanned my ID chip in my right arm, and began filing my reports. While I filed the proper paperwork and put in the orders I needed for more medical supplies than what this small-town doctor would have on hand, I looked through the news articles from the last eleven days. My heart broke to see the footage of Lance's funeral, including the faces of his wife and young daughter as they laid him to rest. I should have been there to comfort them and present them with the Crimson Division flag.

A notification on the upper left screen let me know that my field reports had processed and that my seven-day quarantine period began at sundown. With a sigh, I dialed my father's number; while it rang, I added clothing and a new plex to the shipment. My father's voice mail picked up the call, and I hung up and dialed again while finalizing my shipment. The voice mail picked up again, and with a sigh, I left a message, saying, "Hey, it's me. I just made it somewhere I could call and wanted to let you know I'm alive. You probably already got a message letting you know, but I thought you should hear it from me. I will try calling you later when I get my new plex in a couple of days." I paused for a moment before ending the call.

*It would have been nice to hear from you, Dad. I'm stuck here and don't know what to do. I'm afraid and miss you, even though we probably wouldn't talk if you were here.* I couldn't stop the thoughts that raced through my mind as I blinked back tears. It was hard not to feel abandoned again because he wasn't there for me when I needed him. I stood there for about twenty minutes, hoping he would call back, but nothing happened, so I powered down the holoplex station, left the outpost, and headed toward the doctor's office.

I was about five hundred feet away from the outpost building, when someone shouted at me to wait. I turned and watched as the short, scruffy-looking man from the outpost came huffing after me. I held my breath for a moment, hoping my father had called back. Anticipation was killing me by the time he caught up to me and wheezed out a brief statement about a message left for me. He handed me a small military-grade graphic recorder. It was a holographic message recording device usually used to hand out orders for soldiers.

He left me alone as I pressed the small green dot in the center of the two-inch-by-two-inch recorder, which was about as thick as my fingernail. I was always afraid I would break the thing when I used one. Within seconds of my thumb leaving the green dot, a holographic projection of the proxy high commander, who was doing my job while I was unable, came into view.

"Asherex Reach, I am glad to hear that you are alive, and I assure you I will be personally overseeing the shipment you have placed and will have it to you within the next forty-eight hours. Since you are in the outpost area that I am in charge of, I have a mission for you while

143

you are in quarantine. I have had many reports over the years of a terrorist organization of religious rebels. While you are in the area, I want you to find and infiltrate their organization. Find out who is in charge, and report back to me so that I can eliminate the threat once and for all. I will be expecting status reports from you after you receive your plex. Recover quickly, and peace to you, brother."

Anger coursed through me as I shoved the recorder into my pocket and continued to the doctor's office. How dare he think he could order me around like that! He was a *proxy*, not a real high commander! I outranked him, and even if he was my high commander, as a Crimson Soldier, I still outranked him. He didn't even respect me enough to call me by my title of high commander. *Who does he think he is?*

I was still seething with rage when the doctor took me into the exam room. He helped me out of my clothes so he could examine my infected wounds. I could tell by the look on his face that he had come to the same conclusion I had about the nasty-looking shrapnel wound in my side.

"So," he said, opening the wound back up to scrub it, "are you going to refuse pain meds on me again?"

"I don't use meds if I don't have to. I would rather be in pain than be hateful and angry at everyone I see."

"Looks to me like you're already angry." He said it in the usual monotone doctor's voice, as if he were reading the list of ingredients in a vaccine.

I sighed, attempting to calm down, and said, "Have you ever had someone with a lower position try to order you around when he had no authority to do so?"

He laughed and nodded. "It happens all the time, kid; get used to it."

"Not in the Adreian military it doesn't."

He sucked in a sharp breath and let it out before shaking his head and scrubbing my wound. I clenched my teeth at the fresh pain and forced myself to take deep, even breaths. This wasn't as bad as when I'd been tortured, so I could take it.

"You going to turn him in?" he asked.

"I'm thinking about it but not sure what his endgame is. He's involved in the political world and wants a high commander position, so he could be dangerous. He doesn't know it, but he's under investigation right now, so I don't want him escaping that. I will let it slide for now, but if he thinks I'm going to turn in the religious people so he can slaughter them, he's got another thing coming."

"You just be careful around them, soldier. I spent my residency in Adreia, and those people you are with watch me closely when I come around. Adreians abusing their power have bullied and pushed them around a lot. They might throw you out on the street if they find out you're a soldier. If that happens, you just come here, let yourself in the back way with your ID chip, and get a hold of me. I will take you in if I have to. This whole place is crawling with gangs who come through here, terrorizing the locals and robbing folks. Those Torah people in that little community aren't messed with much unless they are in town when the raids happen, so the locals here are not very fond of them. We are a small town with big drama."

I thought about what the doctor had said while he finished up with my wounds and gave me the only nano shot he had before sending me on my way. West and Earl waited for me outside and helped me into the death trap, and we headed back to the community. When we returned, I was exhausted and headed straight to bed, throwing the recorder onto the dresser by the bed as I crashed. Tomorrow was the Sabbath; it was hard to believe I had been here for a little more than a week.

# Chapter Twenty-Five

## Roark

After parting ways with Brashex in the trading-post town, I was finally heading home. The last couple of days had passed in a blur as I underwent several rounds of nano treatments and repaired my cruzer. Brashex had bought the parts to fix the damage, helped me repair the beast, and even paid for my medical treatment. When I'd protested, he had responded that since I'd saved his life and he should have owed me a life debt, he was doing this instead of owing me for the rest of my life.

I hated to admit that I liked the guy, and I almost had asked his name, but I'd decided I liked the idea of keeping the mystery alive. The guys were going to have a conniption fit when I told them the story and didn't have a name for the Brashex soldier. It would eat at them for the rest of their lives, and I couldn't wait to reveal my tale to them.

The nearly seventeen-hour flight was almost over, and I could see the World Above. Relief washed over me as I entered Adreian airspace, but I soon found myself surrounded by a squadron of pilots. The commlink buzzed, and I answered it, more confused than ever. Two hours ago, I had been given clearance to enter Adreian airspace. What was going on?

The holoplex windshield of my cruzer activated, showing me the fleet leader. He looked at me, shook his head, and said, "We have orders to escort you to the nearest hangar bay and arrest you when you disembark."

"On what charges? I haven't done anything illegal."

"I'm sorry, Roark; we are just following orders. They are transferring you to the Secret Service prison after your arrest. Do you understand?"

I nodded as disbelief flooded through me.

"Do you agree to be escorted and swear not to resist arrest?"

"Yes, I agree to your fleet escorting me and willingly surrender."

With a nod, the fleet leader ended the call and led the way through the tunnels and into the first hangar bay we came across. The Secret Service for the war council were waiting for us the moment the electromagnetic cuffs clicked into place. Without a word, they loaded me into a Ravager, and off we went to some secret prison. Thoughts raced through my head as I tried to figure out what I had done to deserve being locked up.

I was still in shock when they stripped me of my armor, jacket, and boots before they locked me away in a five-by-seven cell with a small toilet in the corner. The only light came from a dim recessed light in the ceiling that would go darker as if it would go out and then flicker and start over again. The room consisted of solid gray concrete walls with a rusty-looking steel door; if I'd had to guess, I would have said it was around sixty-eight degrees consistently. I wondered how long they were going to keep me here.

I didn't know how much time had passed. My stomach cramped in hunger, and I resisted the urge to drink out of the toilet. I had at least a day's growth of stubble on my face and regretted not eating before leaving the Surface, but I had been in a hurry to get the black box back to the war council. *I should have taken my time.*

The violent full-body shivering had been going on for a while, keeping me from sleeping. It took everything I had not to get up and beat on the door, demanding answers. How much more of this were they going to force me to endure? This wasn't legal. No one could be held for more than twelve hours without being given a reason for imprisonment. No one was in prison for longer than a couple of days before being sentenced and punished immediately. *What's going on?*

The clang of a key in the lock drew my attention, causing hope to flare to life. Bright light flooded into the room. I shrank back from the onslaught before rough hands jerked me to my feet. They returned my clothes and boots, told me to make myself presentable, and locked me inside the shower room with a disposable razor. I had ten minutes to shower and shave before they came for me again.

We headed up six flights of stairs without a word spoken, and the silence was killing me. The stairs ended in front of a large, blast-proof black door with massive double locks that required two people to use their keys simultaneously. That opened a scanner bar that checked everyone's ID chip and ran us through facial recognition; I was surprised it didn't require a blood sample as well. What was beyond the door that required such security?

Finally, the door opened, and we walked down a hall lined on either side by Secret Service soldiers in full armor before coming to another door. This one, plated with gold, was so shiny that I could see my reflection. A light above the door blinked green, and the door opened. *Because let's face it: we need one more security measure because the double-key scanner door just isn't cutting it back there.*

They removed the cuffs from my wrists before we walked into the war council's dome-ceilinged meeting hall. I was confused as to why I was being escorted in a back way like a criminal. The entire war council, their assistants, six rows of important military officials, the high commanders, and Senator Reach sat around the circular room, watching me walk to the platform in the middle of the room. My heart pounded in my chest, and it took all my willpower to keep a calm demeanor.

The war council's main speaker, a man in his mideighties who looked better than most fifty-year-olds, stood, commanding attention. He looked around before addressing me. "Unit Leader

Roark of Crimson Division unit C1086, you have been brought before a council of witnesses to have your life reviewed. We have spent countless hours reviewing your personal life and your flawless military career. It has not gone unnoticed that you have refused to advance rank for the last ten years and instead have remained a unit leader. Since you took command of your unit, it has suffered only two losses and has seen many advance to rank because you force them to be the best Adreia has to offer. Seventeen men have served under your command and entered retirement, with many more requesting a transfer to your unit. Enemy soldiers have captured neither you nor anyone under your command, and you have successfully carried out every mission handed down to you."

The council member to his left stood and spoke. "Unit Leader Roark, you have displayed courage under fire and brought honor to Adreia that few men ever dream of obtaining. Though your tactics are unorthodox, you have led your unit in battle to more victories than any other unit in the Crimson Division. And it is with great honor today that I stand before you and call you my brother." He traditionally bowed to me, and the rest of the war council stood and followed suit. What parallel universe had I just walked into?

"It"—the booming voice of Commander in Chief Vaxis came through the opening doors—"is a great privilege to be present today to present you with a promotion that few in the history of Adreia have received." He walked toward me, and Senator Reach stood and took his place at Vaxis's side. "It has taken several months for us to review your life." He stopped twenty feet from me and gestured up at the ceiling, where images from past battles played all across the vaulted dome like thousands of tiny moments in a never-ending war movie. "No longer will you be called a unit leader, and no, you cannot refuse this promotion, Roark. From now on, you will be Crimson Soldier Roark."

He bowed to me as Crimson Soldier Reach removed his senatorial robes and handed them to Vaxis, revealing his full body armor, with his Crimson Soldier patch tied on the right arm. He walked to me, and his face relayed the seriousness of the situation. He stopped a foot from me and said, "Roark, too long you have hidden in the shadows. From now on, you carry the weight of Adreia wherever you go. This mission you have returned from was one I picked to prove that given the chance, you would go above and beyond the call of duty. You have earned this position just as I did, just as Asherex did. Wear this"—he pulled a Crimson Soldier patch out of a small box and tied it to my right arm—"knowing that you are a Crimson Soldier."

I was speechless as he took a few steps back and then got down on one knee and bowed his head to the ground. A mighty sound like the rush of roaring waters sounded in the room as everyone present knelt down before me. I blinked back tears as fast as I could. *How could this happen to me?*

As quickly as it had happened, it ended. I was numb as the ceremony continued, with each council member taking turns informing me of the requirements of my new role. I couldn't remember their words; I was too shell-shocked.

The numbness still filled me as I walked out the main hall doors into the capitol building. I couldn't believe it wasn't a dream. In a daze, I walked through the bustling halls, hoping I didn't crash into anyone, but they seemed to part around me like a stream around a rock. A gentle hand on my arm snapped me out of my numbness, and reality came crashing down around me as I turned to see Senator Reach. His gentle smile comforted me.

"Come, Roark. Have lunch with us. I've already put the orders in and have been waiting for you to get out. We have a few things to discuss, you and I."

With a nod from me, we headed down the hall but turned into another set of hallways instead of going out the main doors. Senator Reach unlocked a door and led us inside his office, where he told me to go change into the new armor in the bathroom. I closed the door to the private bathroom and couldn't believe what I saw: hanging on the back wall was the latest model of body armor, the most expensive thing on the market, and it had my name and rank inscribed upon it.

I put it on, looked at myself in the mirror, and couldn't stop the tears that spilled down my face. I'd never owned something so nice. There was no way I could accept this gift.

I walked out in the armor, looked at Reach, and said, "I can't wear this. Do you know how much it costs?"

"Yeah, I paid for it." He walked toward me. "And you will take it. The former commander in chief presented me with new body armor when I became the first Crimson Soldier in decades. I did the same for my son after his promotion. We've done this for you, but my son has other things waiting for you after he is found."

"How did you know I was getting promoted? And what do you mean by 'after he is found'?"

"Asherex is the one who brought it to my attention that you were more than qualified for this promotion, but because of Lillie's death, we were prevented from further investigation. Luckily for you, Asherex's best friend is our commander in chief, and he has poured countless hours into researching dangerous missions to send you on to test you. As for your second question, Asherex went missing over a week ago while attempting to locate and capture a terrorist. I haven't heard anything in two days because when they heard you were returning to Adreia, they pulled me into solitary to await your arrival. Now I'm hungry, and I know you are, so shall we go?"

We walked out of the office and back toward the main entrance to the capitol building, but the senator's assistant stopped us. The young man was breathing heavily and held a plex out to Reach, who took it and listened to a briefing of the messages he'd received while he was away. In particular, the assistant said he should listen to the one voice mail he'd left for him. I watched in fascination as Reach was patient and kind to his assistant before sending him back into the senate hall to stand in for him while we were out. It was strange to see what a good political figure looked like after years of dealing with Rayas.

We finally made it into the restaurant, and it took everything I had not to moan at the wonderful smells filling the room. My stomach, on the other hand, rumbled in unrestrained protest of being empty. Reach listened to the voice mail using the earbud, and instantly, all the tension in his body drained away. For a brief moment, I thought he might collapse on the floor. What had he just heard?

The hostess of the five-star restaurant led us to a secluded room on the second floor with walls of windows on three sides. Some type of climbing vine plant covered in tiny purple flowers provided the only shade in the room. It was peaceful, and I felt myself relaxing just from the ambiance, even though the place was way beyond my price range and social status. As we neared the table, I heard Keller Thaz's laughter fill the room, followed by Victor Rayas's voice. I stiffened up a bit and felt Reach grab hold of my arm as he told me to play nice.

As soon as the hostess left us at our table, Keller stood, saluted me, and then came and hugged me. He gave me a good squeeze and whispered, "I'm so proud of you, son."

I bit back the tears that threatened to break free because he hadn't called me *son* since I threw Tess out of my life. She had taken me out to her favorite place to stargaze and brought a bottle of wine stolen from her dad's collection. After we'd drunk the wine, she'd tried to seduce me, but I'd refused. I had ended up passing out, and when I'd woken up in the morning, she had been gone, and I'd had to walk back to the orphanage twenty-eight miles away. Some of the popular guys Tess hung out with at school had driven by, and instead of offering me a ride, they had run me over and beat me unconscious. If a truck driver hadn't stopped, I'd have been dead. A week later, I had walked out of the hospital only to discover no one had known I was there.

I had ended up losing my job because of it, and when I'd shown up at school, the administrators had yelled at me for not informing them I wasn't attending. It had been one of the most stressful days of my life, and when I had seen Contessa in the hall, talking to the boys who'd put me in the hospital, I'd nearly lost my temper. I had tried to ask her to talk to me in private for a minute, but she had refused and joined her friends in making snide remarks about me just because I was an orphan with no social status. At that point, I had lost my temper and called her out on how terrible she was as a friend and how she couldn't have cared less about me in front of her fake school friends.

I had called her a spoiled rich girl and many other things right there in front of everyone. I had publicly shamed her. It had been wrong, and I was still ashamed of it. Everything I had said was true, but I knew I should have gone home and tried to talk to her about how I felt when she was alone. Instead, I had ignored the principal's call for me to come to his office and walked out the doors and straight into the basic training camp without taking a single personal item with me.

Keller released me and took his place at the table once more. "So, Rayas, what do you think about Adreia's newest Crimson Soldier? I think he looks dashing in that armor."

Keller's question hung heavily in the air as Rayas eyed me with a murderous gleam in his eye. "It makes me question the leading authority's ability to make good, rational decisions regarding our nation's future. Allowing someone with unstable mental capabilities to hold such a position of power is absurd."

"Well"—Senator Reach's calm voice commanded attention— "neither my son nor I was considered stable or sane when we were promoted, and we haven't burned Adreia to the ground, so I think we will be fine. Besides, the fact that Roark here hasn't attempted to murder you before indicates that he has much more patience than I. I would have silenced you long ago if I had to put up with you as much as he did, but that's just me. I really, really love violence."

Victor's eyes widened a bit before he stood, made a snide remark about Reach's father not approving of him, and stormed out of the room.

I took my seat as Keller shook his head and said to Reach, "I can make him disappear for you if you would like."

"No, we need him alive—for now."

Keller nodded as the waiter brought out two plates of food and one to-go box. The food was placed in front of Reach and me, while Keller accepted the box before excusing himself. Finally, we were alone, which I could tell had been the plan all along.

"Asherex reported in and began quarantine yesterday. My son survived falling into a raging river and going over a waterfall. What are the odds?" He blew out a relieved sigh and then looked at me. His demeanor changed, and in a businesslike tone, he said, "I'm sure you are aware of the attempted assassination of the high commanders during the summit meeting a few months back." I nodded, and he continued. "That very day, Lillie, Asherex's wife, was involved in an accident that led to her death, and we were forced not to pursue an investigation. After a week, Asherex filed for a work petition, and they granted it to him for the investigation only. See, Asherex is extremely meticulous about where his water comes from. He bought the company, changed the bottling process, and only drinks that brand while in Adreia. He had a personal supply of it delivered to the summit meeting for his use and then shared it with the other high commanders when they learned that he had it.

"Anyway, there were only six people with access to the water. The first was the man who loaded the water for shipment, the second was the delivery guy, the third was Asherex, the fourth was Proxy High Commander Uriah, and the fifth and sixth people were servants Asherex took with him to see to his food since he can't cook. Asherex's servants were thoroughly vetted; they love him as if he were their son, so it was easy to see that they didn't do it. Asherex isn't going to try killing himself or anyone else. If he wanted to kill someone, he could get away with it right in front of the entire nation.

"Asherex had his employees fully vetted with the best lie-detection programs, and they had to spend some time in the Secret Service prison before being cleared and released to return to their families on the Surface. This leaves Proxy Uriah, who is still under secret surveillance. Asherex seems to believe that Uriah isn't smart enough to come up with something so complex on his own or get his hands on the black-market poison, let alone the radioactive isotopes found in the water."

"What does all this have to do with me?" I asked as I finished all the food on my plate. The meal had hit the spot, and I couldn't help but enjoy the five-star cuisine, which probably cost a small fortune.

"Because, Roark, it is the Crimson Soldiers' responsibility to combat threats to national security and eliminate terrorists. Asherex believes—and I agree with him on this theory—that poisoning him was a test to see how effective the poison was before giving it to our commander in chief."

# Chapter Twenty-Six

## Roark

I sat back, trying to process everything Reach had just told me. He let me think while he finished his plate, and then he sat back and waited for me to comment. After carefully considering the weight of my words, I asked, "So why do we need Victor alive for now?"

He smiled at me with a predatory look in his eyes before answering, "We both know that Rayas has connections with the black market and loose ties to Uriah. I believe he may be the one who orchestrated the attack during the summit meeting. With it being a failure because my son didn't go crying about not feeling good the moment he felt the effects of the poison and instead held off until it nearly killed him, I was certain there would be another attempt. Two days after the crane explosion, an assassin attempted to kill Drayen, but because he was visiting my son at the time, the assassin found an empty house. The security system that Asherex insisted he install just a few days prior captured the whole thing.

"I hacked the city's surveillance system and tracked down the assassin. Within hours, I captured the man, brought him before the war council, and participated in the interrogation. He didn't exactly come out and say who'd hired him, but he hinted that it was an upcoming political figure. That, combined with the rest of the evidence Asherex collected from the botched assassination attempt during the summit meeting, led me to believe that Rayas was involved. The only downside is that Asherex refuses to allow me to capture and interrogate Rayas without at least one solid piece of evidence.

"This is why no one will cross Rayas right now. No one is reviewing the abuse cases filed against him or willing to arrest him. Asherex is calling all the shots on this investigation and wants everyone involved taken down, not just the obvious ones. I'm sure you can understand how frustrating this is."

"Victor is going to think he can get away with anything."

"Yeah, he is, but that line of thinking will cause him to be less cautious in the future, and when he slips up, you'd best believe I'm going to enjoy taking him down."

I shook my head at the wistful look on his face.

He pushed his empty plate out of the way and, with a sigh, said, "I need to get back to the senate so we can actually get something done. I have a goal to see every contract through this year so no one has to suffer because those ignorant fools in there can't make up their minds about farm equipment. Very few of them even understand the basics of farming."

We talked for a few minutes longer while the waitress brought by the scanner and scanned Reach's ID chip, and he put in the tip before we left the restaurant and parted ways. I called a cab, and after a few minutes of waiting, I was finally heading home. Relief washed over me when I arrived and saw my airship on its pad. At least they'd had the decency to bring it back instead of making me pay to have it towed.

The neighbors stared at me as I walked to the front door. I waved at them, and they quickly got back to their yard work and attempted to pretend they hadn't just been spying on me. Before I could open the door, a mower stopped near my front porch, and I turned to see the boy I paid to mow my grass. He had a big smile on his face as he hopped off the mower he had just bought on his own not long ago.

"Hey, Mr. Roark, I'm so glad to see you!" He ran up to me, shook my hand, and said, "Congratulations on your promotion, by the way. I took care of everything for you while you were gone and cleaned your house so you wouldn't have to when you got back."

"I guess you want me to pay you then?" I teased.

He shrugged and replied, "You are too good to me, Mr. Roark. You can pay me whenever you have time. I know you are good for it."

I smiled at the kid and shook my head. It was hard to believe he was only ten, but then again, I had taught him how to act like a businessman. I even had shown him the value of going the extra mile and being honest when something went wrong. The kid mowed ten lawns a week at thirty dollars per acre. He saved up everything to buy the best equipment he could, and the last time I had talked to him, he had been about to hire another person to help him because he had more people wanting him to mow their yards in the neighborhood. He was an intelligent kid and had a real future as an entrepreneur.

"I'll tell you what. I just got this promotion, so I get paid more now. I will go ahead and pay you for your services."

"Okay, Mr. Roark." He held his arm out to me.

I pulled out my plex, scanned his chip, and paid the bill for the yard work and housework he had done for me. It looked as if the kid had even restocked my pantry while I was away. Man, this kid was something else.

"Mr. Roark, if you ever decide to do some landscaping, just let me know. I also want to get into that, but I need a couple of clients to showcase my talents. I would give you a good discount too." He winked as he finished speaking.

"All right, kid, if I decide to have it done, you'll be the first one I call."

He smiled before saying goodbye and heading back out on the mower to finish my yard. I walked inside my house, and I felt out of place for the first time. It bothered me to see it empty and void of personal belongings. *Maybe I should save up some money and buy furniture or something.*

I headed toward my bedroom to change out of my armor, but someone knocked on my front door before I made it to the closet. With a groan, I walked back to the door and opened it only to have my breath catch in my lungs from surprise. I found myself staring into the dark green eyes of my Brashex soldier friend. This was weird.

"You going to invite me in or keep me out on the porch, Adreian?"

I quickly stepped back and motioned for him to come in. "What are you doing here?"

He wandered around my living and dining area as if he hadn't heard me and pondered some grand secret. After walking the length of the rooms, he turned to me and said, "You know, I was expecting there to be more black and some really expensive, ridiculous furniture. The house is beautiful, by the way, but the inside is severely lacking."

"What are you—some kind of interior designer?" My sarcastic question seemed to hang in the air.

He turned to me with a grin and replied, "Nope. I just like to have—I don't know—a little bit of furniture and maybe a painting on the wall. Most people actually hang these things called curtains on their windows too. It's a very primitive practice, but it helps to brighten up the place and has the added benefit of helping to regulate the temperature. They block cold in the winter and heat in the summer. You might want to look into it."

I stared at him for a moment before bursting out laughing. Once I caught my breath, I found him in Emet's room. "You never answered my question about what you are doing here."

He turned to me and replied, "I like this room. It feels like there is something good and pure about it that lingers; it's so peaceful." He closed his eyes for a moment before letting out a content sigh and continuing. "Roark, I am the ally from Brashex who was working with the Adreian war council to bring back the black box." He opened his eyes and pierced me with his gaze. "You could have left me there to die, but you didn't. You showed me mercy that very few have ever given me. I still don't understand why you did it, but I am grateful and wanted to come by to see you before I head home to my wife. She came here a few weeks ago to settle into our new house and finish the naturalization process for us to become citizens of Adreia.

"She called me the day you were arrested to tell me she was pregnant. We've been trying for six years now to have a child, and if you hadn't spared me—" He looked away with tears in his eyes. "I know I said we were even for the life debt, but I cannot leave my side of the debt with so much more to pay, knowing that you brought me back to my wife and child."

"Nope. No way. You paid your debt in full. You did more than anyone ever has for me by paying for those parts and the hospital bill. I know how much it costs and won't take anything more from you. If you feel like you still owe me, you can pay me back by raising that kid to know that his dad loves him, and whatever you do, do not spoil him so that he grows up to be a little terror. Deal?"

He took my outstretched hand, shook it, and said, "Deal." He pulled me into a hug and thanked me again. This day was getting weird, with so much physical contact with people. He pulled back and headed to the front door, but before he walked out, he turned and said, "Maybe I'll see you around, Adreian."

"That would be nice, Brashex."

He gave me a mischievous grin before walking out, and I caught a glimpse of his state-of-the-art, top-of-the-line airship parked out on the street. *Man, this guy has to be loaded. No wonder he got so upset about my old beast.*

I watched through the window as he flew away and had to admit he was right about the curtains. Perhaps it was time to look into furnishing my house, but that would take a lot of money I didn't have. With a wistful sigh, I turned back to my room, changed out of my armor, and crawled onto my pallet on the floor. Man, it was good to be home.

# Chapter Twenty-Seven

Asherex

It was the first day of the week, and West was taking me back to town to collect supplies and see the doctor again. The Sabbath day had gone by fast, and I had done my best to learn something about what the people in the community believed instead of sleeping the day away. Unfortunately, I had missed out on the Friday night festivities because of the nanos, which had forced me to take pain meds. The meds the doctor had prescribed for the excruciating pain the nanos caused while repairing internal damage had knocked me out and left me feeling as if I had been run over.

The road seemed bumpier today, and I did my best to ignore the pain of my wounds. The nanos repaired the bruises all over my body and improved the minor injuries. The larger shrapnel wound in my side still seemed as nasty as before, but with a few more days of nano treatments, I would be as good as new.

West dropped me off in front of the outpost station and headed to the store where the people from the community sold their goods. A military-issue airship landed a few minutes later and began unloading supplies for the outpost, so I walked over and waited for my stuff to be unloaded. They dropped off two wooden crates before leaving me to open them myself. It was strange, but whatever. I needed to get the nanos unloaded so I could see the doctor.

It took me a few minutes to pry open the crates, which caused my body to protest. I surveyed the medical supplies and frowned at what I saw. I had paid for specific brands, and the items in the crate were not what I had ordered. I didn't even recognize the packaging on the box containing the nanos. It was an odd brown box with no brand logo on it.

"Excuse me." I got the attention of an older soldier. "This isn't what I ordered."

"Well, tough luck, kid; this is what you got. Take it or leave it."

I couldn't believe the guy. "I believe your job is to deliver exactly what was paid for, down to the serial number and everything. I'm not paying for this."

"You've already been billed, kid, and we ain't taking it back."

My temper flared, and it took all my self-control not to unleash it as I replied, "Who do you think you are? You cannot disrespect—"

"Who?" He interrupted me.

I felt the switch flip in my mind, and all my emotions drained away in an instant, leaving me with nothing but the cold, calculating feeling I usually had when I was about to assassinate someone.

"Who are you to speak to me—"

I cut him off before he could say another word, and my deadly calm tone caused his face to pale as I said, "I am High Commander Reach of the Crimson Division, and I will not tolerate disrespect from an underling. Where is your unit leader?"

"H-h-he's out sick, sir." His stammered voice was full of panic, as it should have been for such disrespect of a ranking officer.

"Under normal circumstances, I would have you put on probation for your insubordination. Instead, I will hand you over to your head of a hundred and let him deal you a punishment he deems worthy of your crime. Now, remove my payment from this shipment of medical supplies, and leave them."

"I'm sorry, High Commander Reach." He bowed to me in the traditional fashion.

For a moment, I thought I should feel a little guilty, but right now, I was unable to feel emotions like a normal human being. *Emotionless robot.* My father's words echoed in my head, and I knew I would feel guilty later. This man had probably served in the military longer than I had been alive, and now he was groveling like a child.

He looked me in the eye and continued. "I will return with the correct shipment as soon as possible."

"No. If I need anything else, I will have one of the units under my command see to it."

With that, I ordered them to take the medical supplies to the doctor's office and the boxes of clothes and other personal items to West's truck. They left as soon as they finished, and I finally saw the doctor. He had to take blood samples before and after every nano treatment because I was in quarantine, which meant I would have to come back for the next three days for the nano shots. Hopefully, West would be willing to drive me back to town each day for them.

We made small talk as we waited the required time after the nano shot before taking another blood sample. He added that one to the others he'd taken from me on the first day he treated me and on Friday before he gave me his last nano shot. By the time I walked out of the doctor's office, my whole body felt as if it were on fire from the nanos, and I couldn't wait to get back to the bed-and-breakfast and eat so I could take the pain pill and pass out. At least I could feel things again.

I asked West to tell me about their Passover celebration on the ride back in an attempt to keep my mind occupied. It worked for the most part, but by the time we were back at Kyandra's house, I was sweating and shaking from the pain. Man, I hated nano shots. Once we were back in the community, West helped me to my room, where I took the much-needed pain meds and lay down, hoping to sleep the pain away.

I awoke at precisely 3:45 and just stared at the ceiling, waiting to see if the pain would return. When I was satisfied that the only pain I felt was from my wounds, I climbed out of bed, feeling completely drained of all energy and sick to my stomach. I hadn't eaten when I took the pill, and I was regretting that decision now.

It seemed to take forever to make it down the stairs and into the kitchen. I found a note letting me know there was food for me in the fridge and giving directions on how to heat it up in the toaster oven. I watched the vegetable-and-rice meal heat up in the small oven, afraid I would catch something on fire if I didn't. *Maybe I should have just eaten it cold.* That was what I did when my servants left food for me at home.

A small eternity passed before it was time to remove it, stir it up, and then put it back in for another fifteen minutes. I waited about eight minutes before deciding I couldn't handle it anymore and took it out before pouring the food into another bowl that Kyandra had left on the counter. With a bottle of water in one hand and the food in the other, I made my way to the front porch to eat. It was a peaceful day, even though it was a little on the chilly side.

I was sitting there enjoying the sunset, when Kyandra walked out of the house and handed me a blanket with a smile. I accepted it, realizing how cold I was only after I wrapped up in it. She sat on the other side of the doorframe and watched the sunset with me. We didn't say a word as the sun sank out of sight, and I once again became aware that I was alone with her. This wasn't right. I hadn't been alone with my wife until our wedding night; there had always been someone with us, even though we had grown up together. Even when she had babysat me when we were younger, one of her siblings had been there too. Lillie had been four years older than I, and even when we were children, our parents had insisted we be supervised at all times to ensure that nothing inappropriate happened.

My heart beat faster as I glanced around to see if I could see anyone else walking around, but there was no one. A quick glance at her let me know she was still watching the last of the light fade into darkness, oblivious to my inner turmoil. I felt as if I were about to have a panic attack and knew I needed to get my mind off it. I couldn't just go inside, because we would still be alone if she came inside, and it didn't matter if we were in different rooms; that wouldn't stop other people from gossiping.

A glint caught my eye, and I turned my attention back to Kyandra. The small flash of light had come from an engagement ring on her finger, which both calmed me and caused me to be even more on edge. The whole time I'd been here, I hadn't seen her speak to anyone as if she were engaged to him, but maybe he didn't live here.

"Kyandra, I've noticed that you wear an engagement ring. May I ask where he is? I haven't seen you interact with anyone in a way that would suggest he is here." Well, that was one way not to bring attention to the fact that I was studying her—not.

She looked at me for a moment and said, "I've noticed that you have a wedding band on, but you haven't spoken about your wife since you've been here."

I twisted the band around on my finger and replied, "Her name was Lillie."

"Was?" Kyandra's question was soft, almost as if she didn't want to know the answer.

"She died fifty-five days ago. I know I should have removed the ring during the forty days of mourning, but I couldn't bring myself to do it. I don't think I'm strong enough to remove it."

"I'm sorry, Ash. I can't imagine what you've been through." She was silent for a while before saying, "I was engaged ten years ago, when I was twenty-one, to someone who was very kind and considerate. He studied with the rabbi and was almost done with the discipleship program, but eight years ago, a group of Adreian soldiers came through and drafted the men of our community who could fight. Steven was one of them, and he never came back. I don't know if he died or is out there somewhere."

"I'm sorry to hear that. You would have been told if he had died, since he lived in the community." If the enemy had captured him or he had deserted the battlefield, someone would have filed a report. But then again, if he had been swallowed up by the river, as I had, it was unlikely the soldiers had gone looking for his body. "Have you tried hiring a private detective to find him?"

Kyandra looked at me, shook her head, and said, "I can't afford that."

"You can now."

"I couldn't do that with the money we need to put back into this place. It belonged to our grandparents and needs too much work. If Grandpa could see what it's become since he's been gone, he wouldn't be happy."

"I understand, but you should at least consider it. You deserve to be happy, and you can't put your life on hold for someone who might never return. I admire your commitment to this man, but even if he came back to you today, war changes people, and he might not be the same person you once knew."

I stood, using the doorframe to pull myself up, and walked inside, carrying my bowl into the kitchen. Kyandra was still outside, so I went to my room and rifled through my bag until I found my new plex. After powering it up, I called customer service to have all my old information transferred to the new plex and the new number replaced with my old one. After two hours of being put on hold and transferred to seven different people, I was finally on hold with the district manager.

A cheery female voice came through my earbud, saying, "Sorry for your wait, Mr. Reach. I've been looking over your records, and your insurance seems to be in order, but unfortunately, your request to have information transferred will take a couple of days to review."

"I've transferred information more than forty times since I bought my first plex, and it never took more than a few minutes. All you have to do is put in your clearance codes and follow the dialog boxes until it finally asks you to input the current and previous numbers. After that, you click the Transfer button, and everything switches over at that point. It's effortless."

"I'm sorry, Mr. Reach, but I cannot do as you requested." Her voice had a bite to it. "The process isn't as simple as that."

"Yes, it is." I did my best to keep my tone level as I spoke. "It is so easy that a child could do it."

"I don't appreciate your tone, Mr. Reach."

"I don't appreciate that you are telling me you cannot do your job correctly." I kept as calm as possible, but I wanted to throw the plex across the room. "Like I said, I have done this many times in the past, and I am looking at your policy on transferring information right now. It says that the process only takes five minutes maximum, so I would like you to do your job so I can call my father."

"I don't know what you are looking at, Mr. Reach, but that is not and has never been our policy and—"

Frustrated, I cut her off and said, "Have a nice day, Mrs. Thayer. I will be contacting your boss later to let him know how incompetent you are. I will transfer the information myself."

I hung up, hacked their database, and did the transfer. It took twenty minutes total before all my old information popped up on my new plex. There were hundreds of messages, so I spent the next couple of hours going through them and replying. Once everything was settled, I pulled up my dad's number, but I hesitated so long that I had to wake the screen up four times. I wanted to call him but was afraid he wouldn't answer.

The screen darkened again, and I hastily woke it up, punched in Drayen's number, and called him. It was three in the morning in Adreia, but I needed to talk to someone who wouldn't give me the runaround. It rang five times, and I was about to hang up, when he answered. His holographic image popped up on the screen.

"Asherex! I can't tell you how happy I am to see you. What's going on? How are you feeling? Are you healing up all right? Who are you staying with? Are they good people?"

I chuckled at my friend's worried tone. It was easy to see that he was a parent who had asked these questions before. "I'm doing pretty good. My wounds are healing up as well as expected. The people I'm staying with seem decent and have been super friendly and accommodating. They are a little strange but genuine people." I let out a little sigh before saying, "I spent two hours trying to get my plex transfer done and finally gave up and hacked them and did it myself."

"Who did you talk to? I want every name to ensure that it doesn't happen again. You are a high commander and Crimson Soldier, so they never should have disrespected you like that. It should have only taken like five minutes to transfer your information. I should know; I was there yesterday getting it done."

I shook my head and gave him the names. Sometimes it was good to be best friends with the commander in chief. I watched him write the information in a notepad program on his plex and noticed that he looked as if he hadn't slept in days. "Is everything all right with you?"

He looked up at me and, with a sigh, said, "Our best pilot was shot down three days ago, and we haven't found his cruzer. About a week ago, Adreia and the Brashex started having problems with a new-age airship shooting down everything that tried to leave the World Above. It was undetectable to our radar systems and had some sort of camouflage system that made it nearly invisible to the naked eye."

A chill ran down my spine at the mention of the camouflage system. I knew that system better than anyone because I'd designed it and was in the process of building a warship and remote-piloted drones with that feature, to be revealed at the next weapons convention. About a year ago, my company had been hacked, and some information had been stolen. I had reported it to the war council and been assured they would look into it.

Oblivious to my inner monologue, Drayen continued. "Jayce noticed something unusual and called it in just in time to get his fleet out of there before the thing opened fire on them. The young commander shot the airship down but sustained heavy damage. We found the enemy airship, but it's unsalvageable. Because of the nature of the attack, the Brashex commander in chief is working with us to locate Jayce's cruzer, which crashed in their territory. It's a total nightmare."

Jayce the Ace was the youngest pilot in Adreia's history promoted to commander of a thousand. He had led hundreds of firefights and had to retreat only six times from battle. I had met him once, and he had been an exceptional individual with a ready smile. He reminded me of Jonathan with his cheery attitude, and he never spoke ill of anyone. In fact, the entire Jasper Division had requested his promotion to commander of a thousand with the hope that one day he would lead the whole division as their high commander. It was a shame to lose such a talented young man. The kid was only fifteen but well respected by everyone he met.

"I wish I could help you, but without my equipment at home, I couldn't hack the satellites and track him on the way down. I'm sure my father could, but I know the senate is busy this time of year, and he won't have much time for anything else."

"Have you talked to him yet?" Drayen's question hung heavily in the air for a small eternity.

Finally, I replied, "Not yet. I tried calling him but couldn't hit the button, so I called you. I will call him, but maybe I should get some sleep first. I've had my second round of nano treatments today and am worn out." It was an excuse, and we both knew it.

"Please call him when you wake up. If he doesn't answer because he's in the senate chamber, leave a message and wait for him to call you back. I know you don't believe me, but I promise you that he is worried about you and loves you. Don't make him wait to hear from you; even if it's only a quick conversation, you both will feel better afterward. Then you should call Aiden, since he's like your child, to make sure he knows you are safe and alive.

"And, Asherex, if I were you, I would do it before you get your nano shot tomorrow, because you turn into a monster when you are drugged up, and no one needs that kind of attitude from someone they thought might be dead a few days ago. Lazerick might get a kick out of it, but the rest of us seminormal people don't appreciate it. However, if you are in a lot of pain in the morning, wait until after your treatment and after the pain meds wear off before you call. I know you don't like people worrying about you and don't want them to see just how much pain you are in, so that's all the advice I will give you. I will check in with you tomorrow night, unless I pass out from lack of sleep. Good night, Asherex."

"Good night, Drayen."

He hung up, and I walked into the bathroom, cleaned up, dressed in my pajamas, and headed to bed. I lay there for a few minutes before remembering the recorder message I had intended to bring up to Drayen. I reached over in the dark to find the disk. It bounced off my fingertips and fell behind the small dresser. With a sigh, I lay back in the bed; I would look for it in the morning.

# Chapter Twenty-Eight

## Roark

I had been dead asleep, lost in one of those deep sleeps in which I drooled all over myself and soaked my pillow. I rolled over to find a dry spot and was almost asleep, when my plex rang for the second time. I wanted nothing more than to go back to sleep, but it seemed whoever was calling me wouldn't have it.

Frustrated, I grabbed the plex, noticing that it was almost dawn. I had slept for more than a day. The holographic screen flared to life and immediately dimmed to adjust to the low light in my bedroom. I found myself looking at a number I didn't know. I had four missed calls from it and several voice messages. With a sigh, I touched the holographic screen to answer the call, and immediately, Proxy High Commander Uriah came into view.

"Good morning, Roark."

I corrected him on my proper title, saying, "It's Crimson Soldier Roark."

"Excuse me?" He sounded offended.

I responded, "It's Crimson Soldier Roark now. My military title has never been just my name; I've always been Unit Leader Roark, but now it's Crimson Soldier Roark."

He looked at me as if he had sucked on a lemon.

I continued. "The sun isn't even up, so I wouldn't call it morning yet or say that it is good either, seeing as how you woke me up."

"So you haven't received a message from Asherex Reach yet?"

"Do you mean High Commander Reach? My high commander?"

He was silent for several moments. Displeasure burned in his eyes.

"Proxy High Commander Uriah, you are being extremely disrespectful of your higher-ranking officers today. And to answer your question, no, I haven't read the message yet. After returning from a top-secret mission and being promoted to Crimson Soldier, I've been asleep, so I haven't had time to do anything yet."

"High Commander Reach," he said with contempt in his voice, "has selected your unit to oversee his quarantine proceedings, but I am assigning another unit in your place."

"No." I cut him off and smiled at the anger that covered his face. "If my high commander—who is also a Crimson Soldier, if I may remind you—wants my unit, then he will get my unit. To oversee a man's quarantine is a very high honor, and I will not refuse his request. On the other hand, you are standing on very thin ice with me right now and should watch your tone and think very hard about what you say next. After all, I have the power and authority to kill you, and there would be no investigation into why. Disrespecting a higher-ranking officer is a punishable offense too, and you have disrespected High Commander Reach and me. Is there something you want to inform me of? If not, I would like to get back to my day."

"Since you insist on proceeding to oversee your high commander's quarantine without your medic, one will be assigned to you during the duration of his quarantine. Also, your third private, Nathan Press, has been promoted to unit leader in another section of the Crimson Division, and Kale, a fourteen-year-old ward of the state, is taking his place. He will be with you until his contract is up in three months, and if he does not show signs of improvement with his court-appointed shrink by that time, he has been commissioned to be put down.

"While you were away, your team met the kid, and your medic has spent a lot of time with him. Perhaps your team will be able to bring Kale out of his shell and help him to become a productive member of society. You are scheduled to meet him later today and officially make him part of your unit. I sent you all the details. Don't be late."

With that, Uriah hung up on me. *How rude.* He acted as if he could boss me around. Before my promotion, I probably wouldn't have said a word—no, I would have mouthed off, but now I could back up my threats. The war council had given the wrong man the promotion of Crimson Soldier, because I wasn't afraid to do what I thought best for my team or do what was necessary to protect the people I cared about.

With a sigh, I got out of bed, dressed in workout clothes, cooked a light breakfast, and then pulled out my treadmill and began running. While I exercised, I went through my messages from the last week. I had several messages from Emet, with the last voice message from him letting me know he was going to some third-world country I couldn't pronounce to volunteer his time building a school for some ministry he volunteered at around this time of year. He would be gone for two weeks, and I felt terrible that I wasn't going with him. Last year, I'd told him I would go with him if I was able, but with the recent mission, the national security issue, and the oversight of High Commander Reach's quarantine, I couldn't join him.

I still wasn't sure he would have wanted to be around me if I had shown up. The urge to tell him about my promotion was strong. But I knew that was something I should share face-to-face and not through words on a screen. Uncertain, I messaged him back, knowing he wouldn't have service where he was, and told him I'd just gotten back from a solo mission.

An hour and a half into my workout, the doorbell rang. Frustrated, I powered down the treadmill and answered the door. A well-dressed deliveryman in a fancy suit with a fully automatic rifle slung across his back greeted me with the warmest smile I'd ever seen. He pulled up his electronic clipboard and said, "Mr. Roark, I'm Davien of Reach Consolidated Arms and Outfitters. We supply the latest and greatest in firearms, armor, and armored vehicles; whether for land, sea, or air, if you have a need, we have a product. I'm here today to deliver a package from President Reach to congratulate you on your promotion to Crimson Soldier."

I was impressed. Davien wasn't reading from his clipboard during his speech, and he even shook my hand to congratulate me on the promotion. He seemed so happy to be delivering the package to me that I had to wonder what it was.

"If you will just follow me to my cruzer, I will have you sign for the products and allow you to test them."

At my nod, we headed toward his airship, and I asked him if he enjoyed his job. He had nothing but good things to say about the company and was quick to inform me that he had personally tested every weapon I would receive today, to ensure they held up to the company standard. Obviously, he loved his job, but if I'd gotten paid to go around shooting guns and blowing things up, I would have enjoyed it too. Who wouldn't have?

Once inside the cruzer with its own gun range, I signed for the package. Davien pulled out seven guns from locked safes and placed them on the table in front of me: an automatic rifle; a sniper rifle; a tactical shotgun; dual handguns with the same caliber as the one I carried; a specialized flare gun and laser cutter that could cut objects up to fifty feet away; and, lastly, every soldier's best friend, a combo gun that launched grenades and served as a shotgun with a second barrel for smaller armor-piercing rounds. Everything came with the latest and greatest accessories, and it was all free for me to customize. My high commander sure knew how to give a gift!

We spent the next two hours shooting the guns and trying out every option I had to customize each weapon. We talked about everything from politics to the latest news, and Davien told me about the massive-scale operation working with the Brashex to find

Adreian pilot Jayce Quest. I couldn't believe Adreia had lost its best pilot, and I felt bad for Jayce's sister. His parents were from old money and hadn't approved of Jayce's career choice. They had wanted him to become a lawyer or a doctor, and I was sure they were telling everyone that if Jayce had only listened to them, he wouldn't have been missing now. That kid had saved my backside many times, and I hoped he either had survived the crash and was all right or had died upon impact. The rocky outcroppings he had crashed on were out in the middle of the ocean, and drifting out at sea on a life raft didn't seem like a good way to die.

We finished up with the last weapon's customizations, and I looked over at Davien and asked, "So we have tested everything except for the grenade launcher. I don't suppose you can test that on your cruzer?"

He gave me a big grin, showing his perfectly white teeth, and said, "Not on the airship, but we can go outside for that."

"Oh, I'm sure the neighbors will love that."

"I make a living annoying neighbors all over the country. Since you don't live within city limits, we can fire off a total of fifteen grenades before we are breaking the law."

I smiled at him as he wheeled out a large metal-framed box about the size of a small shed and set it up in my yard. My neighbors gawked at us as Davien pulled out his gun he called Buddy, pressed a couple of buttons on his clipboard that caused holographic targets to appear in the box, and then let loose with a barrage of gunfire, followed by a grenade. He nodded for me to have at it, and the targets began moving in the box, only disappearing when shot. It was the most beautiful thing I had seen all day.

The bunker box withstood all fifteen grenades and probably a thousand rounds before we shut it down. Davien smiled at me and said, "Well, how do you like your weapons?"

"I don't know what to say, to be honest. I've only ever had used weapons, and this all seems like too much. I expect to wake up any moment and find that it's been a dream all along."

175

He reached over and pinched me hard, causing me to flinch and look at him in shock. He smiled at me again and said, "You're not dreaming. This is as real as it gets. Mr. Roark, you don't know how much of an honor it is to be your deliveryman today. You are a Crimson Soldier and the epitome of what it means to be an Adreian soldier. When I started working for Reach Consolidated, our president was only fourteen. Everyone thought he would run the company into the ground before it started, but look at us today; we have taken over thirteen companies and are the only firearm business that brings the gun to the customer.

"I love my job, and people like you make it worthwhile. Most people I deliver to tell me how unhappy they are with their jobs or complain about their lives, but you haven't once complained about anything and have made my job easy. I can tell that you have a passion for your unit, and I leave here knowing that they will be safer because you have the best weapons on the market today. I may not be on the front lines, putting my life on the line, but I get to be the guy who tests every weapon to ensure it doesn't fail in the field. Because of you and your men, I look forward to going to work every day."

Davien's passion touched me. I wasn't used to being around people who cared so much about Adreia's military who didn't work for it. "Davien, you said you were honored to be my deliveryman today, but the truth is that I'm honored to have such an outstanding and well-mannered man before me. Most people around me only see that I have one name and use it as an excuse to ridicule me, but you have been so respectful that I can only ask that you allow me to shake your hand."

He smiled, nodded, and shook my hand. We talked a bit more about the five-year warranty on the weapons while he helped me carry them inside and loaded me up with a month's supply of ammo. I watched him fly off in his cruzer as my plex rang, and I answered it without looking. The holographic screen displayed the image of my high commander, and I quickly bowed in the traditional manner.

"High Commander Reach, how are you?"

"I am doing well, Crimson Soldier Roark. I still have a hole in my side, but it will soon be healed." Asherex sounded different than I had imagined he would. His voice was full of kindness, and the smile on his face hid his pain. "Have you had a chance to review my messages about the quarantine yet?"

"No, I haven't. I went straight from the war council's promotion ceremony to lunch with your father, where he briefed me on the national security threat and ongoing investigations, and from there, I made my way home and went to bed. I started going through my messages this morning, but a delivery from your company interrupted me. Thank you for the weapons. They are more than I ever thought I would own."

"No need to thank me. I reviewed your financial records and tracked every credit you have spent since joining the military. You have provided for your unit since Head of a Hundred Zeth took over and cut the budget for your unit. The discovery of his misappropriation of military funds ended in his termination. I refunded every credit you've spent of your private money. It turns out Zeth has been intercepting all your mail going to the higher-ranking officers, and if I didn't have specialized software in place to protect my email account, you never would have been able to reach out to me either. I have recommended that he be publically executed as an example of what happens when you tamper with military affairs."

*Wow.* I knew Senator Reach loved violence, but it seemed out of character for his son to recommend that someone be executed on live television. Then again, he had broken several laws, and that was the punishment.

"Proxy Uriah tried to have my unit removed from your quarantine care," I said.

"I thought he might try something like that. He sent me the wrong supplies and has disrespected me as well as ordered me to hunt down religious people in the area I'm staying in so he can murder them. He called them terrorists, but they are probably the nicest people I have ever met, and as far as I can tell, their beliefs look down

177

upon violence. I would have reported him if I wasn't investigating him already." Asherex let out a sigh, and weariness was evident in his eyes. "When you come later this week, I want you to ensure that everything coming here is exactly what I ordered and destroy anything that doesn't have a brand logo on it."

That seemed like an odd request, but I nodded and said, "Anything you need, High Commander, I will do it."

"You can call me Asherex. There is no need for us to be formal since we are at the same level of authority and rank."

"I can do that, Asherex." I smiled at how weird this was. I had spent my entire military career trying to get people to call me by my official title, and now I had been given the high honor of calling someone by his first name. It was surreal.

"You have no idea how nice it is to have someone agree to that request on the first try. Usually, I have to argue for a bit to get others to forsake formalities. Thank you, Roark."

"Asherex, you look like you need to get some rest, so I'm going to get off here and get ready for my meeting with the newest addition to my unit."

He nodded, saluted me, and hung up. I showered, hand-washed my workout clothes, and hung them to dry before dressing and donning my new armor. I flew the two hours to the capital city, grabbed a bite to eat, and then went to the barracks to meet Kale. A well-dressed woman was waiting for me when I arrived and introduced herself as Kale's social worker. She was nice as far as social workers went, and I was glad she seemed to genuinely care for the kid. None of my social workers had given me a second glance; they had treated me as if I were infected with Zeron's disease.

"Where is Kale?" It was strange that the kid wasn't there to greet me, but I was willing to give him the benefit of the doubt.

"He said he wasn't feeling well and went to the bathroom before you got here. I'm sure he will be right out, Unit Leader Roark." She bit her lip and looked around nervously before whispering, "Kale has been through so much, and he doesn't like talking to anyone.

I'm afraid he already gave up because they put him on death row instead of giving him a chance. He went straight from a bad home situation into forced military service. He's a good kid and doesn't deserve this."

"His records are sealed, so I don't know what he's been through."

"Yes, he is protected under the Criminal Minor Act, and other than myself and his court-mandated shrink, no one else knows what he has been through. I wish I could share it, but I can't. Kale won't talk about it with anyone, and he's had to participate in front-line battles since he graduated from basic. He hates violence, and I had to pull a lot of strings to get him into your unit. I know you take care of your men in ways no one else does. I know you will do your best to keep him safe and protect him, and that's all I ask."

"I will try, but if the kid doesn't want to talk, there isn't much I can do."

She nodded with tears in her eyes as Kale made his way across the room to us. He was five foot nine, an inch taller than I was; his eyes looked gray; and his side-swept, shaggy strawberry-blond hair hung in his face, nearly concealing his left eye. He looked skinny, as if he hadn't eaten well during his last two years in the military, and his face looked like skin stretched over his skull. Man, I was going to have to fatten this kid up.

When he neared us, he bowed to me with a clenched fist over his heart and, in a barely audible whisper, said, "Unit Leader Roark."

I dismissed his bow while his social worker began talking to him about my unit and our history. Kale kept his eyes down, refusing to look anyone in the eye, but I could see that he was constantly scanning the entire room. Someone had beaten this kid badly for looking at him. I had my work cut out for me and would have to watch my temper so I didn't scare him off.

The social worker left us alone, and I looked at the kid and asked, "What unit did you serve with last? I heard you were on the front lines."

He stared at my boots and replied in that small voice, "C0995 with Unit Leader Tao."

"Unit Leader Tao is a tough man to get along with. He rules his men with an iron fist and can be quite harsh. I'm nothing like that, and if anyone gives you any grief from now on, you tell me. I will take care of it, okay?"

He nodded, and I gently placed a hand on his shoulder and said, "We won't be seeing any combat for a while. My unit has been honored to oversee High Commander Reach's quarantine, so I'm sorry to say that you will be spending at least a week in the quarantine facility in the underparts of Adreia alone after we get back from his checkup later this week."

"I like being alone."

I almost didn't hear him, and my heart broke. I had been in and out of many orphanages, some of which had had cruel people running them. I understood wanting to be left alone. "When you are not on a mission, where do you stay?" I asked.

He took an involuntary step back, fidgeted with a strap on his pants, and said, "In the Marshfield orphanage."

"There are miniature apartments available for military personnel here on base if you want to stay in one. It's just one room with a twin bed, a small closet, a kitchenette, and a tiny bathroom. I stayed in one straight out of the orphanage in my early military days."

He looked at me without making eye contact, shrugged, and said, "No one told me about that."

"I can get you set up if you want. My unit's budget allows for my men's accommodations and basic supplies, like food and clothing, if needed. No one will be there to tell you how to spend your free time or force you to do anything you don't want to do. You will be set if you can cook your own food."

"I can cook ..." He trailed off, and I wasn't sure he was going to say anything else, but then he looked back at me and said, "I would like that."

"Follow me, and we will get you set up with everything you need."

Kale didn't say a word as I spent the next couple of hours securing his room and signing as the responsible party for any damages. If he trashed the place, I would have to pay for it, but the kid needed to know I had his back if he trusted me. With the paperwork done, we went to his room, which looked exactly like the one I had lived in when I joined the military. Kale looked around, turning on every light, testing the stove and oven, and trying out the faucets. He seemed satisfied with it, so we left to go get his personal belongings from the orphanage.

The Marshfield orphanage looked awful and in desperate need of repair on the outside. When we walked inside, a young boy on his hands and knees was scrubbing a stain out of a rug that looked as if it belonged in a dumpster. Other kids of various ages ran around mocking the boy and being obnoxious. The scene brought back many horrible memories.

"Volan!" A shrill, angry-sounding woman's voice pierced through the din of noise, and the young boy winced at the sound. "Who opened the door?"

"Kale an—"

The woman cut him off as loud footsteps headed our way, and she said, "It's about time that worthless kid showed back up!" She finally came into view, and for a moment, I could only stare in shock as the extremely overweight woman wearing clothing two sizes too small marched into the room, nearly knocking Volan down as she came huffing after Kale. I was amazed she fit through the doorway. She eyed me with contempt and, with attitude, said, "Who are you?"

"I am Unit Leader Roark, and Kale is here to get his belongings."

"I don't think so. That boy is a ward of the state. He ain't going nowhere, and if—"

"Actually"—I cut her off, and if looks could kill, I would be dead—"he is the property of the Adreian military, and since I'm his unit leader, he has to do everything I say. Besides, I am a certified warden, meaning I can legally take any ward I want from any orphanage, and there's nothing you can do about it." She opened her mouth to say something, but I quickly shut her down by saying, "And I am a Crimson Soldier on top of everything else, so you have to do everything I say or be arrested for disobeying direct orders from one of the highest-ranking people in Adreia."

The look on her face was priceless. From the corner of my eye, I caught a glimpse of Kale relaxing before I continued. "I know that because Kale is in the military, you get paid ten thousand dollars a month to provide for him. Yet I can take one look at him and see that he has not received proper nutrition while in your care. I could file a suit against you for neglect and have an investigation launched into how you are providing for the kids you get paid to care for. I also know that because Kale only has a few months left before he is scheduled to be put down, the investigation would be delayed unless I forced it to go through. So if you don't speak another word to me while I'm here, I won't file a suit."

She looked between Kale and me before huffing and walking back into the other room. Kale left to get his things, and I was left alone with little Volan. I got down on my knees in front of the six-year-old and asked, "What's your name, kid?"

He looked up at me, pushed his glasses up, and quietly said, "My name's Volan. It used to be Volan Isran, but my parents died, so now it's just Volan."

"Well, Volan, it's nice to meet you." I shook the kid's hand. "The woman in charge—is she mean to the kids here?"

"Joanna yells a lot, but she usually isn't mean to most kids. Just the ones she thinks are dumb."

"Is she mean to you?"

He looked away and started scrubbing the stain again. Before I could question him further, a young couple walked through the door. It was obvious they were there to adopt, and little Volan jumped up, greeted them, and led them down the hall. I was about to peek around the corner, when Kale showed up, holding a black backpack that didn't look full.

We didn't say much as we waited for the cab, but he looked at me in confusion when I told the driver to take us to the shopping district instead of to the apartments. I told him we were going to get him a new wardrobe and pick up some furnishings, such as curtains, for his apartment as well as some groceries.

We spent a couple of hours buying clothes and then ate at the food court in the six-story mall before going shopping for his apartment.

He picked out a bedspread, curtains for the three windows in the apartment, and towels for the bathroom. He surprised me with the color schemes he picked out. I never would have tried putting those colors together and thought about how hard it would be when I furnished my house. Kale had an eye for odd things that looked out of place but, when put together with the other furnishings he picked out, went well together.

After he picked out a small sitting chair, end tables, a lamp, and paint for the new place, we paid. I had everything shipped to his apartment, so it would be there when we arrived later. On the way to the grocery center, we passed by an art store, and he asked me if we could go inside. I, of course, wasn't going to tell him no, so I found myself in a store that I didn't recognize anything in. I watched Kale as he wandered around. Occasionally, a brief smile would skirt across his lips before disappearing, and I knew this would help him more than anything I could have done.

"Get whatever you want from here, Kale."

He looked at me in surprise before going back through the store and picking out exactly what he wanted. I paid for his sketchbooks and the rest of the artsy paraphernalia I knew nothing about—a bunch of chalky crayons, charcoal sticks, and other things that looked like old trash but probably had a purpose.

It didn't take us long to get groceries after that, and the kid clung tightly to the bags full of art supplies as if his life depended upon it the entire time we were in the store. I called a cab while we checked out and then headed back to his apartment. Once there, we carried his boxes of furniture and things up the four flights of stairs to his apartment, but he wanted to paint the place before he did anything else, so I left him to it and headed home.

# Chapter Twenty-Nine

Asherex

I woke up coughing so hard I thought my lungs would rip out of my chest. Downing two bottles of water finally put an end to the coughing, but the healing wound in my side was throbbing now. I was on the third and final day of nano treatments for my injuries and the fifth day of quarantine. I was ready for my wound to heal so I could take a shower instead of taking sink baths and washing my hair over the side of the tub.

Speaking of which, I needed to wash my hair today. I knelt down beside the tub, started the water, and got my hair wet before turning the water off to scrub the natural shampoo into my hair. Another coughing fit hit me as I turned the water on, causing me to drop the long-hosed showerhead. Soap got in my eyes, and I was drenched by the time I could shut the water off. It took me a couple of minutes to stop coughing before I could rinse my hair. Frustrated, I peeled off my wet clothes and dried off. The bathroom floor was wet, and after getting dressed, I mopped it up and completely dried it to avoid water damage.

I gathered all the towels and my wet clothes and headed downstairs to put them in the wash. The coughing started again, nearly causing me to spill the laundry soap, and Kyandra rushed in and took over, telling me to go get something to drink. I left the laundry room, trying to suppress the violent cough, and headed to the kitchen. I drank another bottle of water and sat down at the bistro table, feeling sick. What was going on? I'd had a slight cough yesterday and felt a little nauseous after my nano treatment, but it had seemed to clear up after I took the pain pill and slept. Other than that, I hadn't done anything except call Roark yesterday.

"Are you all right, Ash?" Kyandra walked into the room, looking concerned. "You were coughing all night; are you getting sick?"

"I—" *I shouldn't be sick with the nano treatment, unless ...* A cold chill ran down my spine. *Zeron's disease.* I was a second-generation Adreian, so I should have been immune to Zeron's, but here I was, showing the early signs: a persistent, violent cough and nausea. Maybe I was wrong. I hoped I was wrong.

"Ash? What's wrong?"

I looked up at Kyandra. I must have looked worried, because she suddenly looked terrified. "I don't want to say it, but I shouldn't be sick with the nanos I've been taking."

She looked at me, and I could tell her mind went right to where mine had been just moments ago. I had one more day after today to monitor myself before Roark's unit came to perform the final test to confirm if I had Zeron's or not. I was afraid I was infected. *There's no cure.*

Before either of us could say a word, Jonathan came in the back door, letting me know he was going with West and me to town. Jonathan's cheery attitude snapped me out of the shock I was in, and Kyandra quickly turned away, as if she were afraid to ruin his good mood. He started humming one of their worship songs while I forced myself to eat a banana, even though I wasn't feeling hungry. I hoped my stomach settled down later so I could take my pain pill after the nano shot.

A few minutes later, we were loaded up and heading to town. Jonathan and West talked about a truck that Jonathan had been working on for the last couple of days at his shop and the parts he had ordered for it, which should have been delivered today. The conversation ended, and the quiet was killing me, so I looked at West and asked, "Westly, how did you come into faith in this Yeshua and belief in Torah?"

He looked at me with a big grin and, in his southern drawl, answered, "It's a bit of a long story, but believe it or not, I haven't always been this way. I grew up deep in the South and worked as a security guard for one of the largest private firms around. We could pick where we wanted to work as long as it was within our territory's borders. Anyway, I worked in the big city, where I had a nice apartment, a fancy car, and a smokin'-hot girlfriend.

"Me and my girl lived together for five years, and everything seemed like it was going really good, until she started coming home super late on Friday nights. After a couple months of it, I believed she was cheating on me, so I started following her on Friday and learned that she was going to this Sabbath church for services and a shared community meal to usher in the Sabbath. I would go to the service, sit in the back so she wouldn't see me, and then leave before all the dancing started.

"I didn't say a word to her, because I wanted to see if she was going to tell me she was going to church, but she never said a word. Six months passed, and I could tell she was growing more distant. Then, one day, she told me she was going to move in with her best friend because her friend just got out of a bad relationship and needed support. A few months later, she called me at work, and I was fully expecting her to tell me she was breaking up with me, because we barely saw each other. Imagine my surprise when she told me that her best friend's boyfriend had beaten her up, and she wanted me to come sit with her at the hospital while she waited to find out how bad her friend was hurt.

"I traded my double shift that night with a coworker, Roy, who never stayed late. When I got out to the parking lot, someone was waiting and shot me, thinking I was Roy, so I ended up in the hospital and nearly died. My girlfriend took care of me for a few weeks. After that, I confronted her about the church thing and told her she had to choose between God and me. Well, she didn't pick me."

He trailed off as if the thought were amusing before continuing. "Roy transferred to another site after apologizing to me for getting me shot. He had been having an affair with the shooter's wife. Fast-forward ten years, and I was thirty and in a different city, staying in a hole-in-the-wall apartment with a junker car and no girlfriend. And to top it all off, I had become a bit of an alcoholic. It was late, and the bartender I was friends with took my keys away from me and told me to go home at two in the morning. Instead of calling a cab, I decided to walk ten blocks to my apartment, and it started stormin' something fierce.

"The streets were hauntingly empty, and I was cursing up a storm of my own, when a car pulled over, and the guy offered me a ride. It was a nice car, the kind of car you wouldn't want a soggy drunk to ruin, but I took the offer, and off we went. At first, he stared at me for a bit. Then he told me he was my former coworker Roy. Turns out that after I got shot, he turned his life around. He remembered me complaining about my ex going to church, so after he moved, he started going to one. He was a disciple under someone there and then was put in charge of the place while the guy was off building another community.

"He gave me a pamphlet about the church before dropping me off. I woke up the next morning with a massive hangover and his pamphlet on my fridge. I decided I would go on Shabbat, and if I didn't like what I heard, I wasn't going back. For the whole service, I sat there feeling like I was being beaten up, and I hated every word he spoke, but when the service was over, I couldn't make myself leave. Roy sat with me for hours, not talking, until I finally broke down and started crying like a baby about how awful I was and how I didn't want to stay that way. He spent the rest of the day walking me through the scriptures, and after a couple of weeks of studying what he said, I discipled under him.

"A couple of months later, I tracked down my ex-girlfriend and asked her out to lunch to talk. I apologized for how I'd treated her and asked for forgiveness before tellin' her about my dramatic life change. I married her a few months later, and we've been together ever since. We moved out here twenty years ago, and we now have been married for twenty-six years, with two kids. I couldn't be more blessed if I tried."

Jonathan was smiling from the backseat, and I could tell he had heard this story a few times but still loved it. I wondered what the other people's stories were in the community. It was fascinating that West had given his life over to something more without fully understanding what he was doing, and I had to wonder if this religion was the answer to my own questions. Why else would I have been there, if not to learn about it?

"So, Ash, why are you so curious about my story? I didn't think Adreians cared about this stuff."

"We don't have religion in Adreia. It isn't illegal anymore, but no one knows about it, and there is no way to find out about it unless you come to the Surface and read books or talk to religious people. I am very interested in what you people believe and why. It's so different from anything I've ever known."

West looked away from me and back to the road, as if he were satisfied with my answer. I was sure he was still being cautious since he didn't know much about me. Of course, he didn't ask me questions or try either. Jonathan seemed open and willing to talk about his personal life and faith with anyone who would listen. I was not the kind of guy to go around gushing out my life story to everyone, and I wasn't sure what type of protocol these people went by when they interacted with outsiders like me.

"What about you, Jonathan?" I asked.

"I grew up in the community, playing with the other kids and attending services with them. My parents didn't believe, so I couldn't talk about it at home. Several things happened that I believed could only have come from Elohim, because there's no natural explanation for them, but I wasn't fully committed at the time. After my parents died, I prayed for a way to stay here, and a week later, a check came in the mail with no return address. It was from some Adreian group that helps the families of the people drafted to serve in battle. The scary part is that the check was for the exact amount I'd prayed for, down to the last cent. Because of it, I paid off the house and the shop and stayed here.

"From that day forward, I studied the scriptures and prayed constantly. Even though I was ten, I obtained a minor's driving license for special scrapping vehicles and kept the business going. I have never gone hungry and always have what I need. Yehovah is faithful even when people are not."

"Why didn't anyone from the community take you in?" The truck was silent, and my question hung heavily in the air. What was going on? Jonathan had a sad look on his face, and West concentrated harder on the road than before.

"I don't really have an answer for that, Ash. I've never had a handout a day in my life, and I work hard for everything I have."

My heart broke for the kid. No one had wanted him to be part of their family. He was sweet and kind, but I could see the brokenness inside him now. He was lonely and had been alone for five years, having to work hard for every meal. How could this community of people claiming to serve such a loving Elohim have abandoned a child? Maybe this religion wasn't the answer to all the questions I'd had all my life. Perhaps this Yehovah was just made up and an excuse for these people.

If I could have taken Jonathan in, I would have in a heartbeat. He was kindhearted and eager to learn. He would have fit right in with Aiden; the two of them probably would have worked well together in the airship repair business. I looked back at Jonathan in the review mirror, and my heart sank at the realization that if I was right about having Zeron's, I wouldn't be able to explore the option of adding him to my family. *Who would want a dying man to adopt him only to leave him an orphan again in a few months?* With a defeated sigh, I settled back into my seat and stared at the road ahead.

The rest of the ride was quiet, and the doctor's visit was uneventful, except for the coughing episodes. The doctor seemed worried, and when I left his office, I was even more convinced that I had Zeron's. The longest anyone had lived with the disease was sixty-one days. 76 percent of people drowned in their own blood by the end of the second week, and 97 percent of those who survived died within the first thirty days. The symptoms got worse the longer one lived, starting with a cough and nausea and then progressing to coughing up blood, random bouts of paralysis, loss of appetite, and feeling completely drained. The symptoms came and went. A person might experience partial paralysis one day and feel like running a marathon the next.

Tomorrow was going to be one of the longest days of my life, and I couldn't wait for the final test on Friday to find out if I was indeed infected. As we drove back to the community, my mind replayed the moments I'd spent with those infected with Zeron's. I was numb and decided to sit on the back patio of Kyandra's house instead of going inside.

Two and a half hours passed. I couldn't take it anymore and took off walking through the community toward their fellowship hall. My body was on fire from the nanos, but I didn't want to waste time in a drug-induced sleep. Once inside the empty building, I headed up to the piano, closed my eyes, and began to play. I played several songs before my fingers found a familiar tune, and I lost myself in it. Playing the piece I had written so many years ago took thirty-two minutes and forty-five seconds.

Exactly thirty-two minutes and forty-five seconds later, the final note filled the air, and I sat there defeated. I didn't know what else to do. A sound drew my attention, and I looked up to see Avdiel walking toward me. He sat next to me and said, "That was a solemn song you just played. What's it about?"

I looked away from him and down at the keys. "When I was

fourteen, my cruzer was shot down, and I ended up in a Borderland prison across from a Brashex soldier. He ended up with Zeron's disease and was sick for about three weeks before I figured out how to pick the locks, and we escaped. We took refuge in an abandoned neighborhood that looked as if everyone in it had just walked out the door without taking anything and never returned. It took me a couple days to turn an old radio into a walkie-talkie and call Adreia.

"Because we were still in the Borderland, they couldn't send an extraction team, so I was left with Brandon. One of the houses we stayed in had an old piano, and since I knew how to play, I would play for him every day." I smiled at the memory. Brandon would hum a tune he made up, and I would use his tune to write a whole song. Parts of those songs had made it into his song I had just played. With a sad smile, I continued. "He got sick really fast after a month, and I watched him slowly die. It was probably the most horrible thing I've ever seen, but he refused to let me mercy him. He didn't want to leave me alone, and part of me didn't want him to go, but the other part wanted his suffering to end.

"One day he asked me to write a song about his life so he could hear it. I spent about six hours working on it in my head before I played it. The first twenty minutes of the song I just played were about his life, and the rest was my struggle after he died and I made it home. I was in quarantine for two and a half months after escaping the Borderland, and Brandon's death affected me so much that I went to my piano mentor with the song. He is famous, and he now plays Brandon's song when he plays for charities. He told me he cries every time he plays it, and there isn't a time when people don't come up to him after the concert to tell him how much they were moved."

I got quiet after that. I wasn't sure what to say. Confusion, fear of the unknown, and numbness fought for control over me. Frustrated, I propped my elbows on the piano and put my face in my hands before saying, "I just don't know what to do. I have Zeron's—I know it—and I don't know how to tell my dad."

Avdiel put a hand on my back and said, "Ash, you don't know for sure yet. Wait until the tests are done before you despair."

"I've watched seventeen people die from this. I know the signs and symptoms, and with all the nanos in my system the last five days, I shouldn't be sick, but I have a persistent, violent cough, which is the first symptom." I sat up and looked into his dark blue eyes. I wanted him to understand, but perhaps I was also searching for something more, something real within the depths of his soul. "How do you know that your faith is real?"

He looked surprised by my question before answering, "Faith doesn't have to have a rational reason behind it. I have faith because of something happening to me that I cannot explain. Every human being has faith in something. People have faith that their cars will work properly when they start them. Some believe that if they are good people, they will be all right after they die, and others believe in a higher power that holds them accountable. Whatever it is, everyone has faith in something. The question you have to ask is, what do you have faith in?"

# Chapter Thirty

## Roark

My unit had spent the entire day running drills and routine training exercises. We were worn out and a man down since Emet was gone, but the kid had proven himself to the team today, which was all that mattered. I came out of the shower room into the bunkhouse to change and found Unit Leader Tao talking to Kale. The kid looked as if he wanted to be anywhere else, so I walked up to them.

"Is there a problem, Unit Leader Tao?"

He looked at me and sneered. Sure, I was still in a towel, and some would have found that disrespectful, but he had no business talking to my soldiers. I hoped he said something smart and gave me the chance to deck him. I was in one of those moods.

"Unit Leader Roark, this doesn't concern you."

"I beg to differ on the matter. Kale is mine now, so you don't get to talk to him unless I approve it beforehand. Do you understand?"

"I will speak to this worthless ma—"

I cut Tao off by grabbing him by the throat and slamming him into the lockers. The guy was six inches taller than I was, and his shocked look brought a smile to my face. I kicked his legs out from under him so that my hand was the only thing keeping him from falling onto his backside and said, "You will not speak to Kale again. To disrespect one of mine is to disrespect me. Do you understand?"

He choked out a yes, and I released him. He fell to the ground and sat there trying to catch his breath. I looked around the room at all the soldiers gawking at us and said, "Anyone else want to test my patience today?" They all looked away and slowly returned to whatever they had been doing before I caused a scene. "Come on, kid; let's leave this trash on the floor, where it belongs."

Kale quickly followed me and didn't look behind him. I probably shouldn't have let my temper get the best of me and attacked Tao, but I had been pushed around enough by people like him and was finally able to put my foot down. Things were going to change in the Crimson Division, whether everyone else liked it or not. As a Crimson Soldier, I was responsible for ensuring things ran correctly.

After I dressed, I dismissed the rest of the unit and took Kale home. He, of course, didn't say a word the whole flight back. He spent the entire three-hour flight coloring in his book, and I was pretty sure he didn't look up from it once. How was I supposed to save him if he didn't try?

Before I left him, I tried to encourage him by telling him how well he had done today, but it didn't seem to faze him. Maybe my outburst had scared him away. It wouldn't be long before his time was up, and I wasn't sure he wanted to live.

I powered up my cruzer and was about to take off, when my plex rang. I quickly dug it out of my pocket, saw that it was Keller Thaz, and answered it. His black hair was expertly combed out of his face, and his stormy blue eyes danced with laughter as he said, "It's good to see you, son. Where are you?"

"I'm outside the apartments in the capital city's military base. Why?"

"Good. You're in town. Can you meet me at Challan's in fifteen minutes?"

"Yeah, I guess I can make it there."

"See you when you get there!" With that, he hung up.

*What was that all about?*

I flew to the most expensive restaurant in the city and parked on the sky deck, where my cruzer would be stored in one of the lower parking garage levels. The valet exchanged my keys for a number and escorted me inside. I felt out of place in my body armor amid all the fancy-suited men and dolled-up women in dresses that probably had cost more than I made in a year. *Thaz had better have a good reason to drag me into this awful place.*

The maître d' looked up from her holoplex station, looked me over, and smiled before saying, "My name is Kyaria, and welcome to Challan's. How may I serve you today, Crimson Soldier Roark?"

It was a pleasant change from the usual greetings I was accustomed to. "I'm supposed to be meeting High Commander Thaz."

She smiled before looking down at the holoplex station for the reservation. "If you will follow me, Mr. Thaz is waiting."

Kyaria walked me to a secluded table in the back of the restaurant that offered a full view of the place. It was the perfect spot to see an ambush coming, which was why Keller had chosen it. Thaz stood as we drew near and bowed to me before kissing Kyaria's hand and sending her away. His charm and infectious smile made her blush as she walked away.

"One of these days, some poor girl will faint on you if you keep that up," I said.

Keller laughed as he took his seat.

I joined him. I looked at him intensely before saying, "So what is all this about? You know I hate these fancy places."

"I know you do, but you are going to have to get used to it. Fancy dinners, charity events, and many galas are in your future as a Crimson Soldier."

"I don't belong here, Keller."

"Roark, just because you lack an inherited social status does not mean you don't belong. Your lack of faith in yourself to fit in is what

holds you back. I saw it when you were a kid, and it is still in you."
His scolding tone did little to ease my nerves.

Keller gave our orders to the waiter, ordering for me because
I hadn't bothered to look at the menu. The waiter returned with
water and a bottle of costly wine a moment later. Keller sampled and
approved it before having our glasses filled and the bottle left in a
bucket beside the table.

Keller drank half his glass before looking at me and saying, "I
went to the capitol building today and spent most of the day there. I
know you are leaving tomorrow to see Asherex Reach, and I wanted
to give you this before you left." He pulled a paper envelope out of
his inside jacket pocket and slid it across the table to me. "You've
tried for years to get the documentation from when you were given
over to the system as a baby and have been unsuccessful so far. It
costs a lot of money, and if you don't know the right people, it is
nearly impossible to get your hands on it."

I looked at the envelope, afraid to peer inside it. I had wanted
to see who had given me up for adoption for so long. Now that the
information was in front of me, I was too terrified to look. This
would tell me who my parents were, and maybe I would finally find
out why they hadn't wanted me.

"Roark?"

I looked up at Keller and opened my mouth to say something,
but for once, I was speechless. He smiled at me before picking the
envelope up and saying, "I already read it, and I know that the
answers you are looking for are not inside. If you want me to, I can
help you find those answers, but you have to read the paper inside
first."

I accepted it from him and, with a sigh, opened it. It was a
military report from a soldier:

> I, Commander Lou Verity of the Crimson
> Division, during a routine scouting mission of
> Solis, discovered a child thrown into a dumpster

and buried beneath several feet of trash. The infant is less than a month old, and its gender is male. Our medic examined the child and deemed him in good health, except for being underweight and slightly dehydrated. Several attempts to track down the parents were unsuccessful. When the child did not cease to cry for three days, refusing formula and sleep, the men brought him to me because of my experience with my own difficult infants. The child stopped crying immediately and accepted the formula from my hand.

The child, whom I am now calling Roark, was with me for a week and gained weight, but my time on the Surface ended, and they urged me to take the child. My high commander gave me leave to care for Roark until he reached a suitable weight before turning him over to the state. I cared for the child for two months before handing him over to the Haitfield orphanage, where he would receive the necessary care, as my military court-appointed shrink deemed me unfit to care for a child.

I read the letter twice before it sank in. Had Lou Verity wanted to keep me but been unable to? Had he been counting down the hours before he could hand me over? Based on his report, it seemed he was trying to keep his distance from me, but then again, the last paragraph seemed to imply he didn't want to hand me over.

"Keller, I don't understand what this is supposed to mean."

"I know, kid. I know. I know Lou Verity, my former commander of a thousand in the Crimson Division. He lost his wife and three daughters, all under the age of two, three months before he found you. I can't speak for him, but if I had lost Contessa and found another child abandoned like that, I don't know if I could have taken that baby and raised it. That loss will mess with a man, even driving him to madness."

I couldn't help but think about Victor Rayas as he spoke. From what Emet had told me, Victor had been a different person before his son disappeared. It didn't excuse what he did now, but he was a good example of what a desperate man would do after his child was gone.

"Roark, if you want to meet him and ask him, he is hosting a charity event four days from now. It's an art gala to raise money for the homeless shelters in the region. Lou is a wealthy man who goes around doing these charity events all over Adreia. This might be the only chance you get to talk to him."

"How would I even get tickets to it? And if I did manage to make it there, what would I say to him?"

"I've already bought tickets for us. I'm not going to make you face this alone, son. As for what to say to him, well, you have a very unique way with words, so I know you will figure out what to say when the time comes." Keller's smile turned mischievous as he spoke.

The food was set before us, and we started eating while my mind replayed what had just happened to me. I finally had a chance to find out where I was from and ask the man who had given me up why he had done it. I had wanted this my whole life, but what if it didn't change anything? What if Lou hated me for bringing up his past? What if he threw me out of the gala?

All the questions chasing themselves around in my head came to a crashing halt as I remembered that tomorrow I would be doing the quarantine check for Asherex. Afterward, I would have to spend a week in quarantine myself, so I wouldn't be able to go to the gala. I sighed and said, "It doesn't matter, Keller. I won't be able to go, because I will be in quarantine."

He chuckled, causing me to look up at him. He set his silverware down and said, "Roark, what part of 'scouting mission of Solis' did you not understand? Solis is a small desert town on the border of the Wastelands on the Surface. You didn't read past the report, did you? You had blood tests done, and they confirm that you are 100 percent from the Surface, so you are immune to Zeron's disease. That means no quarantine for you."

I looked at him as his words sank in. I was from the Surface and immune to the incurable disease that killed Adreians. I couldn't possibly be a carrier for the disease. Both fear and relief coursed through me at the thought of being able to go to the gala and meet Lou. The next four days were going to be an emotional roller coaster.

Shock still gripped me as we finished our meal and parted ways. I flew the two hours home and sat in my cruzer for a long time before pulling my plex out and calling Emet. I knew he couldn't get my message for a while, but I had to tell him, even if it would be a few more weeks before he heard it.

The plex seemed to ring for an eternity before his voice mail picked up. At first, I didn't know what to say. Then I opened my mouth, and the words flowed out. "Emet, it's Roark. I know you won't get this message for a while, but I wanted to call anyway. So much has happened since I got back, and I just found out tonight that I am from the Surface. Keller got the paperwork for me. Turns out an Adreian commander found me in a dumpster. I'm going to meet him in a few days, and I'm terrified. I don't know what's going to happen. I will tell you about it when you get home." I paused for a long moment and sighed. "Emet, I'm sorry I haven't been a good friend lately. I should have told you what happened while I was tortured. Can you forgive me? I guess I will talk to you when you get back, and please don't hesitate to call me if you need anything, no matter what time it is."

I hung up and went inside. Too wired to sleep, I lay on my floor pallet, replaying the last week in my head. How could all of this have happened to me?

# Chapter Thirty-One

## Roark

After sleeping for four hours, I stepped out of the shower and took my time getting ready for the day. Last night, I had cleaned and polished my armor and weapons, and now I carefully put on every piece as if it were the last time I would wear it. Today I was meeting my high commander for the first time, and even though he was five years younger than I, I respected the man and didn't want our first meeting to disappoint him.

I was more nervous now than ever, and my hands shook as I buckled my boots. As soon as I was official-looking, I grabbed an apple for the road and headed out to pick up Kale. The rest of the unit were going to meet us at the base, and I was sure they were as nervous as I was, except for Doug, who had been part of a quarantine unit before. This was going to be nerve-racking, to say the least.

My neighbors gawked at me again as I walked to my cruzer, and for the first time since moving here, I realized I had never gone over and introduced myself to them. They had been in and out so much when I first moved in. Then I was gone more than I was home and always rushing out the door when they were out. Maybe it was time to introduce myself.

I walked across my well-maintained lawn to their side of the street. They were all outside; the wife and husband were sitting in chairs, watching their three little girls jump around in a small plastic pool. The husband stood up and walked over to me. I held out a hand as he approached, and he took it as I said, "I've never properly introduced myself, and for that, I'm sorry. I'm Roark."

He smiled and said, "It's no problem, Roark. I'm Case, and this is my wife, Lena. Over there we have the twins, Liza and Lana, and our youngest little girl, Mackenzie. Don't ask me which of the twins those names belong to, though, because I still can't tell them apart, unless they have different-colored hair bows."

His wife eyed him, and I bit back my laughter. I hoped if I ever had kids and ended up with identical twins, I would be able to tell them apart.

"You know, Roark, when we saw the news earlier in the week about you becoming a Crimson Soldier, we were shocked to see that it was you. How many people can say their neighbor just became one of the most powerful men in Adreia?"

Feeling suddenly embarrassed by Case's question, I replied, "It was a huge honor to get the promotion, and I don't think I deserve it, to tell you the truth. That's a lot of weight to put on one man's shoulders."

Lena spoke up. "We see you come and go a lot wearing your armor; my dad was in the military for most of my childhood, and he spent more time at home in one month than I've seen you at home for the last six months. You are a very busy man."

"Roark," Case said, "the other day, when the guy from Reach Consolidated was here, we sat back and enjoyed the show when you tested the grenade launcher combo gun. That made our day, and I wanted to let you know that we like having you as a neighbor, even though we haven't met you before today. We feel safer knowing there is a soldier next door. Maybe we can have you over for dinner sometime?"

"I would like that." My reply surprised me. Other than the few times with Contessa and her father, no one had invited me into their home for dinner. "Once things settle down a bit, we can make plans."

"Sounds good to me." Case shook my hand again, and I headed back to my cruzer.

The day had started well. I hoped it stayed that way.

Two hours later, I landed outside Kale's apartment, and we flew across the base to pick up the rest of the team with our stand-in medic. Ethan, well known in the medical community, had served in many mobile mediunits over the years. I had never worked with him before, but Doug had assured me he was almost on the same level as Emet when it came to being a field doctor, so that was good enough for me.

We walked into the quarantine preparation room, where the overseer handed us specialized gear to wear while they loaded up my airship with sanitization equipment. Everyone stored his standard gear in a locker and replaced it with the quarantine garb, but I didn't bother messing with it. The instructor finally noticed that I wasn't falling into line and walked up to me. In a drill sergeant voice, he yelled in my face, "Put your gear up, soldier! This isn't a joke; this is life and death right here."

"Actually," I replied in the most serious tone I could muster, "Adreian law states under sanction fifty-two of the Quarantine Law that all Adreian-born individuals must wear the required gear when interacting with those in quarantine. People proven through blood tests to be from the Surface are exempt from quarantine laws under sanction fifty-two, article six. I have paperwork that proves I am from the Surface and, therefore, exempt from the law; thus, I will not be wearing the gear."

I handed him the official letter certified with the capital's seal. He read it twice before handing it back to me and walking off in a huff, mumbling under his breath. My team just looked at me in disbelief, and I assured them I would fill them in later. I then left them to oversee the cargo load going into my cruzer, as Asherex had commanded me. I got there to find that they hadn't figured out how to open the back hatch. These poor people didn't know how to operate a manual; it was the funniest thing.

Asherex had ordered a bunch of medical supplies for the small town's doctor, so there was a lot to go through. I opened the hatch and reviewed the supplies, paying close attention to each serial number. Seven crates passed inspection, and I opened the last crate and found a couple of boxes of nanos in brown packaging without brand logos or names. A chill went down my spine as Asherex's warning to destroy anything like it filled my mind.

"What is this?" I asked one of the order fillers.

He looked at me as if I were a moron and replied, "Nanos."

"These are not what High Commander Asherex ordered."

"Well, these are what we have to get out before we can open up another batch of nanos for shipment."

I tried arguing with the guy, but it was obvious he wasn't going to take them back and give me the right thing. I did the only thing I could: I picked up the wooden boxes filled with nanos and threw them as hard as possible against the concrete floor. Every eye in the place was upon me, so I gave them the biggest grin I could muster and said, "Oops." The sound of crashing wood and breaking glass had never been sweeter.

The order filler came out of the warehouse, cursing me for mishandling property. He was three feet from me and said, "That's coming out of your paycheck, and you can pay for the replacements as well."

"I don't think so." I tapped my Crimson Soldier patch on my right arm and said, "I ordered you to replace these with the correct serial-numbered items, and you disobeyed a direct order. I could consider that treason, you know. I'm not going to pay for these or the replacements, and neither is my high commander; in fact, I think you should because your incompetence caused this mess in the first place. You are in charge here; thus, you are responsible and liable for any and all mishaps and damaged goods."

The guy looked at me, and I smiled at him and handed him

the paperwork I had with the correct serial numbers, saying, "Make sure it is right this time, or else I will have you arrested for treason."

My guys stood around watching the scene, and Doug wore a big grin; he was amused, to say the least. The others seemed to be holding back laughter; they had sat back and watched me mouth off for years without being able to do much else, and now all I had to do was mention committing treason, and I got my way. *I seriously think they let the wrong guy have this kind of power, but hey, I'm not in charge of the country.*

Soon enough, we were loaded up and heading out on the four-hour flight to where our high commander was. On the way, we, with the exception of Kale, discussed what we'd been up to since I had gone on forced leave. Of course, the guys were dying to know how I'd gotten my promotion, and I happily told them about my solo mission and the Brashex soldier I'd saved, who'd ended up being our undercover ally. My boys were upset with me for not getting the guy's name, and I could only laugh at their reactions.

The flight passed quickly, and as we began the last twenty-minute stretch, I looked back at Kale, who had his sketchbook three inches away from his face. I didn't understand how he could reach out and pick up the other colored chalk-looking things without looking away from his drawing. The kid had a meeting with his shrink in two days, and it didn't look good if he wouldn't talk to the guy. Kale hadn't spoken a single word to his shrink from the start, so even if he just said hi, it would be an improvement. Instead, he had another reason to be antisocial, and I was slightly tempted to take the sketchbook away from him, but I was afraid he would completely shut down if I did. What was I going to do?

With a sigh, I called our man at the outpost and uploaded the landing coordinates he gave me. Doug took his place as my copilot, and we landed in the most rundown town I'd ever seen. The buildings were old wood, except for our outpost station, which was made of stone and looked out of place in the dusty town, with its gravel roads. *Of all the places in the world for Asherex to end up, why did it have to be here?*

I helped the guys unload the supplies and stock the doctor's supply cabinet while our stand-in medic went to talk to the doctor. Kale disappeared after the second trip inside, and I could tell everyone else was annoyed that he wasn't pulling his weight. Once we were down to the last crate, the guys told me to go ahead and meet up with our high commander, so I headed into the doctor's office.

Asherex's voice carried through the building, and soon another deep male voice joined him in conversation. I wondered if he was talking to the doctor, since I didn't recognize the voice. Laughter erupted from Asherex's room, and I walked in to find Asherex and Kale sitting next to each other with the sketchbook open in Asherex's hands.

Asherex had a special respirator on that was standard protocol, and it covered half his face, but I could still tell he was smiling. He looked up at me with those sky-blue eyes that seemed to pierce through me and into the wall behind. It was intense and intimidating at the same time.

"Roark, it's nice to finally meet you in person. I've been looking forward to meeting you since I started my military career at twelve."

I was shocked. He had wanted to meet me? "Why?" It was all I could say.

"Well"—he sat up, handing the sketchbook back to Kale—"you were the reason I pushed so hard in basic. I wanted to beat your records and be the best. Unfortunately, I didn't manage to beat them all, but I made a good effort to."

I shook my head, amazed at how down-to-earth he was, and found myself relaxing completely. Something about him drew people in, and now I understood what the others had meant when they told me Asherex seemed to have some magical power that made people like him.

"Roark, would you excuse me for a moment so I can finish my conversation with Kale before we get down to business?"

"Sure, go ahead." What else was I supposed to say? "I've got all the time in the world."

Asherex looked at Kale, pointed at his sketchbook, and said, "These drawings are outstanding, and with your talents, you could make big money in advertising. No one does freehand anymore, because it is easier to use software, but I know of several companies that would pay big money for something new and innovative like this."

"I didn't think anyone would care about my doodles." Kale spoke in a normal tone, and I was shocked. He had a deep, masculine voice, and hope flared within me that he might have found a reason to start talking to his shrink.

Asherex put a hand on Kale's shoulder and looked him in the eye. "They are not doodles, Kale. These drawings are so detailed; I can take one look at them and know that you spent hours on them. They are beautiful, and I can tell you have a passion for drawing that can become a career. Don't let anyone tell you that you cannot do this, because I went to college and ended up with a PhD in musical arts. I've composed several songs that top musicians play all over the world. If I can do that, you can do whatever you want."

"Nobody has ever told me I could be something before."

Kale's words pierced my heart. No one had told him that he wasn't worthless. He had only known cruelty and hardship, and his words brought back memories from my childhood, when I'd been bounced around among orphanages. The adults told many kids in foster care and the orphanages that they were not wanted and were worthless. I had been on the receiving end of many of those comments until I became a permanent resident of Hawkinger orphanage and met Contessa. Her father had been the first adult to speak to me as if I could be someone, and in this moment, I knew that somehow, Kale was in my unit just so he could be here with

Asherex. If Emet had been here, he would have told me there were no coincidences, only divine appointments.

Asherex's voice was soft and full of compassion. "Well, Kale, you can be better than just something. You have the opportunity to be you. So many people out there just coast through life and are dead inside because they are trying to be something they are not. Don't be like them; choose to live inside and out. Chase your dreams, take risks, and don't be discouraged when things don't work out. I've failed more times than I have succeeded, and I chose to learn from my failures and be better than I was before.

"This life is full of hard times, and bad things happen, but I learned a long time ago that it's okay to share the darkest parts of myself with those who are trying to help. Believe it or not, I tried to kill myself once because I was hurting and didn't think anyone could understand. Someone saved me that night, and that was when I learned that I had to make the decision to let people close. Let them see me vulnerable. I've never regretted my choice, and now I am happier than ever and have a family I've built for myself. When the right people come into your life, you will want to share yourself with them, so trust me when I tell you to go all in and not hold back."

Kale looked away from Asherex with tears brimming in his eyes, and I had to look away. That was deep, and I could tell he was speaking from experience. *This got intense fast.*

"I think I know what you are saying, Asherex." Kale's voice was full of unshed tears and years of pain. If I had been a praying man like Emet, I would have prayed for the kid.

Asherex gave Kale a gentle hug before releasing him, pointing at the sketchbook, and saying, "If you are interested in a job in advertising, apply the design you have on page three to the Traderex logo. After you have it, take it to the Traderex office, and take the elevator to the fifth floor. Ask for Sherri from marketing, and tell her I sent you. Show her the design; if she likes it—and I know she will—you'll have a job. Once you are established with the company, your opportunities will be endless."

Kale nodded as Asherex dismissed him from the room a moment before the doctor and my medic walked in. Ethan briefly spoke with Asherex before he started preparing to collect the necessary blood samples. Ethan seemed slightly nervous while pulling the needle out of its sterile packaging. Asherex gently took it from him and stuck it right into his vein as if he had done it a thousand times.

"You should have let me do that, High Commander Reach," Ethan said as he quickly began filling the vials with blood.

"There's no need for you to risk getting infected while taking my blood."

Ethan and I both looked at Asherex as if he'd lost his mind.

There was a smile in Asherex's eyes as he continued. "I started showing symptoms a couple days ago. I have Zeron's disease."

"You don't know that for sure, Asherex," I said, and he gazed at me with a calm, almost peaceful look.

"I know, and I am infected."

Ethan started to argue with Asherex, but Asherex politely shut him down. I wouldn't have been so calm or polite if I'd thought I had that death sentence. Once he filled all six vials, Asherex removed the needle, stopped the bleeding, and disposed of the biohazardous materials in the proper bins. Ethan and the doctor loaded all the carefully labeled blood samples into a cooler, when Asherex started coughing so violently that he nearly fell down.

My heart stilled as the doctor caught him. I had never been around someone who was infected. Sure, I had seen the training videos that every unit leader had to watch to know what to look for if one of his team became infected, but seeing the violent cough in person was different. I hoped Asherex was wrong, but I knew he shouldn't have been coughing like that with all the nanos injected into his system over the last several days.

Asherex settled back on the hospital bed and waited patiently as the doctors finished what they were doing before leaving and shutting us in the room alone. The quiet was deafening, and I could see the calculating look in my high commander's eyes. Finally, he looked up at me with a blazing intensity that seemed to change his eyes to a pale green color and said, "I spent most of yesterday trying to come up with a solution to a problem I have now that I am not going to live much longer. I believe you, Roark, are the answer."

"What are you talking about?"

He grabbed his plex and brought up six small screens at once. I immediately recognized one of the papers: it was my warden certificate. I'd paid lots of money and spent countless hours in classes to obtain it so that I could legally care for Emet when Rayas threw him out of his house. What was Asherex doing with it?

"When my wife died, I met your medic, Emet, and the moment I laid eyes on him, I decided I was going to buy him and set him free."

The breath in my lungs rushed out at once while the hair on the back of my neck stood up as he continued.

"I started the paperwork as soon as I was discharged from the hospital, and one of the requirements of releasing a slave is that a certified warden has to care for him until his family can be found and prove that they can provide for him. Originally, I had planned on taking Emet in and finding his family, but I won't live long enough to see that happen. You are already established as Emet's secondary caregiver, and he has spent considerable time under your roof. I want you to become his warden when he is freed and hunt down his family in Yisra'el."

"Of course I will do it. Emet is like family to me." I was surprised I still had a voice with all the bizarre things my body was doing at the moment. I felt as if electric tingles were pulsing over my skin, and my heart was beating rapidly.

"You cannot speak a word of this to anyone, not even Emet. Do you understand?"

"Why?" How could I not tell my friend that he would be free and able to return to Yisra'el?

"If Victor gets word of what I plan to do, he will drive up Emet's price, and the paperwork will have to be restarted. The paperwork to free a slave you don't own is very finicky in that an expected price range has to be put down, and if it costs more than what is written, then you have to start back at square one. It can take two to six months to set a slave free."

I sat down hard in the plastic chair next to the door and said, "I can't lie to him."

"If you cannot do this, I will find someone else."

I looked up at him in protest. How could I let someone I didn't know take Emet in? What if the person was cruel to him and didn't try to find his family?

Asherex must have noticed the look on my face, because he said, "I know this is going to be hard for you, but if you want to do this, I can order you to remain silent, and since I have slightly higher seniority than you, you will have no choice but to obey."

I nodded at him. It was the only way I wouldn't feel guilty about the whole situation; I just hoped Emet would forgive me when I was finally able to tell him the truth. This month had been full of shocking, life-changing events, and I wasn't sure I could handle much more.

Asherex walked me through what I had to do to be up to his foundation's standards for keeping a ward. He would give me a budget of $2 million to do home repairs and make my house a home for Emet while he was with me. I was not sure if $2 million would be enough, but Asherex seemed confident in my ability to do the task with that amount, so I would find a way. The rest of it was to go toward finding Emet's family in Yisra'el. It was expensive to go to Yerushalayim, where I would be able to access records to find his family.

We talked about it for an hour or so, when Asherex changed the subject by asking, "Did you find anything unusual with the order you delivered?"

I looked him in the eye and replied, "There were two boxes of nanos in brown packaging without logos or brand names. I smashed them to pieces just like you asked me to."

With a sigh, he said, "That is what I received the first time. I think they contained the Zeron's virus."

A chill ran down my spine at his words. If they contained the disease, someone was using biological warfare, which I feared could be running rampant in Adreia. *The whole nation could be at risk.*

"Roark, I am a second-generation Adreian. My grandfather was a full-blooded Surface-dweller taken as a citizen slave. My father was his only child with an Adreian woman. I've been exposed to Zeron's seventeen times and even had infected blood enter my system without it adversely affecting me. Whoever manufactured the disease strain most likely modified it, which means someone specifically targeted me. It is the only logical explanation I have.

"When the blood samples get back to the quarantine zone beneath Adreia, personally see to it that they are delivered to my father's laboratory. I don't want the samples being tampered with, and his people fear him more than anyone else, so they wouldn't dare compromise the tests. I want to know the moment my blood had traces of the disease in it. I'm betting the sample before my first nano shot from the delivery will be clear, and the one after will have it."

"I will make sure nothing interferes with the tests. You have my word."

# Chapter Thirty-Two

Asherex

My conversation with Roark still played through my mind six hours later. There was so much more I had wanted to say, but I hadn't known how to bring it up after seeing the shock on his face that I was buying and freeing Emet. I was sure he had developed a deep bond with the slave doctor and probably never had imagined he would see freedom.

Speaking of freedom, I was in my room, feeling as if I were trapped in a cage. The blood samples should have been at the lab two hours ago and been tested already. Each sample took about fifteen to twenty minutes to test, and I was dying of anticipation. I had to know what they found out.

With impatience getting the best of me, I fired up my plex and hacked my father's lab to see the results. The last sample was being analyzed now, and the Zeron's virus was in my system, just as I had expected. Knowing it didn't make the blow any easier, and I sank down onto the bed, feeling numb. With shaking hands, I looked through the samples and confirmed my suspicion that I'd ended up with the virus after the first unmarked nano shot.

*At least it was me and not someone else.* The thought crossed my mind, and I relaxed a bit. I could go after whoever had infected me and ensure that it didn't happen to anyone else. If it had been any of my soldiers, no one would have thought twice about the unmarked nanos or the soldier getting sick.

I took a deep breath, backed out of the system I had hacked, and called my dad. I knew I should have done so days ago, but every time I had brought up his number, I hadn't had the strength to follow through with calling him. It rang and rang; with each unanswered ring, my heart sank. After what seemed like an eternity, my father picked up with voice only, saying, "Asherex? Can you hear me?"

"Yeah, I can hear you." Through his earbud, I could hear the chaotic sounds of the senate chamber, and guilt pierced me. I was taking him away from the busiest time of year, and every minute he was away could mean life or death for a Surface farmer. Should I have called him?

A few moments later, the holographic video feed kicked on, revealing my father hidden away in his private office. "How are you?" My father's question hung heavily in the air, and it took a moment before I could answer.

"I have Zeron's." It was all I could say.

He looked at me with fear in his eyes. I had never seen that look in his eyes before.

"I hacked your lab and found the results. I …" My voice trailed off. I didn't know what else to say.

"I'm coming to see you." His voice choked up a bit, causing pain to lance through my chest.

"No, Dad, you can't. You have to stay in Adreia and take care of things." I couldn't speak further as the tears began to fall. We both knew he couldn't afford to take the four-hour flight to come see me, let alone the return trip. If he was gone for a full day, millions of people wouldn't get their contracts renewed and would suffer. I couldn't let him do that to come see me. If he did, all the people whose contracts weren't renewed would haunt him.

"Asherex, I'm sorry." He buried his face in his hands, and I could tell he was crying.

A few minutes went by with no words spoken, and then a knock at his door broke the silence. They needed him back on the senate floor. "I will call you later if you are awake, and we can talk then, Son."

"Okay, Dad."

He ended the call, and I was alone. Kyandra was downstairs, preparing dinner, and even though it wasn't right for me to be alone with her, I went to the kitchen because I didn't want to be alone. She took one look at me, and tears filled her eyes before she came over and hugged me. The emotional dam broke as soon as she touched me, and I wept like a child on her shoulder.

# Chapter Thirty-Three

## Roark

I'd had an exhausting nine hours since leaving Asherex. After dropping the guys off at the quarantine center, I delivered the blood samples to the lab that belonged to Azriel Reach. A couple of workers tried to take the samples from me to test them in another facility, but I not-so-respectfully declined them. They weren't happy, but I didn't care. The incident made me wonder if Asherex was right that someone was trying to assassinate him.

Now I was finally home, and the knowledge that Asherex was infected kept swirling through my thoughts, along with our conversation from earlier. I still couldn't believe he was trying to buy and free Emet and had been trying since he first met him. Why did he feel so compelled to do it?

*If your God were real, He would set you free. You are so devoted to Him, yet He has left you utterly alone. How could anyone believe that your God is real if He can't even take care of you?*

My own words speared through the chaos of my thoughts. The night I had come home from the hospital after being tortured hit me like a ton of bricks. After all these years, I knew that Yehovah was real, but Emet's abusive slavery had been why I refused to believe He was who Emet said He was. But now how could I deny it, knowing that Asherex had been plotting to set Emet free all along?

*Yehovah doesn't need me to be who He is, and He takes care of me. I might not understand why I am here, but He will turn it to His purpose.* Emet's words crashed around me as if he were standing beside me. *His ways are higher than my ways, and His thoughts are higher than my thoughts. Who am I to question Him?*

I stood and began pacing the length of my living room. My steps were edgy and violent as I fought with myself. There was nowhere for me to run where my thoughts wouldn't go, and deep down, I knew Emet was right. Yehovah alone was Elohim, and there was no other. But I had denied Him for so long that I figured there was no way He could want me now.

*Whoever conceals his transgressions will not prosper, but he who confesses and forsakes them will obtain mercy.* Emet's scripture quote brought me to my knees.

With tears in my eyes, I looked up at the ceiling and said, "Yehovah, I'm so sorry." I buried my face in my hands and sobbed harder than I had in my whole life.

# Chapter Thirty-Four

## Roark

I awoke from the most peaceful night of sleep I had ever had, only to find that it was nearly noon. The gala started in six hours, but somehow, I wasn't afraid anymore. After taking time to stretch, I spent time in prayer and then made breakfast. I didn't really know what I was doing, but I was going to make an effort to try. I had heard enough of Emet's prayers over the years, so I just modeled mine after his.

Yesterday's Sabbath had been the most challenging day of my life. Before it had started, I had bought a digital Bible for my plex and spent most of the Sabbath reading it. Well, I'd read it some, and then I'd had to put it down for a couple of hours to process what I'd just read. Knowing some of the stories and little bits and pieces hadn't prepared me to read it for myself and have my preconceived notions shattered like thousands of tiny pieces of glass. I hadn't done anything else aside from that and repenting of my sinful ways. I hadn't even eaten yesterday.

With a sigh, I finished up the last report I had to review and did Kale's daily evaluation. It seemed pointless since I hadn't been around the kid since returning from the Surface, but I had to do it. An hour had passed since I started doing paperwork, and I was about to head to my room to see if I had something nice to wear to the gala, when the doorbell rang. Confused, I answered the door and found Keller standing on the other side, looking as if he had just walked away from a fashion show.

"Good. You're not wearing anything bulky."

I must have had a dumbfounded look, because Keller smiled at me before turning to someone else and calling him over. He rushed me inside and held the door open for a man wheeling a large trunk that could probably have held three bodies, and several young men followed him. All of them were well dressed. Keller said, "I told you, Glenn, that you would have plenty of space to work in."

Glenn looked around as his assistants took the trunk from him and began setting up. He looked at me, put one arm across his chest, rested his other elbow on his arm, and waved the length of my body with his free hand. "Well now, I know exactly what I'm going to do with this canvas. You have the perfect body to wrap one of my suits around."

Keller laughed, no doubt from the look on my face. When he caught his breath, he looked at me and said, "Relax, kid. Glenn is my tailor and the only man who can get you into a proper suit before the gala tonight. He's the best."

Keller's plex rang as Glenn and his assistants began taking measurements. We talked the whole time, and although he was a little off, I liked the guy. I had a feeling that if being a homosexual hadn't been a crime punishable by death, he would have been the most openly gay man I ever met.

Hours passed while they worked on the suit, and Keller was on his plex more than he was off it. It seemed there might have been a break in the case of High Commander Bane's wife's murder and his disappearance. Some tampered-with security footage had caught a glimpse of three men carrying something out of Bane's house. It might have been his body, but they didn't know, and several people were attempting to recover the footage.

Two and a half hours before the gala, my suit was finished, and

I had to admit I looked like a snobby rich person in it. I walked out of the bathroom to face Keller, Glenn, and his minions. They eyed me the way a hawk eyed its prey before attacking.

"Well," Glenn said, "I think it's my finest work yet. You just make sure that everyone knows I designed this masterpiece tonight."

Keller assured Glenn that everyone would know he had made the suit and then saw them out to their van. Keller and I left for the capitol shortly after that, and on the way, Keller told me he would have to join me later at the gala, because he had to stop by the office to check in on the investigation, but he promised he would be there. He landed his cruzer outside his mansion before looking at me and, with a soft sigh, saying, "Contessa is my date for the evening, but she's going to have to go with you. She's been dying to see the art on display tonight, and I don't want her to wait on me, so you will be borrowing my date for a couple hours until I get there. There's a limo waiting to escort the two of you; all you have to do is go inside and get her."

I nodded at him and disembarked from his cruzer. The walk up the stairs seemed to take an eternity. The last time I had walked up these steps had been the last good night I spent with Contessa. My heart tried to pound its way out of my chest as I let myself into the house and informed one of Keller's servants I was there to get Contessa. She left me and hurried off to get Tess, and every second I stood there caused me to want to bolt out the door and just run off.

My nerves were about shot, when Tess appeared at the top of the marble staircase. She was wearing a beautiful deep blue dress with glittering diamonds across the chest and down the sleeves to the elbows, where the material draped down with large openings that hung past her hands. When she lifted a hand to grasp the railing, the sleeve remained at her side, and she looked like a fairy-tale princess. She was beautiful.

She looked at me with a smile that lit up her stormy blue eyes, and my heart melted at the sight. Her blonde hair was curled, and every step caused the curls to bounce a little, reminding me of when we had been kids playing in her backyard.

As she reached the last step, I held out a hand, and she took it without hesitation. I placed her hand properly on my arm and escorted her to our waiting limousine. Once we were inside, I looked at her and said, "You look stunning."

She smiled back at me and replied, "And you are actually wearing a suit. I never thought I would see you in one, and it looks good on you."

We were quiet for a while, but even though it wasn't an awkward silence, I felt I needed to break it and put my foot in my mouth again. With a sigh, I said, "Tess, I need to apologize."

"For what?" She looked at me with confusion written all over her face.

"What don't I need to apologize for? I've been aggravated and belligerent with you since high school. I never should have said anything to you at school that day, and I'm sorry I did. I meant to call you to apologize, but I kept finding excuses while in basic training, until I figured it wouldn't mean anything by the time I graduated. And it seems like every time I've been around you since, I've lashed out at you for something that happened years ago. Emet tells me it's my coping mechanism, but that doesn't make it right.

"And the day we were abducted, I should have kept my mouth shut and not said what was on my mind. Then I insulted your religious views because it seemed like every time I turned around, something God-related was going on, and I didn't want to see it or have anything to do with it. I've hurt you and Emet because of your relationship with Yeshua, all because I was afraid to believe He would actually want me."

Contessa took my hand and was about to say something, but I stopped her and said, "I need to get all this out before I chicken out and don't say it." She nodded, and I continued. "The truth is that I don't deserve friends like you and Emet, and I haven't appreciated either of you. I didn't realize how blessed I was before I went to see Asherex."

I paused for a moment, feeling unsure and a little afraid, before sighing and continuing. "Now I know that Yehovah is the living Elohim, and Yeshua is the Messiah. I know I don't have to be the man I've been, and the road ahead of me terrifies me like nothing else ever has. So now I need to ask you: Will you forgive me and give me another chance? I can't promise that I can change overnight, but I know I don't want to be who I was before."

Tess looked at me with tears in her eyes and answered, "Of course I forgive you. I've spent the last five years praying for you. Yehovah has heard my prayers, and now I have the greatest blessing anyone could ever ask for: I have gained a brother in the faith and a chance to restore our friendship."

I released a breath I hadn't realized I was holding and pulled her into a hug. This woman surprised me at every turn. She had held firm while interrogated and hadn't ceased to pray for me for five years without seeing a single sign that her prayers were effective— five years of enduring my temper, attitude, and insults. I didn't deserve her in my life.

Releasing her from the embrace, I said, "We should pray for Asherex and his family."

She agreed, and I let her take the lead in the prayer since she had more experience with it. After a few minutes, she fell silent, and I took over. The feeling that came over me was the most indescribable thing I'd ever felt. A boldness I'd never known washed over me, and scripture verses I hadn't even realized I knew came to my mind. It was awe-inspiring.

We finished praying as we pulled up in front of the multimillion-dollar art gallery. Tess squeezed my hand as the driver opened the door, and I helped her out of the limo. There were reporters everywhere, and camera flashes blinded us as we walked up the steps and entered the building. I was sure everyone was dying for an exclusive interview with me after my promotion to Crimson Soldier.

I had been effectively ignoring them so far, but eventually, they would end up cornering me. *Maybe I should just get it over with and pick one of the ones who will actually not embellish the story.*

The gala had started half an hour ago, so there wasn't much of a wait for us to hand over our invitations and walk down the massive staircase. Nervousness filled me as the herald announced us to the crowd as we descended into the main hall. He called me by my proper title of Crimson Soldier and introduced Tess as Ms. Thaz, daughter of High Commander Thaz. It was strange to me, but Tess's reassuring hand on my arm gave me the confidence to walk through the throng of wealthy people.

We spent several hours mingling, and the number of people who left their conversations to speak with me surprised me. Out of the six hundred people there, only a few seemed bothered by the fact that I didn't have a last name and, thus, had no official social status. These people showed me more respect than I received in the military. It was strange to think that if I had remained friends with Contessa, her father would have introduced me to this world long ago.

Tess and I left the dance floor and looked at some art hanging on the walls. She told me about each painting, and what I saw didn't match what she was saying. The work was just a bunch of random colors blurred together, with a few paintings depicting beautiful scenes. I was out of my element with the art stuff, but seeing Tess's amusement to my reactions was priceless. I would call it like I saw it, and then she would tell me about the brushstrokes and how each one spoke about the artist. I didn't see it, but hey, if people wanted to throw paint onto a piece of canvas and call it art, then who was I to judge their work, even if it looked as if a three-year-old had spilled paint on it?

"Well now, this is a remarkable sight."

I turned at Keller's remark and watched as Tess's face lit up before she left my side to hug her father.

"Dad, I'm so glad you made it."

"I wouldn't miss it for the world, cupcake. The two most

important people in my life are here and probably the most adorable couple in the building."

Tess blushed, and I opened my mouth to say something, but Keller cut me off by saying, "I just spoke to Lou's assistant, and he is on the balcony. If we go now, we just might catch him alone."

I nodded as Tess slipped away, and we set off. My heartbeat quickened with every step we climbed. Once at the top, we discovered that the balcony was empty except for an older gentleman with silver hair. He was leaning on the balcony rail, looking down at the people below. All I could see was his side profile; he looked as if he were searching for something or someone, and sadness rested on his face.

"Good evening, Mr. Verity. I hope we are not intruding, but I have someone with me whom I would like to introduce to you."

Lou turned to us at Keller's announcement and walked toward us with the aid of a cane because of a limp. Faint burn scars covered the left side of his face. His smile broadened as he reached us, lighting up his hazel eyes, and he took Keller's outstretched hand and said, "Keller, my old friend, how nice to see you again."

"The pleasure is all mine. You know I can't resist coming to one of your charity events." Keller gestured to me and said, "This is a friend of my daughter's and Adreia's newest Crimson Soldier, Roark."

He shook my hand, and a strange look crossed his face. "It is a pleasure to meet such a fine young man as you. If you don't mind me asking, how old are you?"

Keller excused himself to rejoin Tess, leaving us alone, and I replied to Lou's question. "I'm thirty-one years old and still a ward of the state, if you didn't figure that out from my lack of a last name."

"You were never adopted?" His question hung heavily in the air between us for a long moment.

I took a breath, released it, and decided to speak the truth. "No, I wasn't adopted. I had thousands of interviews with potential adopters, but no one took me. They bounced me around between orphanages in different cities, and I even went to a few foster homes.

Then I reached the age where it is nearly impossible to get adopted, so I ended up in one orphanage where I lived until starting my military career at seventeen."

I paused for a moment before pulling out the envelope containing his report about finding me as a baby. I released a sigh and said, "It isn't a coincidence that Keller brought me to see you today. This"—I held the letter out to him—"is why I'm here. I received it about four days ago."

He took the envelope from me, and I observed him closely as he read it. He didn't get far before he stopped reading it and just stood there staring at it in disbelief. A shaky breath escaped his lips as he looked up at me with tears and said, "Roark, I've been searching for you for years."

I couldn't believe what I was hearing as he pulled me into his embrace. His body shook with emotion, and it took everything I had not to get my hopes up. I wanted to give in to my longing to have someone want me, but I had to know the whole story before I would allow it.

He pulled back from me, handed me the envelope, and said, "That day when I found you in the dumpster, I went out with the intention of not coming back. Solis was a very violent place, with gangs, and not a day went by without a shooting. I was about to walk through an alley into the midst of a group of gang members, knowing they would start shooting at me. My wife and three daughters had died three months before, and I had made everyone believe I was okay and ready to return to work. Little did they know I had planned where I was going so I could get myself killed because the emptiness and grief were crushing me, and I couldn't bear the weight any longer.

"When I first heard your cry, I thought I was hallucinating from lack of sleep. My youngest had been four months old, and there were many nights I woke up thinking I heard her crying, so I ignored you at first. Before I made it to the end of the alley, I heard it again and doubted myself for a moment before I decided I could wait five more minutes to die."

Lou trailed off for a moment, as if he were back in Solis. I couldn't imagine what he had been going through when he found me—the emotional turmoil of loss and the desire to end his life. As hard as my life had been, I never once had felt the need to end it. Instead, I pushed people away and turned them into enemies.

"Roark"—he put a hand on my shoulder and looked me in the eye—"you saved my life that day and kept me from going back out there to try again. I told myself that I would try again after I knew you would be fine and safe. When you refused to eat from anyone other than me, I was a little annoyed, and I couldn't wait until they let me drop you off, but the longer I had you, the more I came to love you. You were so tiny, and I was sure you had been born prematurely like my oldest daughter. I was afraid I would break you when I picked you up.

"A few weeks before I was supposed to give you up, I decided I didn't want to, and I set about the process to adopt you. I had to go back for an evaluation, and one of the men I served with in Solis told someone that I had been trying to kill myself there. Of course, he didn't know that was what I was doing, but he suspected it. Because of that and that alone, they deemed me unfit to adopt and forced me to give you up. I was so brokenhearted about it that I hardly ate or slept for two months.

"Keller had been in one of the units under my command, and when he found out what had happened, he came to see me." Lou smiled at the memory, and I did my best to remain silent and let him finish, even though all I wanted to do was ask a thousand questions. He closed his eyes, opened them again, and continued. "He was all fire and fury when he came to my house and walked in like he owned the place. Keller refused to take no for an answer and forced me to get out of the house and contest the ruling that I was an unfit parent. I went to so many doctor appointments and had to see a therapist to prove that I had suffered severe emotional trauma from the unjust ruling. It didn't matter that I had intended to kill myself that day, because I never made it known to anyone or put myself in a suicidal situation, so there were no grounds for the initial ruling. It all came down to the fact that I couldn't afford a good lawyer to defend my case, so I lost you, Roark.

"With Keller's financial assistance, I was able to get the ruling overturned, but by that time, you had disappeared into the system. At my lawyer's urging, I sued them for what had happened and won several million credits from it. I invested that money and became quite rich, which I used to foster several children over the years and continue my search for you. Everyone told me that after thirty-one years, I should give up, but here you are, and Keller kept his promise that he would help me find you. I know this will sound awful, but I am glad no one adopted you, because I have thought of you as my son all these years."

He had tears running down his face, and I couldn't hold back my own. I hugged him and said, "You don't know what hearing that means to me. I grew up hearing that I was worthless and that no one would ever want me, but you've been searching for me. You wanted me."

Lou clung tightly to me for several minutes and released me only when his assistant showed up, telling him it was time for him to start the auction. He reluctantly left, assuring me that he wanted to talk after he was done. I stayed there watching from the balcony as the charity art auction began. Releasing a shaky breath, I bowed and thanked Yehovah for the incredible evening. *What a blessing this evening turned out to be!*

# Chapter Thirty-Five

Asherex

I t was the day after the Sabbath, and the evening seemed to drag on as I spoke with Kyandra about the possibility of staying there for the duration of my quarantine until I died from Zeron's. I had a few options for places I could go to live out the remainder of my days in specialized facilities in areas called neutral zones. A designated neutral zone was a sovereign nation ruled by a man referred to as a king. The purpose of a neutral zone was to provide a safe place for both Adreian and Brashex citizens infected with Zeron's to live out the last of their lives.

As long as the king followed the fundamental laws, he could run his city in whatever way he saw fit. The king had to provide a housing facility with everything the dying person could have wanted, staffed by Surface residents because they were immune to the disease. A state-of-the-art hospital and an Adreian and Brashex embassy were mandatory in the city. Every neutral zone had a sizeable military police force due to the strict antiviolence policies. A neutral zone's king had to punish violent crimes to the full extent of the World Above's laws.

I knew I could check into one of the two neutral zones within a thousand miles, but I wanted to stay here and find out if Yehovah was the one I had been talking to all these years. I hoped Kyandra and her brother were willing to take on the honorable role of being my caretakers during that time. It was a lot of work, but the compensation for their service was generous. There was a good chance they could also apply for grants to remodel their house while I was here.

Kyandra returned to the room after spending the last forty-five minutes on the phone with her brother. She sat at the dining room table and said, "Michael says he is sorry to hear about your medical condition and will pray for you. He's going to come home next week and says you are more than welcome to stay here. It's what our dad would have wanted—to help someone in his time of need and share the gospel with you. As for taking care of you, I'm not sure I will be much help, but you can include Jonathan in the caretaking position and pay him for his time. He has been so helpful already; it isn't right that he's not being paid for it, when I am. I haven't done much."

"I think Jonathan would help just because he loves to, but you are right that he should get paid. I can ensure that happens. If you agree, my quarantine unit will have to come out, install a specialized air-filtering system, and redo your ventilation system. Any repairs associated with it are covered, like a new central air unit and installation of solar panels to run the air filter. They can add more panels to run the AC as well."

"Wouldn't that be taking advantage of your situation?" Kyandra sounded hesitant as she spoke.

"Actually, it is all part of the Quarantine Provisions Act passed about one hundred years ago. Not many people pay attention to it, so they don't know that there are many benefits to hosting a quarantined individual. Once you're approved, other people in the community can apply for grants as well, because you all work together and have shared community meals. You can have your roads repaired and a bridge put in where the floodwater usually cuts you off. It falls under the Provisions Act because the roads are my ticket to see the doctor."

Kyandra looked at me with her bright green eyes full of concern. "I guess it's up to you if you want to stay here or go somewhere else. No one here would think it right to profit from your sickness, but you are right about the roads needing to be fixed so that we can get you into town when we need to."

"I would love to stay here, but it is final once the decision is made. I cannot go somewhere else later on." I tried to make her understand the seriousness of the situation but wasn't sure she comprehended it.

"If you want to stay, I will sign the papers you need, and Michael can sign his part later. When Jonathan gets here, you should talk to him about paying him to be a caretaker since he does most of the work. Don't make a final decision before tomorrow night, so you and everyone involved can think things through."

I nodded at her in agreement and said, "There is one more thing I need to tell you, and it's important that you know. My primary job is—"

The slamming of the back door interrupted me from telling Kyandra that I was an Adreian soldier. Jonathan walked in with an apologetic look before saying, "It's so windy out there. I didn't mean to slam the door. I'm sorry."

"It's all right, Jonathan." Kyandra stood from the dining room table and went to start dinner.

Jonathan removed his boots and then joined me at the table. He looked at me for a moment before whispering, "Were you about to tell her that you are a soldier?"

"Yes," I whispered back at him, "she should know if I'm going to stay here."

"And there will be a good time to tell her but not now. Tomorrow is the anniversary of when her fiancé was drafted and never came back, so not exactly the right time to say anything."

"Can you guarantee that I will have a place to stay when it might be the right time? Once I turn in the paperwork to stay here, I cannot go anywhere else. This is the rest of my life we are talking about, Jonathan. It isn't going to be easy for anyone involved, and as much as I want to stay here to learn more about your religion, I don't want anyone to get into trouble for breaking their promises, nor do I want them to resent the decision they made. It would be better for me to die out in the wilderness alone than be stuck somewhere I am not wanted."

Jonathan looked away as the weight of reality came crashing down on him. *Maybe it would be best to leave since these people don't like Adreian soldiers, I thought. My soldiers would have to come here to do the necessary repairs on the house, and I wouldn't be able to contain my anger if the people in the community mistreated them. I should go.* Pain lanced through my chest at the thought. If I left, I would never know if Yehovah was the answer to all my questions.

"Ash, I can't make any guarantees, but I know Yehovah will make a way. I know you don't believe, but trust me when I say that you are here for a reason, and I believe you should stay. If something happens and you can't stay here, we will figure something else out."

With a sigh of resignation, I replied, "Okay, Jonathan, I won't tell her yet, but I will tell her."

# Chapter Thirty-Six

## Roark

The art auction went on for several hours, and I joined Keller and Contessa after the first hour had passed. Lou was an enthusiastic man who stood up to speak about several pieces of art being auctioned off, while another guy took the bids and was the main speaker. Lou was welcomed back to the podium to give the history and background of another painting yet to be unveiled, so everyone was eager to see it. A kid from the Surface, Vick Maras, was the artist. He was the son of a famous artist and had been her apprentice. She apparently never had taught anyone else, so he was already renowned just for that. His mom had died a few years ago, and the one painting of hers he'd donated had already sold for nearly a million credits.

I was amazed that people would spend so much on a painting, but then again, I didn't know anything about art. They unveiled the two-foot-by-three-foot canvas, and my breath caught in my lungs. Instantly, my eyes gravitated to it. It captured my attention, and I didn't know why. It looked like a massive storm cloud that took up all but a couple of inches of the canvas, and it had eerie blue-green coloring in it, with purplish-gray clouds toward the outside. Lightning lit up portions of the cloud. Beneath the cloud was a green windblown field. But that wasn't what caught my eye the most. The few inches not covered by the storm cloud drew me to the painting. The spot was bright, sunny, and peaceful, as if the approaching storm couldn't shake it. It was stunning.

Tess whispered something into her father's ear, and when the bidding began, he was quick to raise his paddle. He had bid on a few paintings but had backed down when the price was higher than a quarter of a million credits. Keller and two other people were bidding on the artwork, and the price quickly climbed to a quarter of a million credits. Once it reached that price, I was surprised to see that Keller continued bidding. One of the other two quit bidding, leaving everyone to watch the unfolding race to half a million credits.

The call for half a million credits hit, and the other guy had the highest bid. Keller looked at me and then at Tess and raised his paddle to meet it. The next-highest bid was called out, but the other guy shook his head, and the auctioneer called the painting sold to Keller for half a million credits. Tess hugged her dad with the happiest look on her face. I couldn't believe he was willing to pay that much for a painting that probably would not have sold for that price anywhere else.

The last six paintings sold quickly after that, and Lou returned to the podium to give his closing speech. He took a moment to look over the crowd before saying, "I could not be more proud of you tonight; we not only met our goal for the night but exceeded it by six million credits." He paused for applause before continuing. "Many of you have become friends of mine over the years as we have come together to provide for those less fortunate than us. Many of you have heard and been moved by my own struggles, and through our stories of loss and triumph, we have forged bonds that transcend mere friendship. Tonight I stand here before you in complete awe of that bond and want to thank an old friend of mine for keeping his promise made over thirty years ago. Would everyone here give a round of applause to Keller Thaz?"

The room erupted, and Keller bowed to the people before he looked at me and smiled.

The room fell silent again as Lou continued. "As many of you know, thirty years ago, I lost the child I had fought so hard to adopt, and I have searched for him ever since." My heart stopped; I couldn't believe he was doing this in public. "But tonight Keller has returned him to me. My long-lost son has become an exemplary man, a man of valor and one of Adreia's greatest warriors." Lou waved me to the stage as he said, "May I present to you, my family, my son, Crimson Soldier Roark."

As I walked onto the stage, the room erupted in cheers and clapping. The sound was almost deafening. Lou pulled me into a hug in front of everyone, and I couldn't believe I was turning into a hugging person. I had never been a fan of people invading my personal space, but I found I was warming up to it.

"Roark"—as Lou spoke, the room quieted, and his assistant handed him his plex—"would you honor me, an old man, by allowing me to officially adopt you as my son here before these witnesses?"

I had to clear my throat because of the emotions threatening to choke me before I could say, "You've got it all wrong, Lou Verity. It would be an honor on my part to be called your son."

He smiled, brought up the adoption papers on his plex, and handed them to me. I signed my old name on the first line before signing my new name with my last name on the second. Lou signed his name to the document before sending it off and making it official. Roark Verity—that was my name now. Emotion nearly brought me to my knees as he pulled me in for another hug.

*Thank You, Yehovah, my Father and King, for this unexpected surprise.*

Lou turned back to the crowd, took my hand, and held it high before announcing, "I present to you for the first time Crimson Soldier Verity, my son!"

The cheering was overwhelming as we walked offstage together, and everyone waited to congratulate us. These people had known about his quest to find me for years and were overjoyed to see us together at last. It was hard to believe that just a few weeks ago, I had thought no one wanted me, and now I had been accepted not only by my Father in heaven but also by the man who had wanted to be my father my whole life. It was almost more than I could take.

Keller left Tess and me to get back to work while the party wound down. After everyone had gone home, we sat with Lou and discussed our lives. We stayed until two in the morning before we parted ways, and I helped Tess into our waiting limo. Once we were inside, Tess laid her head on my shoulder, threaded her fingers with mine, and said, "Roark, I had fun with you tonight. Usually, when I come to these functions, my dad ends up being pulled away, and I'm stuck on my own, but tonight I enjoyed the whole evening."

I gave her hand a light squeeze and replied, "I've missed doing things like this with you, Tess. I'm sorry I was such a fool and pushed you away for so long."

"It's not all your fault, Roark. If I had been more concerned about you than my reputation at school, we would still have been friends, and you would have met Lou sooner." She squeezed my hand as she spoke and leaned in closer, causing my heart to beat faster.

"But then I never would have gone into the military and had Emet put under my care. Never would have heard about Yeshua, and I wouldn't have been able to introduce Emet to you, which means you wouldn't have heard about Yeshua either. I'm starting to look back and see Yehovah's hand in everything now."

She looked up at me in the dimly lit partitioned backseat and asked, "What are we going to do now? I don't want you to disappear on me again, but I know you are busy and live two hours away." She laid her head back on my shoulder and let out a little sigh. "I'm not going to let you walk away this time."

"Are you asking me out, Tess?"

"If I waited for you to do it, I would die of old age, Roark."

Her teasing tone brought a smile to my face, and I replied, "Well, we could make your dad happy and just get married like he wants us to."

Tess sat up suddenly, looked at me, and said, "No, he didn't. Really?" Her voice was full of shock.

"Oh yes, he did." I mustered up my best Keller impersonation. "He said, 'When are you going to call my daughter? Have you asked my daughter out? I'm not getting any younger here, Roark, and I would like grandchildren before I die.'" I ended the impersonation, and Contessa shook her head with a smile. "Emet told me that Keller threatened Victor if he came after me and called me his future son-in-law."

"Of course he would! I'm going to kill him." Tess covered her face with her hands. "Why would he say that to you?"

She was embarrassed, and I knew she would bring it up to Keller and give him an earful. *What I wouldn't give to see her rip into her dad about this.*

"Well, in his defense"—I couldn't believe I was defending Keller—"he knows I'm stubborn and foolish and put my foot in my mouth a lot, so he feels like he needs to push me. You just said that you couldn't wait for me to ask you, because I wouldn't do it."

Tess scooted across the bench seat, leaned against the door, and looked out the window. Our ride would be over soon, and I couldn't tell if she was mad at me or just thinking. I waited a few minutes for her to say something, but she didn't, so I moved next to her, reached out, and gently turned her chin to face me.

"I'm not going anywhere, Tess. I love you. I've always loved you, and after that day, I thought it best for me to keep you away because I was tired of being hurt. All I ended up doing was hurting us both more, but I'm not going to do that anymore. If you think you are ready for a relationship, I will do my best to be open and honest with you about everything. I recently heard a very wise man say that when the right people are in your life, you will want to share yourself with them and not hold back. Contessa, you are the right person, and I don't want to let you go or hold back from you. If you can have patience with me as I learn who I am in Yeshua and break free from the lies of the past, I promise I will protect you, provide for you, and become a man you will be proud to follow."

I hesitated, and my heartbeat was deafening in the silence as my unorthodox proposal seemed to fill the empty space in the limo. I wasn't looking for a dating relationship with Tess; I didn't have time for that, and neither did she. If we were going to do this, it would be all or nothing. It didn't matter what I had to do to get ready for marriage, even if it meant hours of counseling and therapy.

With tears in her eyes, Tess hugged me and whispered, "I can do that, Roark, but you have to tell Dad that we are getting married."

*Well, so much for not having any more life-changing events in my life.* I couldn't believe I'd just gotten engaged to my childhood best friend, but as I held her, I knew I had made the right decision. All I had to do now was get our silver engagement bands fitted for our right hands. I was sure her father would insist we have our six-month courting process before he provided us with our gold wedding bands for our left hands, since it was Adreian tradition for the bride's father to buy the wedding bands, while the father of the groom paid for the wedding.

I released Tess from the hug as the realization that Lou would be paying for our wedding crashed down on me. Looking at Tess, I said, "I have a feeling this will end up being the biggest wedding ceremony in years with Lou organizing and paying for it."

Tess closed her eyes and covered her face with her hands. "Oh no! This is going to be insane with both our dads involved. Maybe we should just run off."

I laughed. "Keller would murder me if I deprived him of the chance to attend his only child's wedding. I'm not afraid of many people, but your dad would hunt me down, and no one would ever know I was dead."

"He would not, Roark. He might be mad at us for a while, but he wouldn't hurt you because of me. But you are right; we have to have a ceremony. It isn't right for us to deprive Lou of one either, not after he spent so long trying to find you."

I sighed as we pulled up in front of the mansion. Tess was right that we had to endure our fathers' extravagant wedding ceremony. It was going to be a long waiting period full of talk of fancy wedding plans. *Ugh.* I hated fancy and expensive places and ceremonies. I liked simple and easy things.

The driver opened our door, and I helped Tess out of the limo before escorting her inside. Keller was still awake and sitting in his office just off the entrance. He asked me to join him, and Tess smiled at me before making her way upstairs to her room. I walked into Keller's office to find him with his hair a mess, as if he had been running his fingers through it repeatedly, and his reading glasses on. He still looked ready to have his picture taken for an ad, even with his dress shirt wrinkled and undone slightly.

"Sit and tell me how the rest of your night went." Keller didn't even look up from his holoplex station as he pointed to the empty chair across the desk from him with a stylus pen.

I sat down and was quiet while trying to find the right words.

I must have been silent too long, because he shut down the holoplex, removed his glasses, and said, "Well? I don't have all the time in the world here, so spit it out, son."

"I asked Tess to marry me." I didn't know why I said that. He wanted to know how things had gone with Lou, but that was fresh on my mind.

"It's about time. Her ring size is six, by the way, and if you go to Vallan's and give my name, they will take good care of you. Now, how are things with you and Lou?"

"We have a lot to catch up on, and I'm not sure how everything will fit into my busy schedule now that I'm Asherex's official quarantine provider. I don't know if I will be escorting him somewhere else or if he'll stay where he is. Then I have to go at least once a week for routine checkups and supply deliveries, not to mention that so many things have to be done if he decides to stay where he is."

With a smile, Keller replied, "I'm sure Asherex will make things easy for you. He always finds the most efficient way of doing things, so you will have more free time than you think."

My thoughts turned to the task Asherex had given me to find Emet's family, and I doubted I would have free time between doing that and trying to save Kale. I would have to spend a lot of time in prayer in the coming months, because I felt that Asherex wasn't going to die quickly from Zeron's. Things were just too complicated right now.

"Anyway"—Keller broke through my thoughts—"back to my daughter. I will discuss the wedding with Lou after you tell him that you are getting married, but I don't think you should have a long, drawn-out courtship. My daughter is thirty, and you are thirty-one, which means you will be in your fifties by the time your first child is old enough to be out on their own. The sooner you are married the better. I want young ones running around and all the chaos that comes with them."

"Keller, you're only forty-seven. You could have more kids if you want them that badly," I said with a hint of teasing.

"And be seventy when they start having families of their own? I don't think so."

I laughed at him, and he didn't look amused. "What will you do, Keller, if you meet a nice young woman and get married, and she wants kids?"

"That's not going to happen." His quick reply was sharper than I believed he intended, and in a lighter tone, he quickly added, "I've been divorced for twenty-three years. If I was going to find a good woman, I would have by now. Besides, I work too much to make a woman happy, so it wouldn't work out anyway in the long run."

"Sounds like you are in denial. If you found the right woman, you would spend less time working and make time for her."

He gave me a look like he wanted to knock me out of the chair before letting out a sigh and saying, "It's late. You can sleep in the guest room across the hall from mine, and I will take you back home in the morning. And don't argue with me; you are not taking a cab home and wasting your money. You will sleep here and have breakfast with us. Now, if you will excuse me, I'm going to bed."

With that, Keller left me alone in his office. I waited a moment before heading to my guest room, showering, and pulling the blanket from the bed to sleep on the floor. I prayed for a while, including a prayer for Keller to find a good woman so he wouldn't be alone when I married Tess, before letting myself sleep.

# Chapter Thirty-Seven

Asherex

Two weeks had passed since I decided to stay in the Torah-observant community. Michael's truck had broken down, delaying him, so he still wasn't home. Until he signed the paperwork, the necessary work to prepare the house for my quarantine couldn't begin, so I was stuck with nothing to focus on until Michael got here.

My coughing was more severe, with blood coming up every time. It was hard to keep my fears of drowning in my own blood to myself. I'd spent most of the last two weeks talking to my family and friends while making the necessary arrangements for people to take over my businesses when I died.

The people of the community were eager to share their testimonies with me, and just about every evening, I found myself the center of attention with the children. The children would come over while I was outside enjoying the late-afternoon sun, wanting to play. I never wasted an opportunity with them unless I wasn't feeling well, because I had always wanted kids, but now that wasn't going to happen.

Roark and his unit had been a welcome reprieve from the chaos my life had become. It had been an exhausting and draining two weeks, to say the least, and as West brought me back from my weekly checkup with Roark's unit, I felt utterly drained. I just wanted to sleep, even though I had spent the last three days bedridden because of debilitating nausea.

During that time, Kyandra sat with me, and we talked for hours about the things she had wanted to do but never had because of her fiancé, who hadn't come back from war. She had put her whole life on hold for him, and I wanted to help her find out what had happened to the man she had planned to marry. Kyandra was a remarkable woman who had wanted to open a bakery and use the trading post to sell her goods to the nearby cities. She had a solid business plan, and I believed she would be successful if she left her brother to run the bed-and-breakfast and pursued it. Unfortunately, she had let her fiancé's disappearance deter her, because it had been their dream, and she hadn't wanted to do it alone.

I let out a sigh, drawing West's attention. He was concerned because I hadn't said a word about his truck being a metal death trap, but I was too tired to be concerned about being in a gasoline-fueled fire. I wanted to talk to him more about his belief in Yehovah and what made him want to study the Torah, but my mind wasn't working properly today. I had spoken with many of the townspeople about their beliefs and was almost convinced that this faith was genuine and not something made up by people to make themselves feel good about their actions.

I was almost asleep, when we hit the worst part of the road just as we got into the community, causing me to bang my head on the window. With a yawn, I sat up, gripped the handle on the cab's roof, and held on to keep myself from bouncing around on the bumpy road. The roads desperately needed to be repaired.

As we pulled into the little town, West sat forward, pointed at one of the houses, and said, "Looks like they are having a meeting at Rob's place. I wonder what that's all about."

West dropped me off in front of Kyandra's before going over to Rob's to see what was going on. I went to let myself in, only to find the door locked. She never locked the door. I went around back and found that door locked as well. With a sigh, I sat down on the patio furniture, wishing I had brought my plex with me when I went to town.

My father would be calling me soon, and I didn't want him to worry if I couldn't answer it. We talked for a few minutes almost every day, and even though we didn't talk about anything important, it was nice to have those few minutes. I felt as if we were finally starting to build a relationship that would allow me to be able to speak my mind about all the things I had been putting off for years. *Perhaps now would be a good time to bring it up and get it out of the way.*

The slamming of the back door jerked me awake. I hadn't realized I had fallen asleep and didn't know how long I'd been asleep, which scared me because I had always been aware of how much time passed while I was unconscious. Kyandra stood there looking angry, so I attempted to stand, but nothing happened. My legs refused to move, so I took a deep breath, tried again, and was able to force them to bear my weight despite the numbness in my feet.

"You're a soldier?" Kyandra's question was more of an accusation full of contempt.

"Yes." Over the last two weeks, I had tried to tell her that I was a soldier, but the conversation never had made it that far, due to interruptions.

"I found this." She held up the holographic recorder from Proxy High Commander Uriah.

I'd completely forgotten about it after being diagnosed with Zeron's.

She put one hand on her hip. "I found it when I was cleaning your room today. We trusted you. I trusted you, and it's been nothing but a lie this whole time. You need to go."

"Can I at least explain bef—"

She cut me off. "You have to go now!"

I tried to say something else, but she cut me off again with tears in her eyes and went off on me, telling me I was a liar and a horrible person for what I had done. I stood there for a few minutes until it was obvious she wouldn't let me say a word, and then I just turned and walked away.

Pain speared through my chest as I headed through the countryside toward the trading post. Based on the map, I knew the shortest way into town from here. It was going to be a long walk, but if I kept going, I would reach the trading post by midnight.

I walked for hours through the thickly forested area and crossed the last stream I would have to go through before I made it into town. It was a little after ten o'clock. The numbness in my feet was spreading into my legs, and my hands were completely numb. I wasn't sure if it was because of the chilly night air or if I was beginning to show signs of the random bouts of paralysis that came with Zeron's.

The sound of a stick snapping on the ground caught my attention, and I suddenly found myself face-first in the dirt. I wasn't sure if I had tripped or had lost control of my motor functions entirely, but when I attempted to reach out to catch myself, my arms didn't move, and I hit the ground hard. A cracking sound filled my ears a moment before my nose started bleeding, making breathing difficult.

I couldn't move, and fear gripped me that I would die out here alone. My heartbeat quickened, and little black spots filled my vision as the sound of an animal walking through the brush drew closer. A violent coughing fit overtook me, and I began choking on the blood draining down my throat from my broken nose. I was utterly helpless as darkness descended upon me.

# Chapter Thirty-Eight

## Emet

I unsuccessfully attempted to sleep for most of the twenty-hour flight home, only managing to nap for a couple of hours at a time. I knew that falling asleep on a transport flight like that could spell disaster for an unsuspecting traveler. I didn't have much to steal, but the thought of someone trying to take my one small bag with my plex and some clothes in it terrified me. I didn't want to explain to my master what had happened if the plex was lost.

We finally pulled into Adreian airspace, and my plex began chiming with messages people had left me during my mission trip. I listened to the ones from the guys in my unit first, smiling at their stories. Every year, when I left for several weeks, they would leave messages telling me how much they missed me.

After getting through all twenty-seven messages from them, I listened to the newest message from Victor, who told me he didn't want me back at the mansion when I returned. I had to find somewhere else to go. The news shouldn't have stung as much as it did, but I'd looked forward to going home and reading more of the Bible Victor had bought for me. I couldn't buy a digital copy without him beating me and forcing me to delete it.

With a sigh, I deleted his message and went on to the next one, which was from Contessa. It was a blessing to have her as a friend, and I could hear the smile in her voice as she talked about a charity art gala she had gone to. She spoke in Hebrew for most of the recording, until she wanted to say something that she didn't know how to communicate. Before she hung up, she told me she had some big news to talk to me about when I got home.

The last couple of messages I listened to were from Roark. I was surprised to hear him apologize to me; he wasn't the apologizing type, and I wondered what had happened to my friend. I was even more astonished that he was from the Surface, and I couldn't wait to hear more about what had happened with the guy he'd met who'd given him up for adoption.

I called Roark's number the moment we docked at the shuttle station. It rang for an eternity before he answered with audio only on his end. "Hey, can you hear me, Emet?"

"Yeah, I can hear you. Are you busy?"

"Not anymore. Why? What's up?"

"I'm not allowed to go home, and now I'm sitting here at Coxus Station, wondering if you could give me a ride."

"If you want to wait, I can be there in half an hour. If not, I can order you a cab."

"I can wait. There's no reason to waste money on a cab when you are already that close. Besides, it sounds like we have some catching up to do."

With a chuckle, he said, "You have no idea, Emet. I will see you soon."

After he hung up, I found a bench outside the station and scrolled through media feeds to catch up on the latest news. I was shocked that Asherex Reach was in quarantine for Zeron's. It seemed he and his family couldn't catch a break, so while I waited for Roark, I bowed my head and prayed for Asherex.

When I finished praying, I lifted my head to find Roark leaning against a pole nearby. He had his arms crossed over his chest and that quirky smile on his face. I hadn't realized how much I'd missed him until then. He pushed away from the pole, and I noticed he had new body armor embroidered with the name Verity.

"Well, are you going to just sit there staring at me, or are we going to go home?"

His teasing tone brought a smile to my face as I got up, slung my bag onto my back, and walked toward him. When I reached him, he pulled me into a hug, surprising me. Roark didn't hug people.

"Are you all right?" I asked him.

He laughed and let me go. "You already know the answer to that. I've never been all right and will always be a little off."

We laughed as we boarded his airship, buckled in, and headed to his place.

"Emet, tell me all about what I missed out on this year. I've been so busy lately that I need a little bit of normality right now. After dinner, I will get into all my craziness with you."

With a smile on my face, I started telling him about building an eco-friendly school for the town, repairing the roof of the orphanage, and training the young doctors to handle the more severe medical emergencies. The two-hour flight home seemed to pass quickly as I relived the past couple of weeks. I had made many friends, and I showed Roark the pictures I had taken of the beautiful landscape and the projects we had worked on. There was a slideshow with hundreds of pictures the kids had made for me while they had my plex. It was precious to see the world through the eyes of a child.

We sat in the dimly lit cruzer while the slideshow finished up, and then Roark flashed his famous smile at me and rushed us out of the airship so we wouldn't be late for dinner. I was a little confused but went with it. He was about to unlock the front door, when he spun around, putting his back to the door, and said, "I should warn you about the house."

What had he done? The last time I'd heard that statement, I'd walked in to find that he had taken his frustration out on the wall that once divided the dining room from the living room, without cleaning up the mess.

Roark bit his lip, shook his head, and said, "I guess you will see it when you get inside."

I was nervous as he turned back around, unlocked the door, and walked inside. I first noticed a small wooden table about three feet high with a potted plant sitting on top of a decorative draped piece of cloth beside the doorway. Beneath it was a place to put shoes, and it looked as if it had been there for years. Had Roark gone insane while I was gone? Why was there a piece of furniture by the door?

"Are you coming all the way inside, Emet?"

Roark's question jolted me out of shock, and I looked up at him. Immediately, I saw him standing next to a sofa. I closed the door behind me and walked into the house I'd been in thousands of times over the last ten years as if I were walking into a minefield. Besides the sofa, there were a recliner, matching end tables, a holographic projector to watch things on, and curtains hanging on the windows of the newly painted room. The living room, once solid white, was now a light gray, with copper designs that looked hand-painted. Around the room were several sconce lights that made the place feel ready for lazy afternoons in front of the television.

"What the—" I couldn't find the words to describe the room, and out of the corner of my eye, I could tell the dining room had been redone and furnished as well.

Roark chuckled. "I hired Kale to come paint for me while I was running around for the last two weeks. I pulled some strings to exempt him from quarantine duty for a bit so he could settle into his new place. He still doesn't talk to anyone other than Asherex Reach, but I told him what I wanted, and he made it happen. He even sent me pictures of furniture that would work in the rooms."

I couldn't believe it, and with an anticipation I never had thought I could have, I turned to see the dining room. It was done in a pastel pink with a teal marbled look. Upon closer inspection, I discovered that it was all paint, without a trace of wallpaper. The opening to the room made me feel as if I were stepping through sliding garden doors broken up into tiny windows, with sheer gray-and-pale-pink curtains draped on the dining room side. The divider both broke the two rooms up and tied them together.

The table was a fancy floating-top one. The base was platinum, and the top was clear crystal quartz, with a holographic projector giving it the appearance of water trapped inside the quartz. A chrome rose with a six-inch stem complete with thorns sat on top of a single white satin cloth on the table. It was stunning. The matching chairs held small traces of pink in the quartz seats.

"I thought you didn't believe in furniture, Roark." It was all I could say.

"Well, I've made a few changes and decided to give furniture a try."

I turned at his teasing tone and finally took a good look at him. What had I missed? I couldn't believe I hadn't noticed the patch sooner. Without thinking, I reached out, grabbed his arm, and said, "You're a Crimson Soldier!"

He laughed and then flashed me his signature smile. "Yeah, I got promoted just after you left, but that isn't the biggest news I have for you. We will be late for dinner, though, and I need to change. There are new clothes in your closet, if you want to change too."

With that, he left me alone in his beautiful dining room. I peeked into the kitchen as I passed and noticed that all the cabinets were off the walls. He was remodeling, and I couldn't wait to see what he did with it. Feeling overwhelmed, I entered my room and found a new bedroom set waiting for me. It took me a moment to realize Kale had repainted the wall opposite my bed to look like a photograph of a beach I had gone to with my parents as a kid on Lake Tiberias. The beautiful view of the sea with the sun shining on it brought tears to my eyes.

There was a note on the dresser from Kale; he wanted me to know how much he appreciated my spending time telling him about Yisra'el and my childhood memories. It had meant so much to him that he had wanted to bring me closer to the place I loved by painting it for me to see every day until I could see it again in person with my own eyes.

I heard Roark in the other room and quickly threw on clothes before going to meet him. He pulled a bottle of wine and a covered dish out of the fridge as I walked out. He must have seen the confused look on my face, because he handed me the container and said, "The neighbors invited us over for dinner tonight. They are really awesome people, and once the house is finished, they will come over for dinner."

"Since when do you talk to the neighbors?"

"A few weeks back. They were outside, and I stopped by to introduce myself since I'd never done it. It turns out they are some of the nicest people I've ever met, and I should have met them sooner. Oh, by the way, I made chocolate truffles for dessert."

My mouth instantly began to water, and I looked down at the covered dish in my hands. Roark's truffles were the best I'd ever tried, and I'd been to many five-star restaurants over the years with my master. He put theirs to shame.

Roark motioned for us to head out, and as we walked back into the living room, I stopped dead in my tracks. There was a painting hanging on the wall that, in my shock, I hadn't noticed before. It was a massive storm cloud that looked as if it could drop a tornado at any moment. Lightning arced through the cloud, whose eerie blue-green color was wrapped by ominous purple-gray clouds. The green wheat field, blown about by strong winds, was awe-inspiring. It was a piece of Elohim's creation frozen in time, and it brought a smile to my face.

"Tess and her dad bought it for me at the gala."

I turned at Roark's confession before replying, "It is a reminder of Yehovah's power."

He smiled at me for a moment and then said, "They are waiting on us now. We should get going."

We didn't say much as we walked across the street and knocked on the neighbors' door. A small child opened the inside door and yelled for her dad, who soon showed up. Roark introduced me to Case, and once we were inside, Case introduced me to his wife, Lena, and their kids. The twins, Liza and Lana, wore matching dresses, but Liza had a red bow in her hair, while Lana had a pink one. The youngest, Mackenzie, was wearing a dark gray dress and jabbering away as if everyone knew what she was saying. It was adorable.

Dinner was honey lemon chicken cooked with onion and garlic, with sides of green beans and mashed sweet potatoes. Apparently, Roark had been talking to them about my religious beliefs, because they asked me if I wanted to say the blessings before we ate. They were eager to hear them, and I wasn't going to pass up an opportunity like that. After the prayer, Case carved up the bird, and we enjoyed the meal together. The food was delicious, and Lena asked me about the mission trip I had gone on.

We talked the entire time we ate, and I could see why Roark liked these people. Once we were finished eating, the kids ran off to play, and we sat around playing card games, drinking wine, and eating Roark's truffles. Case and Lena asked me many questions about my religion, and I was surprised by how much Roark would respond to fill in the gaps in my answers. I wasn't used to him bringing it up in front of other people.

At eight thirty, Roark and I left while Case and Lena put the kids down for the night. Once we were back home, Roark took the empty dish to the kitchen, came into the living room, took a couple of throw pillows off the sofa, piled them against the recliner, and sat down on the floor, using the pillows as a backrest.

*I guess some things don't change after all.* I reclined on the couch and handed Roark the half-empty bottle of wine. He took a swig, and I noticed a silver ring on his finger. *When did he get engaged?*

Roark let out a contented sigh before saying, "I guess I owe you some explanations."

"Uh, yes! I've been very patient, waiting and not asking questions."

"Well, I got sent out on a solo mission a few days after you left me here because I didn't talk to you, which I should have done because you are my best friend, and you didn't deserve to be treated like that."

What was wrong with Roark? He kept apologizing and admitting he had been wrong.

He sighed and continued. "Anyway, I completed my mission and made friends with a Brashex soldier who is now an Adreian citizen, and as soon as I landed, I was arrested. They threw me into the war council's private prison without telling me why. When they finally pulled me out of that place, they took me to the war council's chamber and promoted me to Crimson Soldier. Apparently, Asherex recommended me for the promotion and brought it up to his best friend. Our commander in chief began the investigation into my life.

"After that, Keller gave me the paperwork I've been trying to get forever that would tell me who put me up for adoption. Turns out I am from the Surface, and the soldier who found me wanted to keep me but was accused of attempting to kill himself and had to give me up. His name is Lou Verity, and Keller was under his command at that time. He forced Lou to go to court to try to get me back. By the time it all was said and done, I was lost to the system, but Lou never stopped searching for me.

"I met him at the gala, and he is the most amazing person. He adopted me right there in front of everyone." Roark trailed off, and his eyes shone with tears as he took another swig from the wine bottle and passed it to me.

I had seen Roark drink only twice in the ten years I'd known him, and I could tell he was close to being drunk, which only added sentiment to his words.

"So my name is now Roark Verity, which is still weird, but I've managed to spend more time with Lou the last two weeks and really get to know him. He wants to take me to some private beach house he has on the Surface for a few days next week, so we can bond without distractions. It's all a little strange because I never thought anyone would want me, and now here I am with a father and"—he looked me in the eye—"a brother. Oh, and let's not forget that Tess and I are engaged now, so soon I will have a wife."

Shocked to my core at his confessions, I did my best to maintain control as I replied, "I'm glad you two have finally put your differences aside and decided to be together. She used to ask me about you all the time." I trailed off for a moment before continuing. "Well, Roark, it looks like you've been through some life-changing things since I've been gone."

"That's not even all of it!" With a smile, Roark abruptly stood and said, "I stopped fighting it. I finally gave in, Emet, and I've never felt so free. My life is no longer my own; it belongs to Yeshua HaMashiach! Hallelujah!"

I couldn't help but jump to my feet at hearing his loud declaration.

Roark pulled me into a tight hug and said, "Thank you, Emet, for never giving up on me. I've said so many hurtful things to you because I was fighting what Yehovah was trying to do. I'm so sorry. Can you forgive me?"

I tightened my grip on him and answered, "You have already been forgiven, Roark."

"I understand now why you wouldn't let me kill Victor, and I will do my best not to kill him in the future and will just pray for him." His words were barely a whisper.

Tears spilled down my cheeks at my hearing that from Roark. Now that he was a Crimson Soldier, he would have been able to kill my master for any reason he chose and get away with it, and the fact that he was willing not to kill him spoke volumes. If Yehovah could turn Roark's heart to him, I knew it was still possible for Victor to be saved.

Roark released me from the hug and took the wine bottle from me before finishing it off. "Well, I've had too much to drink, and I've spent all day with the war council, so I think I'm going to go to bed now. I will see you for breakfast, Emet. Good night."

With that, he disappeared into the bathroom for a bit before shutting himself in his room. I sat back on the sofa, trying to process everything I had heard, before bowing my head to pray and thank Yehovah for answered prayers. After praying, I took a shower, went to my room, dressed, and called Contessa. I had to know exactly what had happened between them to get them to the point that they were getting married.

She answered on the first ring, and we talked for hours about her engagement to Roark and the work I had done while away. Around midnight, we said our goodbyes, and I looked around my room, which seemed like a completely different place, with new carpet, new furniture, and a beautiful mural across from my bed. When the sun rose in the morning, it would light up the scene and bring it to life. Kale was amazing, and I sent up a quick prayer for him.

I turned and noticed something on top of my large dresser with a mirror behind it. Curious, I walked over to it only to discover it was a book chip. It was white with an aqua-blue spine, and I picked it up and activated it. The full-size book projected out of it, revealing a complete Hebrew Bible with the option to change the language to one of three hundred languages listed. I smiled as I took the book over to my new bed, settled in for the night, and began reading Elohim's Word.

# Chapter Thirty-Nine

Asherex

I had been in and out of consciousness for the last two days, nine hours, and thirty-six minutes. The paralysis had crippled me and kept me down the entire time. I was still facedown in the dirt and increasingly aware of a weight pressing down on my back as I slowly tested my fingers and toes for mobility. Once I was sure the paralysis was gone, I slowly pushed myself up, and the weight on my back quickly disappeared.

My stiff body protested as I sat up on my knees, looking around for whatever had been on top of me. A dirty, matted dog that looked as if it once had been white stood behind the nearest tree, watching me with wary eyes. It obviously once had belonged to someone but had been lost or abandoned. There was no doubt the dog was what I had heard in the brush before I collapsed.

Ignoring the dog, I gave myself a quick examination, and when I looked up again, the dog was just inches away from me. I spoke softly to it, and its tail began to wag. As slowly as I could, I lifted my hand for the dog to sniff while talking to it. After what seemed like an eternity, it licked my hand, and I attempted to pet it.

The dog knocked me to the ground within moments of the first stroke and began whining and licking my face. The poor thing was not much more than skin and bones, and I knew she must have been starving. I took time petting her before leaning on her to pull myself to my feet. She stuck close to me as I backtracked to the stream I had crossed two days ago and cleaned the dried blood off the best I could. I was sure I looked worse for wear, but my nose wasn't broken, so that was a bonus. Now I just had to walk another two hours to get to town.

By the time the trading-post town came into view, I was parched. The dog followed as I walked on the gravel road into town but stopped just before the first building. Several men stood outside the shop, loading up an old military truck, and the hair on the back of my neck stood up. The doctor's warning about raiders coming into town filled my mind, and I wondered how they would greet me as I continued toward the store.

I noticed West's truck parked across the street, next to another much newer truck. A man came out of the store as I neared it. The men carried semiautomatic rifles, except for the guy who had just walked out of the store. He carried a handgun. There were ten men total, and I noted where they were and what kinds of guns they were packing, while calculating how many rounds each held and the rate of fire of each. This was going to get messy.

"What can I do for you, stranger?" the guy with the handgun asked as I came to a halt in front of him. "You look like you've had a rough go of it, kid." He turned toward the man beside him and whispered in his ear, flashing his gang tattoos, before looking back at me. "Why don't you sit down and have a drink?" the gang leader asked.

"I would appreciate that, sir." I sat on the wooden porch in front of the store while another guy brought me a bottle of water. I guzzled it down and continued my scan of the town. Across the street, a guy was holding two people from the Torah community hostage with West: Kyandra and another man I didn't recognize. Kyandra locked eyes with me; from here, I could see the tears shining in her green eyes.

The man in charge handed me another bottle of water and offered me something to eat, but I declined because I knew I would end up throwing it up. He smiled at me and said, "I haven't seen you around these parts before. Where are you from?"

"I'm just passing through. I don't belong here." I kept my reply short and devoid of emotion.

He gazed at me with an odd look in his eyes as his men resumed loading their truck with stolen goods from the store. I rested there, making small talk with the guy in charge, rehydrating, and waiting for the right time to make my move. There was a good chance I would end up dying once I started the fight, but death by firefight was preferable to the slow death this disease had waiting for me.

Once rested, I stood up, and the man in charge walked over to me and said, "Where do you think you're going?"

"I won't let you steal from these people."

The guy laughed, pulled his gun, poked me in the chest with it, and said, "And what are you going to do about it, boy?"

"If you pull a gun on someone, you'd better be ready to pull the trigger."

He waved the gun in my face, making a show of it for his guys, and started mocking me. I took a deep, controlled inhale; flipped the switch that turned off my ability to feel; and released my breath. In one fluid motion, I snatched the gun from him, smashed the buttstock into his throat, and knocked him unconscious by slamming him headfirst into the wooden beam holding the porch roof up. Without blinking, I turned, firing a round into the chest of the man holding Kyandra captive, before turning on the man inside the store.

The guy inside was definitely dead from the shot, and as I turned toward the center of town, where the sheriff was hanging upside down from the fountain, I took a hit to my left shoulder. I didn't feel any pain, but tightness pulled at the injury.

I headed for a wooden shipping crate for cover while firing rounds at the remaining seven men. With three rounds left in my gun, I waited patiently for them to fire off enough to reload. These men were not military-trained and were just firing off rounds like they were in unlimited supply. Once they stopped to reload, I stood, firing a round at the nearest guy who was attempting to move to a better vantage point. It was a headshot, and I knew I would feel guilty about that later. *Stop killing people, Asherex.* The thought swirled through my mind while I fired the last two rounds at number five, hitting him through his wooden hiding spot.

With my last round spent, I made it to number four's gun and quickly swapped out my useless gun for his semiautomatic rifle and the extra magazine. Rounds whizzed past my head as I rolled behind a parked car, hoping the gasoline-powered vehicle wouldn't catch fire somehow while I was near it, before letting loose a volley of fire and putting six and seven out of commission. They were both screaming and moaning in pain, letting me know they were alive for now.

Guy number eight came out of the alley behind me, forcing me out of my hiding place and back into the street. I took another hit in my abdomen from number nine before I could put two rounds in him, ensuring he wouldn't be able to pick up another gun. Number ten made a beeline for the military truck, so I turned on number eight and put him on the ground with rounds to his firing hand and both his legs.

The truck fired up as I slapped the spare mag into the rifle. It roared down the gravel road, swerving all over the place, and I opened fire on it, aiming for the tires. The already unstable truck blew a tire, causing it to jump a ditch and slam into a power-line pole. Smoke billowed as the engine sputtered and died a moment before the pole fell over, dragging live power lines on top of the vehicle.

An angry shout drew my attention as the man in charge shot a round into my leg, bringing me to my knees. I looked at him while he walked toward me, took aim at my head, and squeezed the trigger.

The gun jammed, and he cursed while trying his hardest to fix it. I forced myself to my feet, even though my leg did not want to hold my weight. I could see an airship heading our way in the distance, but it was about five minutes out.

I walked toward him and fired a round into his leg, causing him to scream and fall down. He clutched his injured leg, and tears streamed down his face as I approached. I stood over him, and in a whimper, he asked, "Who are you?"

"I am High Commander Asherex Reach of the Crimson Division."

His face paled as the reality sank in that he hadn't stood a chance. I almost felt sorry for him, but this was the reward for those who stole from people and attacked ranking officers. No doubt when whoever was flying in got here, everyone I hadn't killed in the firefight would be hung for his crimes.

Without an ounce of compassion, I slammed the buttstock of my rifle into the guy's face, knocking him unconscious, before turning back toward the fountain in the town square. As I walked toward the sheriff, I tore the rifle apart. It was obvious the sheriff had suffered from a nasty head injury before he was strung up by his ankles from the statue fountain. He was conscious now as I, despite my body's sluggishness, untied the rope holding him. Once he was safely lowered to the ground, I limped over to the fountain, rested against it, looked at him, and asked, "You good?"

"Yeah, I think so. Are you?"

"Nope. I'm going to pass out now."

He nodded as I closed my eyes and let oblivion take me.

# Chapter Forty

Asherex

I awoke abruptly, knowing I had been out for three hours, and it was a little past noon. I was in a cruzer medical bay, covered in grime, a feeling that only came from being in a recovery tank. Why was I here instead of being dead?

"It's about time you woke up."

I looked over to see a Brashex commander I had once spared in battle. "Commander Haran, how nice to see you again."

He chuckled behind his specialized respirator. "It's Head of a Hundred Haran now. I demoted myself after the baby came, because the wife wanted me to live long enough to help her change diapers."

I smiled at him, shaking my head, and said, "You are not supposed to give life-saving medical aid to people infected with Zeron's, so why would you do it?"

"Kid, you are not the only one who occasionally bends the rules, you know. When you filed your wishes for your care, you indicated that you didn't want a mercy bullet or pain meds to ease you through the disease. That alone tells me that you have some unfinished business to take care of before you die on us, so I took the liberty to see you patched up so you could finish it."

"You ruined a fourteen-million-dollar piece of equipment to patch me up? Why would you do that?"

"It's not ruined. Just because no one from the World Above can use it doesn't mean it isn't working. I'll leave it here for the doctor after it has been tagged to ensure that no one who isn't you or a Surface-dweller uses it." He stood and motioned to some of his men, and they brought in Kyandra, West, and the guy I didn't recognize. "I've spent the last two hours interviewing these people while my men went to their little town and spoke with the people there. You see, your father informed me that you haven't checked in for three days now, and I had to ask why you would be here in town while your plex is back at your hotel room. Then it occurred to me that you are not dumb enough to be wandering alone with Zeron's as far along as it is now, when you could suffer from paralysis. Now, I'm going to ask you this once, and I expect an honest answer: Did they throw you out of their little town?"

"No." I didn't hesitate, and the look on Kyandra's face was pure shock. "I went for a walk by myself to clear my head and was struck with paralysis that kept me out for two days."

"Asherex, if they threw you out, the penalty is death. Don't try to cover for them."

"It's either High Commander Reach or Crimson Soldier Reach to you." I had to ensure they knew I was serious right now. There was no way I was going to let Kyandra and the others die because they had made a decision while emotional. People made mistakes, and even though it meant I was left with no place to stay, I wasn't going to let them pay for something that, in a few days to a month, wouldn't matter because I would be dead anyway. I let out a breath and continued. "And I stand by my word. I simply went for a walk and wanted to be alone, so I didn't take my plex with me."

His anger exploded, and in a harsh tone, he said, "If you lie to me and I put it in my report even though we both know what really happened, if it comes back on me and my men, we will be the ones hung for it, and then they will punish these people anyway. Is that what you want? You want more people to die because *they* broke the law?"

I looked him in the eye and, in my most authoritative tone, said, "You dare question me? I am a Crimson Soldier, which means my word is law in Adreia and here. Let me fill you in if you don't know the laws concerning temporary neutral zones; the one infected is in charge unless a specified caretaker has that authority. That means my word is law here. If I say something happened, you cannot question it. Do you understand?"

He let out a shaky breath and replied, "Yes, sir."

"Good. Now we can end this conversation, and you can file your reports." I looked at Kyandra, who quickly looked away from me.

Without glancing around, I walked past everyone and exited the airship. I sat down on the store's porch, and a man I knew all too well joined me. He was a Brashex assassin I had saved from an underground prison and nursed back to health. His parents had named him Revenge, but he went by Rev because he thought his name was ridiculous.

Rev looked at me and said, "Reach, I'm not here to argue with you. I just wanted to say that I'm sorry you are sick, and if there is anything I can do for you, just let me know." Rev believed he owed me a life debt for saving him, and I knew how important it was for an honorable man to repay a life debt.

"You are retiring soon, right?"

My question caught him off guard. "Yeah, why?"

I released a breath before saying, "I need you to track someone down for me. He may or may not be dead, but he's been gone for twenty-seven years. His name is Asheron Rains. He and his adoptive father, Xerxes Rains, were drafted twenty-seven years ago to fight in an Adreian-Brashex battle, and they both are listed as MIA. Xerxes was a former Shadow Soldier who left Brashex after getting divorced. That's everything I know about them."

The soldiers escorted Kyandra and the others off the airship. As

Rev looked at Kyandra, he asked, "Does this have something to do with the beautiful girl you are staying with?"

I looked at Kyandra as she walked to the newer truck across the street from us and then back at Rev. "Yes, he is her father, and she deserves to know what happened to him. You cannot tell anyone what you are doing, but your debt is paid in full if you do this for me."

"Reach, we both know she threw you out, and you still want to help her. I can't say I'm surprised, since we are supposed to be enemies, and you saved my life, but are you sure you want to waste your repayment on this?"

I looked him straight in his hazel eyes and said, "I am absolutely sure this is what I want. If her dad is still alive, I want him brought back. If he is dead, they deserve to know so they can properly mourn for him. He was a temporary Adreian soldier, and it is the honorable thing to do."

Rev nodded at me and said, "I retire in two months and will do this for you. You are a good man, Reach."

I closed my eyes at his statement. Was I truly a good man? I had lied to Kyandra and the people in the community by not telling them I was a soldier, but then again, if things hadn't gone down the way they had, everyone here would have been robbed blind, and there was no telling if they would have been left unharmed.

He cleared his throat, drawing my attention, and said, "When we leave here, we've been given permission by the Adrian government to hunt down the rest of the gang and execute them for violating the terms of a neutral zone. I just thought you should know." He trailed off for a minute before adding, "A Brashex scientist is studying Zeron's inside the body. His research led to the recent early detection tests allow monitoring for four days instead of waiting a week. If you are interested in joining his study, I can hook you up with his company, and they can put the sensors and other monitoring devices inside you to give live feed data of your brain and body functions. Not a lot of people each year get Zeron's, so there is a lot they still don't know. With a small data set from just a few consenting adults, they cannot study the disease's effects on the body that thoroughly."

I thought about it for a moment, terrified and intrigued at the same time, before I replied, "It sounds like something that could potentially help others in the future. I will do it if they will allow me to be part of the study."

"Your hair will have to be shaved off for the procedure," he teased, causing me to shake my head.

"Good riddance. It was getting too long and curly for me anyway."

Rev laughed before pulling out a piece of paper, scribbling down the information I needed, and telling me he would arrange things for me if I wanted to call them sometime after tonight. Not long after that, Rev boarded the airship, and they departed on the hunt for the rest of the gang, leaving me alone on the store's porch.

I closed my eyes and rested against the wooden beam holding the porch roof up, feeling completely drained from the last couple of days. Twenty minutes went by before I felt the presence of someone else standing in front of me. I opened my eyes to find myself staring into Kyandra's beautiful green eyes brimming with unshed tears.

She released a pent-up breath and said, "Ash, I'm so sorry. I never should have thrown you out; none of us should have. We—I was upset and irrational, and I'm so sorry."

The tears fell down her cheeks, and I could tell she meant every word she said as she continued. "A few hours after you left, Jonathan came and rebuked us for what we had done, and we realized we were wrong. You should have been given a chance to explain everything, but we robbed you of that, and I'm sorry, Ash. We've been looking everywhere for you. The whole town has been searching the woods, and we've been coming to town every day in case you showed up here."

I let out a breath and patted the spot next to me. Kyandra sat down, and I looked her in the eye as I said, "Believe it or not, I don't blame you. Of course, things could have been handled differently, but they weren't, and we cannot change that. That recording from Proxy Uriah makes everything I've been asking over the last couple of weeks look like I was attempting to do as he ordered, but the truth is that I've had this burning desire for as long as I can remember to find out if there is more to this life."

I shook my head and stared into the distance with my heart in turmoil as the events of the last couple of months played through my mind.

With a shaky breath, I continued. "At first, I didn't understand why I was here, but I believed I was brought here for a reason. Everything was so new and confusing, and if it wasn't for Jonathan, I wouldn't understand a thing about your faith. I sat back and watched the people in the village to see if what they said they believed came out in what they did. I was starting to see that maybe there was something about this Yehovah and Yeshua. I observed some things that made me question the validity of your faith, but when I was out there on my own, the strangest thing happened: a stray dog found me and kept me from getting hypothermia during the time I was paralyzed and unconscious.

"There are too many coincidences that led me here, and hearing you apologize and seeing the true remorse in your eyes, the kind that cannot be faked, has let me know that this is what I was searching for. There is no doubt in me that Yehovah is Elohim, and Yeshua is the King of kings, the One who saves. If I hadn't caught Zeron's, I would have gone home with questions and no answers, but now I have the truth, and nothing and no one can take that from me."

"How can you be so forgiving after what I did? You lied to those soldiers to save our lives. Why would you do that?" Her words, choked with emotion, broke my heart.

"Kyandra, that is the kind of person I am. Besides my pride keeping me from having a serious talk with my father, I easily let things go. Everyone says I'm too nice, and who knows? Maybe I am. But I would rather see people get a second chance for a mistake they made than see them punished. I've won more battles by offering to spare the lives of my enemies if they surrender instead of killing them. The truth is, despite what you witnessed here today, I truly hate violence. I want to make peace with my brothers in Brashex, but I've felt like being in the army was my calling since I was five, and if I hadn't listened to that little voice telling me to become a soldier, I wouldn't be here today to believe in Yeshua."

Kyandra looked at me, and I turned to face her. She had a half smile on her face as she said, "Yehovah works in mysterious ways." We sat there quietly for a few minutes before she said, "Michael and I would love for you to come back with us and stay. Everyone is willing to listen to what you have to say if you want to; if not, we won't ask questions."

"I would like that very much. I'm tired, and I know today is preparation day, so perhaps after the Sabbath, I can explain to everyone."

She nodded, stood, and motioned for me to follow her to the trucks parked across the street. Once there, she introduced me to Michael. We talked for a few minutes before loading up and heading back to the community. I rode with West, while the others climbed into Michael's truck. The ride back was quiet, but West apologized during the last few miles and explained that he'd had nothing to do with my expulsion. I knew that he hadn't known about it until after we got back from the doctor's place, and it touched me that he was willing to take part of the blame because he was part of the congregation.

Once we were back at the bed-and-breakfast, Michael and I spoke for an hour before he signed the quarantine paperwork, and I headed up to my room to shower. It took three attempts to get the dried goo from the recovery tank out of my hair before I stepped out of the shower. My ash-brown hair was a curly mess, so I grabbed the scissors from my shaving kit and trimmed it down to a quarter of an inch. Satisfied that the messy curls were gone, I shaved my face, dressed in lounge clothes, and lay in bed. I was ready to get some proper sleep.

Before I allowed myself to nap, I messaged my dad to tell him I was okay and would call him later when I had some free time. As the message sent, I couldn't help but wonder how my dad would react if I told him about my revelation of Yeshua. There were times when all I had to do was tell him something, and he wouldn't question it, but there were other times when he would silence me on the matter before I could explain anything about it. I supposed I would have to learn how to pray so I could ask for guidance and for him to hear what I was saying. I had a lot to learn.

A knock on the door woke me an hour before sunset, and Michael peeked inside before letting me know that he and Kyandra were heading over to the main hall in twenty minutes, if I wanted to walk with them. I gave a nod and then dressed in something more appropriate for the Sabbath before joining them. The main hall was bustling with last-minute plans since most of the people who usually helped to set up had been out looking for me. As people passed me, they stopped to express their remorse for what they had done, and their genuine repentance once again blew me away.

I scanned the crowded building for Jonathan, but he wasn't there. My heart sank a little when I learned that he hadn't shown up today. It wasn't like him not to be there to help them, and I could tell that the ladies in the kitchen were getting flustered at the men trying to help. They were used to Jonathan knowing what to do and not needing instructions.

I sat there as the festivities began with the band and dancing while fighting the urge to go find the kid. After thirty minutes, I walked away, letting someone know I was heading back to the house, so they wouldn't go looking for me. Once back at the bed-and-breakfast, I grabbed my plex, wrote a note for Kyandra, and headed to Jonathan's house. It was fourteen miles away, but a couple hours' walk while enjoying the beautiful, starry night seemed like a good way to start my first Sabbath.

The walk seemed to go by quickly as I focused on the scriptures I had heard and read about the creation account and how every created thing glorified the Creator. As I neared Jonathan's house, I felt more freedom than I'd had in my life, as if a massive weight were lifted from my shoulders, and just the thought of knowing that I wasn't in control elated me beyond measure. There was something more to life than just living to die, and that voice I'd heard all my life finally had a name and attributes to go along with it.

Jonathan's house was a small one-story place with an attached garage and a large building with rolling doors about five hundred feet away. The building doors were slightly ajar, and Jonathan's quad bike sat inside with the back end gone; no doubt he was working on the thing. In the house, flickering candlelight shone through the massive bay window, and I could imagine Jonathan sitting there reading by candlelight.

I knocked on the front door, and within moments, Jonathan opened it. As soon as he saw me, he pulled me into a hug and said, "Ash, I'm so glad to see you!" He pulled away and asked, "Are you okay?"

I smiled at him and replied, "I'm good, Jonathan. I missed you tonight at the service, so I thought I would come spend Shabbat with you."

He invited me inside and asked, "How long have you been back? Everyone has been looking for you. My four-wheeler broke down, and I had to push it back here yesterday, or else I would probably still be out there."

We sat down at his dining table while I told him about the last couple of days and the shootout in town. He looked as if he were sorry he had missed the firefight but relieved at the same time. I told him about everything except my new faith. I wanted to know why he wasn't with the rest of the community for Shabbat first.

"Jonathan, why are you here alone instead of with everyone else? They missed you tonight."

He smiled at me, but it was a sad smile. Then he looked away and said, "I just needed a break. They weren't thrilled about me rebuking them, and I got the feeling they didn't want me around anymore."

I reached out and touched his shoulder, causing him to look at me, and said, "Jonathan, they asked me to come back, and I believe they regret what they did. They said your rebuke caused them to realize what they had done. Please don't be mad at them, because all of this happened for a reason."

Confusion filled his eyes, and he asked, "For what reason?"

I smiled at him with the most gentle smile I could muster, when all I wanted to do was jump up and shout. "All of this happened because I had doubts about Yehovah being who I was told He was, but after seeing true repentance from them, my doubts are gone."

"Are you saying what I think you're saying?" His question was full of hesitation and restrained hope.

"I believe Yeshua is the Messiah, the Son of Yehovah."

No sooner had the words left my mouth than Jonathan was suddenly there, pulling me into a deep embrace and shouting for joy. His enthusiasm was infectious, and I soon found my own voice joining his. When we pulled apart, he had tears of joy flowing down his face, and I knew that when the time came for me to share my faith with my father, I wouldn't have anything to fear.

# Chapter Forty-One

## Roark

My unit and I flew toward the little nowhere town Asherex was staying in to install the specialized ventilation system and solar panels. I knew how to do the solar panels, but even though I'd spent fourteen hours going through the instruction manual, I still didn't know what I was doing with the ventilation system. The conversation behind me seemed to echo my thoughts about how unqualified I was to do the install.

Zach was attempting to explain the mechanics of the installation, but Varkas obviously wasn't getting it. Finally, after listening to them argue for forty minutes straight, I spoke up with the most stern, fatherly voice I could muster and said, "Okay, kids, don't make me pull this thing over now."

"He started it," Varkas said.

I replied, "I don't care who started it; I'm finishing it. Doug, if they argue one more time, smack 'em upside the back of their heads."

"Can do, boss." At Doug's remark, the cruzer fell silent, and it stayed that way for about fifteen minutes.

Then Zach asked me, "Roark, why do you think Reach would have us do the install if none of us know what we are doing? I can figure it out, but it's really complicated."

"I don't have a clue why he does what he does. What do you think, Kale?"

Kale had been silent for the whole ride so far—not a surprise to any of us—and had been drawing since takeoff. He set his sketchbook aside and said, "If High Commander Reach believes we can do this, then we can." Everyone else was shocked to hear him speak, and the looks on their faces were priceless. I had to admit that his deep voice still surprised me.

"You're right, Kale; he knows what he is doing." As soon as the words left my mouth, Kale had the sketchbook back in front of his face. I shook my head as my conversation with his shrink two days ago played through my mind. Apparently, since coming to my unit, Kale had been even more unresponsive to his shrink. The guy was concerned that I had fed an addiction by buying the art supplies, but I believed there was something more going on. I wasn't ready to give up on the kid.

Doug and I navigated the airship through the vertical descent on a lawn outside a two-story house. It was an old house with a large, beautiful front porch. No wonder Asherex had chosen to stay here instead of going to a quarantine facility, where he would have been staring at four gray walls in his room and had limited outside access.

I left the men to unload the crates, headed onto the porch, and knocked on the gorgeous hand-carved wooden door. A moment later, a beautiful woman with curly honey-brown hair and bright green eyes opened the door. She was about three inches taller than I, and her eyes held a sweet gentleness. Maybe my high commander had decided to stay here for the girl. *I mean, who wouldn't?*

"Ma'am, I'm Unit Leader Verity, head over High Commander Reach's quarantine unit." I held out a hand.

She shook it and said, "I'm Kyandra Rains. Come on in. Ash will be down in a minute."

*Ash?* These people were on a deep level of respect with Asherex if they called him by a nickname instead of his full name.

I walked into the room and immediately saw something that

caught my eye. I quickly removed my boots, walked toward it, and asked, "Is this a menorah?" I reached out and gingerly touched the beautiful gold-and-silver seven-branched candelabra with oil cups sitting on top. I turned around to see Kyandra standing there looking a bit shocked.

She answered, "It is a menorah. I didn't think Adreians knew about religious stuff like that."

I smiled at her before saying, "My medic, who is also my best friend, is a Messianic Jew from Yisra'el. He's spent the last ten years telling me about Yerushalayim, his faith in Yehovah and Yeshua, and the scriptures. I've learned a thing or two over the years. Went to Yisra'el once and even spent a Shabbat there with a very nice older couple and their kids."

"What was it like?" Her question was full of longing, as if she wanted to go there and see it for herself.

"They mostly spoke Hebrew, and I only know a few words, but the atmosphere of it all was surreal. Looking back now, I wish I had been a believer when I went, but everything worked out the way it was supposed to when it was supposed to, so I can't complain."

Kyandra's smile lit up the whole room, and I wondered again if Asherex was staying here for her. I couldn't imagine being here and not falling for her inner beauty. I didn't blame the man if he wanted to spend the rest of his short life with someone like Kyandra.

"You're early, Roark."

I nearly jumped at Asherex's statement and turned to find him standing at the bottom of the stairs, wearing a plain olive-green shirt and blue jeans. It seemed out of character for him, and it surprised me to see him look like a civilian. He smiled at me, brightening his eyes, which were more green than their usual blue.

"Well, Asherex, if any of us knew how to do the job today, I would have come on time, but you decided we needed to do it, so here we are at eight o'clock in the morning instead of two o'clock in the afternoon."

"You won't have to worry about it. I know how to install it, and I prepped the existing ventilation system over the last two days."

I crossed my arms over my chest, looked at him, and said, "You're not supposed to be doing any work like this right now."

He shrugged. "It's never stopped me before." He mirrored my pose and waited for me to say something.

I shook my head and replied, "Don't let me get in your way. Just tell us what to do, and we will help as best as we can."

With a smile, Asherex led me outside and began ordering everyone around. I understood now why Asherex was a high commander. He was bold, fierce, and compassionate all at the same time. He was probably the most respectful boss I'd ever seen, and the guys were quick to do as they were told.

He split us up, leaving me in charge of the solar-panel installation with half my unit while the other half helped him. Not long after we started, a fifteen-year-old kid showed up and jumped right in alongside Asherex. I figured he must have been learning about the install before we arrived, because he seemed to know what he was doing. I watched Asherex and the teenager interact. It was like watching a father teach his son. Maybe Asherex was staying for the kid as well.

We worked well into the afternoon before Kyandra and her brother, Michael, brought us lunch. They served freshly picked garden salads with apple slices, grilled fish, and asparagus. Michael blessed the food before we ate. My guys made me proud by not shoveling the food down and, instead, showing manners I'd never seen from them. *Maybe I should expect them to act like this when I cook for them.*

The conversations that flew around the table surprised me as my guys asked Kyandra and Michael about their faith and shared the stories of Emet telling us about the scriptures. Asherex didn't say much, but I could tell he was listening intently. I wondered how much he had learned since coming here. We hadn't really talked the last couple of times I had come for his quarantine checks.

As we finished eating, Asherex and Jonathan cleared the table and began doing the dishes. While they were doing that, the rest of us removed the older central air unit from behind the house and hauled it to the barn, where an old harvester was parked. Varkas immediately took an interest in the old beast and began rattling off everything he knew about it. His dad owned the company that had made it 157 years ago. He was impressed that it was in relatively good condition and still ran. He wanted to buy it to put it on display in the company showroom.

Jonathan found us in the barn and told us he and Asherex had repaired the harvester a few weeks back, and he told Varkas whom to talk to about buying it. I watched as Jonathan conversed with Kale, even though Kale didn't reply. Jonathan asked him questions, unfazed by the shrug, nod, or headshake for an answer. Kale never made eye contact with him, but I could see him relaxing, and eventually, a smile crept onto his face. *Man, that kid is the happiest person I've ever seen.*

Asherex finally called us back to work, and we finished installing the new air conditioner and hooked it up to the solar cells before it was dark. We had another full day of work to complete the install, and Asherex was set to have surgery tomorrow for some kind of Zeron's testing, so we decided to camp out and get an early start on it in the morning. Kyandra and Michael provided dinner for us, and we sat outside under the stars, eating by candlelight. It was a change from the normal and made me want to build a patio on the back of my house so I could start having people over for outdoor dinners. I never had thought I would want stuff like that, and I had to praise Yehovah for all of it.

After supper, Kale and Jonathan did the dishes while the rest of us sat and talked. The guys turned in for the night at ten, but I was too wired to sleep. I sat out under the stars, praying for a while, before I noticed Asherex sitting on the front porch, sipping a cup of tea. I joined him, and we talked for several hours about our past war campaigns before he surprised me by telling me that he had come into faith in Yeshua. He told me he always had believed there had to be more to life than what he'd learned growing up, and when he'd come to the community, he finally had found the truth.

His story was still bouncing around in my thoughts as I returned to the airship. I was ready for bed but stopped short of the hatch when I noticed Kale sitting there with an odd look on his face. Without thinking twice, I sat down next to him but didn't say anything. If he wanted to talk, he would start the conversation, I hoped.

It seemed like an eternity passed before he sighed and said, "Roark, can I talk to you?"

"Of course you can, Kale." I was afraid to say too much, in case I scared him off. I was known to put my foot in my mouth a lot.

"I've never told anyone this, but you are the first person to show me that you care, and Asherex was right that you will want to share with others when the right people are in your life." He was quiet for a while, as if trying to find the words, before saying, "My parents were drug addicts, and when I was two, they sold me to their dealer to pay off their debt. At least that's what he told me. Carson was his name, and he had a massive drug and prostitution ring. I was raised by the working women, and when I was around five, I was given the job of lookout. I had to memorize every face that walked through the doors and learn what cars they drove. If someone I didn't know showed up or a car I didn't recognize stopped or drove by, I had to report it.

"I wasn't allowed to talk unless I was telling Carson about people and vehicles that didn't belong in the neighborhood. If I was caught talking to anyone or making eye contact, I was beaten. One of the male prostitutes took me under his wing when I was six, and he secretly taught me to read and write between his clients. That went on for about two years, until one day, a well-dressed man showed up in an expensive car with one of our frequent visitors. The guy was there to buy some drugs, and Carson had a thing about new people buying from him; they had to stay there long enough for Carson to see how they reacted to the drugs."

Kale trailed off and bit his lip. I wasn't sure what was going through his mind, but my heart sank at the look on his face. Something terrible had happened to him, and I had a sinking feeling that he had suffered sexual abuse.

With a sigh, Kale continued. "When the guy in the suit came in, he saw me outside, and after he was all drugged up, he convinced Carson to let him pay for my services. I was eight years old and knew what sex was because I grew up having to be in the same room as the woman raising me while she serviced her clients. None of that, though, prepared me for what that man did to me."

Kale leaned forward, propped his elbows on his knees, and buried his face in his hands. "After that day, I lost all my freedom and was up for sale. I had to learn how to be a good prostitute and pretend like I enjoyed it, but I had such a hard time faking it that I had to be given drugs. That man visited me three times a week for a year before he stopped showing up. I was so far gone that I would do anything for my next fix."

He blew out a shaky breath before continuing. "I was twelve when the Opal Division raided the place. Carson handed me a gun, and everyone was there waiting to fight so that he could escape. I had a moment of clarity; if I didn't stop him, then more people would end up like me. Somehow, I managed to fight my way to his room, where he kept all the cash and had an escape tunnel. I don't remember much of what happened. We fought, and when the soldiers busted down the door, I was lying in a puddle of my own blood—Carson had cut my throat. I remember watching in slow motion as he shot two soldiers, and I looked up to find the gun he had taken from me. I grabbed it and shot him in the back.

"When I woke up, I was in the war council's private prison and all healed up. They kept me there until I detoxed from the drugs before bringing me up for a hearing. I was the only one left alive from the drug house. If I was willing to cooperate with their investigation and help round up the suppliers, they were willing to put me into a rehab program in which I would serve three years in the military and be evaluated to see if I was fit to reenter society."

We were quiet for a bit while I let everything sink in. It was hard not to get angry about what had happened to Kale, but I had to remind myself that there was still hope for him. All I had to do was get him approved by the shrink. I broke the silence by asking, "Why haven't you told the psychologist about this?"

Kale looked me in the eye and said, "I can't say a word to him. He doesn't recognize me, but I know him. He's the guy in the suit who raped me."

# Chapter Forty-Two

## Roark

I sat on the front porch while the sky grayed with the coming day. My mind still reeled from the conversation with Kale. He had been so upset that he immediately got up and stormed off to his bunk, leaving me alone. I knew it hadn't been easy for him to tell me about his past, and my heart was still hurting as I continued to pray for guidance. I didn't know the proper protocol for something like this, and I feared it could take weeks of research to find the solution. I didn't have that kind of time. Kale didn't have that kind of time.

I was so deep in thought that I didn't notice Asherex sitting beside me until he handed me a cup of tea. We sat there in silence, watching the sunrise, and once the color display was gone, he asked, "What's on your mind, Roark?"

"How do I get Kale a different psychologist that I can trust?"

He pondered the question for a moment before answering, "Well, right now, he and Emet are not serving together, so Emet can legally be his court-appointed shrink."

I thought about it for a minute, knowing that Emet was the only one I trusted, but I would need Rayas's permission, and I knew he wasn't about to help me. With a sigh, I said, "Rayas would never do a favor like that for me."

"You will never know until you ask. My dad hates Victor, yet he keeps him close and doesn't hesitate to ask him for favors. Just ask him, and tell him about the situation. He might surprise you, but if he says no, you are a Crimson Soldier and can do it anyway. My advice is that it's always better to ask first before asserting your power; that way, if it blows up, people can't say that you didn't try to do it peaceably first."

"I will try it. Maybe Yehovah will show me favor in this, and Kale won't be put to death."

No sooner had the words left my mouth than an old pickup pulled up, and Asherex left me alone. He was about to have one of the most invasive surgeries ever done, and I didn't envy him in the slightest. If he survived the surgery, he would send live feed data straight to a facility in Brashex in the hope of learning more about Zeron's. I didn't think I would have had the courage to do it if I had been the one infected.

As the smell of fresh bread filled the morning air, my men, minus Kale, joined me in the front yard. Doug pulled me aside and told me that he had sedated Kale early that morning due to a PTSD attack, so we would be a man down for a while. I couldn't help but feel responsible because of his trip down memory lane last night.

We ate breakfast with Kyandra, Michael, and Jonathan before heading out to continue working on the install. Asherex had left Jonathan in charge and given him full access to his plex. The kid was a natural-born leader and wasn't afraid to boss us around. He made sure we took breaks and kept hydrated, and he even asked us to stop working to help move the heavy appliances into their main hall. After we finished moving in the new appliances and storing the old ones, we were back at work with extra hands. Some of the men from the little town came to help us finish up, since we helped them.

Around four o'clock, Asherex returned. He looked worse for wear. His shaved head made him look much older and added to the weariness etched on his face. It took two of us to get him out of the truck and up to his room, where he passed out from all the drugs he was on. My heart broke for him, but there was nothing I could do but pray. If ever a man deserved to live, it was him. He did so much good for the homeless, poor, and orphaned and for fallen soldiers' families that I knew it would be devastating for many Adreians when he died.

It didn't take us long after that to finish the installation and test it before we packed up and headed out. On the way home, we ate the sandwiches Kyandra had made for us, and we listened to Varkas talk about the ancient harvester and how he was negotiating a price for it. I was sure his father would be ecstatic to find out about it. An hour into the return trip, I decided to let Doug take over and went to my private room to take a much-needed nap. I prayed for Asherex until I passed out.

Fifteen minutes before we landed in the quarantine sector of Adreia, Doug woke me so I could safely land us, because Doug was used to being a copilot and didn't know how to land my airship. That was something I had to fix in case I was unable to pilot the beast.

After dropping them off, I did the unit-leader-designated paperwork I had to fill out every time I brought the guys back before I gave a report of what we had done. It took about five hours to get everything finished, and I had to wait until seven o'clock in the morning for clearance to leave the quarantine zone. Apparently, the hangar doors from the quarantine sector were open only during the daylight hours, so I decided to get some sleep until then.

As soon as seven o'clock hit, I made my way through the maze of flight tunnels to the entrance of the above-ground hangar. I was hungry and wanted nothing more than to go home, shower, and change clothes, but instead, I made a beeline to Victor's sprawling mansion. I didn't even know if he was home or not, but I went there anyway, hoping that everything would work out in the end. As I landed my cruzer, I noticed his limo parked in the driver's private residence toward the end of the drive. Rayas didn't go anywhere unless he was in that armored vehicle.

I made my way to the front door and knocked. A surprised-looking servant girl greeted me and invited me in before running off to inform her master of my arrival. Rayas appeared in the entryway like an apparition, looking ready for a fight. He crossed his arms over his chest and said, "What do you want, Verity?" His words were full of venom, and I couldn't blame him after I had attacked him the day of the crane explosion.

"I'm sorry." I was just as surprised as he was by my apology. I hadn't intended to do it, but I was just going to roll with it and see what else came of it. "Mr. Rayas, we once had a professional relationship when Emet was first put under my care. I let my emotions and attachment to him cloud my judgment, causing strife between us. I'm sorry that we haven't had a civil conversation in eight years, and I am also sorry that I let my temper control me and hurt you. I never should have allowed it to happen.

"I give you my word as Crimson Soldier that I will give you all the respect you deserve, just as you respected me when our arrangement first began ten years ago. I was young and arrogant and took your trust and respect for granted, treating it like it was commonplace instead of the honor it was. I know my apology doesn't mean much to you now, but I truly desire peace between us if you will have it."

He eyed me like a wary predator before saying, "Is this some kind of trick?" I didn't blame him for his distrust.

"Trust me, the last thing I wanted to do was come here and ask you for a favor, but Asherex convinced me that this was the right course of action."

He nodded, walked across the foyer, and unlocked his office. He motioned for me to follow him before he sat down. I stood until he gave me permission to sit, just as I had nine years ago when he called me here to ask me to be Emet's secondary warden.

"What is this favor that would have you coming here while my slave is living under your roof?"

"I have a kid in my unit who is a ward of the state and will be put down after his military contract is up unless I can get him a different psychologist. It has to be someone trustworthy, and Emet is the only person I know who will remain unbiased." I sat there quietly for a few moments while he stared me down. He could tell there was more to the story than I was saying, and I had to decide if I should proceed with telling him what Kale had told me. With a sigh, I told Victor that Kale had grown up being used as a sex slave and that his current shrink was the man who had first bought him. If the guy discovered the truth about it, he would have the kid executed so that no one found out he not only had broken the law by having sex with a child but also had had homosexual relations with him as well.

Victor was quiet, but his eyes held a rage I didn't understand. Perhaps he was thinking about his son and wondering if something like that could have happened to him. Whatever it was, it was enough to get him out of his chair and heading out of the room. As he entered the doorway, he looked back at me and said, "I will take care of it."

"Are you going to kill him?" I didn't know why the question came out, but the evil smile that crept onto Victor's face told me he intended to do just that.

"Now, Mr. Verity, that is illegal, and I would never entertain the idea." With that, he left me to find my own way out.

# Chapter Forty-Three

Emet

The lukewarm water washed over my overheated flesh, bringing relief to my bruised body. Roark had come back from the Surface yesterday while I was at work, and after a double shift in the OR, I had decided to take the thirty-minute cab ride home instead of flying two hours to Roark's house. It was now two o'clock in the morning, and I regretted the decision to come here. My master had come home shortly after I arrived and found me praying in my room. I guessed he had been in one of his moods, because he had attacked me, dragged me from the room, thrown me down the stairs, and then forced me into his office, where he'd chained my hands and feet to his desk and continued to beat me.

Somehow, he hadn't managed to break anything, but bruised ribs weren't much fun. After he'd left, I'd spent several hours attempting to pick the locks to the chains, which had cut into my wrists and ankles. Sadly, it felt as if it had happened to someone else, and my injuries didn't bother me more than the annoyance of tight muscles and the inability to take a deep breath. I didn't know how many times I had suffered like this, and the fact that it didn't seem to faze me much scared me. I didn't want that to be my normal.

*O Yehovah, I don't know how much more of this I can take. I'm just tired and ready for it to end.*

A strange sound like that of bare skin slipping on wet tile snapped me out of my thoughts, and fear blossomed in my chest. I cut off the water with shaky hands and slowly slid open the frosted-glass shower door. My heart pounded, drowning out every external sound, as I looked around the large, undecorated white bathroom, with its black-and-white tile floor. A bright crimson trail drawing closer to the sink captured my attention. Adrenaline flooded my system as I stepped from the shower and rushed around the half wall next to the sink.

My breath caught in my throat at the sight of my master on the floor, gasping for breath while clasping his side. Blood covered him, and without thinking, I pulled him farther into the bathroom, grabbed my towel, and put pressure on the wound on his side. He muttered something I couldn't understand as I attempted to examine him, and I nearly jumped out of my skin when he grabbed me by my hair, pulled me face-to-face with him, and sputtered out, "He's still in the house."

As soon as the words left his lips, he passed out. I jumped into action, springing into my bedroom and locking us in using the locks Gavin had installed to keep Victor out. I grabbed my medical bag out of the closet and then ripped up one of the floorboards to retrieve the handgun Gavin had bought for me before heading into the bathroom and locking us inside.

I attempted to call Roark, but he didn't answer, so I called Saz and explained what was going on. I told him Victor needed blood now if he was going to survive. Saz assured me he would take care of it and hung up, leaving me alone with my master. I spent the next twenty minutes stabilizing him with what I had and giving him the nanos and pain meds I had in my bag. I knew Roark wouldn't be happy to find out I was using our unit's medical supplies on my master, but right now, saving his life was more important than their grudge match.

A loud banging on my bedroom door nearly caused me to jump out of my skin. A thousand scenarios swirled around in my mind as I pulled the handgun up and realized for the first time that I was completely naked. I sat there kneeling next to my master, fully prepared to defend him with my last breath, when I heard Saz say from the other side of the door, "Open up, Emet. It's me—Saz."

With a sigh of relief, I grabbed the pair of sweatpants I had put on the bathroom counter, pulled them on, and went to the door. I slowly unlocked the door with my gun drawn and ready to fire in case someone else was standing there, and I came face-to-face with Saz. He looked at my weapon with his pale blue-green eyes and then back at me in surprise before pushing past me and making his way to the bathroom with his suitcase filled with blood. I shut and locked the door behind us and watched him start working on Victor. For some reason, he reminded me of an armed robber with his black clothing only a few shades darker than his skin and his buzz-cut black hair.

He motioned for me to join him, and I returned to work. I did my best not to look at Saz or talk to him, because for some reason, my master didn't like it when I was alone with him, and if I was being honest, I didn't really want to be alone with him either. The things he did made Victor look like a child who spilled juice on the carpet.

It took a while to get my master stabilized, but once I was sure he wouldn't die, Saz looked at me, reached out, and touched my bruised face. I involuntarily flinched back from him, not from pain but from his touch—it had felt as if something evil touched me.

He dropped his hand and said, "I always hated it when he hit you. I've tried for years to get him to stop, but nothing I say or do will change his mind."

The quiet that followed his unexpected statement made me uncomfortable and hyperaware that I was half naked and that he was attracted to men. I wanted to run away but feared what he would do if I did.

"I need to apologize to you, Emet." His booming voice filled the air, bringing with it a heaviness that hadn't been there before. "For what happened to you the day I was scheduled for surgery. I knew that Victor intended to kill me that day, so I hired a man to ensure he never made it to the hospital with you. I didn't know that he would blow up the crane or that he was tired of our fighting." He looked down at Victor, brushed a lock of hair from his forehead, and continued. "He fully intended to kill everyone in the car, but by some miracle, no one died."

That wasn't true. Many people had died that day from the explosion and the crane crashing to the ground. Some people had died in the triage tents while waiting for help to come, and others, trapped in buildings and cars, had suffered from the toxic fumes of the melting crane and broken gas lines. Saz and Victor didn't really care about the collateral damage when they decided to fight. At least my master had planned to have me kill one man instead of hiring a psychopath who'd murdered nearly one hundred people in a reckless assassination attempt.

"I'm not the one you need to apologize to. I didn't die that day, but others did."

He looked at me with dead eyes, as if he couldn't have cared less if people died as long as he kept breathing. We didn't say anything else as I helped him take Victor to his room, where Saz sent me away so he could tend to Victor and clean him up. Before I walked out the door, Saz grabbed my arm in a tight grip, causing me to turn around in surprise. He was reaching out to touch my chest, and the icy fingers of fear clenched around my heart, so I violently jerked away, wrenching my arm from his grasp, before rushing back to my room and locking the door.

A servant girl was in the bathroom, cleaning up the bloody mess, and I joined her. We didn't talk the whole time, and as she went to leave, she looked at me with tears in her eyes and, in an accusing tone, asked, "Why didn't you let him die?"

She stormed out of my room, and I locked the door behind her.

Her question bounced around my head as I showered the blood off me, dressed, and crawled into bed. I felt numb and couldn't find the words to pray. *Why didn't I let him die, Yehovah?* The question went unanswered as exhaustion finally overtook me.

# Chapter Forty-Four

## Emet

A rough hand on my shoulder startled me awake, and I was shocked to find Victor's brown eyes staring into my own. He looked as if he never had been hurt, except for a slight bruise on his forehead, below his hairline. Fierce anger burned in his eyes as he eyed me and said, "Did *he* touch you?"

"What?"

"Did Saz touch you?" The fury in his voice made me wonder if he would attack me again.

I sat up carefully, trying not to hurt myself or provoke him, and said, "He didn't touch me."

Victor looked at the bruises on my arm where Saz had grabbed me, and the anger in his eyes deepened. I had never seen him this angry before. I wondered, if I hadn't pulled away from Saz last night, would he have attempted to sexually assault me? That was the one thing Victor drew the line at. He hadn't allowed any of his questionable friends to molest me and had killed several who tried.

"He won't be coming back here again. Do you understand? Go to the hospital to have your injuries treated, and then go to Roark's until I call you back. Don't come here without permission again. Understand?"

I nodded, and he walked to the far corner of the room, opened a secret panel I hadn't known existed, and disappeared as it closed behind him. I wasted no time in dressing and calling a cab, uncertain of what was going on.

It was a quick ride to the emergency room, where they took x-rays of my chest to ensure my ribs weren't broken and gave me nano shots to speed up the healing process. I was surprised my master had signed off on it and even had them provide me with pain meds for the nanos.

When the last bag of fluids mixed with nanos and drugs was emptying into the IV, I knew my discharge time was fast approaching. I grabbed my plex to call Roark, when there was a knock at the door. Before I could say a word, the door opened to reveal Roark. With a surprised look, I said, "I was about to call you. How did you know I was here?"

"I called him."

Roark jumped at the unexpected voice behind him, and I couldn't hide my smile. I looked past Roark to see Dr. Chase standing in the hall. His blond hair shone in the lights, and amusement danced in his blue eyes. I had mentored young Chase for the last five years, and the kid was probably the most dedicated man I'd ever met. He'd first shadowed me when he was fifteen and aspiring to be a spinal surgeon. Apparently, where he was from, he had grown up learning about the medical world and assisted the doctors there from a young age.

He walked into the room, closed the door behind him, and said, "I had hoped to see you again before I left, Emet, to thank you for all the time you've spent teaching me all these years. Even though I haven't been able to perform many spinal operations, my time here hasn't been wasted."

"Where are you going?"

He smiled at me before sighing and replying, "My king has called for my immediate return home. There's been an accident with my uncle, and they want me home to assist in the recovery process.

I'm not sure if I will be able to return in the future, so I wanted to tell you that I've enjoyed learning from a brother in Messiah."

"Wait a minute!" Roark cut in, surprising Dr. Chase. "You've been a follower of Yeshua this whole time and kept it to yourself?"

"Yes, I was under orders from my king to do so. We have to keep our kingdom's secrets, so everything about us is a made-up image designed to allow us to come here and learn from the best so we can return home and teach others. Everything is done for the good of the kingdom."

"Thank you, Riley, for sharing that with us. It has been a blessing to have you disciple under me for the past five years." I tried to keep my voice calm as emotion threatened to overcome me at his confession that he was a brother in Yeshua.

He smiled at me. "My first name is Azaryah."

"Well, Azaryah," Roark said, "I hope your uncle gets better. We will pray for him, and if you need anything, just let me know."

Azaryah smiled as he crossed the room, unhooked me from the machines, and removed the empty bag of fluids. After performing the required exam, he officially discharged me, and we embraced for the first time in five years. I had always felt connected to him, and now I knew that he was my brother through faith. Even though I was going to miss him if he didn't return, I was glad he was going to be with his family. Five years was a long time to go without seeing them but twice a year. If I had been paying attention, I would have noticed that he returned home for Pesach and Sukkot.

"Azaryah, if you can come back, I will gladly let you shadow me and will see to it personally that you take part in more spinal surgeries. You are a very talented young man, and they never should have kept you from the OR, but unfortunately, when we have talented young men like you who will leave after you gain the skills you need, we tend to keep you from perfecting them, so you have to stay longer. It isn't fair to you or your family to do it, and if I could, I would change it."

"I know you would, Emet. You are the best teacher I've ever had, and when things change for you, I will be the first one in line to work by your side." He smiled before leaving us alone.

*Yehovah, be with Azaryah and his family. Provide for their needs, and bring healing to his uncle. In Yeshua's name, amen.*

After we left the hospital, Roark bought me lunch before we boarded his airship and headed home. We didn't speak during the trip, and I replayed last night's events repeatedly in my mind. *Why didn't you let him die?* The servant girl's question chased itself around my head. Why hadn't I?

"Emet!" Roark's shout snapped me out of my thoughts, and I realized we were parked in his driveway. Where had the two-hour flight gone? He looked at me, a little concerned, and asked, "Are you all right?"

I looked him in the eye and felt a soul-deep weariness creep over me before I answered, "No. I'm not all right."

He knelt before me when I didn't elaborate, and I could tell he was doing his best to be patient instead of demanding answers like usual. I shook my head and buried my face in my hands. He knew from my fading bruises that Victor had beaten me again, and I didn't want to see him get angry over something neither of us could control, but I had to tell him what had happened last night.

"Someone broke into Victor's house last night and tried to kill him. I was in the shower, trying to find some relief from the beating he'd given me earlier, when he crawled into the bathroom, covered in blood. I didn't even think twice, Roark. I just—why didn't I let him die?" I pushed my fingers into my hair and stared down at the floor. Tears spilled from my eyes and dripped off my nose onto my shoes. "I could have ended this whole nightmare, but I didn't let him die. Why didn't I just let him die?"

I felt Roark's hand touch my arm before he made me look at him and said, "Because that's not who you are, Emet. You know that it isn't your job to judge who lives and dies. Not trying to save someone is just the same as killing them yourself, and you are not a murderer. You are a good man, Emet, a much better man than me."

"I can't take this anymore, Roark. I just can't."

"Hold on a bit longer. Everything is going to work out. Trust me, and trust Yehovah. I don't know what the future holds for either of us, but look back at what your faithfulness has brought you so far. Yes, you have suffered, but you planted seeds in me that brought me to the place where I was so broken that I couldn't run from God anymore. You helped Contessa and Lillie to find Yeshua and have comforted many who were dying by sharing the gospel with them.

"You are a walking blessing to everyone around you, and I look at you and am inspired every day to be a better man than I was before. If you can keep your faith through everything you have suffered, then there isn't anything too big for me to overcome with Yeshua by my side. Without your living testimony, I wouldn't be right here in front of you right now. You once told me that life is harder to live without faith, but I wouldn't know it until I tried it. Well, I tried it, and I have to say that you were right. I can look back over the last couple of months and see where the Father has been preparing me to turn to Him and equipping me for the task ahead of me. Please don't give up. If you need prayer warriors fighting for you while you rest, I will make a call and have an entire community praying for you. Let us carry your burdens for a while so you can come back strengthened."

I pulled him into a hug and managed to whisper, "I need that right now."

# Chapter Forty-Five

Asherex

I had slept for nearly two days after my operation and finally woken up an hour ago. After talking to my dad for a few minutes, I came downstairs to have a late lunch with Kyandra. I wasn't hungry, but I had to eat something with the pills I had to take for the first week after having the medical-grade sensors implanted throughout my body.

"When's your friend coming, Ash?" Kyandra's question drew me from my thoughts.

"Drayen? He's on his way and will be here any minute now. I should probably be outside waiting so I can direct him to the landing zone." Drayen had insisted on coming to see me today, so he had cleared his schedule except for one meeting later that night and jumped in his airship to fly out. I was looking forward to seeing him.

The back door burst open, and Michael walked through looking as if he were about to panic. He looked at me and said, "It looks like we are about to be invaded out there."

I jumped up and ran outside, calling Drayen on my way out the door. His personal cruzer, escorted by six units of Adreian pilots, gave the midafternoon sky an eerie, apocalyptic feel. Drayen answered my call, and I directed him to his landing zone before directing the pilots to the trading-post town, where they could wait for our commander in chief to take off later for the flight home.

"Who exactly is your friend?" Michael's awestruck question drew my attention as I ended the call with the commander of the pilot squad.

I looked at him and said, "Drayen is the commander in chief of Adreia."

He looked at me in disbelief as the airship's engines powered down, and a few moments later, the back hatch opened, revealing my friend. He was wearing armor, no doubt at the request of the war council, and was well armed, as if going to war. The quarantine respirator covered the lower portion of his face, even though I was past the airborne stage of transmitting the disease. His jet-black hair was longer than he usually kept it, giving him a shaggy appearance that was at odds with all the gear he was wearing.

He walked toward me as his cruzer hatch closed automatically behind him. I couldn't hide my smile as he neared me, and as soon as he was within arm's reach, he pulled me into the tightest hug I'd had in a long time. There was something therapeutic about a hug from my best friend. I needed this.

He pulled away, looked me over, and said, "You know, for a dying man, you sure are looking pretty good. And"—he grabbed my face, looking deep into my eyes—"there's something strange in your eyes." He released me. "What's your secret?"

"If you are a good kid, I will tell you later." I winked at him teasingly, bringing a smile to his face.

Laughter danced in his gray eyes as he slung his arm over my shoulders and turned us to face the house. Kyandra and Michael were on the patio, looking as if they didn't know what to do when we walked up. It was a little amusing, but at the same time, I remembered how nervous I had been at the summit meeting when I met Drayen for the first time in person. He could be intimidating, standing at six foot five and dressed for war.

"Drayen, this is Kyandra Rains and her brother, Michael.

Kyandra, Michael, this is my best friend, Commander in Chief Drayen Vaxis."

We spent fifteen minutes talking with Kyandra and Michael before I pulled Drayen into the house. He took his time removing his armor, respirator, and weapons before walking with me into the living room. As soon as we were alone, I looked him in the eye and asked, "So when are you going to marry Nayomi?"

He looked at me as if I'd lost my mind as he sat down and replied, "I don't know, Asherex. We've only been dating for a few months now and haven't talked about it much. Besides, I've been through the marriage and divorce game a few times and am not looking to repeat it."

"That's because you married the wrong women. From what you've told me, they all believed they could change you into their version of you and left when it didn't work out for them, but Nay knows who you are and isn't trying to change you. I've never seen her this way with anyone, and when we talk about you, she always brings up your good qualities instead of pointing out your flaws. Drayen, you just turned forty, and I know that Nay is ten years younger than you, but you make her happy, and from what your daughter has said, she makes you happy as well.

"You might have some experience with being married. Nayomi has never dated anyone, but I assure you she learned how to sit down and negotiate on a man's level instead of getting emotional. She has four brothers around her age and had to put up with me, so she understands that a man doesn't change unless he wants to. Don't let the past keep you from moving forward and being happy."

"Every time I'm around you, you open your mouth and tell me something I don't want to hear but know is right. Sometimes I hate having a genius for a friend." He smiled at me teasingly, and I shook my head. He let loose a sigh and said, "Like I said, we kind of talked about it a bit, but with you being sick, it's not something we want to get into yet."

"Or maybe you should hurry up and get it over with before I

die, so you can legally be there for her without having to be dragged off to work."

He gave me both a horrified look and one that told me I was a genius. I smiled back at him and changed the subject. We spent the next several hours catching up before I brought up the recording from Proxy Uriah and his plot to destroy the people in the Torah community just because they were religious.

Drayen sat back on the couch, looked at me, and said, "This is a problem. He cannot terrorize people just because they have weird beliefs. These people are not violent or causing problems, so they should have been left alone." He sat forward and looked at me with an intensity that came only from serving as a judge in the Adreian courts. "You don't know how badly I want to kill this guy, Asherex. Just let me take him out."

"Normally, I wouldn't impede justice like this, but if I am correct and he did infect me with Zeron's, he must be left alone so we can link him to the others involved. I'm sure Rayas had something to do with the black-market purchasing of the contaminated nanos, but I don't know if Rayik Saz is involved or not. I want everyone involved taken down for this and interrogated thoroughly to ensure that it never happens again. They got the nanos into our supply warehouse, so there's no telling where else they managed to smuggle them. This goes far beyond just me and the people here; we are talking about the possible infection of billions of innocent people. As long as I'm alive here, everyone is safe from him, and I know that when I die, you and Roark will ensure that it stays that way."

"I know you're right, but I don't like it. You know that before I joined the military, I was a judge for ten years, so letting criminals and terrorists go like this kills me. I'm used to the final end of the chase and have to say that playing the long game is awful."

"I still think the main play is to remove you from office, and I am just a double win for Uriah. It's no secret that he hates being a proxy and wants my high commander position. He was agitated when I was promoted over him, since I was only twenty-two. Now he runs around with a private military company and corrupt politicians. Still, someone else is pulling the strings, and him killing me off will slow down any investigations and allow his promotion to my position of high commander of the Crimson Division. It's a win-win situation for him, but he didn't count on one thing."

Drayen looked at me suspiciously. "What wasn't he counting on?"

"I'm a stubborn, hardheaded Reach who's tasted death six times and come out swinging on the other side."

Drayen laughed because he knew it was true, and it scared him a bit. He had joked about me dying from Zeron's and then coming back as if nothing had happened. If Yehovah decided to heal me of Zeron's or bring me back to life after I died from it, it was all His plan, but my purpose was to bring Torah to Adreia. Yehovah had already put me in a position to influence the commander in chief and my father, one of the most highly respected senators. I wasn't going to pray for a longer life beyond freeing Emet and didn't know if I wanted to return to my old life if He extended my days.

"Well, I can't argue with you there, Asherex, but my time is drawing short, and you still haven't told me about this strange thing I see in your eyes and how you are so at peace right now. I've seen my fair share of people dying from this and have to say that you look the healthiest for as far along as you are. Sure, you've lost some weight, but if I hadn't seen the blood test results with my own eyes, I would say you didn't have Zeron's. What is going on with you?"

I stood, walked over to the bookcase, and pulled a Bible off the shelf before sitting back down across the coffee table from him. He took the Bible from my outstretched hands, and I started explaining to him about Yehovah and Yeshua. I directed him to verses and had him read them for himself. An hour passed before I asked, "Drayen, do you remember when we first talked all those years ago on that broken plex, and I asked you if you ever wondered if there was more to this life?"

"How could I forget? I was terrified you would die on me, and several times, I thought you were hallucinating and talking to someone who wasn't there. Then you started asking me if I ever thought about what happened to us when we die, and I've been thinking about it ever since."

"Well, I found the answers to those questions right there"—I pointed at the Bible in his hands—"in that book and here in these people."

He stared me down hard and then looked back at the Bible before telling me I had better explain and not leave anything out. Twenty-five minutes later, I finished telling him everything I had gone through since coming here and about the road that had led me here. Drayen sat back with a stunned look, not saying a word.

Kyandra and Michael had sat at the dining table a while back, and I knew they'd listened to my story from the other room. Drayen finally looked at me and said, "How can I deny what you are saying? If you say this is true, it must be; you're the smartest person I know, and you would never lead me astray. Even if I wanted to deny what I've read and the things that have happened in your life lately, I cannot ignore the changes I see in you, both the outer change and the peace you have inside."

"So what are you going to do about it, Drayen?"

He looked at me and then shook his head and said, "You are really pushy, you know?"

I leaned forward so he would know I was serious and replied, "You already knew I was like this, so it shouldn't surprise you."

He sighed and said, "I will answer your question before I leave. I need a little more time to think about it."

As I nodded, I noticed Kyandra walk out the front door and was curious to know what she was up to, but before I could investigate, Drayen asked, "So how are things with your dad? Have you had a real conversation with him yet?"

"Not yet. We have been talking a little every day, and I think we just might be able to have a conversation without fighting and maybe talk about the things we haven't been saying to each other since Mom died. I'm ready for it, but I'm afraid I might not find the words to say, like I've done every time before."

I trailed off, thinking back to all the times I'd attempted to have the one conversation with my dad that would change our relationship from formal and nearly nonexistent to deep and meaningful. I could address ten thousand troops, negotiate peace treaties with the enemy, and go face-to-face with the war council but couldn't seem to say two important words to my dad: "I'm sorry." It could have been just that easy, and everything after that would have explained why I was sorry, but those words had never left my mouth. Those two words had kept me from really knowing my father.

Drayen crossed the space between us, firmly grasped my hands, and said, "Asherex Reach, you are the strongest person I've had the privilege to meet, and I know that when the time comes, you will be able to have that long-awaited conversation with your dad. The most important things are the hardest to say, but once you've said them, you will feel much better. I lost that opportunity with my brother when I defeated him and took his place as commander of a thousand in the Crimson Division. I thought I was doing it to save him because he was sick, but all I did was drive him further away. If I can talk to him again, there are a thousand things I want to say, but for all I know, he is dead, and I will never get the chance."

Kyandra came inside, interrupting us, and said, "Ash, there's someone outside asking for you. He wouldn't tell me who he was."

The look on her face told me she didn't trust whoever it was, and Drayen and I were on our feet in a matter of seconds. As soon as I walked out, I saw him sitting on a hoverbike with a five-by-four-foot covered wagon. He was wearing a black armored riding suit with an emblem on the back and an expensive-looking black-and-chrome helmet.

"Well, isn't this a pleasant surprise?" The man's voice sounded familiar.

*There's no way it could be—*

"Seth-Lucius?" I heard his laughter as he pulled off his helmet, revealing my old friend. He looked at me with mismatched eyes, one gray blue and the other green.

He smiled at me before dismounting the bike. "I have a present for you, Asherex." He looked past me at Drayen and said, "Hello, little brother."

I looked between them. Seth-Lucius looked as if he were enjoying himself a little too much, and Drayen was stunned. They both had jet-black hair and were about the same height, with only an inch of difference between them; Drayen was taller at six foot five. Drayen was larger in build, while Seth-Lucius was much leaner because of his chronic illness, but he looked healthier than I did now.

Stepping off the porch, I approached Seth-Lucius, and he bowed to me in the traditional military fashion before pulling me into a gentle hug. After he released me, he pulled out a holographic recorder chip and tossed it to Drayen, saying, "I guess since you're here, both of you can share my present. Everything you need is on that recorder, so don't lose it now, Brother."

Drayen didn't say a word as Seth-Lucius pulled off his glove, scanned his handprint on the wagon lid, and pulled the top up. In one fluid motion, he replaced his glove, reached in, and pulled out a beat-up-looking man before tossing him to the ground. It took me a minute to realize that Veris, my father-in-law, was bound and gagged on the ground in front of me.

"After I heard about what happened, I asked my boss if I could hunt him down for you while you were missing. It took me a while, but I finally got him. But by that time, I'd learned you had Zeron's, and I was too late."

He trailed off, as if somehow he could have prevented me from getting sick.

A few moments passed before Drayen finally spoke up. "How did you learn about Veris? It was a closed op with only a handful of people in the loop."

Seth-Lucius smiled at his brother in a mischievous way before saying, "My people—they know things."

Another hoverbike pulled up beside Seth-Lucius, interrupting us. The man spoke to him in a language I didn't understand but recognized as Hebrew. They argued back and forth for a few minutes before Seth-Lucius looked at me and said, "Well, kid, I guess I've got to go. My king demands my immediate return home now that I've delivered Veris to you."

"So that's it then? You disappear for years after making everyone think you're dead and then show up for less than five minutes before vanishing again?" I said.

He looked at me with compassion in his eyes and replied, "Things are different now, Asherex, and I don't have the luxury of being in one place too long without risking the lives of my people. I should have come sooner, but I was trying to find out where the infected nanos came from that Victor Rayas purchased from the black market. I managed to track them to a Wastelands trading post but lost the trail there. I'm sorry I couldn't do more."

I looked at him in disbelief that he knew about the investigation into Rayas and the nanos. Who were his people, and how could they hack our system like that? *My father was a hacker and taught me, Asherex. Now I'm teaching you. We come from a long line of hackers and programmers. It is crucial that you learn everything I know so that one day you can teach your children.* My father's words from long ago ran through my mind. Was it possible that the people Seth-Lucius worked for had the same skill set that my family from the Surface had?

The man on the other hoverbike released a frustrated sigh; removed his helmet, revealing a kid probably around thirteen; and said, "Dad, we have to go now. If we miss the transport ship back home this time, they'll throw us into the detention center again. Let's go."

"All right, Katri'el, we are going."

Katri'el seemed satisfied with his response and replaced his helmet before starting his bike and driving off. Seth-Lucius turned to grab his helmet, when Drayen stopped him, saying, "Wait, Brother."

Drayen crossed the distance between them and stood a few feet away before continuing. "There are a few things I need to say to you. I'm sorry I tried to kill you the last time we saw each other. I was angry at you for leaving me and returning to Brashex without telling me you were going. I'm sorry I defeated you and took your place as commander of a thousand in the Crimson Division because I was afraid you were too weak to do the job. The thought that I needed to protect you because of your medical condition blinded me so much that I didn't see you could take care of yourself. I never should have pushed you into running off, and I'm so sorry for doing it. I see now that I was trying to be like a parent to you, when all you wanted was for me to be your brother."

Drayen pulled Seth-Lucius into a fierce hug, and Seth-Lucius looked at me like he didn't know what to do. I smiled at Seth-Lucius and mouthed to him to hug his brother back. It took a moment before he finally brought up one arm and lightly embraced Drayen before saying to him, "You're not the only one who messed things up. I wanted to prove to you that I could take care of myself, and I pushed too hard. If it hadn't been for Asherex saving my life, I would have ended up getting myself killed, but now I have people who look after me and force me to have routine medical workups to prevent me from pushing myself too far. Besides, I've adopted Katri'el, so I have to live for a few more years for him."

They released each other, and Drayen said, "Is this your way of apologizing? Because it was terrible."

"Yeah, I guess it is. I'm sorry, Brother, for everything and for attempting to kill you that day you ended up in the copper mine. No one believed me that you were there after Asherex surrendered to us, and I guess it's a good thing because I would have just killed you on the spot instead of taking you captive."

Drayen shook his head and said, "Tell me one thing. Did you go back to our father's house when you went back to Brashex? After the way he treated us, I couldn't imagine you returning."

"I did. We had a sister too, but he killed her, so I went out and challenged the high commander of the Shadow Division, took his place, and then came home and let him hit me so I could kill him. The worst part was that after all that, Mom still cried over him and hated me for killing him. I don't know what happened to her. After that, I moved into the barracks, and I stayed there until I met Asherex. I haven't been back to Brashex since and honestly never want to set foot in the World Above again. I am happy serving my king, and I have a large extended family who seem to care about me for reasons I don't understand. They are very religious and caring, and let's face it: I'm the extreme opposite of them.

"Well, I'd better get going before the kid yells at me again or gets caught up having to do another remote drone strike for one of our guys, like he did earlier. I'll call you sometime, and we can catch up, Brother."

"You don't have my number."

Seth-Lucius looked at Drayen as he put his helmet on and straddled his bike before saying, "My people can get it for me." He started his hoverbike, waved goodbye to me, and took off without another word.

We stood there watching him disappear before Drayen said, "Give me a digital copy of that Bible of yours, and I will study it."

"What made you decide you believed it?"

He looked at me with an expression of disbelief in his eyes and replied, "Earlier, I silently asked this Yehovah to do something that would let me know He was real, and then my long-lost brother showed up out of nowhere. How can I ignore that?"

I smiled at him and sent him the digital copy I had on my plex. Shortly after, he geared back up to leave, and I walked him to his cruzer. He stopped at the bottom of the ramp for the back hatch, looked at me, and said, "Call your father, and tell him everything. If I could talk to my brother, you can say what you need to say to your dad. Yehovah is with you, so you have nothing to be afraid of."

I nodded at him with tears filling my eyes and replied, "I will first thing when I get up. I'm worn out now and need to go rest."

"Your dad has been pushing the contracts through the senate and is about ten thousand ahead of where he needs to be to stay on track, so you can have him come out to see you in person without them falling behind."

Joy filled my heart at the thought of seeing my dad again before I died, and I pulled Drayen in for a final hug in case it was the last time I was able to do so. "Thank you for being my friend, my brother Drayen."

"I should be saying that to you, Asherex. You've changed my life in more ways than you could ever know. I don't want to say goodbye. My only regret is waiting so long to meet you in person. I'm going to miss you." He tightened the hug before releasing me and walking up the ramp to his airship with tears streaming down his face.

I walked back to the front porch and watched him take off, not knowing if I would see him again.

*Yehovah, see Drayen home, and open his eyes to see and his ears to hear so that he will surrender to You and walk in all Your ways. Teach him to love what You love and hate what You hate; guide him as he leads the country, and let Your Torah spring forth from his mouth and overflow to those around him so that all may come to know You through him. In Yeshua's name, I pray. Amen.*

# Chapter Forty-Six

## Roark

I was sitting in the middle of one of the most expensive restaurants in the capital city with my father, but my mind was miles away. At that moment, Kale was having his first appointment with Emet, and I was so worried the kid wouldn't talk to him that I couldn't concentrate on what Lou was saying to me.

"Roark." Lou's concerned tone drew my attention. He looked at me with hazel eyes full of questions and asked, "What's on your mind, Son?"

I pushed my barely touched appetizer plate away from me, laid my forehead on the table like a child, and sat there silently for a minute, debating whether I wanted to speak my mind. I was still learning how to act right in the upper-class circles and didn't want to do or say something that would embarrass my father. At the same time, the emotional turmoil tore me up from the inside out. I hadn't slept well since coming home, and I hardly ate, because I was concerned for Kale. If not for the fact that I was only certified to care for one ward at a time, I would have taken the kid in and cared for him as if he were mine, but I couldn't do that if I was going to have Emet with me once Asherex freed him. This was killing me.

"I don't know what to do," I said finally.

"I don't believe that for one second, Roark." Lou's statement caused me to lift my head and look at him before he continued. "I've only known you for a short time now, but it is quite clear that you are a very decisive man and, at any given time, have various plans in place to take care of whatever is in front of you. Tell me what's bothering you, so we can work out a solution together."

I let out a breath and told him everything about Kale's situation and how I could not take him in because Emet was my ward. I poured out my heart about Kale and told Lou that I felt connected to him in a way I hadn't felt since Emet came along. Earlier that day, the review board had informed me that it might be too late for Kale even if Emet signed off on his release—all due to the evidence that he'd been involved in the prostitution ring and not just the drugs when he was under Carson's thumb.

"Pretty much as long as he is a ward of the state, they are not willing to pursue rehabilitation beyond his contract, which will soon come to an end. I can't adopt him and don't know what to do. I've prayed about it nonstop since coming back from our last run to the Surface. If he dies because of me ..." I trailed off as nausea threatened to overtake me again. What could I do?

"I see this is very important to you, and the fact that you love him so dearly moves me. If adopting him is the only way to save his life, why not consider having him as a brother instead?"

Surprised, I looked up at my father in disbelief. "Are you saying you would adopt him?"

He smiled at me, reached across the table, and took my hand. "Roark, you are my son, and watching you become physically ill because someone you love is being threatened hurts me too. I've fostered many children over the years while I searched for you. I never thought I would officially adopt anyone else, but Kale is part of the family you've made, which makes him one of my children, as well as Emet. Why not make it legal and official and give him the loving home he never knew he could have?"

I stood, walked around the table, and hugged my dad hard,

not caring what anyone else thought about us at that moment. Everything seemed to drain out of me as he embraced me back, and I could feel the weariness of the last few days creeping up on me. I had barely sat down before our waiter brought us the main course, and I found myself starving.

"When are you going to adopt him?" I made myself hold off on eating until I had an answer, even though all I wanted to do was shovel the food in.

"How about I go in first thing in the morning and take care of everything? I might meet with some resistance, but if you are willing to throw around your Crimson Soldier authority, we can have everything taken care of by the afternoon, and he can be your brother before the day is over. Now, eat your dinner."

With a smile and an elated heart, I dug into the gourmet meal in front of me. Tomorrow I was going to be a big brother. I had never thought I would have a family, and I couldn't believe how blessed I was. *Thank You, my Father and King, for the family You have given me. I pray that You guide us as we begin this journey together and teach me Your ways so that I might be a light before them. In Yeshua's name, I pray. Amen.*

# Chapter Forty-Seven

Asherex

I awoke for the first time in five days with feeling in my arms and legs and took my time stretching every muscle I could before opening my eyes. The last five days, during which I'd been bedridden, nearly had crushed me and caused me to miss Shavuot. I was thankful Lazerick had come with Aiden to assist Jonathan and Michael with my care. During that time, Aiden and Jonathan had bonded over their mechanical abilities, and last night, Aiden had spent hours talking about how much he admired Jonathan.

"It's about time you woke up." Lazerick's teasing tone drew my attention, and I could see the laughter dancing in his champagne-colored eyes. He was in one of those moods again, and it showed as he pulled his curly, shoulder-length silver-and-blond hair into a ponytail and said, "I was beginning to wonder if I needed to drag you outside for the buzzards."

I threw a pillow at him, and his mischievous laughter filled the air. Within moments, Aiden burst through the door with his plex in hand and earbuds in, blaring music that everyone could hear, like a typical teenager. He smiled at me as I sat up and motioned for him to come close, and as soon as he was within arm's reach, I snagged his earbuds and said, "Are you deaf, boy? Just because you can have your eardrums repaired doesn't mean you are free to damage them."

"Sorry, Dad." He shut off the music and asked, "How are you feeling today?"

"I'm ready to get out of this bed and take a proper shower. No offense, but the two of you are lousy at giving sponge baths."

Aiden scrunched up his face at me before Lazerick said, "Well, if you would've let us put you in the tub"—my heart skipped a beat at the thought of being immersed in water—"we wouldn't have had that problem."

He knew I was terrified of being in water, and he was using it as a way to get under my skin, but before I could snap back at him, Jonathan appeared in the doorway and said, "Lazerick, Michael was wondering if you could help him adjust one of the solar panels on the main hall's roof. I already told him you would, so he's waiting for you."

Lazerick looked at him with an evil smile before he turned back to me and, with an exasperated tone, said, "Master, can you believe the nerve of this kid?" Lazerick was on his feet and out the door before I could toss the covers aside.

Aiden couldn't stop laughing. "The two of you crack me up."

Aiden's voice, mixed with laughter, made me smile before I grabbed him and pulled him into a headlock. We wrestled for a few minutes before Aiden broke free, rushed across the room to the door, grabbed Jonathan, and ran off with him so I wouldn't come after him for slipping away. I had missed that boy.

After taking a quick shower and dressing, I called my dad. I had talked to him a few times while paralyzed but hadn't asked him to come see me, because I hadn't wanted him to see me like that. He answered on the last ring, and I smiled as he came into view, tucked away in his office. He never let the senate chaos interfere with our conversations.

"Asherex, how are you feeling?"

"I'm doing a lot better today. Dad, can I be selfish and ask you for something?" My heart pounded as I prepared to ask him to fly four hours to come visit with me so that we could have the heart-to-heart talk I'd been putting off since Mom died. He didn't know it was going to happen, and I wasn't about to tell him, in case he didn't come.

"Whatever you need from me, consider it done."

"Come spend the afternoon with me."

My father was on his feet as soon as the words left my mouth. He told me he would see me in four and a half hours, and we ended the call.

Shock filled me as I made my way to the kitchen. It was a little after seven o'clock in the morning, and it was preparation day, which meant my father would get here around noon, and we would have only a few hours together before he had to leave.

Kyandra surprised me at the foot of the stairs with a smile on her face as she asked me to join her in the kitchen for a late breakfast. I sat at the bistro table while she danced around the kitchen, cooking pumpkin pancakes while humming. She had spent a lot of time with me over the last five days, and we had talked about almost everything we could think of. She knew everything about me except for my fear of drowning, which had kept me from taking a bath my whole life.

During our conversations, I had convinced her to hire a private investigator to find her fiancé. Part of me wanted her to know what had befallen him, and a small piece of me wanted to be selfish and have her for myself for what little life I had left in me. It was dumb to be falling in love with a woman, when I was just going to die on her and leave her with nothing more than a few months' worth of memories, but I couldn't help myself. I figured I was dying anyway, so why hold back?

We ate together and talked about the music they were thinking about playing tonight. I looked at Kyandra and asked, "Do you think they would let me sing a song I wrote?"

"You can sing?" Kyandra looked surprised.

Aiden popped his head into the room and said, "Dad's going to sing? Now I have to stay to hear him. He hates singing in public. I've only heard him a few times in my life, and man, can he sing!"

"Don't let him lie to you." Lazerick's unexpected voice coming from the other room caught us all off guard as he entered the kitchen. "Asherex is very modest and thinks he has an average voice, but he could have made a career of it had he wanted to. The kid can sing like a pro without ever having to practice."

"Thanks a lot, Dad. Now she's going to be expecting something spectacular and be disappointed," I said.

He seemed unfazed by my sarcasm. "You're welcome." Lazerick turned to Kyandra before continuing. "Like I said, don't let him lie to you, and if he is offering to sing, don't let anyone stop that."

I shook my head at him, and he responded with one of his toothy smiles that made him look like a child. Then he turned his attention back to Kyandra and said, "Do you and Michael care if Aiden and I stay for the Sabbath? The kid has his heart set on staying, and he is the pilot, so I don't have much say in the matter."

"Of course both of you can stay. It is the least we can do after you guys flew here to help us with Ash during Shavuot."

Lazerick's plex rang, drawing him out of the kitchen, and Kyandra picked up our conversation as if it had never been interrupted. We were so engrossed in conversation that we didn't notice that several hours had passed, and it was time for Kyandra to make lunch. While she prepped the barbecue chicken flatbreads with greens and some kind of dressing, I decided I should go upstairs and grab my plex in case someone had been trying to get in touch with me.

I had more than a dozen messages from Larissa, Nayomi, and the triplets, so I sat on the bed and responded to them. I didn't realize how tired I was until I had the holographic screen in front of me, and I decided to lie down to rest my eyes for a moment. If I fell asleep, my dad would call me when he was close and wake me up.

A gentle hand on my shoulder pulled me out of deep sleep, and I opened my eyes while my foggy brain attempted to find out what time it was but failed. That was happening more and more lately. As soon as my eyes focused, I saw my father's light blue-green eyes staring back at me. Without a second thought, I sat up, pulled him into a hug, and felt like a small child being comforted by his father after being sick, instead of a twenty-six-year-old.

I pulled out of the hug and asked, "How long have you been here?"

"I got here an hour ago and have spent that time talking with Kyandra and Jonathan. I didn't want to wake you." He smiled at me again, and I could tell he wanted to say something, but he held back and said, "Jonathan is extraordinary. I see why you love him. He's so respectful and kind—something I'm not used to seeing in teens these days—and Aiden has taken quite a shine to him." He was quiet for a minute with a soft smile before he continued. "Kyandra seems like a very genuine woman, and she cares for you more than she realizes."

I couldn't help the butterfly feeling that filled me upon hearing my father say that about Kyandra. Even though I had loved Lillie, I had never felt like this before with her. I thought I felt bad about it, but I didn't. With a wistful sigh, I looked at my dad and said, "I'm not sure staying here was the best idea, because I'm just going to hurt her when I pass away."

My dad touched me on the shoulder and said, "Son, one thing I've learned over the years is that you cannot make decisions for other people like that. If she already had feelings for you before you decided to stay and you'd left, she would have been here wondering if you had died. It would have eaten her alive, not knowing."

"Perhaps you are right." I smiled at my father before saying, "I slept through lunch and am starving. How about we sit downstairs at the dining table and talk while I eat?"

We headed downstairs and sat at the table while Kyandra heated up some lunch for me. I ate everything she had left, enough to feed four people, while I caught up with my dad on the latest news in

Adreia. An hour into our conversation, I finally found the courage to say what I needed to say. It was now or never.

"Dad, I need to talk to you about something I've put off for a long time."

He looked at me. His eyes were emotionless, no doubt because we hadn't argued about something yet, and that was how all our conversations had ended over the last seventeen years since Mom died.

I let out a breath and said, "I'm sorry for everything that has kept us apart all these years. When Mom died, I didn't know what to do, and I needed you, but you left me with Veris and Larissa for a whole year. It was like I lost both of you at the same time. When you finally came back, I was so hurt that I didn't want to be around you. Then you were so focused on your political career that I got left behind, and you didn't have time for me. When I turned twelve, I was surprised that you signed the waiver for me to go to basic and then start a military career, but then you didn't show up for graduation, even though I had pushed myself to break most of the records and graduated with honors.

"I resented you after that and got to the point that I hated coming home on leave, because I was forced to be part of your political career. I was nothing more than the savant child with a prestigious military career ahead of him for you to show off to your friends, benefactors, and rivals. I did it because you were my father, and I didn't want to ruin your reputation, but I despised it so much. It's why I moved out to be on my own when I turned seventeen.

"When I was promoted to unit leader at fifteen and you were finally elected to the senate, I could tell you were ready to try being my dad, but I was indifferent by then. I thought I knew better and didn't need you in my life. After I married Lillie, I started to see just how wrong I was, but I didn't know how to fix it. Every time I tried to bring it up, we just argued, which was entirely my fault because I wasn't ready to let go of the past."

"It wasn't all your fault." My dad's voice choked up, and I forced myself to look into his eyes while mine filled with tears. "I never should have left you. I was being selfish and grieving for everyone I had lost all at once. Some secrets had been kept from you, and I couldn't bear them after she died. I should have tried harder."

"I wouldn't have let you even if you had. I wasn't exactly being rational. You tried harder than you think, but I refused to let you close, and I'm sorry."

My father stood and said, "Asherex Gid'on Reach, this is not your fault; it's mine. I should be the one apologizing to you. I'm so sorry that I made you feel abandoned. Can you ever forgive me?"

I stood and walked over to my father, pulled him into a tight embrace, and said, "Yes, you are forgiven." The tears fell when he wrapped his arms around me, and something inside me broke. We hadn't embraced like this since before Mom died. In fact, we hadn't been all that close while she was alive. He had kept his distance and watched me with wary eyes, as if he were expecting me to kill him at any moment.

After what seemed like an eternity, he released me, and I sat back down, feeling weary. He looked at me with a deep sadness in his eyes and said, "There is something I have to tell you." He was quiet for so long that I thought he wouldn't continue, but finally, he sighed and said, "After the accident when you lost your memory, your mother and I consulted with many doctors and decided not to tell you anything about who you had been before the accident. Asherex, you had a twin sister who was dragged off by wolves with the other fourteen children who disappeared the day you fell through the ice."

All the breath in my lungs exploded out at once. I'd had a twin sister, who was gone, and I never had known about it. Was that the reason I had been searching so hard for something more?

"What was her name?" A part of me hoped I would recall something about her, but after twenty-one years, I hadn't remembered a thing from before the accident.

"Her name was AnnaLee. It was the name my father wanted to use if he had a girl. The two of you were identical in every way except for your attitude. She was calm, loving, sweet, curious, outspoken, and always smiling."

My father closed his eyes as if the memory was just as painful now as it had been all those years ago. I couldn't imagine being unable to talk about losing a child while having to look at her identical copy every day. It was heartbreaking, and I wasn't sure what to think about the fact that my parents, Larissa and Veris, and all six of their older children had kept this from me my whole life. They had acted as if I were a complete stranger to them when I first met them after the accident.

My father shook his head, drawing my attention, before looking me straight in the eye and saying, "Asherex, you were as different from your sister as the day is from the night. You never spoke to anyone or looked others in the eye. When you decided to communicate, it was through screams, growls, and this awful noise that gave people nightmares. We couldn't control you, and you became more and more violent the older you got. We had to pull you and your sister out of public school because you put kids in the hospital, and no one would tutor you, so your mom quit her job to teach both of you.

"Because of everything you were doing, you were forced to see a shrink, but all you did was become violent, and he stopped seeing you after you bit him. After that, you were put on a watch list. If you put one more person in the hospital, you would be moved to the decommission list, and if you didn't improve, you were to be put down when you turned six. We thought you were doing better for a while, until your mother and sister went out of town, and you found a kitchen knife and broke into my room."

My father closed his eyes again, and I could tell this was difficult for him to say. I couldn't believe I had been such a monster as a child.

"You stabbed me three times in the chest before I broke free. I threw you into the bathroom and locked you inside by knocking over the gun safe. I could hear you screaming in pain from your broken arm and fractured skull because of me while I ran away. I managed to drag myself to the front door. You hid my plex before attacking me. I tried to get out to the car so I could call for help, but I passed out as soon as the front door opened. If it hadn't been for a neighbor coming home and seeing that the door was wide open, I would have died.

"They wanted to put you down that night instead of taking you to the hospital, but your mother made it back before they could make the decision and convinced them to put you on the decommission list. She tried so hard to rehabilitate you, but it was obvious that you would not change."

"The accident was six weeks before my sixth birthday." My voice filled the still air between us, and he looked at me as if I were a treasured possession. He nodded, unable to say anything else, due to the overwhelming emotion welling up inside him and spilling down his cheeks. I couldn't imagine having to keep that kind of secret for twenty-one years, and suddenly, Veris's actions to sterilize Lillie made sense. He knew what I had been like and probably had feared any children we had would be just like I had been. I felt sadness creep up on me, knowing he had died a few days ago. He had just been trying to protect his family and had ended up causing Lillie's death.

"Is that why you wouldn't stay home alone with me for years and why Mom wasn't allowed to be left in a room alone with me?" I whispered the words, unable to say them louder. I hadn't understood why my parents were so distant from me while I was growing up, but now I knew. It wasn't every day that children were deemed unfit to enter society and sentenced to death. I must have been an absolute monster.

"Yes." He was quiet for so long that I was afraid he wouldn't say anything else, but he finally broke the silence and said, "We never should have treated you like that."

I stood up, pulled him into a hug, and whispered in his ear, "I forgive you for everything." He tightened his grip on me, and even though it was too tight of an embrace, I relished it.

# Chapter Forty-Eight

Asherex

My father and I spent all afternoon walking around the community while I told him about my new faith. I could talk to him about it on a different level than Drayen, and it was refreshing to talk to my dad like that. Our conversation was predominantly intellectual, without either of us bringing up feelings, until the end, when he shared that his father, Yo'ash, had become religious when my father was ten years old. I tried not to feel as if he'd cheated me out of something that important about our family history, but I still felt a little betrayed.

The Shabbat service had been such a blessing tonight, and I was thoroughly worn out by ten o'clock. I had spent the last thirty minutes sitting in a chair with a six-year-old girl asleep on my lap while watching my father interact with the people of the community. They'd asked me to open the music service with my song. Halfway through it, I had realized that my father had never heard me sing before. After I'd finished the piece and sat back down, Dad had told me he was proud of me. I had heard that from him only one other time in my life, a year after I had taken Aiden in and transformed him from a stubborn, wild child into a happy, eager-to-learn boy.

I looked down at the beautiful blonde-haired girl sleeping on my lap, and for a moment, pain lanced my heart at the thought that I had no child of my own. My line would end with me. I was leaving my father without an heir, and even though he was going to have a child with Larissa, it wouldn't be the same unless he stepped up and took responsibility for his actions and her father and the judges decided to pardon his crime. Having an affair with a married woman was one of the things a Crimson Soldier couldn't get away with.

I closed my eyes only to have my father gently shake me awake. The girl's uncle took her from me before Dad helped me to my feet, and we walked back to Kyandra's. As we walked, I looked up at the stars and asked my dad, "What did you think about the service tonight?"

"It was different. Kind of reminded me of being in the Wastelands with Tarren."

I smiled as a thousand memories of hearing his adventures in the Wastelands swirled in my mind. I could tell he was battling with himself after the service, but I didn't know how much more I could talk to him about it before he started pulling away. Maybe if we had known each other better, I would have known just how much I could lay on his shoulders. With a soft sigh, I sent up a quick, silent prayer that he would come to know Yeshua before I died and find comfort.

Once in the house, I took a shower, dressed in pajamas, and lounged on the bed while Dad finished a call with his assistant. He hung up and sat on the other side of the bed with sadness filling his eyes, knowing that our time together was drawing to a close since he was leaving at midnight. I looked him in the eye and asked, "Dad, can you tell me more about Grandpa?"

With a smile, he lay back against the pillows. I moved over to lay my head on his shoulder as I had done as a child. I grabbed his hand, linking our fingers together—something I'd never been able to do with him—and he let out a sigh, relaxed, and said, "My father was kidnapped and forced to become a citizen slave in Adreia after he helped some soldiers fix their airship. He started out with nothing and had no family to help him. I guess his family back home was religious, just like these people here, but he didn't really believe it himself and didn't until after my mom walked out on us when I was ten.

"He worked hard to afford a place to live and food to eat. He only had three outfits and took care of them better than most people take care of their cars. Yo'ash was very intelligent, almost on the same level as you, Asherex. Everyone knew it, but he refused to give his captors what they wanted, so he had to struggle for everything because they made his life a waking nightmare. He met my mother a few years later, and they got married. After they had me, Dad started questioning his religious upbringing. He wanted to raise me with their traditions, but Mom wasn't going to have it, so I didn't even know about it until he started homeschooling me. But even then, he was very cautious about sharing with me. I think he was afraid he would lose me if Mom found out.

"When I was five, his workplace sent him to a convention where he met Victor Rayas. They ended up becoming friends and going into business together. Less than a year later, Victor lost his wife in childbirth, and my father spent a lot of time consoling him and trying to help him with the lawsuit and his hearing-impaired infant. It put a lot of strain on his marriage, and when I turned ten, Mom walked out on us. She committed suicide a few months later. I hated him for that because he told me it was his fault. I didn't learn until after he died that he had told me that so I wouldn't blame myself for her leaving.

"After she was gone, he started digging into his family's religion and tried teaching me, but I didn't want to hear it. He had to put me in public school because his business demanded his presence, and without a second income, he couldn't afford to homeschool me. I met Veris, and we became friends. At least I thought so. Now that I look back on it, I realize he was just using me because he thought my dad was rich, and he didn't want to be the poor kid anymore. I was a fool to believe he was ever my friend, but I wanted a friend so badly that I was willing to turn a blind eye to his usury.

"Dad tried many times to get me to see Veris's true nature, but I was rebellious, and whatever he told me to do, I would do the opposite to spite him." He trailed off, as if reliving something from the past, before he looked me in the eye and said, "When I look back on it now, I am ashamed because I was so hateful and disrespectful of my father, and I didn't care if we were in public when I went off on him. The only time I didn't act out in public was if Victor's son, Kress, was with us. Asherex, as much as we fought and argued, you never once said one negative thing to others about me or raised your voice to me in public. Every time we would fight, no one would bring it up later, because no one knew about it. I relived all the public fights I had with my dad, and I started hating myself more and more. I don't deserve you."

He wrapped his arms around me, pulling me close, as silent tears streamed down his face. I didn't know what to say. I had been afraid that if I damaged my father's reputation, he would throw me out of his life entirely, so I hadn't dared to say a word about him to anyone outside of my most trusted friends. I couldn't tell him that without him thinking worse about himself, so I lay there quietly while gently touching his arm.

It was now past eleven, and we hadn't spoken any more about Yo'ash. I wanted to bring up Larissa and the pregnancy but wasn't sure how to go about it without starting a fight. I let out a sigh and said, "Dad?"

"Yes, Asherex?"

"Can I give you some advice about Larissa?"

He stiffened up a bit before saying, "I don't want to fight about it, but I am willing to listen to what you have to say."

"You need to do the right thing. Now that Veris is dead, she needs strong support for what lies ahead, and raising her kids on her own will be really hard. I know her dad loves you, so you need to talk to him and tell him the truth about Larissa being pregnant with your child. I'm confident he won't press charges, and after that, you have to hold a press conference to announce it to the whole country before any news channel can grab a hold of it and twist the story.

"The people of Adreia elected you, and you haven't even tried to get reelected since the first time, because they vote for you regardless of whether you are running. The people love you, and they know that you fight for them every day, so they deserve to hear the truth from you. No one will demand your arrest, knowing that you and Larissa both were grieving and made a mistake. It happens all the time, and the people will sympathize with you. It's a political move but also the right thing to do; all you have to do is listen to whatever Larissa's father tells you to do."

He sighed and said, "I hate to say it, but you are right. You would have made a great politician, Asherex."

"Just because I know how to play the game doesn't mean I want to."

He chuckled. "You're right." He moved so that he could cup my face in his hand and look me in the eye before saying, "You would have been an amazing commander in chief one day, Asherex; you are a born leader."

I smiled. "Yehovah has other plans for me."

He sighed hard and replied, "If only they were plans to prosper you and not to kill you."

"I will live, Dad, whether in this life or the one to come. I've been more alive now since the moment I started dying. Everything before I knew Him seems like a distant memory, a dream. I wouldn't trade it for anything, and I want you to know this kind of joy and peace that I have found."

There were tears in his blue-green eyes again, and I laid my head on his chest. My own heart pounded as I lay there listening to his heart beating, something I had never done in my life. He had never let me get that close, and as I listened to his strong heartbeat, my mind returned to the first time Aiden had done this with me. He'd crawled onto the couch to watch a movie, but halfway through, he'd turned away from the holoprojector and rested his head on my chest, above my heart. After ten minutes, I finally had asked him what he was doing, because he was missing the movie. My heart had nearly broken at his reply: "Dad, I wanted to hear what home sounded like." He had never known his father, and when I first had taken him in, he had started calling me Dad as an insult to push me away. That moment on the couch had been the first time he called me Dad and meant it. That night had changed everything between us and made me realize I wasn't as close to my father as I'd thought I was. There were a thousand little things I never had known parents did with their kids until Aiden came into my life.

I closed my eyes and just enjoyed the moment. It was hard to believe I was twenty-six years old and was just now the closest I had ever been with my father. Jonathan had been right that I had an opportunity with my dad that few ever got, and I would cherish this moment for the rest of my life.

My father shook me awake more forcefully than he had before. It took my foggy, disoriented brain a few moments to realize another coughing fit had overtaken me, and I had to fight for every breath. The fear of drowning tried to overtake me, and then my father's face came into view. His calm voice brought me back from the brink of panic. He was wearing the quarantine respirator now and had put on the protective suit to prevent my blood from contacting his skin; only part of his face was exposed now.

It seemed like hours passed before the coughing subsided, and I could only take shallow, wheezing breaths. All my strength was gone, and my dad was the only thing holding me in a position that allowed me to breathe. I looked over at the clock and stared at the numbers for what seemed like an eternity before I could tell that it was a quarter after two in the morning.

"Dad." I barely managed to wheeze out the whisper.

He quickly grabbed my hand and said, "I'm here, Son. I'm here."

"You're going to be late." I wasn't sure if he heard me.

Then he whispered back, "I know. I'm not abandoning you again when you need me."

I squeezed his hand and weakly said, "I need you to go now. I'm going to be okay. It's not time yet."

He unwrapped his arms from around me, stacked pillows up in his place, crawled off the bed, and came around to look me in the eye before taking my hand and saying, "Asherex, I—" His words were choked off.

I squeezed his hand with all the strength I could muster and whispered, "I love you, Dad."

Tears spilled down his face as he told me that he loved me. I could see on his face that the decision to leave tore at him, but I was too tired to fight through the weariness to ask him to go. Lazerick appeared in the doorway with sadness in his champagne-colored eyes. He was leaving with my dad, and I knew I wouldn't see him in person again. Lazerick, with all his quirks, had been like a father to me over the years. Now everything I had belonged to him and Aiden.

I had asked him to finish the citizenship paperwork for Aiden's father to be able to move to Adreia from Brashex so the kid would finally meet him. I respected Aiden's father more than anyone could understand, and all he had ever wanted was to be able to see his son. I regretted that I wouldn't be there to introduce them. I should have fought harder for him to move sooner.

My dad gently stroked the side of my face, drawing my attention. He removed his respirator to kiss my forehead and told me goodbye, but I stopped him before he moved away. I pulled my wedding band off my finger. It was the first time I had ever removed it, and I felt as if I were closing a door that I had been forcing to stay open. I placed the ring in his hand and whispered, "Give that to Larissa." It was customary to return the wedding band to the bride's parents whenever a marriage ended, but I hadn't been willing to say goodbye yet.

"I will, Son. Don't you worry about it."

"Take care of Aiden, and be there for my baby brother or sister. Don't hold anything back this time, Dad."

"I won't repeat my mistakes with them. I promise. I will take care of them, so don't you worry." He kissed my forehead again and then walked away with tears streaming down his face.

Lazerick sat on the edge of the bed, took my hand, and said, "I'm not going to kiss you." His teasing tone made me smile. He shook his head before saying, "I think he will be all right; your dad is very strong, but I'm going to miss you. I never had a kid before you came along, and it isn't right that a father has to bury his son. I love you, kid."

"I love you too, Dad."

He smiled at me before pulling a syringe out of his pocket and said, "I know you don't want it, but I can't leave knowing that you are in pain. You say it isn't your time yet, so I'm believing you and leaving knowing that you are sleeping peacefully."

I weakly nodded at him before he injected me with whatever was in the syringe. Warmth spread throughout my body, and my heavy eyelids closed, dragging me into sleep.

# Chapter Forty-Nine

Emet

It was the Sabbath, and my master had summoned me back to the mansion. I sighed when Roark dropped me off and left me standing on the stone steps. I didn't want to be here and was tempted to call Roark back and just leave with him, but I knew I had to do what my master asked of me. It took me several minutes to finally walk up the last six steps and go inside.

I was halfway across the foyer, when the doorbell rang, and I quickly turned to answer it. Shock flooded through me when I saw Senator Reach on the other side, looking as if he'd slept in his clothes. He pierced me with his intense blue-green eyes and asked, "Is your master home?"

Before I could answer, Victor's voice boomed across the foyer. "What do you want, Azriel?"

Azriel walked past me into the room, and I closed the door behind him, waiting to see what would happen. I knew he always carried at least one gun beneath his senatorial robes. They stared each other down like two predators sizing each other up before Azriel finally said, "I have some questions for you."

"About what?" My master's dark brown eyes were full of venom, and his tone was anything but friendly.

"My father." As soon as the words left Azriel's mouth, the fight drained out of Victor, and something flickered in his eyes that I hadn't seen since before I was officially his property. Azriel took a step toward my master and said, "I didn't come here to fight with you; I just want answers. You were closer to him than I was."

Victor looked at me and then back at Azriel before motioning for us to come to his office. I stood, unsure why I was there, while Azriel sat. My master looked him directly in the eye before saying, "Why now? It's been almost thirty years since Yo'ash died, and you haven't asked me a single question about him in all that time."

"My son is asking questions I don't have answers for. I need to know about his faith and how he came into it. He tried telling me about it, but I didn't want to hear it at the time. Now my son has given in to this illusion, and I at least owe it to him to tell him his grandfather's legacy before he passes away."

I was surprised to hear that Asherex had come into faith in Yeshua, and I remembered the kid I had set free the day while we were looking for my high commander. Could it be that he'd found Asherex, as I had asked him to? I had only wanted the kid to leave so I wasn't tempted to run away.

"Yo'ash often told me about his family back on the Surface. They were all devout followers of the religion he never named. He only said he was a Yisra'elite. When we first met, he talked about it because it was what he had grown up with, but he didn't believe any of it, at least not until after his wife killed herself. After that, something changed, and he started living his life following the traditions of his family.

"I thought it was all nonsense, but I didn't try to stop him, because that's not what a friend should do. He was a lot happier because of it, and even though it drove me mad and he convinced Kress to believe it, I only rebuked him to keep it quiet in public. It's not illegal, but many would have taken offense to it and put a target on his back if he had talked about it publicly.

"The truth is that I didn't pay much mind to his craziness, and if you want to know more about that religion, you should ask Emet. As for your father, he wholeheartedly believed that it was real for seven years, and I watched him change so much in that time before he died."

I watched my master's eyes lighten and fill with compassion with every word that proceeded from his mouth. It was awe-inspiring to see the darkness disappear, and I could see the deep sadness within from the loss of his friend. My heart hurt for him, and I silently prayed.

They continued to talk for nearly an hour before Azriel had to leave and get back to the senate. Azriel made it to the office door, when my master spoke up, stopping him dead in his tracks, saying, "I didn't kill your father, Azriel. I know you think I did, but if it wasn't an accident, I had nothing to do with it."

Without looking back, Azriel shook his head and walked off. My master had been Azriel's patron, a role most on the Surface called a godfather, but he had been unsuccessful in stepping into that role because of Azriel's hatred toward him. I wondered if things would have been different if Azriel had stayed with Victor. I knew that being around Azriel was always bittersweet for my master, and no matter how much Azriel embarrassed him, he never beat me on a day when he had been around Azriel. Even now, after nearly thirty years, Victor kept his word to Yo'ash about protecting his son.

My master looked at me as if just realizing I was there, and I could see the darkness overtaking him again. I released a shaky breath and asked, "Are you mad at me?"

The surprise on his face seemed out of place for him, and he shook his head and said, "I'm not mad at you, Emet. I seem to have forgotten why I asked you here today." He trailed off, reached into his pocket, and withdrew a prescription bottle before taking the cap off and looking at the dwindling pills inside. With a sigh, he replaced the cap and handed me the pills, saying, "Dispose of these for me. I don't need them anymore."

I looked at the label as he walked away and was surprised to find that they were for helping an addict recover from drug addiction. I had written that prescription for him in my first year as a doctor, and he should have had only one round with three refills and then been free from his addictions. I knew he hadn't been using drugs since then, so why was he taking the pills?

"Why are you still taking these?"

He was nearly in the other room, when my concerned question stopped him. He turned and said, "They didn't work the first time around, so Saz has been supplying me with them. They help me stay levelheaded, but now that he's not going to be around anymore, it is time to move forward and get rid of them."

It was impossible for someone to become addicted to the pills, and long-term exposure to them caused so many health problems for the user that there was no way the substance in the bottle was the labeled prescription drug. Saz had lied to him all these years, but why? What did Saz have to gain from keeping my master drugged up?

Before I could say a word, the front door burst open, and Proxy High Commander Uriah walked in as if he owned the place. He disregarded me as if I were nothing more than dirt on the floor and then looked at Victor and said, "We have a problem, and you're going to have to do something about it!"

"You had better watch your tone with me, Uriah." My master's voice was full of icy authority, and a murderous gleam shone in his eyes. This was the man I had known my whole life. He was ready for a fight, but for once, someone else was the recipient of his hostility.

"The nanos have been destroyed by that worthless piece of garbage—"

"Crimson Soldier Verity"—Victor interrupted Uriah, enraging him—"is off-limits now, thanks to you. I told you that storing the nanos was your responsibility in exchange for a high commander position—a position you rejected, by the way. I removed Bane from office, but you were too greedy."

"I told you that the Crimson Division was what I wanted, not the Opal Division!"

"You insolent, impatient child! How dare you come in here blaming me for your incompetence!"

Uriah pulled out a gun at the same time my master lunged at him. I didn't stick around to find out what would happen next. Without thinking twice, I bolted outside and kept running. I ran until I couldn't run anymore and collapsed on the sidewalk outside the shopping district. My whole body ached, and I trembled as I called Roark. He looked at me without asking any questions and told me he would come get me.

I spent the next two hours replaying what had happened and wondering if someone had died back at the mansion. Surely by now, someone had discovered a bloody scene, and they would see that I had fled the mansion. Paranoia set in, and with every Opal Division soldier who passed by me, my fear that the authorities were coming for me grew.

When Roark found me, I was shaking violently and felt sick. I didn't know how he managed to get me into his cruzer. He kept talking to me, but I didn't hear a word he said. I was still in shock and didn't start coming back to myself until we were nearly home. My plex chimed, drawing my attention, and I opened the messages to see that Victor had messaged me several times, asking me if I was okay and if I had made it out safely. I sent him a quick message telling him I was at Roark's now and closed down my plex.

"Do you want to talk about what happened?" Roark's voice was both authoritative and concerned.

"I don't know. It doesn't make sense." I shook my head. I couldn't tell Roark what I had heard. Had my master killed High Commander Bane? If he had, Roark would kill him because he and Ezekiel had been friends. I didn't know enough to accuse anyone of anything. What had they been talking about concerning nanos?

"Maybe you should go take a hot bath and lie down. You look like you're not feeling well."

"Okay."

That was the end of our conversation, and I went inside and did as he suggested, but all I could do was stare at the wall, reliving the events of this strange day. *O Yehovah, strengthen me, and guide me. Tell Your servant what to do, because I don't know what I'm doing.*

# Chapter Fifty

## Roark

It was the day after the Sabbath, and I was on my way back home from a lab where I had taken the little whitish-green pills Emet had asked me to get tested. It turned out the pills were a nasty street drug called VX-473, but because I didn't have the proper clearance, the lab couldn't tell me what the drug did. Apparently, one had to be a specialized rehabilitation doctor like Emet or be part of the Opal drug division to get the details on it without filing a petition. I decided not to file and just to ask Emet how he'd ended up with the drugs in the first place.

I did my best to control my temper and keep my frustration in check as I landed my cruzer and went inside. I yelled for Emet, but there was no answer, and the house was eerily quiet. Panic started to set in after I yelled for him a few more times only to have silence greet me. With my heart pounding in my chest, I ran to his room, where I found him on his knees with his face to the floor in prayer.

My temper returned to the forefront, and it took all I had to keep my voice level as I said his name a few more times. He was so deep in concentration that he couldn't hear me. I shook him a little more violently than I intended, and he jumped and looked at me, startled. Bewildered and on the brink of losing control of my anger,

I said, "Did you not hear me? I've been calling for you for the last five minutes! I thought you had been kidnapped or something."

"I'm sorry. I didn't hear you."

Trying not to let my anger explode, I took a deep breath and just walked away. There was no doubt Emet could tell I was angry, since he had seen me like that many times over the last ten years. I paced back and forth through the living room before sitting on the couch—the first time I'd ever sat on the thing—and bowed my head to pray. I knew I should have done that before panicking and probably before I had come into the house ready to attack someone.

I prayed aloud for a half hour, asking for help with my temper, not caring if Emet heard me. When I finally looked up, he was resting against the wall, staring at me with a soft smile on his face. It was probably the first time I hadn't unleashed the full brunt of my temper against him, and seeing him looking at me now made me feel terrible for all the times I had made him flinch back from my words. I was beginning to realize that my words held power and had to be controlled.

"I'm sorry, Emet. I shouldn't have snapped on you like that."

"It's all right. I know that people don't change overnight." He crossed the room and sat in the recliner. "It is a process that takes time."

I didn't deserve a friend like him. I smiled at him and said, "So the drug you had me go test is illegal, and they wouldn't tell me anything about it because I don't have proper clearance. It's called VX-473."

I watched his eyebrows draw down and could see the wheels turning in his eyes as he started connecting dots. After a minute, he looked back at me, his eyes gleaming with tears, and said, "It is known as Vex on the streets, and it is highly addictive. It can open the mind and is favored by inventors and big businessmen who need clarity for a project. Thousands of people get hooked on it every year and end up getting themselves killed while on it, because the side effects are increased libido and aggression. It is the most-confiscated drug in underground prostitution rings, because in low doses like the ones I had you test, it increases the sex drive in the prostitutes, so the ringleader can make more money. When it is taken with another drug that negates the effects of the increased rage, it becomes ten times more likely to kill the user."

"Okay, and why did Victor have them?"

"I don't think he knows what they are. He had a drug problem when I was younger, but as soon as I could write prescriptions, he had me write him one for what was actually on the bottle, so he could break his addiction. Victor told me it didn't work, and Saz has been supplying him with pills since then."

I couldn't believe what I was hearing. It was insane! Victor's friend and business partner had drugged him for all those years.

I shook my head and said, "So Saz has been drugging Victor, which explains the sudden bursts of uncontrollable rage, but what does Saz get out of it?"

Emet gave me a look that spoke volumes. It was full of disgust and embarrassment.

I couldn't help but ask, "Sex?"

He made a face and blushed but didn't say a word. I knew that Saz was an evil monster, and no one dared to touch him after what had happened to him years ago. He had attempted to turn in his higher-ranking officers for participating in human trafficking but hadn't realized the man he went to was also involved. They'd beaten him and left him for dead, but he somehow had survived, and when they'd found out about it, they'd butchered his family in front of him. After that, they'd shot him and thrown him into a river, but he had survived that too and come back with a vengeance. Saz had armed himself after he was healed enough to wield a weapon, walked right into a summit meeting, and shot up the place.

Thirty-six people had died that day, and he had taken out all but two of the people involved in his family's murders. He'd surrendered, and the authorities had launched an investigation into the original matter as well as the murders of Saz's family. By the time the case had reached the courts, a new commander in chief had come into office, and at the request of the Adreian people, he'd pardoned Saz. After that, Saz had been so messed up in the head that he'd started doing his own thing and never looked back.

Emet sighed and said, "Victor shouldn't go through detox alone. I need to be there to make sure everything goes right."

My heart clenched at his words as thousands of past images of Emet coming back here beaten to a pulp flashed through my mind. If Victor was violent on the drugs, how much more so would he be while coming off them? He had years of drug use to get cleaned up from.

"I'm not sure that is a good idea, Emet."

He looked at me with his big brown eyes full of concern and sadness, and I felt bad for a moment about being the cause of it, but it was better that he not get killed. Maybe I was being a little selfish, because it was a massive weight off my shoulders if he stayed here, where I knew he was safe. Besides, I still didn't know what had happened yesterday at Victor's to cause Emet to run off like an escaped convict or if Victor would decide to harm Emet for witnessing it.

"Why don't I take you to work tonight since you are working a double shift at the hospital and get you a nice hotel room so you are in town for your appointment with Kale in two days? That way, you can have a break from everything, like you've been wanting for a while now. If you still want to be with Victor after that, I won't hold you back, but you have to go to the spa and relax while you are there. Deal?"

He smiled at me and relented, saying, "Well, since you are insisting, I guess a day at the spa won't kill me."

I smiled at his teasing tone. It wasn't often that he joked around with me, and I cherished every moment. Hopefully, there would be many more joke-filled days ahead when he was free of Victor for good.

# Chapter Fifty-One

## Asherex

It was 12:03 a.m. on the second day of the week, and I was sitting out on the front porch, watching a meteor shower. I had never done that before. I had to admit it was the most beautiful thing I'd seen in a long time. Then again, maybe it was because my life had changed, and I was seeing everything through new eyes now. It was almost as if everything I had seen before knowing Yeshua had lacked life, and now even just looking at a tree was an experience.

Aiden had left yesterday after convincing Jonathan to think about apprenticing under him in the cruzer repair business. The two of them had become close. Aiden had taken Jonathan out for a cruise in his custom-built airship he had designed, and I was pretty sure Aiden had taught Jonathan how to drive while they were out. I hoped Jonathan decided to apprentice with Aiden, because someone who knew how to repair cars and airships could get a high-paying job anywhere. Plus, learning from the owner of the largest cruzer manufacturer and repair shop in Adreia would play a significant role in landing a job after the apprenticeship was over.

The sound of the front door closing drew my attention. Michael sat next to me on the swing with an open bottle of wine in his hand. He took a swig from the bottle before asking, "Couldn't sleep?"

"I've been sleeping too much lately. Honestly, I'm tired of being in bed and just want to enjoy the beautiful night. You know, back when I was stationed on the Surface, I never really took the time to enjoy the scenery; I was so focused on the mission that I never looked around. I missed a lot back then."

He handed me the bottle of wine, and I took it and stared at the label as he said, "A lot of people do just that, Ash. They coast through life without taking the time to stop and look around at what Elohim has made." Michael watched me for a few minutes while I continued staring at the bottle. "Is there something wrong with the wine?"

"No." I smiled at him. "It's been a few years since I've had alcohol. I promised my wife I wouldn't touch it again while we were married."

"What happened that caused you to make that promise?" Michael's voice was full of compassion. It was nice to feel like I could share with him without feeling judged.

"I was in combat, and our convoy was bombed. I underwent several operations to remove shrapnel, and it took several months to recover, but I kept feeling like something was wrong and had a dull ache in my head that never went away. The doctors all told me I was having a psychosomatic issue because I had been awake and completely aware of my injuries for thirteen hours before I was medevaced and put into a drug-induced coma. As it turned out, I had a piece of shrapnel pressing on my spinal cord, at the base of my skull. I lived with it for nearly a year and turned to alcohol to numb the pain. Lillie and I fought a lot because of it, and I was frustrated that she didn't believe me about being in pain, so our fights often ended with me losing my temper and getting in her face.

"I came home one day to find her with bags packed. She told me I had three days to decide if I wanted her or the alcohol. She went to visit her parents, and on the second day, I decided I wouldn't choose either. If I lost her, I wouldn't be able to function, but if I stopped drinking, I would be in constant pain, so I went out to the house

I was building for us, intending to kill myself. To this day, I don't know how I'm still here. I locked myself in the house, got drunk, went to the master bathroom, and got in the tub with my brand-new combat knife. I sliced my arms to the bone from wrist to elbow. I left a note on the bathroom counter, describing the pain I was in on a daily basis and saying I couldn't live one more day with it."

I shook my head at the images that flooded my mind of being locked inside that dark house alone, with the nearest neighbors six miles away. Somehow, someone had managed to break into my house without leaving a trace, patch me up, and take me to the hospital. My security cameras hadn't been able to capture the guy's face. It was the craziest thing.

"That must have been really hard for you to do, and I can't imagine what you must have felt to not have your wife's support like that."

I looked Michael in the eye and said, "Committing suicide was probably the single most difficult decision I've ever made, not because of my wife but because I've always been haunted by not knowing if there was something beyond death. I was afraid of ending up cursed if I died without knowing. That fear kept me from giving in to the suicidal thoughts after the first couple of months, and it took Lillie's threat of leaving to finally push me past the fear.

"The craziest part of the whole thing is that someone saved my life that night. Whoever gave me nanos removed all traces of blood from the bathroom, except for a few drops near where I had thrown the knife. If not for those few tiny drops near the toilet, I would never have believed I had done it. The guy who saved me busted open my skull and dropped me off at the ER, saying he had noticed a light in my house and found me passed out on the floor with a bunch of building materials on top of me.

"Because of that random faceless stranger, the doctors found the shrapnel and removed it. My wife tried to blame herself for not listening to me, and it took me a long time to convince her that it wasn't her fault. I made a promise to her about not drinking again while we were married, and I made one to myself that I would never again make her regret marrying me. I told her I loved her every day and proved it by showing her how much she meant to me every chance I got. After that, we only fought over me not talking to my dad, but now that's fixed as well, so I guess"—I pulled the bottle up to my lips—"that would be a good cause to celebrate."

I took my first drink of wine in more than four years and savored the smoky cinnamon flavor. The verse I had recently read in the scriptures about wine making the heart glad came to mind as I took another drink before handing the bottle back to Michael.

He shook his head, held up the bottle, and said, "I can drink to that. To restored relationships. L'chaim. To life and to the One who brought forth the fruit of the vine. Blessed be the name of Yehovah forever and ever. Amen!"

"Amen! L'chaim!"

He took a drink and handed the bottle back to me. We didn't talk for a while but sat there enjoying the beautiful display before us and drinking. The bottle was three-fourths of the way gone, and I was feeling pretty good and a bit buzzed, which I was starting to suspect had been his intention all along, when he broke the silence, saying, "Ash, I'm glad I met you. You've challenged me to see things differently, and I'm thankful for that. My family has been through so much. We lost our dad and his adopted father on the same day due to a civilian draft, and they never returned. Our mom couldn't cope without him and died of a broken heart a few years later. She had a mental handicap that kept her from connecting with people, but Dad loved her and chose to be with her. He never left, even on her worst days, and his love for her was the most awe-inspiring thing I've ever witnessed.

"After my father, Asheron, was gone, our mother tried so hard, but she shut down, as she had before my father came around. She loved us so much, but without him setting the example for her, she didn't know how to open up to us. Kyandra was so young that she doesn't remember Mom much, but what she does remember is Mom reading to her from the hospital bed she was confined in during her last few months."

He trailed off and sighed as if getting those memories out in the open were taking a weight off his chest. Michael took another drink and then looked at me and said, "All I ever wanted was for my sister to be happy, you know? There for a while, I thought she was when she met Steven, and they got engaged." He smiled at the memory. "They had so many plans for their future, and right before he was drafted, I finally gave my approval for their marriage, but when he never came back, she started losing hope. If you hadn't come along and convinced her to hire a private detective, she would have been waiting for him for the rest of her life, but now she can move on, knowing that Steven ran off after the battle and ended up marrying someone else."

I couldn't help the smile that crept upon my face as I remembered Kyandra getting the news about Steven yesterday. She had taken it better than I'd thought. She'd removed her engagement ring and told me she was ready to move forward. We had ended up outside on the back patio, talking about Steven and my Lillie, only bringing up the good things, so we could finally close those chapters of our lives. It had been therapeutic for me, and I had watched Kyandra come to life right before me as all the possibilities she had denied suddenly revived. I had almost given in to the urge to kiss her but had stopped myself before she realized what I was doing. She didn't need to get more attached to me than she already was.

"I believe Kyandra will be just fine; your sister is tougher than she thinks."

With a smile, Michael replied, "I know, but you have helped her so much more than you realize. After our grandparents passed away four years ago, Ky was lost and didn't really get excited about much. Then, out of the blue, she called me to tell me that Jonathan had pulled a dying man out of the river, and no one could get him into town, so she had to take him in. She might not have done much to care for your wounds, but just your being here inspired her to start baking again.

"My sister hadn't baked since our grandparents died, and then she called me every day to tell me how well you were doing. The more the two of you talked, the happier she got, and I wanted to come home so badly, but I had already given my word to help our brothers and sisters devastated by the twister. To be honest, I was a little afraid she might be tempted to fall into sin with you, but now that I've had the chance to watch the two of you together, I can clearly see that you are extremely nervous about being alone with her. If you were anyone else, you could have manipulated her with your injuries and convinced her to sleep with you, but I learned from Jonathan that you wouldn't let her near you if you didn't have a shirt on."

He sounded astonished at the thought that a man wouldn't try to trick Kyandra into having sex with him. She was beautiful, and I could see why someone might have tried it, but my father had raised me better. I took another drink of the wine and said, "My parents taught me never to let a woman who isn't your wife see you in a state of undress. Most men in Adreia with ranking military fathers or family members in the political world learn this to keep the family reputation intact. It can make going to the hospital very strange because of the female nurses, and they get very frustrated with us, but it is what it is."

Michael laughed so hard I thought he would fall off the swing. Once he caught his breath, he said, "I cannot imagine you embarrassed to be seen by a woman without your shirt on!"

I chuckled and replied, "Yeah, well, you haven't been around to see it. I don't get flustered like that very often, but I hate to admit it: I have blushed many times since being here, because Kyandra had to change my bandages several times and saw me without a shirt."

He just laughed again, and tears streamed down his face. *He must be kind of drunk, because I'm not that funny.* At least I didn't think I was.

"Oh, Ash, I'm going to miss you. I never thought I would have called an Adreian soldier my friend, but here we are." Michael let out a contented sigh, took a long draw from the bottle, and sat back, watching the peak of the meteor shower.

I started drifting off, when Michael shifted, causing the swing to move. He finished the wine before looking me in the eye and saying, "You know, the first time I saw you, you were walking into town, looking like death warmed over, and I couldn't believe you were an Adreian soldier. I watched you look at my sister and saw the moment you decided to help her, and I had no clue how you planned to help us. Those men were planning on killing us and taking Ky with them, but then you surprised us when you stood up to that punk and took his gun.

"When you took out the guy watching us, I grabbed Ky and ran to safety, only to look back and watch you get shot. I couldn't believe it when you just kept on going like nothing had happened. Then you got shot again, and I thought for sure you would go down, but you didn't even flinch. When you turned around to attack the truck, I saw the expression on your face, as if you couldn't feel a thing, and in that moment, I faced every fear I've ever had of Adreian soldiers. Everyone told me they were emotionless killing machines, and I believed it until I saw you.

"You may not have been feeling anything in that moment, but when I looked into your eyes, it was like looking into a dead man's eyes, and Yehovah revealed to me that you were nothing like what I had been told a soldier would be. You had been sent to us to save us from those thugs, and the fact that you are blessed enough not to be held back by emotions while doing what must be done makes you special."

He got quiet for a moment, as if he were reliving the moment but seeing it from another perspective. I had always thought of my inability to feel things the way a normal person did as a curse, but perhaps Michael was right, and it was a blessing. My photographic memory didn't let me forget the face of any man I'd killed, but the emotional attachments to those memories were nonexistent because there was no emotion in me during that time. Sure, I felt terrible later about killing someone, but it wasn't as intense as it was when I didn't have the switch flipped off and had to take someone's life.

Michael put a hand on my shoulder and said, "Ash, when you lied to those Brashex soldiers about my sister kicking you out, I was in awe because I got to see your heart. You had every right to demand punishment, and the law was on your side, but you took one look at us and saw that we were worth saving. Your mercy reminded me that I too need the mercy of Yehovah, and it is something I will carry with me for the rest of my life. It is quite humbling to see the wages for breaking the law get pardoned."

"What can I say? I was fully prepared to walk off into the wilderness and wait out my days, but when they invited me back, I was humbled. I've shown mercy to hundreds during my military career, and to have someone turn me into an enemy and then repent and seek my forgiveness was almost more than I could take. I knew that Yehovah was telling me He was in control, and it was time for me to accept His mercy and come home to Him. I never would have if I hadn't been thrown out of town like that."

Silence followed my words, and I thought about heading to bed, but there was a desire within me to tell someone other than my father about what I was feeling. I had never been much for talking about feelings since the first four years after the accident that had wiped out my memories, when I'd had to see a shrink almost every day. It had seemed as if the more I shared, the worse things were for me, so I'd stopped talking about all my feelings and just told people what they wanted to hear, so they would leave me alone. I had read through the books that psychologists had to go through to get a degree and had learned how to play the system; it was how I'd managed to keep people from realizing I was a genius until I was seven years old.

I released a deep breath and asked, "Michael, can I share something really personal with you?"

"Of course you can, Ash. I promise I won't tell anyone unless you give me permission."

"I feel like a very foolish man right now and am probably only telling you this because I'm a little drunk."

He chuckled a bit, and I knew he was right there with me on the being drunk part. I must have been silent for too long, because he nudged my arm and said, "Well, spit it out already, Ash."

With a shake of my head, I said, "I am falling in love with Kyandra, but I can't tell her, because I'm going to die very soon."

"You're not a fool, Ash. My sister likes you, and she lights up when you walk into the room. Sure, she will be devastated when you die, but she knows it is coming. I can't tell you to say anything to her about it, but you should pray on the matter, and if you decide to tell her, make sure that your actions match your words."

"I will. Well, I'd better get to bed. Who knows what tomorrow will bring?" I stood up and almost fell over. I wasn't sure if the wine or Zeron's was making me numb, but Michael caught me and helped me inside to my room. He was definitely drunk and had a hard time keeping his voice to a whisper as he stood outside my bathroom door, waiting to see if I needed more help after I had washed up and changed clothes.

He helped me to bed before heading out to his room. I tried hard not to laugh as I heard him stumble down the hall. Maybe we shouldn't have drunk the whole bottle of wine, but for the first time in a long time, I felt relaxed and free of the painful pressure in my chest that had been there for weeks. I closed my eyes and fell asleep praying.

# Chapter Fifty-Two

## Roark

I t was Emet's last day in the hotel, and I knew he was anxious to be with Victor while he went through detox. If it hadn't been for the fact that he was seeing Kale today for his biweekly appointment, he would have called me already to discuss it. As much as I didn't want him to get hurt again, I knew he needed to go be with his master.

I let out a sigh and called Victor and was surprised when he picked up on the first ring. He looked a little worse for wear but still had that evil look in his eyes as he eyed me and asked, "What do you want, Roark?"

"I was wondering if we could meet to talk about something very important."

"I'm going to be in your area today and will stop by around three. Now I have to get back to a meeting with the governor." With that, he hung up on me.

The old me would have been offended, but it didn't bother me today. Victor was busy, considering he was the secretary of defense for Adreia's capital city. His position was similar to what the Surface called a police commissioner. It was his job to police the Opal Division and ensure they weren't operating outside the laws governing the police force to guard the needs of the people.

A knock on my door drew me away from my thoughts, and I was glad to see that the countertops for my kitchen remodel were finally here. The delivery guys brought them to the porch, and I thanked them before they headed off. I got to work measuring everything and set about cutting the holes for the sink. Case must have noticed me out working, because he came over and helped me finish the installation and get the plumbing lined out. We had a long conversation as I gave him a tour of my home, and then he helped me lay the beautiful wood floor in the kitchen.

He cleaned up while I started making chocolate truffles, and we had a couple of beers he had brought over. All I had left to do with my kitchen was to install the knobs on the cabinets and hang the curtains. My house was feeling more and more like home. Case helped me put my tools back into the shed before heading home. Soon I would have a housewarming party and invite them.

Twenty minutes after the truffles were done, I heard an airship land in my driveway. I made it to the front door as Victor walked up, and I could tell he was taking in the sight as if searching for flaws. It was the first time he had been to my house, and I was a little nervous about having him here. He was critical of everything, but maybe that was just a side effect of the drugs.

Victor's greeting was a little gruff as I invited him in and stood there waiting to see his reaction to my home. This was Emet's second home, and I knew it was essential to Victor for him to have a nice place to live, even if he didn't admit it. With a small sigh to myself, I offered to give Victor a tour of my small two-bedroom, one-bath house and apologized for the mess due to the recent renovations.

The look on Victor's face told me he approved, even though he didn't say it, as we returned to the dining room and sat at the table. We made small talk for a few minutes before I brought out the truffles. Before he tried one, he commented that Emet had told him I made better truffles than the restaurants, and I nearly fell out of my seat when he complimented me on them. I had never heard him say something nice to me before.

"What is it that you wanted to discuss? I know you didn't invite me here just so you could feed me truffles."

I breathed out a sigh, hoping he wouldn't lose his temper, and pulled out my plex. As I pulled up the holographic screen with the details of the test done on his drugs, I said, "Emet is really concerned about you because of the prescription bottle you gave him to dispose of." Anger filled his eyes, and I quickly spoke up before he could say anything. "He had a right to be concerned, because I had the pills tested, and they are illegal street drugs called VX-473."

The look on Victor's face was one of pure rage, and his lip pulled back in a snarl as he said, "That vile worm. I'm going to kill him."

I knew he was talking about Saz, and for a moment, I felt sorry for the guy, but the feeling disappeared as quickly as it had appeared.

"Victor, I'm a little concerned that you have been kept drugged because of your position. Just think about it for a moment; Saz isn't exactly a law-abiding citizen, and we both know it. You are the secretary of defense, and if he could manipulate you and keep you blind to what he was doing, you could be helping him smuggle in illegal goods without ever knowing about it. You worked closely with High Commander Bane and could have sent his men out away from any of his shipments coming into the city or going out."

I pushed the results across the table and watched as he read the report. The deep wound of betrayal blossomed in his eyes as he powered down my plex and sat back in the chair. I could see the wheels turning in his mind. No doubt he was looking back through his relationship with Saz and seeing all the things he had ignored that weren't right.

"Emet wants to help you through your detox because there is a good chance it could kill you. I don't think it is a good idea because you have a habit of trying to kill him."

He looked up at me with remorse in his eyes before he shook his head and said, "Emet deserves better, and I don't want him around me right now."

"I promised him I wouldn't kill you, even though I could do it and get away with it. I think Emet is right, and he needs to be with you right now. If you give me your word that you won't intentionally hurt him, I will give him permission to go home and help you."

Victor eyed me warily for a moment before saying, "If I cause him any harm, you have my permission to kill me, and I won't fight you."

I was surprised he would give me an offer like that, but when he extended a hand to seal the deal, I didn't hesitate to take it. He stood up to leave but looked back at me and said, "I've always been able to count on Emet to do the right thing, and I know when the time comes, he won't hesitate to do what is right." With that, he left me confused about why he'd said it.

# Chapter Fifty-Three

Asherex

A loud explosion jolted me awake. I rolled off the table, only to realize that my right hand was stuck. I couldn't remember if I had picked the lock, and I fought back panic as I attempted to free myself. I needed to get out of here before they came back and started torturing me again.

My hand finally came free as the door opened, and the Brashex interrogator entered. Fear coursed through me as I looked into the depths of his dark green eyes. He walked toward me, pulling out a cattle prod.

"Ash? Ash, are you all right?"

Who was Ash, and why was the interrogator asking me if I was okay?

As soon as he was near me, I lunged forward, pinned him against the wall, and wrestled the cattle prod from him. It finally skidded across the room, but the soldier managed to free himself and get me in a choke hold before saying, "Ash, you need to wake up! It's me—Jonathan."

"I don't know anyone named Jonathan." As I said the words, I elbowed the soldier in the stomach and then flipped him over my shoulder. I scrambled toward the door and fell as pain lanced through my thigh. The sounds of the soldier fumbling with something beside the table drew my attention, and I rolled over to see him with a gun in one hand and a syringe in the other.

The wound in my leg throbbed, and I looked down at the bloody mess. He'd shot me. I put pressure on the wound and looked around for a weapon to use against him. Before I knew it, he was there jabbing me in the arm with the syringe, but before he could press it, I kicked him away, pulled it out, and threw it across the room. I stood and limped toward the door, only to be tackled to the ground.

We wrestled for a while before he landed a blow to the side of my head, causing me to lose my grip on him, and he scrambled away. When I could see straight again, he rushed to me with the syringe, and before I could move, he was on me, plunging the contents into my arm. Instantly, fire spread through my veins, and I cried out in pain as he moved away from me. I lunged backward, slamming into something that felt like a dresser, but when I looked behind me, it was nothing but a blank concrete wall.

Something wasn't right. I looked around the room again, and the walls seemed as if they were melting. *What is going on?*

"Ash?"

I knew that voice, but how? When I looked at the source, I saw the face of the Brashex interrogator who had tortured me for the last six days, but that wasn't his voice. I put my face between my knees and clutched the back of my head as I tried to make sense of it.

A loud boom made me jump, and I knew a war was going on beyond the walls, but something about it didn't seem right. The explosion sounded more like violent thunder, but the room was shaking from it. Was it thunder, or had a bomb just gone off outside?

"Ash?"

The voice was closer to me this time. In a half-panicked, half-commanding tone, I said while shrinking back, "Don't touch me!"

My chest hurt, and my leg throbbed. Tears welled up in my eyes and spilled down my face in frustration. A gentle hand on my arm caused my heartbeat to quicken, but I forced myself to sit there and see what happened next. I sat there for several minutes, trying to get my thoughts in order, but it was as if something were blocking me from doing so.

"Ash, are you all right?"

I looked into the soldier's face, but he had brown eyes this time. *What is going on?* He must have seen the confusion on my face, because he closed his eyes and began speaking as if talking to someone else. I heard the name Yehovah, and a light suddenly came on as things started flooding back. The walls finished melting, revealing a bedroom, and suddenly, I remembered where I was.

"Jonathan?" I hoarsely whispered.

Immediately, he touched my face, looked me in the eye, and said, "Here I am."

I pulled him into a tight hug and whispered over and over that I was sorry. I knew I must have sounded like a broken record, but I was finally free from the nightmare. My sense of time was gone, so I wasn't sure how long I sat there clinging to Jonathan for dear life while he continued to pray for me, but after a while, I felt the effects of the PTSD meds kicking in. I needed to lie down before the room started spinning on me.

Jonathan helped me back into bed and spent a few minutes talking about what had happened. He was bruised from the attack but didn't seem concerned about himself. Instead, he wanted to know how my leg was doing, since I'd smashed it against a dresser. I was sure there was going to be a nasty bruise, because of how tender it already was.

My chest hurt worse than it had over the last few weeks, and I wondered if I had hurt myself while trapped inside my memory. It took a while to convince Jonathan to leave and let me rest before he finally relented. With a sigh, I gently rolled onto my side, watched the storm outside my window, and whispered, "O Yehovah, I'm tired of fighting. I'm ready to rest now, but whatever Your will, let it be done."

I closed my eyes, letting the rain on the metal roof lull me to sleep. My plex rang just as I was nodding off, and I grabbed it, thinking my dad might be calling, but I was surprised to see the number for the case worker over Emet's emancipation paperwork on the holographic screen. With my heart pounding in my chest, I sat up and answered it, knowing that Raya wouldn't have called unless there was news about Emet's paperwork.

"Hello, Asherex! How are you doing today?" Raya's cheerful voice brought a smile to my face. She was always energetic and happy.

"It's nice to hear from you, Raya. I've had a rough morning, but I'll be okay."

She looked at me with a genuine smile and compassion on her face.

I smiled back at her and asked, "How are the little ones, and did your husband ever find a new job?"

"Oh boy, aren't you just the sweetest thing? My girls are doing fine; they get bigger every day and are the happiest little things I've ever seen. My husband finally got his lazy self off the couch and got him a job driving a cab. It keeps him busy and out of my way, and my house has never been so clean!"

I couldn't help but laugh at her heavily accented drawl as she dramatized her statement about her husband. He had been unemployed for only three months, but he had driven her wild the whole time.

With a shake of my head, I replied, "I'm glad to hear some good news today."

"Oh, sugar, you ain't heard the good news yet today! I know the last time we talked, I said it would probably be another two weeks before we could get the paperwork for Emet into the final approval stage, but I've spent the last three days here, much to my husband's dismay. He can spend a few days with those kids without me. I have basically been harassing my bosses, and they approved the paperwork this morning! You can now purchase Emet, and he's a free man."

"I don't—" I couldn't find the words. A huge weight lifted off my shoulders, and tears fell.

She looked at me with tears streaming down her face and said, "Oh, sugar, you done made me mess up my face now." She wiped the tears from her eyes with a monogrammed handkerchief before continuing. "You just rest now, sugar, and do something for yourself with what time you've got left. You spend so much time caring for others, and you deserve something for yourself. Goodbye, Asherex. Rest well, and peace to you."

"Goodbye, Raya. May peace fill your house."

The tears streamed down her cheeks in little rivers as she ended the call, and I lay back in the bed, feeling as if I had accomplished my life's mission. Weariness set in, but before closing my eyes to rest, I quickly messaged my father to tell him he could buy Emet on my behalf.

# Chapter Fifty-Four

Asherex

I awoke with a clarity I hadn't had in a long time and knew I had been asleep for twenty-three hours straight. After stretching and taking a shower, I dressed and went downstairs to find Michael and Kyandra sitting at the dining table, discussing something, and Jonathan sitting in a chair nearby, reading something in Hebrew. The atmosphere was grave, and I was almost afraid to interrupt, but after standing there for several minutes, I said, "What's going on in here?"

They all looked at me in surprise for a moment before Jonathan dropped the book he was reading, rushed to my side, and pulled me into a hug. I hugged him back, realizing they had thought I wouldn't wake up.

"How are you feeling?" Kyandra's concerned tone tugged at my heart.

I replied, "Honestly, I feel better than I have since coming here, and I would like to do something today that I've never done before."

Jonathan looked at me, a little confused, and asked, "And what would that be?"

"I want to learn how to swim." My heart skipped a beat at the thought of being immersed in water, but I needed to face my biggest fear. "Besides, I should be baptized as well. Things have been kind of hectic lately, and that is an important part of coming into faith in Yeshua."

Michael stood and said, "West is probably the best we have for teaching people how to swim. I can go get him if you are sure that's what you want to do."

"I'm sure." As soon as the words left my mouth, my body tried to go into panic mode, knowing that being in water deeper than my ankles was in my near future. I had to remind myself that I had fallen into a raging river and even gone over a waterfall and survived that while wearing a hundred pounds of gear. Surely I could handle swimming or at least attempt it.

"I can make some sandwiches and snacks, and we can all go to the lake together. It would be nice to get away from the house for a while," Kyandra said.

A picnic at the lake sounded relaxing. I smiled at Kyandra's idea and said, "That sounds amazing." Her face lit up in a smile that made her green eyes sparkle before she went to the kitchen.

Jonathan grabbed my hand, drawing my attention, before he looked me in the eye and whispered, "I know you don't have much time left, but you should tell her how you feel about her before you never get the chance again. Trust me, she will hold on to that and be strengthened if you do, instead of wondering if she made a difference in your life while you were here."

"You're only fifteen; how did you get to be so wise?"

He smiled at me and replied, "The fear of Yehovah is the beginning of wisdom. Don't you know?"

We looked at each other for a moment before bursting out laughing. It wasn't even funny, but we couldn't stop for some reason. Jonathan dragged me to the floor as tears streamed down his face, because he struggled to breathe through the laughter. When he was finally able to suck in a breath, it sounded like a combination of a hiccup and a snort, which caused us both to laugh even harder.

It took almost five minutes for us to be able to breathe normally again, and my sides were hurting. I had never laughed that hard in my life. The laughter was still dancing in Jonathan's brown eyes as Michael walked in with West, and they gave us weird looks before going to help Kyandra load up the truck. I headed upstairs to grab something to swim in and found myself in the bathroom, on the verge of hyperventilating at the thought of purposely walking into a body of water. What was I thinking?

"I can do all things through Messiah Yeshua because I have not been given a spirit of fear but of power and of love and of a sound mind. I can do this. I will be baptized today."

I repeated it over and over in my head as we headed to the lake. Apparently, the owners of the property with the lake and surrounding 150 acres about six miles from town had moved away fifteen years ago to be with their grandchildren. No one had bought the property from them, and as we passed through the gentle hills and beautiful valleys on the way to the lake, I fell in love with the place. It would have been perfect for starting an orchard and a vineyard. If things had been different, I would have bought the place and lived here.

We parked next to a shed near the lake. Inside were a mower and small changing rooms with curtain doors. West, Michael, and I changed while Kyandra and Jonathan set things up outside and started a fire. As I walked out in my shirt and shorts, I felt as if I were walking to my death. Why couldn't I have been afraid of something other than water?

West was already waist-deep, and I watched the progression of water upon his body while trying not to have a panic attack. Michael touched my arm, drawing my attention, and said, "I'll walk you out just to be on the safe side."

I nodded in relief, knowing I wasn't going out there alone, but I knew he was afraid of the random paralysis hitting me. I took a deep breath and released it slowly as I took my first steps into the lake and had to bite back my panic when the water was deeper than my ankles. With my mantra on repeat in my mind, I forced myself to continue forward. I had served on the front lines since I was twelve, faced death many times, and even been tortured and escaped, but this was the hardest thing I'd done in my life.

For the first time, I noticed the water was warm as it covered my knees and began climbing higher on my thighs. I faltered for a moment, and Michael's touch on my arm reassured me that I wasn't alone, so I pressed on. By the time I reached West, it was nearly chest-deep, and if not for Michael standing right behind me, I would have bolted in the other direction.

West smiled at me and began telling me about baptism and what it meant for me as a believer in Yeshua. It all happened so fast that it caught me off guard when he put his hand over my face, holding my nose closed, and dunked me under the water. I was only under for fifteen seconds, but it seemed to drag on for an eternity while, in slow motion, my memory of being electrocuted and drowning in a frozen lake at the age of five played out before my eyes. Suddenly, I was filled with warmth and peace, just as I had been during that time. This was what I had been searching for, this inner knowledge that I was not alone.

When I resurfaced, I pulled West into a hug, unable to comprehend the feeling inside me. It was almost as if I were finally whole after missing a part of me that I never had known existed. I had been trying to discover that part for twenty-one years, and the tears spilling down my face were the only way I could communicate the joy of finding it.

West spent the next hour teaching me how to swim, and it left me feeling worn out. I left the guys and joined Kyandra on the shore. She hadn't been in the water but had tended the fire, watched us, and read a book. Kyandra smiled as I sprawled out on the grass near her and let out a deep breath I hadn't realized I had been holding.

"How are you feeling, Ash?"

"Completely worn out but in a good way; I haven't exercised in a long time, and I have to say that I actually miss it."

She shook her head and replied teasingly, "Only you would love exercising."

"Well, someone has to around here."

She laughed at my teasing tone, and I was left marveling at this woman who brought out a playful side of me that I hadn't seen before. I had always felt awkward when joking around with others, but with her, it came as naturally as breathing. *Was Jonathan right? Should I tell her how I felt, or should I leave her wondering after I am gone?* If she had been the one dying, I would have thought about every moment I had spent with her and wondered if she had enjoyed our time together.

"Kyandra, can I talk to you about something kind of serious? Something I am torn about sharing with you."

She looked at me with her endless, beautiful green eyes full of life and warmth and said, "Of course you can, Ash. What good are friends if you can't share your feelings and secrets with them?"

I smiled while trying to find the right words to string together. She waited patiently, not trying to rush me, and I finally said, "I was raised not to be alone with a woman I wasn't married to and to have no physical contact of any kind with women other than a handshake. When I started pursuing Lillie, it was easy because we had grown up together and already had an established relationship. It was easy. Don't get me wrong; I loved her, but I didn't realize until after we married just how little I knew about loving someone the way a husband should love his wife. It took me nearly six months before I really loved her like that, but looking back now, I can see that I didn't share my deepest thoughts and fears with her, because I was afraid I would scare her.

"I never genuinely teased or joked around with her, because I was forcing it to happen. When I was in school, Lillie's triplet brothers taught me how to fake being interested in conversations and pretend to joke with others so I could fit in. I've always felt like I was deceiving people when I did, but now things are different."

I got quiet again while trying to put the right words in order.

I hadn't had to work this hard to tell Lillie I loved her, but maybe I hadn't really loved her like this before we married. When had things gotten so complicated? I could tear apart an entire airship, put it back together blindfolded, and solve advanced mathematical equations in a matter of seconds, but telling a woman that I had feelings for her was difficult.

"Ash, we don't have to talk about this if you don't want."

"No, we do. It's important that you know this."

She looked at me in confusion for a moment before nodding and telling me to take my time. A few minutes passed before I reached out, took her hand, and said, "Kyandra, these last few weeks have been a blessing like no other, and if it wasn't for you, I don't think I would have made it this far. I've been able to get to know you better than anyone else, and you know more about me than everyone I know. You are smart, kind, compassionate, and so giving. I don't want you to be left wondering if you impacted my life when I'm gone, so I need to tell you that I have come to have feelings for you that go beyond friendship." I stared into her eyes, watching as what I'd said sank in.

Her eyes filled with tears. "Oh, Ash, I—" She pulled me into a hug and cried. Somehow, she managed to sob out that she felt the same way, and I did my best to comfort her while trying not to get her wet, because she hadn't brought any extra clothes. I was unsuccessful. After she finally pulled away from me, I gave her my dry shirt, and she went to change, while the others decided to come back and sit around the fire.

Kyandra rejoined us, and we made s'mores with kosher marshmallows, because apparently, that was a thing. Michael handed me a sticky mess dripping melted chocolate and marshmallow goo, and I stared at it as if he were giving me poison. They all laughed at me, and West teased me about not wanting all the sugar to go to my hips while working on his second diabetes sandwich.

With a sigh, I decided I was dying anyway, so what could it hurt to have junk food? I took a bite. The flavor combination took me by surprise. I was astonished that it was actually good and not too sweet for my taste, probably because of the dark chocolate they were using. As soon as I finished it, Jonathan handed me a second one, and as I ate it, I realized that if I could have picked a last day to be alive, it would have been this one with these people.

We stayed out past sunset, talking around the campfire, singing songs, and telling stories, but all too soon, we packed up the truck and headed home. On the way back, I pulled out my plex and messaged Aiden: "Aiden, I have to ask you something important. Message me as soon as you get this."

Within seconds of sending the message, he replied, "What is it, Dad?"

"How would you feel if I adopted Jonathan? I haven't talked to him yet, because I wanted to discuss it with you first."

"Honestly, Dad, I'm not surprised you want to do it. Jonathan is incredible, and even though I'm not legally your kid, I would love to have him as a brother."

"If he says yes, you will have to step up and be a good older brother to him. Can you handle it?"

"I can't say I will be good at it, but I will do my best, Dad."

"Aiden, you are going to be an amazing big brother. I couldn't be more proud of you."

"Thanks, Dad. I love you!"

"Love you too, Son."

I put my plex away as we pulled up in front of the bed-and-breakfast. Jonathan walked me inside while the others unloaded everything, and I knew Jonathan could see how weary I was. He had a concerned look on his face as I walked into the bathroom and took a quick shower before dressing in the nicest pajamas I owned.

Jonathan was sitting on the foot of the bed when I walked out of the bathroom. He had pulled the covers down on the side of the bed I liked to sleep on and turned on the bedside lamp, which was now the only light in the room. I propped myself against the pillows and patted the empty spot next to me. Jonathan didn't hesitate to lie down, and I smiled at him before saying, "Jonathan, I've been thinking about what you said to me earlier—about how I should tell people certain things before I die, so they are not left wondering. I asked my dad to look after you when I was gone, but today I realized I didn't want to leave things that way, and I wanted to tell you that since I was a kid, I've wanted to have a large family with a bunch of kids running around.

"Given everything that has happened to me recently, that reality is impossible for me now, but it's not too late. I've come to love you like a son, just as I love Aiden, and I was wondering if you would do me the greatest honor of all and allow me to adopt you as my own."

Tears filled his eyes as he replied, "Ash, why would you want me?"

I touched his face, wiping away an escaped tear, and said, "Jonathan, I don't need an excuse to want you as my son. I chose you just as Yehovah chose us to be called His sons."

The tears streamed down his face, and I pulled him into my embrace. I wondered if no one in the community had taken him in after all these years because he was mine. My only regret was that I was soon leaving him, but Yehovah's will would be done regardless of my feelings about the situation.

I was nodding off, when Jonathan jerked in his sleep, which caused him to wake up. He looked up at me with puffy eyes that told the story of his shed tears before he sat up, rubbing his eyes with his hands and saying, "I can't believe I fell asleep."

"It's been a long day. I don't want to pressure you, Jonathan, but I need an answer soon."

He looked at me for a long time before saying, "I still don't understand why you want me. I've been an orphan for five years, having to work for every cent I can get my hands on to keep the house, and no one here once stepped up and offered to take me in or help me. You've been here less than two months and spent more time with me than anyone has in five years. I just don't understand."

My heart broke at the unspoken words behind what he was saying. Since his parents had died, no one in the community had taken the time to help him, even though it was a Torah command to care for the orphan. Jonathan tried hard to please everyone, hoping they would want him around. He was looking for comfort and affection from those who were supposed to be like family, but he hadn't found it, and here I was, a complete stranger, giving him what he had been searching for all that time. No wonder he was having a hard time accepting it.

"Jonathan, I want you to listen carefully to what I'm about to say, because it is really important," I said, and he looked at me with tears glistening. "If I would've had a child and he'd turned out to be half the man you are now, I would be the luckiest man alive. Unfortunately, I don't have any kids, and no one can carry on my name. I don't want you to be my son because of that; I want you because I have seen your heart and love what I see. If I wasn't dying, I would've asked you shortly after we put the truck together, but I didn't want you to have to bury another parent, so I asked my father to look after you. I never should have done that; I should have talked to you about it, but I was afraid you wouldn't want me to be your dad for what little time I had left.

"I'm sorry I waited so long. I thought I was doing the right thing, but all I've done was rob us of the time we could have had. Jonathan, that day you went into town with West and me, when I asked you why no one had taken you in and you couldn't give me an answer, it broke my heart. You shouldn't have had to go through the last five years alone, and maybe part of the reason I'm here is to take care of you with what time I have left and leave you with a family when I go."

"Okay, Asherex." His voice was choked with tears. "You can adopt me if it is what you want. I never thought I would have a family until after I got married in the future."

"Come here." As soon as Jonathan was close enough, I hugged him and said, "Son, I'm not going to leave you an orphan when I go. Aiden is your brother, my father will be there for you, and Lazerick will care for you as if you were his own, as he did for me."

His grip on me tightened, and I knew I had made the right decision. After we parted, I pulled up the adoption papers Aiden had sent me. It only took seconds for it to become official. I finally lay down to sleep while Jonathan turned off the lamp and went to his room, leaving me to pray for him until sleep claimed me.

# Chapter Fifty-Five

Emet

I was two days into Victor's assisted detox. The worst of it had passed before he finally allowed me to prescribe him the original medication I had given him years ago to help him break his addiction. Things had been interesting, to say the least, with his mood swings, intense hours of being sick, and uncontrollable chills.

Today had been a good day, and I found myself anxiously watching him, waiting for him to become violent. I shouldn't have thought that way, but a lifetime of abuse had trained me well. I truly wanted to believe he could change, but I was afraid it wouldn't happen.

"Emet!"

Victor's angry shout from the foyer caused my heart to skip a beat, and I rushed out of my room and down the stairs as quickly as possible. Proxy High Commander Uriah was standing in the entryway. With a smug smile on his face, he eyed me like a lion stalking its prey. Uneasiness filled me as I reached my master's side, and Victor turned to me with an evil gleam in his eyes and said, "Go into my study. In the safe is a vial of nanos. Get it, and take it to the hospital with you. Our commander in chief has been in an accident, and you will give it to him. Do you understand?"

I started to protest, but he cut me off and, in an aggravated tone, said, "Emet, for once in your life, do what I tell you! Go get the vials, and don't say another word."

My heart tried pounding its way out of my chest as I opened the safe and laid eyes on the small wooden box with a sliding lid containing the nanos. As I slipped it into my pocket, my eyes landed on another vial of something that had a reddish-brown liquid inside. It had a coolant pack around it with its own energy source. *Take it, Emet.* The small voice in my head startled me, and I looked around to ensure no one was watching as I pocketed it. I didn't know what it was, but I trusted the voice in my head more than my thoughts.

Uriah joined us in the armored limousine and started talking about killing Commander in Chief Vaxis. I pulled out my plex and pretended to listen to music while recording the conversation. The nanos in my pocket contained the same mutated strain of Zeron's given to Asherex Reach. They wanted me to ensure that Drayen didn't survive the day.

Victor gave me a gentle smile as he looked at my plex, causing my heart to skip a beat. If he knew what I was doing, I was dead. He shifted in the seat, blocking Uriah's view of me, and I had to wonder if it was intentional or if he wanted to see Uriah's face better. I couldn't tell, and my adrenaline was pumping, causing seconds to seem like hours.

I felt as if a hundred years had passed by the time we reached the hospital. Uriah stayed hidden behind the tinted windows as we got out and headed inside. Once we were inside, Victor pulled me into an empty bathroom and slammed me against the wall by my neck. He wasn't pressing as hard as he'd done in the past, but my head throbbed from smacking the wall. His eyes were completely devoid of emotion as he said, "You will do as you are told. Go into that room, and give Drayen Vaxis that vial of nanos. If you do not do exactly that, you will force me to take drastic measures. I'm counting on you to do the right thing, so you'd better not let me down this time. Do you understand?"

Like a child, I stammered my reply. "Yes, master, I understand."

He released me and walked out of the bathroom, expecting me to follow him. There was no way I was going to be involved in a plot to kill our ruler, and Victor should have known better by now that I wasn't going to kill someone for him. *I guess some people never learn.*

Victor stayed back as I walked down the hallway and entered Drayen's hospital room. Senator Reach stood guard inside, and confusion filled me to see the commander in chief with only a few injuries. I bowed to the two men in the traditional military fashion before addressing the senator, saying, "Azriel, I was sent in here to kill Commander in Chief Vaxis using the same nanos that infected your son."

He looked as if I had just sucker-punched him, and it took him a minute to recover before he replied, "How can you be certain?"

Drayen sat up in bed, eyeing me intently, as I pulled out my plex and played the conversation between my master and Uriah. Drayen cleared his throat and said, "Asherex was right about the two of them."

I nodded and pulled out the small wooden box containing the nanos before handing them to Azriel and saying, "When you arrest him for his part in all this, I will be put to death. Since he owns me, there's no way to prove that I had nothing to do with the biological weapon given to Asherex." Gavin had tried to avoid this before leaving me to protect his family, but for the first time, I didn't fear dying because of Victor. No matter what happened next, I was finally going to be free of him.

"We will see about that. Go tell your master that it is done." Azriel's voice was full of authority but still kind.

I nodded and stepped out of the room, no doubt looking as if I had just killed someone. Victor eyed me warily as I said, "It's done. Just like you wanted."

His eyes softened, and a gentle smile crept upon his face as he replied, "I knew I could count on you to do this."

Before he could say another word, Azriel walked out into the hallway. Looking distressed, he hung up his plex and walked toward us. His eyes glistened with tears, and he had a shell-shocked look on his face. What was wrong?

"Azriel, are you all right?" My master's concerned tone surprised me.

Azriel looked at him for a long time before answering, "No." He looked at me for a moment, as if conveying a secret message, before continuing. "Commander in Chief Vaxis passed away from his injuries. I'm sorry you wasted your time coming here, but it was too little too late." He trailed off before shaking his head. "My son isn't going make it through the day and refuses to let anyone ease his passing, and I'm stuck here in Adreia, unable to go to him."

Azriel choked up and broke down right there in the hallway. This was really happening; Asherex was dying today. I blinked back tears at the news, and surprise filled me when my master went to Azriel's side and comforted him. Victor's eyes had a strange, hollow ache as he held tightly to Azriel. Only a parent who had lost a child knew that feeling.

"What can I do to help, Azriel? Name it, and it is yours."

"I know it doesn't mean much now. My son has never listened to me, but perhaps he would listen to someone else and not needlessly suffer through his last hours. Sell Emet to me so that I might send him to my son, and it might be that he listens to one of his soldiers' pleas to take the drugs or be mercied."

Victor looked at me for a moment before releasing a sigh and telling Azriel that the minimum he could legally sell me for was four million credits. Azriel looked torn for a moment before saying, "How can I put a price on my son being pain-free for his last hours alive?"

The look on my master's face spoke volumes about pain and loss as he agreed to sell me. The transaction took only seconds to complete. Victor didn't even look at me as he turned and walked down the hall as pain lanced through my chest. Just like that, I was nothing more to him than a transaction after serving him for twenty-seven years.

I turned around to find Azriel standing close to me, and before I knew what was happening, he firmly gripped my shoulders and said, "Emet, I wasn't lying about Asherex. I just got the call that he has taken a turn for the worse, and I need you to go be with him, because I can't leave Adreia until after Drayen is safe. Go be with my son, comfort him the best you can, and try to convince him to take the drugs so he can pass in peace."

"How am I supposed to get there? Roark is doing something for the war council, and I don't have a piloting license."

Without hesitation, Azriel put his signet ring on my hand, tied his Crimson Soldier patch on my arm, and handed me his personal handgun before saying, "You go in my authority. If anyone stands in your way, it will be as if they came against me. Take a cab to the base, and commandeer the first airship you see that's about to take off. Do not let them stop you."

"Yes, sir."

With that, Azriel slipped back into the room with Commander in Chief Vaxis, and I ran as fast as possible to carry out his order. Once outside, I hailed a cab, but before the driver could ask me where I wanted to go, I informed him, "I am on a mission from my master, Crimson Soldier Reach, and must make it to the nearest military base as fast as you can take me."

Without a word, the driver turned off the meter, no doubt seeing the Crimson Soldier patch on my arm, and sped off with his emergency lights flashing. It was a wild ride as we raced through traffic and side roads before finally pulling up to the guard shack. All I had to do was show them the signet ring and Crimson Soldier patch, and they let us in without asking questions.

I gave the driver a tip using the last of my disposable credit chip's balance before heading off to where the airships docked. As I ran the half mile across the base, I prayed for favor that the first airship I saw would be the one I would board. Azriel's patch and signet ring gained me access to the docking area, and after taking a few steps inside, I saw a warship towering above the building in front of me. It was one of the newest military models. From what Roark had told me about them, they were the fastest noncustom airships on the market.

"Can I help you with something?"

I turned at the unexpected question and found myself staring into the face of an Adreian pilot wearing a commander-of-a-thousand patch. He wore high-end armor explicitly designed for pilots, and the name on his embroidered patch was Commander Snow. His hair was a rich, deep brown with a burgundy tint, and his blazing green eyes were full of authority.

"I am looking for an airship to take me to the Surface and don't have time to waste. Crimson Soldier Reach Sr. has ordered me to be at his son's side as he passes away from Zeron's. This high honor is one that I take very seriously and not just because Asherex Reach is my high commander."

A smile flashed across his face, revealing his perfectly white teeth, before he said, "Well, that"—he pointed over his shoulder at the airship I had seen when I first walked in—"is my bird, and our training flight got called off today, so we can be in the air in five."

"That would be preferable to commandeering an airship, as he told me to do."

Commander Snow laughed hard as he turned and motioned for me to follow him to where two units loaded gear onto the massive fighter. He pulled up a metallic red whistle and blew three short bursts, followed by a three-second screech, and all twenty-two soldiers rushed into formation. It was impressive how much more organized the flyboys were than the foot soldiers I was used to dealing with.

"I want you boys to listen up." Commander Snow's voice was intense and full of authority. "I'm only going to say this once. This is not a drill. We have orders directly from Crimson Soldier Reach to escort this man"—he gestured to me—"to the Surface for High Commander Reach. I want this bird up in the air in ninety seconds."

"Sir, yes, sir!"

The thundering voices of twenty-two men replying to their commander's order reverberated through me before they broke off to finish loading the gear. Commander Snow walked me aboard while saying, "This beast is the fastest thing in Adreia outside of Asherex Reach's personal cruzer. She demands a crew of at least twenty to keep her up and running and can go for ninety-six hours of continuous flight. She can house up to one hundred twenty men and has seventeen guns capable of firing over one million rounds per minute."

He had me sit in one of the chairs at the back of the cockpit, and as we began our vertical ascent and cleared the buildings so that the wings could unfold, he looked at me with a wolfish grin and said, "The flight there takes four hours, but we're doing it in three."

# Chapter Fifty-Six

Emet

It took just under three hours to get to the tiny trading-post town, but because of the airship's size, we couldn't land it. Commander Snow led me down to the lower bay and opened a drop hatch on the bottom of the airship. He looked at me as he strapped me into a harness and shouted above the roar of the engines, "We can't set down here, so you're going to have to repel! Just hold tight to the grip, and you won't fall. This ain't the infantry, boy. This is the real thing. When you reach the ground, reattach your harness to the rope once you're clear, and give us the signal. After that, you are on your own."

I nodded a moment before he pushed me over the edge of the drop hangar. The descent took only moments, but it seemed like a small eternity, and for the first time in my life, I missed Roark's daredevil driving style. At least he hadn't thrown me out of his cruzer while it was 160 feet above the ground.

My heart was in my throat as I hit the end of the rope, dropped the last couple of feet to the ground, reattached my harness, and gave Commander Snow the signal to take off. The beast crept backward a couple hundred feet, and the pilot dipped the wings back and forth in a show of respect before vertically ascending to get to a suitable takeoff altitude. That had been intense, and I was thankful for the chance to meet the dedicated soldiers of the Jasper Division.

I turned around and walked into town. It was just as small and dusty as Roark had told me, but it held a certain charm. The doctor's office was easy to spot. Several people stood around two trucks parked outside, looking grim, as I walked up. One of the men, who had brown hair and eyes and was maybe an inch taller than I, walked over. He extended a hand and said, "I'm Michael Rains. Are you here for Ash?"

I took his hand and replied, "Yes, I'm Emet, and I'm a doctor. Asherex's father wanted me to come here to see him through to the end. He hopes he can come soon but is currently tied up with national affairs."

Michael nodded and told me to follow him. We walked into the small building, which I guessed probably had only five rooms. Michael stopped, pointed to a room in the back, and said, "He's in there."

"Thank you, Michael."

He nodded with tears in his eyes as I walked down the narrow hallway and into the room where Asherex was. As soon as I stepped into the room, the sound of shallow, wheezing breathing caught my attention. Asherex was lying on the hospital bed, looking as if he'd aged ten years. His closed eyes made him look as if he were already dead while the machines kept track of his slowed heartbeat. He didn't have much time left.

With a sigh, I set my medical kit down on the counter in the corner of the room, and I nearly jumped when I turned around to find Asherex's sky-blue eyes staring back at me with a clarity I'd never seen in a dying man's eyes. He opened his mouth to speak but only managed to say my name in a broken sigh before weakly lifting a hand to reach for his plex, only to lose strength before he could grab it.

"It's all right, Asherex. I've got it." I kept my voice as calm as possible as I grabbed his plex and sat on the edge of his hospital bed.

He opened it up and scrolled through different screens before bringing up one and leaving it open. He looked up at me and mouthed, "Emet, I had hoped I would get to do this in person, and Yehovah has blessed me, because you are here."

He handed me his plex, and it took several minutes before I could comprehend what was in front of me: my freedom papers. I looked up at him in shock.

He stared back at me with a soft smile and mouthed, "It only needs your signature to be made official."

"When? Why?" I couldn't put the words together to ask why he would have done this and when he'd started it.

He weakly grabbed my hand and whispered, "Right after Lillie."

Asherex looked at the plex screen and then back at me, as if to tell me to just sign it already. As reality crashed in on me, I signed the document, and he changed the screen to another page. I signed it without looking.

After that, he powered off the plex and attempted to speak again but couldn't get the words out, so he mouthed them, saying, "You didn't read the last page."

"I trust you, Asherex."

"I've set aside an account for you with your back wages for the military for the last six years that you have served under me in the Crimson Division."

"What?" I couldn't believe what I was hearing. He was paying me for my service, even though Victor already had received payment for it. Why?

"When you buy a Hebrew slave ..." He trailed off and closed his eyes, and I feared he was gone, but he slowly opened his sky-blue eyes again. "You're not going out empty-handed, Emet."

I was speechless, and he knew it. He released a long, wheezing breath, and pain filled his eyes. Pain lanced through my chest at the sight, and I gently squeezed his hand before saying, "Asherex, you don't have to be in pain. Please let me give you something to sleep, or at the very least, allow me to give you something for the pain."

His eyes drifted over to the gun I had placed on the counter next to my bag, and my heart skipped a beat before he looked back at me and whispered, "Sleep sounds good."

I released a breath I wasn't aware I was holding, grateful he hadn't asked me to mercy him with his father's gun. I wasn't sure I would have been able to pull the trigger, even though it was a high honor to end someone's suffering when he or she had Zeron's. It was still murder. He closed his eyes again, and I walked across the small room and rummaged through the medical bag Commander Snow had given me, until I found the right drugs.

Before I could inject the drugs into the IV line, Asherex grabbed my tzitzit, drawing my attention. He shook his head before brokenly saying, "Pray with me first."

He weakly grabbed my hand once again, and I bowed my head and began to pray aloud with him. The first twenty minutes of the prayer were nothing more than praise for the Most High, and after that, I prayed for Asherex and his family. I was so impassioned in my prayer that I didn't realize I was now speaking my native tongue, Hebrew. The prayer lasted almost two and a half hours, but it seemed like it was over as quickly as it had started. Once we were done, Asherex nodded for me to give him the drugs to make him sleep.

It took about fifteen minutes for them to kick in, and I watched as his sky-blue eyes slowly drifted closed. I knew this was the last time I was going to see his eyes staring back at me, unless a miracle happened. I sat on the doctor's stool, only to jump and nearly fall to the floor when something poked me in the thigh as I sat down. Standing, I dug through my pocket and pulled out the vial with the reddish-brown liquid I had stolen from Victor's safe. I looked back and forth from the vial to Asherex's IV line and fought with myself, because I felt I needed to give it to him, but I didn't know what it was. Why hadn't I turned it over to Azriel when I gave him the infected nanos?

I prayed for guidance, and the urge to give Asherex the vial grew stronger, so I finally relented. The drugs had put him into a coma, so I couldn't hurt him with whatever was in the vial. *He's dying anyway, so what's the harm?* With a sigh, I trusted in the little voice that had told me to grab the vial in the first place and injected it into his IV line.

Three and a half hours passed while I watched the monitors as Asherex slowly declined. If not for the sound of the oxygen machine going off, I wouldn't have been aware of the passing of time. Asherex's wheezing breaths became shallower and further between. I didn't want to sit there and watch someone die. I was free now and didn't have to watch every second of someone's passing.

Emboldened by my realization, I turned off the monitors and machines before walking out of the room and closing the door behind me. I had been forced to sit there for every excruciating second while watching and waiting for Asherex's wife, Lillie, and countless others to die, but I had the choice not to watch him die like that. I would remember my high commander as a loving and generous man and not be haunted by the moment of his death for the rest of my life. It was the most liberating decision I'd ever made.

Once I was outside, the small group gathered around. I informed them that I'd put Asherex into a coma so he wasn't suffering anymore and that I would check on him until he passed away. They looked relieved and returned to sitting on the tailgates of their trucks. It looked as if they were not going anywhere until Asherex was gone, and I could hear them joining in prayer together as I walked over and sat down next to a teenager sitting on the porch of the building next to the doctor's office.

It took me a moment to recognize him as the kid from upriver I had helped. He looked as if his world were falling apart, so I nudged him with my arm and said, "I'm Emet, by the way."

He looked at me with a big smile and replied, "Jonathan. Jonathan Reach now." He shook my hand. "I found him, you know. It took me a few days, but I did what you asked, and it's changed everything."

I smiled as my mind replayed the day when I'd sent him off without knowing how much my high commander was helping me. He must have had my freedom paperwork started before that time, and if I hadn't rescued Jonathan from the interrogators, then Asherex probably would've died.

"Yehovah works in very mysterious ways," I said.

"Yeah, He does." Jonathan's voice, though sad, still held a cheerfulness that I knew came only from being a servant of the Most High.

I didn't know what had happened between Asherex and these people, but Yehovah had answered my prayer for him, and he now saw the truth of Messiah. During that time, he'd adopted the kid sitting beside me. I wondered if Jonathan realized he stood to inherit one of the largest fortunes in Adreia.

We sat there in silence for several minutes before I heard what sounded like an airship engine approaching. I stood and walked out into the street just as three airships flew over and landed, folding in their wings just before getting to the top of the buildings. My heart began to pound as Proxy Uriah stepped off the first cruzer with ten armed men, and twenty more came out of the other two. This wasn't good.

Uriah stepped in front of the mercenary soldiers, looked me in the eye, and asked, "Well, is he dead yet, Emet?"

# Chapter Fifty-Seven

## Roark

Earlier that day

I was in the middle of an intense baseball game with my recently adopted brother, Kale, while my dad pitched. It was a charity game; we were down by two runs with two innings left. We were having more fun than I had expected, seeing as how it was the first time Kale and I had played the game.

My plex buzzed in my pocket, and I silenced it, only to have it go off again. Annoyed, I pulled it out of my pocket. Victor was calling me. Part of me didn't want to answer, but if it was about Emet, I needed to know. With a sigh, I put in my earbud and answered the call, saying, "What do you need, Rayas?" I tried my best to keep the annoyance from my voice and wasn't sure if I was successful.

"Emet is in trouble." Victor winced and closed his eyes before dropping his plex, giving me a full view of him lying on the floor of his mansion, covered in blood. My heart skipped a beat, and I quickly got up and walked away from the dugout.

"Victor! Victor! What's wrong with Emet?" I repeated his name and the question several times, but Victor didn't move.

Fear filled me as someone else picked up Rayas's plex and cut off the video feed before saying, "Roark, you might want to get to Asherex as soon as possible." Whoever was speaking now used a voice distorter. He continued. "High Commander Reach isn't long for this world, and Emet is with him now. Proxy Uriah left about twenty minutes ago to destroy the religious community where Asherex has been staying. Uriah will kill Emet without hesitating unless someone stops him."

The call ended, and I ran back to tell Kale that I had to go before rushing off to my cruzer. I quickly started the engines and called for a priority escort through the hangar tunnels below Adreia and to the Surface. It took a half hour to make it to the nearest hangar tunnel. Before I knew it, I was racing toward the Surface with Commander Snow of Adreia's air force quickly on my heels, leading an entire fleet. Uriah wasn't going to get away with attacking those people. I just prayed I would get there in time.

# Chapter Fifty-Eight

## Emet

**"W**ell, is he dead yet, Emet?"

Uriah's question hung heavily in the air as I stood my ground, only then realizing that I had left Azriel's gun in Asherex's room and had nothing to defend myself or these people with if he chose to open fire. *O Yehovah, we need a miracle. Save us from this evil man.*

When I didn't answer him, Uriah turned to one of the soldiers and ordered him to go find out. He disappeared into the doctor's office and returned a few moments later, announcing that Asherex was dead. My heart sank a bit, but I didn't have time to get upset, because Uriah started barking orders at the mercenaries to round up the religious people.

Everyone around the trucks began backing away as the soldiers came forward with rifles in hand. I pulled Jonathan behind me, prepared to fight to the death to protect him. Jonathan's hand clutched the back of my shirt, emboldening me to stand my ground, as Uriah's men advanced.

"Oh, Emet, don't you know it's pointless now? Asherex may have postponed what I'm doing here, but you cannot delay the inevitable.

Your master—or, should I say, former master—tried to keep me from coming here and paid the price."

"You have no authority here, Uriah."

He laughed and said, "With Asherex dead, this place is no longer a neutral zone and falls back under my jurisdiction. I am the only authority here." Uriah pulled out his sidearm and pointed it at me. "I've been looking forward to doing this for a long time."

He leveled the gun at my chest, and I closed my eyes as a gunshot rang out in the deafening silence. I opened my eyes just in time to see Uriah fall to the ground with a bullet hole in the center of his forehead. A glance behind me revealed Asherex standing at the entrance to the doctor's office with his father's gun in hand.

He looked pale and was having difficulty breathing, but he pointed the gun at the soldier closest to Kyandra and said, "Step away from the civilians." His voice was full of authority, and a fire burned in his eyes. The mercenaries looked back and forth between Uriah and Asherex before one of them aimed his rifle at Asherex.

My heart was in my throat as another shot rang out, and the soldier dropped his weapon. A moment later, Roark's ancient cruzer cleared the buildings behind us. He was standing on top, holding his new sniper rifle, while someone else piloted his ship. He looked every bit the Crimson Soldier he was with his face covered by black wraparound goggles and a respirator while his blond hair blew around in the wind.

Before anyone else could make a move, Commander Snow's warship came into view with its guns armed and ready to fire. Snow's authoritative voice came over the loudspeakers, telling everyone to lay down his arms and surrender peacefully. His voice held a threatening promise, and the mercenaries quickly surrendered.

With a sigh of relief, I turned and ran to Asherex's side just as he collapsed in the doorway. Michael and Westly were there within moments and helped me get Asherex into the hospital room, where he passed out. I hooked him back up to the machines and turned them on, only to be left in shock. His heart rate and blood pressure were stable. That was impossible outside of a miracle.

Roark walked in, removing his respirator and goggles, while I started drawing blood. He assisted me while I explained what had happened that day, including the mysterious vial. After the last vial of eight was collected, Roark told me that Victor had called him to warn him that Uriah was coming here, so he had come with backup. He'd even done a midflight boarding with one of the pilots so he could put on his magnetic boots and be up top just in case.

After carefully packing everything, we walked out of the room, and Roark said, "I think Azriel is on his way. They finished up in the senate today and got every contract passed for the first time in forever."

"How's Commander in Chief Vaxis?" I couldn't help my concern for him. I believed Azriel had lied about his being dead, but the news of his death had been all over the media on the flight here, and I'd begun to wonder if it was real or a cover-up.

"He's recovering just fine in a secret location until all this is cleaned up. Apparently, High Commander Bane is alive and in hiding as well, which I didn't find out until after I was halfway here, by the way."

I looked at Roark, thoroughly confused, and said, "I heard my mas—Victor telling Uriah that he removed Ezekiel from his high commander position for Uriah."

Roark shrugged and said, "I haven't a clue what's going on, but Zeke is still hiding in a safe house somewhere while my future father-in-law investigates his wife's murder and his disappearance. Apparently, Keller isn't on the need-to-know list right now, and I probably shouldn't be telling you any of this, but I really hate keeping secrets from you."

"Asherex bought me and set me free." It was all I could say. I was still kind of in shock about it.

Roark suddenly looked as if someone had removed a great weight from his shoulders, and relief washed over his face as he said, "Finally! You don't know how long I've had to keep that to myself.

He swore me to secrecy because he didn't want Victor to find out, and let's face it: I'm a bit mouthy. I've wanted to tell you since he asked me to be your official warden."

Blown away by the fact Roark had known all this time, I couldn't speak. No wonder he'd kept encouraging me not to give up, because he had known something good was just around the corner. I pulled him into a hug and let my tears finally fall.

We walked outside, and Roark greeted the group of Yisra'elites as if they were old friends before Commander Snow and his men pulled him away. They loaded the mercenaries into a smaller airship designed to dock inside the warship hovering outside town. There was organized chaos for the next hour as everyone scrambled around cleaning up the mess Uriah had made while I went every fifteen minutes to check on Asherex.

I spent a lot of time on Roark's plex, talking with the Brashex lab technician overseeing Asherex's internal monitors, all while attempting to get landing-zone permission for their mobile team, who would be landing any minute to check Asherex's blood samples. They had departed Brashex as soon as the call came in that he was finally passing away. They had been as surprised as I was when he woke up after being legally dead for more than ten minutes according to their sensors.

The mobile team finally landed, and I filled them in as they took more blood from Asherex and the samples I had collected earlier to test. They were as anxious as I was to find out what was happening inside my high commander. After collecting the spinal fluid they needed and delivering it to the mobile lab, I stepped out into the darkening evening and breathed a sigh of relief.

"It's been a long day, hasn't it, Emet?"

I jumped at Azriel's unexpected voice and turned to face him. He had a weary smile on his face, and his blue-green eyes were full of questions I didn't have answers for.

"Yeah, it's been a very long day, and I'm ready for it to be over."

"You and me both. I could use a good glass of wine or two right about now." He looked off at the blazing sunset and asked, "Is he going to wake up again?"

I looked at Azriel and must have been quiet for too long, because he finally turned to look me in the eye. I said, "I don't know how he is still alive right now. There is absolutely no medical reason that his heart should have started beating again after ten minutes without activity. Your son is alive right now because it is what Yehovah wills and nothing else."

He looked surprised for a moment before he shook his head and said, "I think I'm starting to understand how my dad was able to be so calm with me while I was rebellious and why he loved sharing scripture with Kress Rayas. There's just something undeniable about your attitude and actions that makes me believe you're right. I believed it after Asherex told me it was true, but seeing it play out in you, after everything you've been through, makes it real."

"It's my job to live out my faith and not keep it to myself, and because of that, I see many answered prayers, even the ones I've prayed for your family since Lillie."

Azriel cleared his throat and said, "I met a man in the Wastelands back when Asherex was five, and he was one of the few who believed in Yehovah and Yeshua. Everyone else in the marauder camp believed that spirits guided them. He dared to stand out, and when I crashed there, he believed it was the answer to his prayers and kept me alive. He called me Uri'kai, which means 'Son of a Star' in their language. Not a day went by that he didn't pray for me, and when the time came for me to come home, he gave me the seal of the Blood Rider and told me he would pray for me for the rest of his life. He was a good friend."

Floored by his story, I stood there in awe of Elohim. Azriel had interacted with believers throughout his life, and I wondered if I was the answer to some of the Wastelander's prayers. *All praise, all glory, and all honor to the One who reigns in the heavens! Yehovah Tzevaot is His name! He is faithful to all who are His and hears the prayers and petitions of His servants! Blessed are You, O Yehovah, ruler of the nations, who hears the prayers of His people, Yisra'el!*

# Chapter Fifty-Nine

Asherex

I t had been seven days since I supposedly died and came back to
life. During those seven days, everyone exposed to me had stayed
in the community for the mandated quarantine. Roark had stayed as
well, even though he was technically exempt. It had been an exciting
time, and I had come to know Roark and Emet well. I was glad I
could call them friends.

My blood tests came back from the Brashex lab. Everyone was
shocked to learn that the virus in my system had died off.

Now that I was considered a carrier for Zeron's, my military
career was over. Of course, I could be a consultant, but it wasn't the
same. Everything was changing for the better, and I believed I knew
what I should do now. I needed to pray about it some more before I
started making preparations; I supposed I could spend a lot of time
in prayer while I finished my two-month quarantine.

My father embraced me one last time and said, "I will see you
back home in eighteen days, Son."

I smiled as he released me, and I told him I looked forward
to it. Then he boarded his airship and took off. Eighteen days
remained before I could return home due to a mandatory specialized
quarantine that lasted seven days past the two-month mark. I

couldn't wait to go home but knew I wouldn't be there much longer before moving on to the next chapter of my life and coming back to the community. If everything I was about to do was Yehovah's will, nothing could stop me.

Jonathan took my hand while we watched my father leave. We'd decided I would live with him for the last of my quarantine and help him get caught up on his repair work. He and I had a lot to talk about before I went into the final quarantine and then to Brashex for testing and to remove the sensors from my body. Jonathan could join me in Adreia when it was finished.

"Come on, Son; let's go home. It's been a long day, and I'm ready to relax without everyone hovering over me."

Jonathan gave me one of his smiles, and we said our goodbyes to the people who had come to see us off. We then headed out on his quad bike. I still had a long journey ahead of me, but for the first time in my life, I knew that everything would turn out for my good. Yehovah was in control, and I had nothing to worry about from this day forward. How blessed was I to have such an Elohim as Yehovah?

# Chapter Sixty

Emet

Roark and I were an hour into the flight back to Adreia, when my plex rang. Victor's number appeared, and I debated whether I should answer it, but I finally accepted the call and brought up the holographic screen. Victor's dark brown eyes were dull with pain. His face was bruised and bloody. A knife handle stuck out of his chest, and the sound of gunfire filled the background.

"Emet, I don't have long, but I have to tell you that I'm so proud of you for doing the right thing and ending this for me. I always knew this was going to kill me."

He closed his eyes, and I asked, "Victor, what are you talking about?"

Someone shouted at him in the background, telling him not to die on him. Victor opened his eyes, gave me a sad look, and said, "I'm sorry for everything. I want to blame the drugs, but I am my father's son, and he was abusive; it's why I killed him after Kress disappeared. Saz covered it up so I wouldn't get arrested and held it over my head all these years. I don't deserve forgiveness, Emet, but if you can find it within yourself to forgive me, then maybe there is hope."

He trailed off, closing his eyes again. My heart stilled in my chest, and Roark sat straighter in his pilot chair. Before I could say anything else, someone forced Victor to his feet and moved him to another location before the firefight resumed. Victor slowly sat up, leaning against a metal crate, before bringing his plex back up and saying, "I failed to keep my promise to Yo'ash. How could I be forgiven?"

"Victor, look at me," I said, and he forced his eyes open again. "You are forgiven. Everything you put me through has prepared me for what is to come, and I wouldn't change a moment of it. It is written that all things work together for good to those who love Elohim, and this is no different. I've forgiven you every step of the way, and I do not hate you in my heart. I love you, and so does Yeshua. You can be forgiven if only you seek it."

He gave me a soft smile as the life faded from his eyes. He closed his eyes and took a deep breath, and when he opened them again, they were filled with the stubborn determination I had seen countless times. In one fluid motion, he stood, grabbed the man defending him, and threw him, along with his plex, into a narrow corridor before slamming the door shut with him on the other side. I heard the heavy-duty blast doors lock and knew there was no way to open them.

My heart sank as the man pounded on the door and shouted, "Rayas, don't do this!" He continued hitting the door before sliding to his knees and saying, "I've lost too many soldiers to this. Please don't make me lose you too."

Muffled gunfire reverberated through the door, and Victor's authoritative voice came through, saying, "I won't make it out, and we both know it, Zeke. Everything you need to know about the terrorist known as the Barron is on my plex. Don't let him win."

More gunfire rang out before silence filled the air. High Commander Ezekiel Bane snatched up Victor's plex before telling me he was sorry and ending the call. Victor was dead. Tears streamed down my face as something inside me broke, and loss crushed me. Victor hadn't been good to me, but he had been my father for twenty-seven years.

Roark pulled me into his chest as I fell apart. Through the sobs, I heard him praying, but I couldn't make out a single word or get my mind to focus on anything past the fact that Victor was dead. I would never see him again. It was too much to bear.

# Chapter Sixty-One

## Emet

I was feeling irritated at Roark, even though I should have been grateful. It was a week before Sukkot, and he was bringing me to Yerushalayim on a specialized working pass to perform a complicated spinal surgery on the elderly man he had stayed with during his first visit there. I should have been grateful that I would be stepping into the Holy City. Still, I felt cheated because I knew that our pass lasted for only a couple of days, and I would be inside an operating room for the duration of the pass. I could only see what was in front of me while walking from the hotel to the hospital across the street. That alone should have been enough, but since we'd started our journey, Roark had babbled on about all the things he had seen in the land of Yisra'el during his seven trips there since Asherex had commissioned him to find my family.

I sighed and replayed a conversation I'd had with Asherex about a month ago. He had acquired the permission of both the Adreian and the Brashex governments to declare the trading post and its surrounding territories a neutral zone that he was to be king over. Part of his responsibility as king was to build and staff a hospital, and he'd asked me to be in charge of the hospital and run it the way I wanted. It was a high honor and a great responsibility. I had prayed about it ever since and had confirmation that this was Yehovah's will for my life. I was meant to be part of this neutral zone that Asherex was going to govern by the laws of Torah that were applicable to life in the dispersion. It was going to be a strange journey, but Elohim had chosen me to walk in it.

"Well, here we are, Emet."

I looked up at Roark's declaration. All the air in my lungs escaped at once as I beheld Yerushalayim for the first time in twenty-nine years. I was in awe of her beauty as we passed the outer defensive walls covered in solar panels. I barely restrained the tears that threatened to fall as we passed over the old city before landing on the parking-garage roof of our hotel. Roark spoke with the valet, and I translated for him so the young man would know how to dock the manual airship.

We checked into the hotel and lay down to sleep. All I wanted to do was wander the streets, touching everything as I passed, but in seven hours, I had to be in the operating room. It wouldn't have been fair to Mr. Britz for me not to rest well before going into the surgery, which they predicted would last fourteen hours. With a sigh, I closed my eyes and prayed for shalom.

Roark's alarm woke me, and I felt as if I had slept for several days. After stretching, I jumped into the shower and then ate lunch with Roark before walking across the street to the hospital. Mr. Britz's family was waiting for us. They welcomed Roark as if he were part of their family. They communicated with him the best they could with their limited knowledge of the common language. It was nice to see them interact, but all too soon, the hospital administrator, who spoke to me in the common language, greeted me. His accent was so thick that I couldn't understand him, so I spoke in Hebrew with him.

He gave me a quick tour of the floor I was operating on before introducing me to the team I was working with. They were all kind and eager to work with me. All of them had, at some point in their medical careers, read one of the many articles I'd published in the Adreian medical journals about complicated, advanced surgery techniques I had implemented both in the field and in a sterile operating room. Apparently, they knew me by name around here, and I couldn't help but feel thankful that Victor had pushed me so hard to be the best.

My heart sank a little at the thought. Victor hadn't been the kindest man, but in the end, he'd seemed as if he were trying to turn his life around, and even now, I still heard his last words to me before he died. Those ominous words hinted at repentance but left me wondering if he'd cried out to Yehovah before he was murdered.

I sighed before going over the plan with the team and praying before scrubbing in for the operation. The grueling surgery lasted sixteen hours. Afterward, Mr. Britz went straight into a recovery tank. The owner of the hospital where I'd worked for most of my career had donated it just for the occasion. It ensured Mr. Britz would have the best possible chance of walking again after twenty-nine years in a wheelchair. Of course, this hospital in Yerushalayim had the best physical therapy department on the planet, with the most advanced technology to aid recovery. Mr. Britz had spent the last couple of months receiving therapy on the muscles in his legs, which had atrophied. He was already at 70 percent muscle mass, but he still had a long recovery process ahead of him if the surgery was successful. I prayed that it would be.

Once I had washed up, I walked into the room where the family was waiting and updated them on Mr. Britz's condition. We spoke for a few minutes before the oldest son led the family in prayer, and hearing them praising Yehovah and calling on the name of Yeshua tugged at my heart and brought back memories of being with my family. I felt a little guilty now for being irritated with Roark on the way here.

Roark and I headed back to the hotel, but two soldiers intercepted us when we made it to the street. One of them looked at Roark and told him we needed to follow them. I gave Roark a questioning look, but he just smiled at me and didn't say a word as we followed the soldiers into the old city. We passed by many things I had never explored as a child, and I wanted to slow down and take my time, but I had to keep up with the soldiers. Distracted, I didn't realize where I was, until Roark handed me a kippah, and I looked up and beheld the Western Wall.

Roark helped me to the wall before I collapsed and began to sob. I couldn't describe the feeling; it was like coming home for the first time in my life. As I sat there sobbing out the Shema in Hebrew, I felt many hands touch me. I figured those people probably came there daily and witnessed many people break down like I was.

When I finally found the strength to stand, a rabbi stepped forward and pulled me aside. He started questioning me about why I was with an Adreian. We sat on a nearby bench as I told him my testimony. He was shocked and praised HaShem for His hand on my life, and before we parted ways, he prayed for me.

My joy was overflowing as we reached the hotel room, and even though our working passes expired in the morning, I knew I would carry this day with me for the rest of my life.

When someone knocked on the door, Roark was on his plex, and I answered it without hesitating. On the other side were two soldiers escorting a well-dressed young man. He told me that the rabbi I had spoken with earlier today was an influential man. Moved by my testimony, he'd called and extended our visitor passes so I could be here for Sukkot. I was speechless, so Roark ended his call, accepted our passes from the young man, and spoke to him for a few minutes before sending him on his way.

"I guess it's a good thing I stepped out in faith and packed us two weeks' worth of clothes. I've been praying for a way to be here for Sukkot since my first visit after Asherex asked me to find your family."

I looked at Roark and asked, "When did you pack us more clothes?"

"While you were sulking about doing the surgery. Don't worry about where we will stay while we are here. I already made arrangements, and we will be staying with Zarek and his family for the feast."

I stared at Roark, no doubt with an odd look. Zarek had been my father's name, and even though there were probably hundreds of older men with that name, hearing it made my heart skip a beat. The day the Adreian soldiers had taken me, my father had died in an explosion when a stray missile hit his truck. At least that was what I remembered. The blast had thrown me from the truck, which was why the Adreians had taken me. Due to a language barrier, they hadn't returned me to my family after I healed. Besides, I had been only five and unable to communicate well enough to answer their questions.

"Are you sure it is a good idea to stay with them? I don't want them to feel obligated because of the surgery."

"Oh, Emet, it's fine! They have welcomed me back into their home every time I've come here. Since I have access to government records to track down your family, they have asked me to find out if there is any information on their second-youngest son, who disappeared after a battle between Adreia and Brashex. They are good people, and two of their older children have homes in the city, so the rest of the family are staying with them, leaving us plenty of space in Zarek's home. Don't tell me you're getting cold feet now that you have the chance to be here for almost two weeks and celebrate Sukkot in the city."

I smiled at Roark's teasing tone and replied, "It's not that; I'm just having a hard time getting past the shock of it all. It seems like a dream, and when I finally come back to myself, I'll probably spend hours praying to thank Elohim."

"That's the Emet I know. Well, I'll give Mrs. Britz a call and tell her that we will be staying with them. Now I have to find parking for the old beast of mine."

I reclined on the bed while Roark made several calls, and I must have drifted off, because he woke me up sometime later with dinner. We talked a bit about his arrangements for us before I jumped into the shower and then headed to bed. We had to be out of the hotel room in the morning, and I wanted to get as much sleep as possible so I could spend the rest of the day exploring. I wasn't sure how I would fall asleep with all the excitement.

# Chapter Sixty-Two

Emet

We checked out of the hotel and spent most of the day exploring the old city. Many childhood memories came rushing back like a flood from the few times I remembered coming to Yerushalayim for the three pilgrimage feasts with my father and brothers. We had lived nine hours from Yerushalayim and had stayed with one of my uncles during those times. I couldn't remember their faces, but the precious moments came back to me with every place I visited.

The sun was setting now, and I could tell Roark was growing impatient, even though he wouldn't say a word. He was anxious to get to the Britzes' place, because the hospital had discharged Zarek that afternoon, and their kids weren't going to be around to ensure he was doing well. It still amazed me that he had grown close to these people even with a language barrier.

With a soft sigh, I returned to Roark, and we left. On the way, Contessa called him, and they talked about some of their wedding plans. They were going to get married in a month, and both complained about all the fanciful, ridiculously excessive plans their fathers had put into place. It was beautiful to see them able to reconcile their past and come together in Yeshua to share their lives together. Yehovah sure had a way of bringing about the unexpected.

Roark ended the call as we walked up the steps. Mrs. Britz opened the door and welcomed us in before we even reached the top step. She embraced Roark as if he were a lost son before pulling me into the warmest, most welcoming hug I'd ever had. It reminded me of my mother's embrace. Since Victor's passing, I'd felt more and more alone, and Gavin had only just come out of hiding with his family. I had met them two weeks ago, but the ache in my heart for a family of my own had only grown.

Zarek sat at the dining table, waiting for us to join him for dinner, and I was in awe of his compassion as we began talking. I translated for everyone as the need arose and found myself laughing more as the night went on. We talked about all kinds of things, and they asked Roark about his military career and the upcoming wedding as if they had been family for a long time. Then they turned their attention to me, and Roark told them stories about me that had us all laughing. I hadn't realized he thought of me like that before. As they poured the fifth round of wine, I saw Roark in a new light. I couldn't believe I hadn't noticed before that moment how much he cared for me.

All this time, I had yearned for the family I'd left behind and hadn't noticed that Roark had been more than just my friend. He had been like my overprotective younger brother, who had stood by my side even when he disagreed with me or was angry with me. I had been even more blessed than I realized, and suddenly, I knew I would be up all night, praising Yehovah for His loving commitment to me. I didn't deserve the slightest kindness from my Elohim, yet He poured out His blessings upon me in abundance.

Mrs. Britz left us to talk while she cleaned up the kitchen. Roark told me that the last time he had been there, he had tried to help her clean up, and she had hit him with a rolled-up newspaper and yelled at him in Hebrew, so now he didn't try, because she scared him. I thought it was funny that this tiny older woman scared him so badly, but I wouldn't have wanted an angry Jewish woman smacking me with a newspaper either.

Roark's plex chimed, and his face turned serious as soon as he opened the message. I touched his arm and asked, "Roark, what is it?"

He looked at me and then at Zarek before looking back at me and saying, "I need you to translate something for me so that he understands exactly what I am saying. This is probably the most important thing he will hear for a while."

I nodded and waited patiently while Roark looked over the holographic document on his plex before saying, "Tell him that I have the report about his second-youngest son."

I translated it, and Zarek sat up straighter in his wheelchair.

Roark continued. "His body was never recovered from the wreckage of the truck that was blown off the road by a stray Brashex missile."

Chills ran down my spine, and all the hair on my body stood on end while I translated for Roark. My heart pounded; this man had lost a child in an accident tied to an Adreian-Brashex firefight. *This couldn't be possible, could it?*

"Zarek," Roark said as Zarek looked at him with a blazing intensity, "I know who your son is."

The sound of a dish breaking in the kitchen drew our attention, and Mrs. Britz quickly appeared in the doorway with tears in her eyes. Roark changed to an unopened message on his plex and brought it up for all of us. It was in both the common language and Hebrew. I immediately recognized one set of DNA as my own before seeing my name below it.

Zarek looked at the holographic screen and then at me before looking at Roark and saying in broken common language, "This is correct?" He looked at me, and his eyes brimmed with tears. "My Emet?"

"It would seem that Yehovah has heard your prayers and brought him back to you."

Roark's words hung heavily in the air before everything came crashing down. The emotional dam broke, and hot tears streamed down my face. I felt Mrs. Britz's arms—my mother's arms—wrap around me, and her joyful sobs filled the air moments before my father appeared beside me in his wheelchair and wrapped his arms around me. I could hear his voice thick with emotion as he praised Yehovah between sobs and began singing joyful songs.

I didn't know how long we sat there like that before they started asking questions. They wanted to know everything, and as I looked around the room, I was disappointed to find that Roark was gone. No doubt he had left to give us space and time to adjust to such life-altering news. The father I'd believed dead all these years was alive, and I had learned how to do the surgery that would enable him to walk again. If I hadn't gone to Adreia, he never would have gotten out of that wheelchair, because no one else would have dared to attempt an operation with so little chance of success.

*Blessed are You, O Yehovah, whose ways are higher and who knows the beginning from the end!*

I hadn't had the chance to answer many of their questions before Zarek, my father, said we should all get some rest and come back together in the morning. With our good nights said, I headed upstairs and was disappointed to find Roark's room empty. Where had he gone? With a sigh, I went to my room, washed up, dressed in lounge clothes, and lay in bed to read the scriptures.

A soft knock sounded at my door a moment before Roark opened it. He smiled at me as he closed the door behind him and flopped down onto the empty side of the bed. There were weary lines across his face, and he looked as if he had just come home from a grueling solo mission.

"Roark, did you know?" I held my breath in expectation of his answer.

"I suspected they were your parents during my third trip here, when they told me about the accident in which Zarek had been thrown from his truck despite being strapped in and become paralyzed. I wasn't sure, though, because they called you by a pet name, not your real name. Tomorrow I will have to go over the paperwork with them so you can officially be free and have the proper permission to come home and be with your family."

My heart flip-flopped in my chest because I knew I wouldn't be staying here, not permanently anyway. I sighed and finally decided to tell Roark what I had been praying about. I looked him in the eye and said, "There's something I have to confess: Asherex asked me to run the hospital in his neutral zone, and I'm going to accept the position."

Roark sat up with a big smile on his face and said, "That's wonderful news!"

"I won't be able to come see my family very often, though. I'm feeling torn about it now, but I know where Yah wants me."

"Do what Yehovah has shown you, and trust that everything will work out. If you are running the hospital, you will have plenty of time to fly back here to see them. It might not seem like you will, but once things are running smoothly, you will see."

"May it be as you have said."

He looked at me for a moment before lying down with a smile. He was still for so long I thought he had fallen asleep, but then he released a breath and said, "Your brothers and sisters are going to be here tomorrow, so if you want me to go, just let me know."

"Roark, you are just as much my family as they are. I don't want you to go anywhere."

He smiled at me and said, "I wouldn't dream of leaving you unless you wanted me to go, Brother." My heart warmed when he called me his brother, and I wondered what our futures held for us.

A soft snore came from Roark's side of the bed a moment before a twitch startled him awake. He looked at me for a moment and said, "I forgot to tell you that Commander in Chief Vaxis asked me to accept Asherex's high commander position. He said it would be temporary, but seeing as how his promotion to commander in chief nine years ago was temporary, I'm not so sure he's a reliable judge on how long I will hold the position. I'm not sure I'm ready for that kind of leadership position."

"You will be a great high commander and be able to build upon the foundation that Asherex laid while in the position. You won't accept a bribe or turn a blind eye to those who misuse their power. You are the perfect man for the job right now, and Yehovah walks with you, so you can do it in the authority of Yeshua."

The smile that spread across his face spoke volumes before he said, "Amen, Brother. Amen. I'm tired, so will you pray for me?"

"Anytime." I sat up and prayed aloud for my brother and best friend.

He passed out, but I continued to pray for a hedge of protection over him and spoke life and joy into his coming marriage. When I finally lay down to sleep, it was an hour until sunrise, and I knew that everything would work out for our good because we feared Yehovah.

# Chapter Sixty-Three

Asherex

It was the preparation day for the first High Sabbath of Sukkot. I was on a conference call during the flight home with six senators from Adreia and Brashex, discussing the few last-minute details about my chosen territory that was soon to be an official neutral zone. The long-forgotten name of the trading-post town, Archwren, named after the man who'd founded it seven hundred years ago, was now the name of my kingdom. Neutral Zone Archwren sounded like something out of a bad movie, but at least I wasn't going to insist it be called by my name, as most kings did.

I sighed as the others continued to bicker with one another. I was anxious to reunite with Jonathan after two months apart. He had come to live with me in Adreia while I recovered from the surgery to remove the sensors for the Zeron's study. His enthusiasm to walk around like a tourist and not have to worry about anything had been rejuvenating, and when I had taken him to Brashex, he had been ecstatic. I was ready to join him in our new home, even if it wasn't 100 percent completed.

As soon as my quarantine had ended, I'd purchased the lake property, with its surrounding 150 acres, and commissioned the building of my house. I'd spent the seven days in quarantine designing it to the smallest detail and paid well for a large crew to begin the work. The only thing left to finish with the house was the inside, but the kitchen, the main living room, my apartment, and three others were completed. The company I had hired to do the job had pulled through and gotten everything done that I had asked of them, even though they'd put in long hours and complied with my wish not to work on the Sabbath. Because of their hard work, I paid them to have the week of Sukkot off to spend with their families.

"We're getting close, Asherex." My father's voice drew my attention, and off in the distance, I saw my towering mansion, which would one day house my Surface branch of the foundation in the east wing. I couldn't wait.

I finally ended the call as we landed, and Lazerick was the first one out of the airship. He hated my father's driving, and it was amusing for the rest of us to see him rush off as if he couldn't get away fast enough. He usually made Aiden fly him places, but the kid was back in Adreia, helping his biological father settle in, and would join us after the High Sabbath had passed.

"Mom, if you want to lie down with the baby and let us bring everything in, it wouldn't hurt our feelings," I said.

Larissa looked at me with that beautiful smile of hers and walked over holding my baby brother, Yehoshua. She hugged me and said, "That sounds wonderful, Son."

My father caught her before she walked off and kissed her. I was still amazed that they had been able to get married after my father held the press conference and announced the affair. My father had officially adopted all nine of her children with Veris as his own. The older kids who were grown had happily taken his last name, except for Nayomi, who'd just married Drayen three days ago.

I was happy for all of them and would soon be a guest of honor at Roark's wedding, but I couldn't help but feel a little envious of them for being able to have that kind of relationship. Now that Lillie had been gone for a while, I found it harder to be around people who were sharing marital bliss. I missed having someone that close, and even though I had kept in touch with Kyandra and talked with her almost every day, I wasn't satisfied with being alone. We had talked about getting married, but she wasn't quite ready for it yet. Why did I fall in love with older women with commitment issues?

The little white pit bull greeted me as I walked up to the house. Jonathan had found her after he came back from Adreia. She was so excited to see me again that her whole body wagged with her tail. She looked a little fat for a dog, and I had no doubt Jonathan had spoiled her while I was gone. She followed me through the house as I went to my room before leaving me to pester someone else. It was a blessing to have the overprotective dog breed as a companion.

"What's on your mind, kid?"

I turned at Lazerick's question and found him putting down the last of my luggage in the corner of my room. We'd unloaded everyone else's stuff first, with mine being last off. There were quite a few bags and boxes because I was moving in and not going back to Adreia for a while. I wanted to ensure everyone else was comfortable before I settled in. I didn't have much time before sunset, and I needed to put some clothes away and make the bed before I left to celebrate with the others. I was starting to regret not bringing some of my servants with me.

"What do you think is on my mind, Dad?"

He looked at me for a moment before shaking his head and saying, "Woman problems. You're just going to have to let it go and move on. Start talking to other women, and see where it goes, because if you dwell on just one and she doesn't want to marry you, then you have just wasted a lot of time. Or your talking to others will make her see that she could lose you, and she might decide to get over herself because she would be the lucky one to have you."

I shook my head at his advice. He had never told me about any relationships he had in Brashex, nor had he attempted to find a woman while under my roof. I wasn't sure he even wanted a relationship that intimate with someone.

"I don't know, Dad. It seems a little wrong to do that. I guess I will see what happens."

"Why don't you go get something to eat? Jonathan stocked us up ahead of time and grilled some salmon and veggies for us, and your father is heating them up. You still have to put on another twenty pounds to be back at a healthy weight, so you need to eat."

"Yes, Dad."

He smiled at me, and I finished putting some clothes away before walking off to the kitchen.

My father already had a plate warmed up for me, and I ate the food quickly. I hadn't realized how hungry I was. I still had a long way to go before I was considered healthy by the doctors, but I was weeks ahead of schedule, and they were baffled by how I could fast for a week here and there and still come out ahead of the curve. It was Yehovah's hand on me that made it possible, and I was able to share my faith with the doctors both in Adreia and in Brashex.

"Your mom's going to stay behind with the baby and Lazerick to sleep, so whenever you are ready to head out, just let me know."

"I think I'll have one more plate before we head out."

Dad laughed. "You know there's going to be food there, right?"

"I know, and I will eat some of that too, but if I'm going to jump in and do some praise dancing with the others, I need all the energy I can get now."

After I ate another plate loaded with veggies and a piece of fish, we headed off in the armored black Ravager my dad had bought for me. He was paranoid that someone would attempt to assassinate me, but I appreciated his vehicle because it didn't run on gas. That alone made it the safest thing with four wheels in a fifty-mile radius.

We parked as close as we could to the main hall, where music was already pouring out from inside. It was about a half hour after dark, and hundreds of people were gathered inside and outside. People stopped us with cheerful greetings as we passed them, and some pulled us into conversation. It was a little overwhelming for me, but Dad quickly moved us along without making it seem as if the conversations got cut short. It was a good thing he was a politician.

Once inside, I scanned the room, looking for my son, but he saw me first and shouted, "Dad!" Jonathan's exclamation caused many to watch as he crossed the room and pulled me into a hug. He pulled back and gave me a questioning look before saying, "I thought you weren't going to make it tonight."

"I finished early and made it back just in time to put stuff away and get here. I wasn't going to miss our first Sukkot together."

The smile on his face warmed my heart, and he pulled me out into one of the dance circles. I had promised him I would give the praise dancing a shot, and he taught me the steps, so it didn't take long to get the hang of it. Time seemed to disappear as I worshipped Yah with all of myself, and for once, I was grateful for not being aware of the passage of time. I finally stepped away from the circle when my stomach reminded me I was still hungry.

I filled my plate with raw veggies and a few dips to try and sat down where I could keep an eye on Jonathan.

Kyandra sat across from me and said, "I didn't think you were coming out, Ash."

"Plans got changed. I'm not planning on returning to Adreia except for meetings I have to attend until the neutral zone is completely established."

She looked at me, confused, letting me know Jonathan hadn't told her anything about it. I had been unable to speak about it to anyone other than family until three weeks ago, when construction on the massive housing facility for the infected had started. It sat on ninety acres and was the largest building of its kind and the most expensive building I'd paid for.

"Jonathan didn't talk to you guys about it?"

She shook her head and said, "He didn't say a word about what you were still doing in Adreia."

Before I could say a word, Michael, West, and two others from the community joined us at the table. I spent the next ten minutes explaining what I had done since I left, and I told them the trading post and all its territories were now a neutral zone under my authority. After I finished explaining, they started asking questions, but Jonathan came over and pulled me away to meet some people he knew from different congregations.

Around nine o'clock, Dad went to get Mom and the baby, and somehow, I ended up with my baby brother because he was fussy. He only settled down when I started singing to him. When I sang, everyone around me went quiet to listen, and I felt awkward. What was it about singing in public that embarrassed me so much?

As the night's festivities wore on, Kyandra convinced me to go sing with the band, and because she was the one asking, I couldn't say no. I ended up playing piano and singing with them for more than an hour before others from another congregation took over the music, and I headed back for more food. I never made it to a table with my plate, because Avdiel, the community's teacher, approached me with several of the congregational leaders from the many communities who had come there for Sukkot and asked me to share my testimony with them.

When my father pulled me away, I had consumed several glasses of wine and was surprised to learn that it was two in the morning. Mom was ready to go home, and I was starting to feel tipsy, so I knew it was a good idea to leave before I made a fool of myself. Now that I was going to be a king, I had to ensure my reputation was full of honor and integrity, which didn't include public intoxication. It was strange that I had tried to avoid politics since my father stepped into that world, and now I was the center of it.

Dad drove us back. It was a little strange that Lazerick and the dog weren't there waiting up for us, but then again, I knew he hadn't slept much for the last three days and was probably in bed. Mom put Yehoshua down and rejoined us in the living room. We talked for a bit, and I started feeling as if we were being watched, but I dismissed the thought because I was a little intoxicated. I was probably just being paranoid, but then again, it wasn't like Lazerick not to be there waiting for me, even if it was only to mess with me. Something was up.

A noise from the foyer drew our attention, and my father and I stood up, realizing simultaneously that we were unarmed. Suddenly, a large man around six foot six, with dark gray eyes and black hair, appeared in the doorway. Black tribal markings covered the left side of his face as well as his left arm. He looked menacing with his broad shoulders and solemn look.

He locked eyes with my father and, in a heavily accented voice, said, "Uri'kai, we need to talk."